A fo... with n... graphic design curren... frame. When she's n... she can be found cooking ... drinking coffee (okay, wine) and eating crisps. She firmly believes God gifts us with talents for a purpose, and with His help, you can create the life you want.

Jessica is a social media junkie who loves to hear from readers. You can learn more at jessicalemmon.com

**Zuri Day** is the national bestselling author of two dozen novels, including the popular Drakes of California series. She is a winner of the RSJ Emma Award, the AALAS (African American Literary Awards Show) Best Romance Award and others, and a finalist for multiple *RT Book Reviews* Best Book Awards in Multicultural Fiction. She wants you to have a zuriday.com!

# CHRISTMAS SEDUCTION

## JESSICA LEMMON

# READY FOR THE RANCHER

## ZURI DAY

MIX
Paper from
responsible sources
FSC
www.fsc.org
FSC C007454

This book is produced from independently certified FSC™
paper to ensure responsible forest management.

For more information visit www.harpercollins.co.uk/green

Printed and bound in Spain
by CPI, Barcelona

**MILLS & BOON**

First Published in Great Britain 2019
by Mills & Boon, an imprint of HarperCollinsPublishers,
1 London Bridge Street, London, SE1 9GF

*Christmas Seduction* © 2019 Jessica Lemmon
*Ready for the Rancher* © 2019 Zuri Day

ISBN: 978-0-263-27195-9

1019

# CHRISTMAS SEDUCTION

JESSICA LEMMON

For all my friends at the lake—you are
the embodiment of a true community,
and I'm so blessed to know you.

# One

Outside the Brass Pony, a five-star restaurant where he'd nursed more than one whiskey at the bar, Tate Duncan stood beneath the canopy and watched the rain come down in sheets.

He'd picked a hell of a night to walk.

But, that's the way the streets here were designed in Spright Wellness Community. With plenty of sidewalks and paths cutting through the woods, making a walk more convenient than a winding car ride to your destination. This was a wellness community, after all.

Tate and a dedicated team of contractors had developed the health and wellness community five years ago. Its location? Spright Island, an enviable utopia thirty-minutes by ferry from Seattle, Washington, and Tate's twenty-fifth birthday gift from his adoptive parents. The island had been, and remained, a nature preserve and was the perfect spot to build a sustainable, peaceful, modern neighborhood that would attract curious city dwellers.

He'd imagined into existence the luxury wellness enclave, which had become a refuge of sorts for those who desired a strong sense of community, and wanted to be surrounded by lush greenery rather than concrete. As a result, Spright Wellness Community teemed with residents who glowed with wealth and stank of wellness. There was a big demand to live small and, even though it wasn't all that small, SWC had that feel about it.

"Umbrella, Mr. Duncan?" The manager of the Brass Pony, Jared Tomalin, leaned out the door and offered a black umbrella by it's U-shaped handle. His smile faded much as it had earlier when he'd attempted to make small talk and learned that "Mr. Duncan" wasn't in the mood for small talk tonight.

There had been a time, and it wasn't that long ago, that Tate would have turned, given Jared a smile and accepted the offer, saying, "Thank you. I'll bring it back by tomorrow." Now, he gave the manager a withering glare and stalked off into the abysmal weather. A twenty-minute jaunt—soggy, chilling and wet—was a good metaphor for the downward spiral his life had taken recently.

Everything in Tate's world had been on an upward track, steady and stable until...

*Until.*

He popped his collar and tucked his hands into the pockets of his leather jacket. Chin down, eyes on the gathering puddles under his feet, he began to walk.

Surrounding neighborhoods were marked by a variety of shops; markets with fresh produce and organic goods, restaurants like the Pony with reputations that drew diners from the coast, plus plenty of service-based businesses like salons, art stores and yoga studios. With its high-end wellness fare, SWC was part luxury living, part hippie commune, but to Tate, simply home.

A rare flash of headlights caught his attention and he lifted his head. Summer's Market stood on the opposite side of the street, the wooden shelves and brightly-colored stacks of produce visible from the windows. The safety lights spotlighted wheels of cheese and boxed crackers arranged near a selection of wine. It was hard to believe he'd once had nothing better to do than pop into Summer's for a wine-tasting and cheese-pairing and have a chat with his neighbors.

*Back when I knew who I was.*

Tate had never thought of identity as a wily thing, but lately his own had been wriggling, slippery in his grip. He'd known once, with certainty, who he was: the son of William and Marion Duncan, from California. Life, apparently, had other plans for him. Plans that had sent him careening, grappling to understand how he'd *become* the son of William and Marion Duncan, right around the same time the woman who was supposed to marry him had walked away.

*I can't do this, Tate,* Claire had told him, her delicate features screwed into an expression of regret. Then she'd given back the engagement ring. That was two weeks ago. Since then, he'd become a ripe bastard.

The rhythm of his breath paced the time along with his steps. Rainwater beat drumlike on his head and soaked into his Italian leather shoes.

On his side of the street, he came upon a building that held an array of businesses, including an acupuncture office, a family doctor and a yoga studio. The yoga studio was the only one lit inside, by a pair of pink hued salt lamps glowing warmly on top of a desk. He peered through the window, wishing he'd have accepted the damn umbrella. Wishing he could absorb the warmth emitting from the place. It was orderly, homey, with its scarred wooden floors and stacks of cubbies for storing shoes and cell phones during class.

He'd been inside once before, to greet the new owner who'd leased the space. Yoga by Hayden was run by Hayden Green, a new resident who'd been in SWC a little over a year now. He saw her around town sometimes. She was the equivalent of looking at the sun. Bright, glowing, joyful. She had a skip in her step and a smile on her face most days. He wondered if yoga was her secret to being happy, if maybe he should try it—make that his new therapy. God knew he wasn't heading back to Dr. Schroder any time soon.

The first-world problems he used to bring to his therapist were laughable considering the *actual* drama surrounding him now. He could imagine that conversation, his doc's eyebrows climbing her forehead into her coifed dark hair.

*Yeah, so I found out I was kidnapped when I was three, adopted out for a large sum of money and my real parents live in London. No, my adoptive parents didn't know I was kidnapped. Yes, London. Oh, and I have a brother. We're twins.*

Eerie. That's what this was. Like a scary story told around a campfire, there was a large chunk of him that wanted to believe it was false. That the repressed memory of big hands cuffing him under the arms and dragging him away from his and his twin brother's birthday party had been a nightmare he could awaken from. That George and Jane Singleton were no more related to him than the Queen of England.

Though he was from the UK, so God help him, he *could be* related to the Queen of England.

Ice-cold raindrops soaked through his hair to his scalp, and he shuddered. His mind had been bobbing in the atmosphere like a lost balloon for going on two months now. He wasn't sure he'd ever get back to normal at this rate. Wasn't sure if he knew what normal *was* any longer.

This entire situation was surreal. And after living an organized, regimented, successful life, a shock he hadn't been prepared to deal with.

What were the odds of two estranged London-born twin brothers bumping into each other in a Seattle coffee shop nearly thirty years later?

*Astronomical.*

He let out a fractured laugh. "You're not well enough to be in a wellness community."

Overhead, he admired a streetlamp like the others lining the sidewalks, remembering how a formerly sane version of himself had commissioned a welder to design them. They resembled tree branches, complete with curling leaves along the top, the lights encased in a bell-shaped flower. Tate mused that they had a fairy-tale quality. Like that smoking caterpillar or the Cheshire cat from *Alice in Wonderland* could appear perched on one at any moment.

"You're losing it, Duncan."

But his smile was short-lived when he abruptly remembered that he wasn't a Duncan. Not really.

He was a Singleton.

Whatever the hell that meant.

The sharp whistle of the teakettle pulled Hayden Green's attention from her book. She made the short trek to her kitchen, flipped the gas burner off and reached for her waiting teacup.

Through the driving rain, she could barely make out the shape of the market across the street and yet her senses prickled. Stepping closer to her upstairs window, she squinted at the street below and found her senses were, as usual, spot-on.

In the deluge lurked a figure. Right outside her yoga studio. It was a man, most definitely, his dark leather jacket unable to hide the breadth of his shoulders.

She pressed her forehead against the pane to get a better look, confident he couldn't see her since the kitchen light was off. He tilted his head back; the street light overhead illuminating him as the rain splashed his upturned face and closed eyelids.

Hayden recognized her unexpected visitor instantly. "Tate Duncan, what are you doing?"

Tate's reputation had reached almost mythical proportions on Spright Island. He owned the island, so everyone knew him or knew *of him*, anyway. Hayden was somewhere in between. She knew of him—of his legendary pushbacks on the laws that stated their community had to have standard streetlamps and ugly yellow concrete curbs. Tate had fought for, and won, the right to design streetlamps that were art sculptures and to install curbs of sparkling quartz. He'd personally overseen every detail because to him, the details mattered.

Hayden had been romanced by SWC. It was a relaxing, serene place to live—a retreat from bustling city life. She had been born in Seattle into a busy, distracting, dysfunctional household, and had longed her entire adult life to be somewhere less busy and distracting.

When she'd learned about Spright Island's wellness community a year and a half ago, she'd come to visit. Days later, she'd taken out as big a business loan as the bank would give her and leased the space for her yoga studio. She'd quit her job at the YMCA, finagled her way out of her Seattle apartment's lease and moved here with minimal belongings. It'd been her fresh start.

Shortly after, Tate had stopped by her studio to personally welcome her to the neighborhood and invite her to a wine tasting happening that weekend at Summer's Market. It was a kindness she hadn't expected, and without it, she might never have met and grown to know her neighbors.

She rarely saw a suit and tie step foot into a yoga studio, so Tate's presence had garnered every ounce of her attention. One of his signature quick, potent smiles later, she'd promptly lost any train of thought she'd had. As it turned out, the legendary Tate Duncan was also stupidly attractive, and when he smiled, that attractiveness doubled.

She'd grown used to his presence around town, if not his mind-numbing male beauty. She and Tate had bumped into each other several times in town, from the market to the restaurant to her favorite café. He'd always offered a smile and asked her how the studio was doing. Come to think of it, it'd been a while since she'd spoken to him. She'd seen him in recent weeks—*or was that a month ago?*—when she'd left the post office. He'd had his cell phone to his ear and was talking to someone, a deep frown marring his perfect brow.

He'd scanned the road and she'd waved when his eyes reached her, but he didn't react at all, only kept talking on the phone. It was strange behavior for Tate, but she'd written it off.

But now, watching him stand in the rain and willingly get soaked, she wondered if his behavior that day had been strange after all. She glanced over at her teakettle, considering. It wouldn't hurt to invite him in for a cup…

Once he'd gone out of his way to make her feel welcome. The least she could do was offer him a friendly ear to bend. Just in case he needed one.

She bypassed her front door for the door next to her coat closet. It led to a private staircase and down to her yoga studio. She shared the building with a few other businesses, but her apartment was in a hallway all its own. The attached studio and private entryway were her favorite aspects of the unique building.

Downstairs, she flipped on the studio's overhead lights and Tate blinked over at her, recognition dawning. He lifted a hand in a semblance of a wave, like he was embarrassed to be caught outside her place of business.

The stirring of her senses reinforced her instincts to come down here. Tate needed someone to talk to even more than he needed a warm space to dry off.

She unlocked the door and held it open for him, tipping her head to invite him in. "Wet night for a walk."

He ran a hand through his soaking hair and offered a chagrined twist of his lips, a far cry from the genuine smile he'd given her almost every other time she'd seen him.

He wore dark pants and shoes, his leather coat zipped to his chin. Her day had been packed with errands, so she still wore her jeans and soft, cream-colored sweater from earlier. If she'd greeted him wearing her usual—leggings and slouchy sweatshirt, minus the bra—he wouldn't have been the only one of them embarrassed.

"My teakettle whistled and then I spotted you down here. You look like you could use a warm drink."

"Do I?" He palmed his neck and glanced behind him. Maybe she'd misread this situation after all.

"Unless you're waiting for someone?"

She'd seen him in town with a waifish blonde woman a handful of times. *Claire*, Hayden had gleaned. Tate's girlfriend and very recently, fiancée. The other woman seemed proper and rigid, and Hayden's first thought was that she was an odd match for the always bright and cheery Tate... though he wasn't bright or cheery at the moment.

"No. I was at the Pony," he said of the restaurant up the hill from here. "The rain caught me."

"I'd offer to drive you home, but I don't have a car." One of the luxuries she'd given up to afford to move to Spright Island, but the sacrifice had been worth it. *Peace* had been worth it.

Every shop or store in the community could be reached on foot if she planned ahead, and she had a few friends in the area or could call a car service if she needed to venture farther.

"But I do have tea." She opened the door wider.

"Of course. Thank you." He stepped into the studio, his shoes squishing on her welcome mat. "Sorry about this."

"No worries." She locked the door behind him and grabbed a towel from a nearby cabinet. "Clean, fluffy towel? They're for my hot yoga classes."

He accepted with a nod and sopped the water from his hair.

"Tea's in my apartment." She gestured to the open doorway leading upstairs. "Don't worry about wet shoes. I'm not that formal."

Tate followed her upstairs and inside her *blessedly spotless* apartment. She'd cleaned yesterday. She was fairly tidy, but some weeks got the best of her and she didn't get around to vacuuming or changing her sheets.

By the time he was in the center of her living room and she was shutting the door to the staircase behind her, she was questioning her invitation.

A man in her apartment shrank it down until it felt like she lived in a cereal box—and this man in particular infused the immediate space with a sizzling attraction she'd felt since he first shook her hand.

*Hayden Green*, he'd said. *You have the perfect last name for this community.*

Now, he pegged her with a look that could only be described as vulnerable, as if something was really, *really* off. She wanted nothing more than to cross the room and scoop him into her arms. But she couldn't do that. He had a fiancée. And she wasn't looking for a romantic relationship.

No matter how hot he was.

"Tea," she reminded herself and then stepped around him to walk to the kitchen.

# Two

Tate slipped out of his leather jacket and hung it on an honest-to-goodness coatrack in between the door and the television. His shirt beneath was dry, thank goodness, and his pants were in the process of drying, but he kicked off his shoes rather than track puddles through Hayden's apartment.

Since he'd personally approved the design of every structure in SWC, he knew this building. He'd expected her place to be both modern and cozy, but she'd added her own sense of unique style. Much like Hayden herself, her apartment was laid-back with a Zen feel. From the live potted plants near the window to the black-and-white woven rug on the floor. A camel-brown sofa stood next to a coffee table, its surface cluttered with books. Oversize deep gold throw pillows were stacked on the floor for sitting, a journal and a pen resting on top of one of them.

"I like what you've done with the place." He was still drying his hair with the towel when he leaned forward to study the photos on the mantel above a gas fireplace. He'd expected family photos, maybe one of a boyfriend, or a niece or nephew. Instead the frames held quotes. One of them was the silhouette of a woman in a yoga pose with wording underneath that read, *I bend so I don't break*, and the other a plain black background with white lettering: *If you stumble, make it part of the dance.*

"Do you have a tea preference?" she called from the kitchen.

"Not really."

He didn't drink tea, though he supposed he should, since he'd recently learned he was *from fucking London*.

"I have green, peppermint and chai. Green has caffeine, so let's not go there." She peeked at him before tucking the packet back into the drawer like she'd intuited a pending breakdown.

*Great.* Nothing like an emasculating bout of anxiety to finish up his day.

"Peppermint would be good if you were nauseous or ate too much, and chai will warm you up." She narrowed her eyes, assessing him anew. "Chai."

"Chai's fine. Thanks again."

She set about making his tea and he watched her, the fluid way she moved as she hummed to herself in the small kitchen. Stepping into Hayden's apartment was a lot like stepping into a therapist's office, only not as stuffy. As if being in her space tempted him to open up. Whether it was the rich, earthy colors or the offer of a soothing, hot drink he didn't know. Maybe both.

He was surprised she'd invited him in, considering she'd found him standing in a downpour staring blankly at the window.

Probably he should get around to addressing that.

She set the mugs on the coffee table, and he moved to the sofa, debating whether or not to sit.

"You're dry enough," she said, reading his mind. She swiped the towel and disappeared into the bedroom before coming back out. Her walk was as confident as they came, with an elegance reminding him of Claire.

*Claire.* Her last words to him two weeks ago kept him awake at night, along with the other melee of crap bouncing around in his head.

*I can't handle this right now, Tate. I have a job. A life. Let's have a cooling-off period. I'm sure you'd like some time alone.*

He felt alone, more alone than ever now that the holidays were coming up. His adoptive parents were fretting, though he tried to reassure them. Nothing would reassure his mother, he knew. Guilt was a carnivorous beast.

Hayden lit a candle on a nearby shelf, and he took back his earlier comparison to Claire. Hayden was completely different. From her dark hair to her curvy dancer's body.

Pointing to the quote on the mantel, he said, "I bet you've never stumbled a day in your life."

With a smile, she sat next to him and lifted her mug. "I've stumbled many times. Do you know how hard it is to do a headstand in yoga?"

"How is the studio doing? I was considering trying a class." A clumsy segue, but that might explain why he'd been lingering outside like a grade A creeper. "I've been... stressed. I thought yoga might be a good de-stressor."

"Yoga's a *great* de-stressor," she said conversationally, as if him coming to this conclusion while standing in a downpour was normal. "I teach scheduled group classes as well as private sessions."

"One on one?" He'd bet her schedule was packed. Being in her presence for a few minutes had already made him feel more relaxed.

"Yep. A lot of people around here prefer one-on-one help with their practice. Others just like being alone with no help at all, which is why I open the space for members once a week."

"That's a lot of options." She must work around the clock.

"There are a lot of people here, or haven't you noticed, Mr. Spright Island?" She winked, thick dark lashes closing over one chocolate-brown iris. Had she always been this beautiful?

"I noticed." He returned her smile. There were just shy of nine hundred houses in SWC. That made for plenty of residents milling around town and, more often than he was previously aware, apparently in Hayden's yoga studio.

"I don't believe you want to talk about yoga." Her gaze was a bare lightbulb on a string over his head, as if there was no way to hide what had been rattling around in his brain tonight. She lifted dark, inquisitive eyebrows. "You look like you have something interesting to talk about."

The pull toward her was real and raw—the realest sensation he'd felt in a while. It grounded him, grabbed him by the balls and demanded his full attention.

"I didn't plan on talking about it..." he admitted, but she must have heard the ellipsis at the end of that sentence.

She tilted her head, sage interest in whatever he might say next. Wavy dark brown hair surrounded a cherubic heart-shaped face, her deep brown eyes at once tender and inviting. *Inviting.* There was that word again. Unbidden, his gaze roamed over her tanned skin, her V-necked collar and delicate collarbone. How had he not noticed before? She was *alarmingly* beautiful.

"I'm sorry." Her palm landed on his forearm. "I'm prying. You don't have to say anything."

She moved to pull her hand away but he captured her fingers in his, studying her shiny, clear nails and admiring the olive shade of her skin and the way her hand offset his own pinker hue.

"There are aspects of my life I was certain of a month and a half ago," he said, idly stroking her hand with his thumb. "I was certain that my parents' names were William and Marion Duncan." He offered a sad smile as Hayden's eyebrows dipped in confusion. "I suppose they technically still are my parents, but they're also not. I'm adopted."

Her plush mouth pulled into a soft frown, but she didn't interrupt.

"I recently learned that the agency—" *or more accurately, the kidnappers* "—lied about my birth parents. Turns out they're alive and living in London. And I have a brother." He paused before clarifying, "A twin brother."

Hayden's lashes fluttered. "Wow."

"Fraternal, but he's a good-looking bastard."

She squeezed his fingers. There for him in spite of owing him nothing. That should've been Claire's job.

"I was certain that I was the owner/operator of Spright Island's premier, thriving wellness community," he stated in his radio-commercial voice. "That, thank God, hasn't changed. SWC is a sanctuary of sorts. There is a different vibe here that you can't find inland."

"I know exactly what you mean. I stepped foot in my studio downstairs that first time, and it had this positive energy about it. Does that sound unbelievable?"

No more unbelievable than being kidnapped in another country and having no memory of it.

"It doesn't sound unbelievable." He took pride in what he'd built. He'd poured himself, body and soul, into what he created, so it wasn't surprising some of that had leaked into the energy of this place.

"I was also certain I was going to be married to Claire Waterson."

At the mention of a fiancée, Hayden tugged her hand from his and wrapped her fingers around her mug. He didn't think it was because she was thirsty.

"When I found out about my family tree, she bailed on me," he told her. "I didn't expect that."

He raked his hands through his damp hair, unable to stop the flow of words now that he'd undammed them. "You invited me in for tea thinking I had something on my mind. Bet you didn't expect a full-blown identity crisis."

Her eyebrows dipped in sympathy.

"I just need... I need..." Dropping his head in his hands, he trailed off, muttering to the floor, "Christ, I have no idea what I need."

He felt the couch shift and dip, and then Hayden's hand was on his back, moving in comforting circles.

"I've had my share of family drama, trust me. But nothing like what you're going through. It's okay for you to feel unsure. Lost."

He faced her. This close, he could smell her soft lavender perfume and see the gold flecks in her dark eyes. He hadn't planned on coming here, or on sitting on her couch and spilling his heart out. He and Hayden were *friendly*, not friends. But her comforting touch on his back, the way her words seemed to soothe the recently broken part of him...

Maybe what he needed was *her*.

He leaned forward, his eyes focused on her mouth and the satisfaction kissing her would bring.

"Tate." She jerked away, sobering him instantly.

"Sorry. I'm sorry." What the hell was he thinking? That Hayden invited him in to make out on her couch? That sharing his sob story would somehow turn her on? As if any woman wanted to be with a man who was in pieces.

He stood to leave. She stood with him.

"Listen, Tate—"

"I shouldn't have come here." He pulled his coat on and shoved his feet in his shoes, grateful for the leather slip-ons. At least there wouldn't be an awkward interlude while he tied his laces. "Thank you for listening. I'm really very sorry."

"Wait." She arrived at the coatrack as he was stuffing his arms into his still-wet leather coat.

"I'm going to go." He turned to apologize again, but was damn near knocked off his feet when Hayden pushed to her toes, cuffed the back of his neck and pulled his mouth down to hers.

# Three

Hayden had fantasized of kissing Tate ever since she first laid eyes on him. She knew he wasn't meant to be hers in real life, but in her fantasies, well, there were no rules.

Of all the imagined kisses they'd shared, none compared to the actual kiss she was experiencing now.

The moment their lips touched, he grabbed on to her like a lifeline, eagerly plunging his tongue into her mouth. His skin was chilly from the rain, but his body radiated heat. She was downright toasty in his arms…and getting hotter by the second.

She tasted dark liquor—bourbon or whiskey—on his tongue, but there was a tinge of something else. Sadness, if she wasn't mistaken. Sadness over learning he had a brother after all these years—a twin brother. Wow, that was wild…

A pair of strong hands gripped her waist. Tate tugged her close, and when her breasts flattened against his chest all other thoughts flew from her head. The water clinging to his coat soaked through her sweater, causing her nipples to bead to tight peaks inside her bra.

Still, she kissed him.

She wasn't done with this real-life fantasy. A brief thought of Claire Waterson crashed into her mind, and she shoved it out. They were broken up—he'd said so himself. Hayden had nothing to feel guilty about.

Besides, he needed her. Whenever she'd been lost or sad, she'd taken solace in her friends. That was what she offered to him now.

A safe space.

She pulled her lips from Tate's to catch her breath, her mind buzzing and her limbs vibrating. His chest and shoulders rose and fell, the hectic rhythm set by the brief make-out session. An unsure smile tilted his mouth, and she returned it with one of her own.

"Better?" she asked.

His low laugh soaked into her like rum on spongecake. He pulled his hand over his mouth and then back through his hair, and her knees nearly gave way. It'd be so easy to lean in and taste him again, to offer her body as a place for him to lay his worries…

"I didn't mean to take advantage of your hospitality. Honest." His blue eyes shimmered in the candlelight.

"You didn't. I always serve tea with French kisses. It's a package deal."

"The best deal in town," he murmured. He stroked her jaw tenderly, those tempting lips offering the sincerest "thank you" she'd ever heard.

"Call a car," she said, before she asked him to stay. "It's pouring out there."

"Actually—" he opened the door that led down to her studio "—I could use a cool, brisk walk after that kiss."

She smiled, pleased. It wasn't every day she could curl a hot guy's toes. She considered this rare feat a victory.

"I'll lock the studio door behind me. There are some real weirdos out there…"

She grinned, knowing he was referring to himself.

Before he pulled the door shut, he stuck his head through

the crack. "You don't really kiss everyone you offer tea, do you?"

"Wouldn't you like to know." She was tempted to put another brief peck on his mouth, but he disappeared through the gap before she could. A fraction of a second later, she was looking at the wood panel instead of his handsome face and wondering if she'd hallucinated the entire thing.

"Hayden, Hayden," she chastised gently as she engaged the lock and drew the chain. She turned and eyed the mugs of tea, Tate's untouched and hers barely drunk. His lips hadn't so much as grazed the edge of that mug.

*But they were all over yours.*

That spontaneous kiss had rocked her world.

She dashed to the window and peered out into the rain, hoping for one more glance at her nighttime visitor. A dark figure passed under a streetlamp, his shoulders under his ears, his hair wet all over again. Before he disappeared from sight, he turned to face her building and walked a few steps backward. She couldn't see his face from that far away, but she liked to believe he was smiling.

She touched her lips.

So was she.


Three wet days later, the rain had downgraded from downpour to light drizzle. Even walking across the street to Summer's Market yesterday for ingredients for blueberry muffins had left Hayden wet and cold. She'd returned home soaked to the bone, her hair smelling of rainwater.

Which, of course, reminded her of *The Kiss* from the other day. She hadn't seen Tate since. Not that she'd expected him to stop by, but... Well, was *hope* the wrong word to use?

Over and over, she'd remembered the feel of Tate's firm lips, his capable hands gripping her hips, the vulnerability in his smile. The ways his eyes shined with curiosity afterward.

Knowing she'd erased some of his sadness made her feel special. She was beginning to think she actually *missed him*. Odd, considering the concept of missing him was foreign until that kiss.

The chilly bite of the wind cut through her puffy, lightweight coat, and she tucked her chin behind the zipped collar as she crossed the street to the café.

Nothing better for walking off sexual frustration than a brisk November stroll.

She had an advanced yoga class in an hour and was tired just thinking about it. A hot cup of coffee would put some much-needed pep in her step.

She wasn't the only resident of SWC taking advantage of the drier weather. Cold drizzles they were willing to brave. Drenching downpours, not so much. As a result, there was a buzz in the air, an audible din of chatter amongst the couples or single professionals lounging in the outdoor patio. It was closed off for the winter, the temporary walls and tall gas heaters making the space warm enough for the overflow of customers.

Inside, Hayden rubbed her hands together, delighted to find that the person in line ahead of her was finished ordering. The only thing better than a Sprightly Bean coffee at the start of a day was not waiting in line to get one. She ordered a large caramel latte and stepped to the side to wait. Not thirty seconds into her studying the glass case of doughnuts and other sinful baked goods, the low voice from her dreams spoke over her shoulder.

"I've seen regret before, and it looks a lot like the expression on your face, Ms. Green."

Her smile crested her mouth before she turned. She thought she was prepared to come face-to-face with Tate until she did. His dark wool coat was draped over a charcoal-gray suit, his hair neatly styled against his head and slightly damp, she guessed from a recent shower. And wasn't that a pleasant image? Him naked, water flowing over lean muscle, corded forearms, long, strong legs…

"Am I broadcasting regret?" she asked, her voice a flirty lilt.

He pointed at the bakery case. "Was it the éclair or the lemon–poppy seed muffin that caused it?"

"Hmm." She pretended to consider. "I could be regretting my impulsive behavior three days ago."

His eyebrows rose like she'd stunned him. She wasn't much of a wallflower, which he should know after she'd grabbed him up and kissed him.

He opened his mouth to reply when a thin blonde woman glided around the corner, tugging a glove onto her hand. *Claire.*

"I'm ready to go," she announced without preamble. Or manners. Or delicacy.

As if her frosty entrance had chilled them both, Hayden's smile vanished and Tate retreated.

He nodded at Claire Waterson, his frown appearing both on his mouth and forehead. "Hayden, this is Claire. Claire, this is Hayden Green. She owns the yoga studio down the road."

"Charmed." Claire nodded curtly as she tugged on her other glove. No offer of a handshake, but Hayden didn't want to shake the other woman's hand, anyway.

"See you around," Tate told Hayden.

She watched them leave, her forehead scrunching when Tate touched Claire's back on the walk out to a car. He hadn't walked to the café today. Hayden would bet *Priss in Boots* hadn't allowed it.

"Grande caramel latte." The cheery barista handed over Hayden's coffee, and she managed a genial smile before walking out the front door, her steps heavy. Tate, in the driver's seat, pulled away from the curb on the opposite side of the street. He didn't wave, but did manage a compressed half smile.

While Hayden didn't have any claim on him, she'd admit she felt like an idiot for believing him. He'd sounded so sincere when he said his relationship with Claire was over. Or had he implied it was over? Either way, if she'd had any idea Tate and Claire would be sharing morning coffee a few days later, Hayden never would have kissed him. From the looks of it, he and Claire were very much *together*.

*Ew.*

She started her march home, an unhealthy dose of anger seeping into her bloodstream. The first sip of her coffee burned her tongue, and the wind blew directly into her face, cold and bitter.

A series of beeps sounded from her pocket and Hayden's back stiffened. That was her mother's ringtone. It never failed to cause a cocktail of panic, fear and resentment to boil over. She ignored the second ring and then the third and, a minute later, the chime of her voice mail.

When Hayden left Seattle, it had felt like more of an escape. Her mother had been—and was still—stressed to the max, refusing to draw boundary lines around the one woman causing problems in their lives: Hayden's alcoholic grandmother. Grandma Winnie favored drama and bottom-shelf vodka in equal measures, and Hayden's mother, Patti, had turned codependency into an art form. Hayden's dad, Glenn, was content to let the matriarchs rule the roost, as if he'd eschewed himself from the chaos in the only way he knew how: silence.

After years of trying to balance family drama with her own desperate need for stability, Hayden left Seattle and her family behind for the oasis of Spright Island.

By the time she was changing for her class, her coffee was cool and her mind was numb. She paused in the living room of her apartment, put her hands over her heart and took three deep breaths.

There was no sense in being angry at Grandma Winnie for being an alcoholic. It wasn't her fault she had a disease. Similarly, she let go of worrying over her mother's codependence and her father's blind eye.

"Everyone is doing the best they can," she said aloud.

But as she trotted down the stairs to the studio and unlocked the door for a few waiting guests, she found that there was one person in her life she didn't feel as magnanimous toward.

The man who'd kissed her soundly, scrambled her senses and then showed up in town with the very woman he claimed had left him behind.

"Hi, Hayden," greeted Jan, the first of her students through the door.

Hayden returned Jan's smile and shoved aside her tumultuous thoughts. She owed it to her class to be present and bring good energy, not bad.

Family drama—and Tate drama—would be waiting for her when the class was over, whether she wanted it or not.

# Four

The bell over her studio entrance jangled as Hayden's evening class filed out of the building. She was behind the desk, jotting down a note for Marla, who'd been coming for individual classes but decided tonight she wanted to join the group. Since Marla hadn't brought her credit card, Hayden had promised to email her in the morning.

Hayden stuck a reminder Post-it note onto the cover of her hardbound planner and looked up, expecting to see the last of her students leave. Instead, someone was coming *in*.

A certain someone who hadn't left her mind no matter how hard she tried to stop thinking about him.

Dressed in black athletic pants and a long-sleeved black T-shirt, Tate shrugged out of the same leather jacket he'd worn the night they kissed. It'd been five days since that kiss. Two days since the coffee shop.

She still wasn't happy with him, but it was impossible not to admire his exquisite hotness.

"Hey," she blurted, unsure what else to say.

"Hey." He looked over his shoulder. "I know I missed class, but I was hoping to schedule a one-on-one."

Her mind went to the last "one-on-one" session they'd

had. She hadn't forgotten that kiss. She probably never would. It was burned onto her frontal lobe.

"Individual sessions have to be scheduled ahead of time," she said as tartly as she could manage. The vision of him with Claire was too fresh in her mind for her to be cordial.

"Are you sure?" He tilted his head as he stepped closer to her.

"If you're here because you feel you owe me an explanation or you need to air your regrets—"

"No. Nothing like that."

She lifted her eyebrows, asking a silent *well?*

"I haven't been in control of my life lately. Everything's moving at warp speed, and I'm caught in the undertow. You ever feel like you've lost control? Once upon a time you had it in your hands, and now…" He looked down at his own fists gripping his coat as his mouth pulled down at the corners.

She knew exactly what that was like, but in reverse order. Her world had been moving at warp speed since birth, and only moving to SWC had stopped its trajectory.

She sympathized with Tate, though she was tempted to cut her losses and show him the door.

"And taking a yoga class with me would help you feel in control?" she asked anyway.

"Ah, well. Not exactly." Palm on his neck, he studied the floor and then peeked up at her with a look of chagrin so magnetic, her heart skipped a beat. "I'm really good at turning you on. At least I think I would be. Are you still doling out kisses with every cup of tea?"

She gripped the edge of the front desk, digesting what he'd just said. He *was* good at turning her on. She knew that, but what was she supposed to do with it? Especially when Tate stood in front of her looking coy and cunning and yet vulnerable and was offering… Wait… Was this *a booty call*?

"Sorry. That offer expired." Not that she was above kissing him, but… "I'm not going to be your girl on the side, Tate. What would Claire say?"

"That's over. It's *been* over. What you saw at the coffee shop was her finalizing things. You know, like you do after someone dies."

He paced to the salt lamp on her desk and stared at it for a beat. "She dropped off a box of my stuff at my house and then asked if we could grab a coffee and talk. I told her she could talk to me there, but she said she preferred neutral territory."

"Oh." It was a breakup. Hayden had misread that entire exchange. Still… "And you didn't feel the need to explain yourself after I saw you at the café? You thought you'd instead come here and…" She waved a hand uselessly, unable to finish her thought, since she wasn't 100 percent sure why he was here.

"I thought we could start with a yoga session." He dipped his chin. "If you have any openings for, say, now."

She tried to tell him no, but found she couldn't. Tate Duncan didn't have to work hard to charm her on any given day, and today he was actually trying.

"How about…" She flipped open her planner and traced her finger down the page. "Tomorrow. Noon."

"Deal."

"I'll need your credit card. I require a nonrefundable down payment for the first appointment."

"Smart."

She hummed. She wasn't so sure this was smart, but was too curious to turn him away.

The morning of his yoga appointment, Tate set out for Hayden's studio. The day was dry if chilly, but he welcomed the burning cold in his lungs as he cut through a path in the woods.

He'd been out for a quick trip to Summer's Market when he'd witnessed Hayden's evening class letting out. He hadn't planned on walking across the street and inside, but when he found himself in front of her, he had to have a reason for being there.

Besides the obvious.

Hayden had consumed damn near every one of his waking thoughts, which was a relief compared to his usual pastime: turning over his parentage, the truth about where he came from, or the disastrous outcome since.

He'd blamed the kiss on whiskey and a need for connection. The liquor buzz was long gone, but the imprint of her kiss remained like a brand. It was reckless to leap into the flames after he'd just escaped a fire—Claire should've rendered him numb. But Hayden…she was different.

Not only had she been there for him when he'd been adrift on his own, but she replaced his tumultuous thoughts with something a hell of a lot better.

Sex.

He wanted her. He wanted her in his arms and in his bed. He wanted her moaning beneath him, her nails scratching down his back.

It was as if he'd devolved to his most carnal desires when she was around, and for a change, he was all for it. He was tired of feeling unmoored, helpless. Sad. With her he felt strong, capable. She'd come apart in his arms during that kiss. She may have put him through his paces last night, but he respected her for it.

Hell, he knew he'd stepped in it with Hayden the moment he left that café with Claire. But he'd owed Claire that meeting. They'd dated for three years and had been recently engaged, though he now wondered if that was more of a technicality. She'd never lived with him—never wanted to. She didn't treasure Spright Island or his community the way he did.

*The way Hayden does.* That kiss with Hayden was about far more than their lips meeting and an attraction they weren't aware of blooming. For Tate, it was about discovering that he'd been sleepwalking through his life.

Tate had never been ill-equipped for a task set before him. He'd accepted the gift of Spright Island from his father without qualms and had set about building an entire town and community even when he'd never worked on his own before. He'd learned by doing. Each time adversity had come up, he'd defeated it.

When he'd found out that Reid was his brother, Tate felt like a superhero who'd stumbled across his fatal weakness. He didn't have a single weapon in his arsenal to handle the situation set before him.

His previously drama-free life had begun to look more like a Netflix feature with him in the center as the hapless protagonist.

Until the kiss with Hayden.

That night had changed him, changed his outlook. And after a numb month of disbelief, feeling something—feeling anything other than stark shock—was as welcome as… well, as the kiss itself.

Yoga by Hayden came into sight and he crossed the street with a neat jog. A smile inched across his face, but flagged when he noticed the Closed sign on the door. He tugged the handle.

Locked.

He checked the clock on his phone. 12:04 p.m. He was late. Maybe she drew a hard line when it came to promptness.

Then he looked up and there she was, her curves barely contained in colorful leggings and a long-sleeved green shirt. She flipped the lock and opened the door, reminding him of the night he'd been standing outside this very studio in the rain.

Reminding him that she'd climbed to her toes to lay the mother of all kisses on him and had changed his life for the better.

"Sorry. Typically, I'm more punctual than this," she said.

God, he wanted to kiss her. The timing was wrong, though. She hadn't yet met his eyes save for a brief flicker that bounced away the second she caught him staring.

She was hard not to stare at, all that silken dark hair and the grace in her every movement...

"I thought maybe you'd changed your mind." He hung his coat on a hook and perused a small display of yoga mats, blocks and water bottles. "I'll have to buy a mat. I don't have one."

"Help yourself." Hayden's gaze glanced off him again, and then almost relieved, she said, "Oh, good, she's here."

A fortysomething blonde woman ran toward the building, her yoga mat under her arm.

"Sherry had a last-minute need for an appointment, so I piggybacked onto your session. With the holiday week being so busy, I couldn't fit her in any other time." Hayden blew out the news in a nonstop stream. "I hope you don't mind."

Of course he minded. He'd scheduled a one-on-one with Hayden, and now he had to share his time with Sherry Baker, SWC's premiere real estate agent.

"Oh, hi, Tate." Sherry patted him on the shoulder before hanging her coat and scarf on the hook next to his. "I didn't know you practiced yoga."

He slid his eyes to Hayden, who bit her lip and locked the door. She'd double booked herself on purpose. *For some reason.*

"You know me," he told Sherry. "I'm always trying to support more local businesses."

"Get this one." Sherry handed him a black yoga mat. "It's manly and the same brand as mine."

"Done." He turned to Hayden with a million questions he couldn't ask. "Mind if I pay you after?"

Her mouth hovered open for a beat as Sherry unrolled her yoga mat. With an audience, Hayden didn't have much of a choice other than being polite.

"Sure."

"Great." He took his spot on the studio floor. He'd won that round. He planned on sticking around after Sherry left. He wanted answers.

# Five

For Hayden, doing yoga was like breathing. She slipped into each pose easily, pausing to instruct Sherry and Tate through the movements.

Sherry was in her midforties with two teenagers. Her son had recently moved to a college campus and her younger daughter was thirteen and embroiled in a teenage spat with her two best friends, Callie and Samantha. Hayden knew this because Sherry hadn't stopped talking since class had started.

Sherry also mentioned her twenty unwanted pounds and a caffeine habit that bordered on addiction, and said she hoped doing one healthy thing like yoga would lead to other healthy things like cutting down on coffee and overtime at work.

Tate remained resolutely silent, though she'd caught a small smile on his mouth more than once as he'd eased from one pose into the other.

During downward dog pose Hayden moved to assist Sherry with her alignment. "Push your five fingertips into the mat rather than the palm of your hand," she instructed. "We don't want compressed wrists."

Hayden turned to Tate next, willing herself to remember she was a teacher and a professional. There was never anything sexual involved in helping a student.

Until now.

One look at Tate's ass, his legs and arms strong and straight, and a wave of attraction walloped her in the stomach. As fate would have it, she was also going to have to touch his hips to move him into more of a V form than a U.

*Dammit.*

One hand on his back, the other on his hips, she instructed him to lower his heels to the floor as much as he was able. He breathed out with the effort, that breath reverberating along her arm and hand, and she became even more aware of him than before.

Who knew that was possible?

Those sorts of thoughts were exactly what Sherry's presence was supposed to *quell*.

She led them from downward dog to cobra, encouraging Sherry to use her knees if she needed to. When Hayden turned to tell Tate the same thing, he lowered into the pushup-like pose with what appeared to be very little effort. A closer look at his biceps and she realized they shook subtly as he took his time, holding himself in plank pose a moment before dropping his waist and pushing up with his arms.

She stared, unabashedly, which he must've noticed a moment later, when he sent her a cocky smirk.

Show-off.

She returned to her mat and walked them through one more sun salutation, ending in mountain pose: standing, hands in prayer pose at the chest.

"Namaste," Hayden said. "That concludes our lesson for the day."

"Woo! That was intense, girlfriend!" Sherry waved her hands in front of her pink face. "I'm sure Tate would've preferred a less chatty partner, though."

Sherry winked at him, and Hayden smothered a laugh. Sherry was happily married and treated Tate like she would a friend or any other familiar resident of SWC.

*You know, the same way* you *should be treating him.*

"I have to return to the office," Sherry announced. "Can I call to schedule a follow-up after the holiday?"

"Whenever you like." Hayden walked Sherry to the door, chatting to stall while waiting for Tate to leave. Instead, Tate was at the front desk, his rolled mat on the surface.

Crap. She forgot he needed to pay.

Sherry left and Hayden made her way to the front desk, her heart hammering.

"If you admit that you booked Sherry because you couldn't trust yourself to be alone with me, I'll forgive you for it," he told her.

"Ha!" She left it at that because any response other than "Yep, that's correct!" would have been a lie.

She *didn't* trust herself alone with him. His kiss the other night had been too welcome, his presence too distracting. She had enough drama in her life without creating some of her own.

Last night after he left she'd thought more about the chaos in Tate's life. Not one parental pair but two. And a surprise twin brother. Hayden had come to Spright Island specifically to avoid drama not become embroiled in it. That, and the fact she didn't trust herself to be alone with him, was why she'd scheduled Sherry for the same timeslot.

Tate wasn't unlike that second serving of ice cream she knew she shouldn't have. It seemed that no amount of will-power could keep her from one more taste.

"Thirty-two dollars."

He handed her his credit card.

"It's a really good mat," she explained needlessly as she charged his card. Anything to fill the dead air between them.

"I wasn't arguing."

"No, I guess you wouldn't." She imagined thirty-two dollars to Tate Duncan must be what thirty-two *cents* felt like to her.

"What's going on, Hayden? Do you find me particularly hard to get along with?"

"I— Sorry. That was rude." She handed his card back and flipped the screen around for him to sign it. When he was finished, she tucked her iPad into the drawer and, with no other task before her, was forced to meet his eyes.

He stood there like he had nowhere else to be.

"I didn't schedule Sherry *only* because I didn't want to be alone with you. It worked well since you're both beginners."

He nodded slowly.

"Plus, what did you expect after you barged in here—"

"I barged?"

"—and demanded—"

"Demanded?"

She huffed out a breath. If was going to continue calling her bluff, she really should stop lying about her true intentions. But there was a nugget of truth she could cling to.

"My schedule has been nuts this week. Everyone's trying to get in before Thanksgiving."

"Ah. And you fit me in." He grinned. "Because you couldn't tell me no."

She made a pathetic choking sound. How arrogant was this guy, anyway? And how did he keep guessing right?

"Because I have to make a living. I don't have billions stashed away…" She almost added "like some people" but she was already protesting too much.

"Right," he agreed, but something in his expression told her he'd gleaned what she hadn't said. "Well, thank you. For the mat."

He went to grab his coat, slipping it over his arms and holding the rolled mat between his knees.

Feeling a dab of guilt, she moved toward him and vomited out a generic nicety. "Thank you for booking your session. I hope you'll consider a membership."

His hand resting on the door handle, he turned as she stopped advancing, putting her mere inches from his handsome face. "I was thinking about another kind of one-on-one session. Are you available for dinner?"

She hadn't been prepared for that. Words eluded her. She knew that agreeing to go out with him was a bad idea, but when faced with his glittering blue eyes she couldn't quite remember why.

"Just so you know—" that blue gaze dipped to her mouth "—if you were ready, I'd kiss the hell out of you right now. Just to make sure I didn't imagine how good you tasted before."

She gaped at him, but he didn't advance to kiss her. Instead he turned around and stepped outside.

Before she could shut the door, he pushed it open a crack. "Think about dinner. I'll ask again."

She locked up behind him, watching him through the glass. He had a sure, strong gait, a disgustingly handsome mug, and looked as good in a suit as he did in sweatpants.

There were a multitude of reactions fighting for first place. She wanted to open the door and yell for him to come back. She wanted to run upstairs and shut the blinds. She wanted to jog across the street and grab him by the ears and kiss the hell out of *him*.

Especially that last one.

While she warred with those options, frozen in stunned bliss at the possibilities, Tate grew farther and farther away until he was a shadowy blur disappearing into a path into the woods.

"Damn him." But she didn't mean it. She was looking forward to next time—when she would leave *him* slack-jawed and without a response.

# Six

Chaz's Pub in Seattle was a far cry from the Brass Pony, with its scuffed floors and beaten tables. Tate walked in for the first time, took in the colorful red and green decorations, and decided he liked the place. Any establishment that decorated for Christmas before Thanksgiving had his undying respect.

His brother Reid had invited him out to celebrate "the biggest drinking day of the year," tacking on, "You're British and it's your duty to get pissed."

As overwhelming as it was to learn he had a brother and a set of parents he'd never met, Tate had to smile. Could've been the yoga. He'd been more relaxed since the session with Hayden, though the buzz afterwards could likely be blamed more on sexual tension than downward dog.

The sexual tension part wasn't entirely her fault. Tate and Claire hadn't slept together since he'd found out about his family, and shortly after that she'd ended their engagement. In other words, it'd been a while.

Plus, Hayden was sexy as hell, had a way of revving him up and calming him down simultaneously. When she hadn't been touching him to move his body into proper form, he'd noticed her sliding from position to position. It'd been like watching an erotic dance.

She was a unique experience, that was for damn sure.

"Tate, hey!"

A petite brunette bounced over to him, pulling him from his thoughts. Reid's fiancée, Drew Fleming was as sweet as she was adorable and at the same time up to absolutely no good. He'd met her before—Reid had brought her when they'd gone out for drinks or dinners.

She looped her left arm in Tate's, and he glanced down at the sizable diamond ring on her hand. Reid had proposed around the time Tate's engagement had ended, as if Reid was an alien who had taken over Tate's life. Wasn't Tate supposed to be the one with the stable family life and fiancée?

"The boys are over there. I'll walk with you. But then I'm returning to the dance floor with the girls. Andy and Sabrina," she reminded him.

"Fiancées of Gage and Flynn."

"You remembered!"

He had. Gage and Flynn were Reid's best friends and coworkers. He'd met the whole gang in passing at one time or another.

Drew guided Tate to a high, round table with several stools surrounding it. Full glasses of Guinness were in front of each of the guys, suggesting they hadn't been here long.

"There he is." Reid wore the wide smile Tate envied. Not that Tate didn't want his brother to be happy, but he'd like to stockpile some of that for himself. Wanted to feel with certainty that tomorrow would come, and things would return to normal again.

"Found a stray," Drew released Tate and laid a kiss on Reid's cheek. He didn't let her get away, snagging her waist and dipping her low while kissing her thoroughly. Next to them, Flynn grinned, but Gage was less enthralled by the PDA.

"Still getting used to that," Gage grumbled as Tate took his seat. Gage was Drew's older brother, and Reid and Drew had kept their relationship from Gage until long after things had gotten serious between them.

"Hang in there, buddy." Flynn slapped Gage's back and let out a baritone chuckle. "Tate, man, how are you?"

Tate nodded, having no other word than a generic "fine."

"You need a beer," Flynn announced, waving down a waitress and to order one.

"Off with you, then." Reid swatted his fiancée's butt and she giggled, radiantly aglow. Once she'd scampered off, Reid's smile stuck to his face like glue. "She's pregnant."

Flynn nearly spit out his beer.

Gage turned an interesting shade of pale green.

"Congratulations," Tate said, figuring that was a safe response given the size of Reid's grin.

"Are pigs flying?" Flynn asked, his eyebrows meeting over the bridge of his nose. "Did hell freeze over? Am I having a stroke?" He turned to Gage and asked, "Do you smell burned toast?"

Gage shook his head, but his color returned. "Maybe we're all suffering from strokes. Reid Singleton: engaged and soon-to-be dad. What gives?"

"Drew. She's… Drew." Reid grinned bigger.

"I know how amazing she is. She's *my* sister." Then, as if it dawned on him at that moment, Gage smiled, too. "I'm going to be an uncle."

"Me, too. Technically." Flynn shrugged.

"And you," Reid dipped his chin at Tate. "Legitimately."

Right. Tate hadn't thought about that. Reid wasn't only a friend he was getting to know. He was a blood relative. The waitress delivered a Guinness, and Tate drank down the top third without coming up for air.

A pair of high-pitched squeals lifted on the air, and the guys turned toward the dance floor, where a brunette with glasses and a tall redhead were hugging Drew simultaneously.

"She told 'em. I knew she couldn't hold out." Reid said that with a smile as well, and if Tate had to guess, he'd say his brother's joy wasn't going anywhere soon.

*"Sláinte."* Flynn held his glass aloft, and the four of them banged the beers together. "So what have you been up to with the wellness commune, Duncan?"

He'd only met Flynn twice, but had determined that joking was Flynn's style. Tate liked Reid's friends and their fiancées. They were good people.

"Planning on a big Thanksgiving dinner Friday for the residents," Tate answered. "Serving Kool-Aid at the end for the really dedicated."

The guys laughed at the cult reference. Tate took it as a win. He knew the way Spright Wellness Community had been perceived it the past, but the place had gained a reputation for luxury living, thanks to Tate. Visitors flocked to the island and filled their community to capacity to eat, shop or simply spend time in nature.

"What about you guys?" Tate asked.

"Family dinner." Reid slid a glance at Gage. "With that wanker."

"I tried to disinvite him, but Mom said it'd ruin the holiday," Gage returned, poker-faced.

"We're going to California to Sab's parents. Her brother, Luke, is flying in from Chicago to join us."

"He's in Chi-town now?" Reid asked. "Sabrina never told me that."

"Yeah. His new gym franchise took off and he moved there to open another one. Rumor has it he's bringing a girl. Another one bites the dust." Flynn hadn't kept it a secret that his family was no longer. He'd mentioned inheriting Monarch Consulting after his father had died. That had brought mention of his late mother followed by a tasteless joke about how his brother was "banging my ex-wife." Flynn didn't seem as bitter about it as he was matter-of-fact, which Tate respected. Here he was trying to handle one curveball, and Flynn had been swinging at them his entire adult life.

"What about you?" Reid asked. "Other than Friday. Any plans?"

"Uh, no. Not really. Couldn't make the trip to Cali to see the parents."

Reid nodded slowly, like there was a thought he didn't want to say aloud in front of the guys. Like maybe he'd figured out that Tate couldn't handle a family holiday with his adoptive parents after finding out they'd basically bought him off the black market. They hadn't known the truth, though, and that was the only reason he was still speaking to them. "The Brass Pony is serving an eight-course dinner. I thought about going."

"You're welcome to join us," Gage said, even as Tate held up a hand to tell him he didn't have to do that. "I'm not asking because you're a charity case. I'm asking because you're Reid's brother. Plus my parents cook enough to feed the county."

As kind as the invite was, a holiday spent with a family he didn't know and as the only single guy at the table sounded like Tate's worst nightmare. Rather than say that, he covered with, "Actually, I have a friend who lives in town. I asked her to join me."

Technically he hadn't asked Hayden out for that specific night but the dinner invitation could have been for whenever, wherever.

"You *dog*. Dating again already?" Reid smirked.

"Claire and I weren't..." Tate took in the three girls who belonged with the men at the table as he tried to decide how to finish that sentence. For lack of a better term, he landed on, "Like you and your girls."

"Enviably gorgeous?" Reid said.

"In love," Tate said, bringing the table's laughter to a halt.

"Damn." Flynn finished his beer and gestured for another round for the table. Tate took another hearty gulp to catch up, but he still wasn't close. "Duncan called us out."

"He does that," Reid said.

"I like him," Gage decided. "Even if he doesn't want to hang out with my loony family on turkey day."

The guys continued bantering, and Tate, for a change, found himself relaxing into the conversation, the beer and the round of appetizers they ended up ordering. He didn't feel like the odd man out with the girls back at the table, tittering about Drew's pregnancy and making sure she had first dibs on every appetizer plate, but it did make him think of Hayden and how well she would've fit in here.

It was time to extend that dinner invitation again. And this time, earn a yes.

# Seven

Hayden, sitting at a table in Succulence, a trendy, gourmet vegetarian restaurant in SWC, waved her friends over. Arlene gave an exuberant wave and pulled Emily in alongside her.

Hayden had met Arlene and Em last year, and they'd become fast friends. In SWC, residents were more interested in what they had in common rather than what set them apart. It made for deep discussions early on and, had cemented the three of them.

Well, originally there had been four. But Bailey had been AWOL since having a baby. Joyously married, she'd always been in a category of her own. Hayden recalled many, many nights when she and Arlene and Em would complain about their recent bad date or #singlelife and Bailey didn't have anything to contribute. Hayden missed her, but was confident Bailey would fold back into the fray. They were too close for their friendship to end over a few lifestyle differences. Besides, one of the three of them was bound to be married or at least happily coupled off eventually…right?

"Girls' night is on!" Arlene, boisterous and bold, had so much confidence it was infectious. She was also hilarious.

More often than not she had Hayden clutching her side in laughter while tears streamed down her face.

"So good to see you!" Emily gave Hayden a tight squeeze. "I feel like I've been gone a year." Emily had recently gone on an excursion to Spain for the lifestyle blog she wrote.

"It felt that way for all of us," Hayden agreed.

"Except we remembered you and you forgot all about us." Arlene threw her purse onto the chair. "First round on me. What's your pleasure? And before you ask, we're doing a shot followed by a cocktail. That's the minimum."

"Uh…" Hayden wasn't exactly a shot kind of girl. Not anymore.

"It ain't like any of us drove here." Arlene's blond hair was big with a lot of volume, like the rest of her. "And it *is* the biggest drinking holiday of the year."

"Because everyone dreads going home to family," Emily supplied. "Peppermint schnapps followed by a cosmo."

"I like your style." Arlene raised her brows at Hayden.

"Well…"

"Tequila," Arlene decided.

"What? No!" Hayden laughed.

"Yes. You can follow it with a light beer."

"I'll have a white Russian." Hayden lifted an eyebrow.

"Vodka shot on the side, then." Arlene didn't wait for an argument, only zoomed over to the bar to place their orders.

"Will you hold my hair?" Emily asked with a bright smile. She was ridiculously adorable with her dark hair in a sassy pixie cut. She folded her arms on the tabletop—white frosted glass balanced on a single silver pedestal. Succulence's mod design resembled a health spa, with its white and silver and neon-green accents. They were also pricey, but Hayden gladly overpaid for the fantastic food and cocktails.

A waiter came by. "Ladies."

"Hi, Josh." Em smiled up at him, as smitten as she was the first time they'd come in here. Hayden took pride in the fact that she'd arrived early enough to request his table.

"Eating or drinking tonight?" Josh was probably five years younger than all of them, but damned if Emily cared. She leaned heavily on a palm.

"Drinking, but snacks later. We'll probably camp here a while, but I promise to leave you a pile of money for a tip."

"Your beauty is enough of a tip for me." His cunning smile scrunched his dark eyes up at the corners. Paired with his tanned complexion and dark hair, Hayden had to agree he was pretty darn cute.

"You are full of it," Arlene told him as she returned to the table, tray in hand.

"Give me that." Josh swiped the tray and pointed at a seat. Arlene obediently sat and let Josh serve their drinks. "I know the peppermint schnapps is Em's."

Emily batted her lashes.

"Arlene has to be the tequila. And Hayden—" he sniffed her clear shot "—vodka. Nice choice. Enjoy, ladies." Then he was off, but not before winking at Emily.

"Oh, will you two screw each other already?" Arlene drank down a healthy swallow of her margarita .

"Shh! These walls have ears. And eyes. And cell phones with cameras." Emily jerked her gaze around the room.

Emily was right. SWC was high-end, luxurious and nature- and wellness-focused, but it was also a dressed-up small town. Everyone knew everyone and therefore knew everyone's *business*.

"We should've gone to the city where we could gossip properly," Arlene said. "Shots, ladies."

"If we were in the city, then I couldn't request Josh as

a server and watch Emily light up like a Christmas tree," Hayden said.

"I do not!" Emily turned a stunning shade of red as she lifted her shot glass.

"Did you think it was coincidence that we're always at his table?" Arlene asked with a raspy chuckle.

"You should ask him out," Hayden said.

"No way. He's just patronizing me."

"He'd like to be doing more than that." Arlene slanted a glance at Hayden.

"Why don't *you* ask someone out?" Em shot back, her shot wobbling at the edge of the glass. "How long's it been since you dated Derek?"

"Not long enough." Arlene held her shot aloft and shouted, "Cheers to years of beers and pap smears!"

Emily turned bright pink, Hayden groaned and hid behind a hand, and Arlene let out a bawdy laugh. That broad. God. Hayden loved her, though. They chucked back their shots, only Em coughing and waving the air like she'd swallowed gasoline.

"What about you, Hayd?" Em croaked.

"What about me what?"

"When are you going to ask someone out?"

"Why would I ask someone out?" Hayden purposely widened her eyes to look more innocent and then tacked on, "When I can kiss…" She looked around the restaurant teeming with their neighbors. Everyone here knew or had at least heard of Tate Duncan, so she couldn't very well blurt out his name. "*Someone* any time I'd like," she finished with an arch of one eyebrow.

"Shut. Up." Emily leaned in. "Who?"

"Someone we know." Arlene assessed Hayden. "But who?"

Unable to resist, Hayden mouthed his name. "Tate."

"Duncan?" Arlene bleated.

"Shh!" Hayden hissed.

"See? It's not fun when she does it to *you*." Em stuck her tongue out at Arlene, who returned the sentiment.

"He was standing outside my studio in the rain one night, and he looked so lost. I invited him up for tea and then…"

"You had sex with him?" Arlene cried.

"Keep it down, and no, I didn't!"

"Why not?" Emily asked with a small pout.

"For the same reason you won't ask out Josh," Hayden answered. "I was too terrified to consider it."

Which was the truth, if not for different reasons than Em. Hayden had fought hard to be fiercely independent, to escape the chaos that bubbled over in her family on a daily basis. Tate wasn't exactly a complete set. Some of his parts were scattered across the damn globe.

"I heard he and the blonde split up," Arlene said.

"Where did you hear that?"

"Naomi. She was at the café and overheard them talking."

Damn. This place really was a gossip mill. Hayden didn't dare mention Tate's learning of his birth parents and a twin brother.

"So, I'd be rebound girl," Hayden said, and it wasn't an entirely bad setup. Seeing how mired her mother was with her father certainly hadn't made it look appealing.

"Sounds like a superhero," Em said. "Rebound Girl! Able to leap tall, handsome billionaires in a single bound."

"I don't think he's a *billionaire*," Hayden said through her laughter.

"Have you seen this place?" Arlene gestured beyond the restaurant to the rows of houses on one side and the retail establishments on the other. "He built it, Hayd. From scratch."

"I have nothing against wealthy men," Emily said. "Except I'm attracted to the ones who aren't." She sent another longing glance to Josh, who was jotting down another group's order.

"He doesn't count, since he owns Succulence. He could be a billionaire restaurant owner. You never know," Hayden supplied.

Em pursed her lips in consideration.

"Well, I wouldn't kick Tate Duncan out of bed for any reason. *Especially* if it was because he was loaded." Arlene waggled her eyebrows, Emily agreed and Hayden found herself easing into the conversation as her mind wandered along the path of what-if and arrived at Tate's bed.

And Tate's couch. And Tate's shower…

"You're thinking about sex!" Arlene said. "Josh! We need another round!"

"No, we don't." But Hayden's smile was too big to be denied. She *was* thinking about sex. Tate was too fun not to kiss, not to do a host of other things to, especially since his last words to her were about kissing the hell out of her when she was ready. "I don't know if I'm ready."

Then again…

Just because Hayden wanted to have an affair with a gorgeous rich guy didn't mean she had to give up her autonomy. Tate didn't *have* to be ice cream. He could be a perfectly reasonable kale salad, which she enjoyed immensely and never suffered cravings for afterwards.

Aw, who was she kidding? Tate could never be kale salad. He was too tempting. Too hot. Too distracting!

But she should give herself more credit. She was independent. She'd moved away from her family and started over with her new family: her friends at SWC. She was a successful business owner, to boot.

Plus she really, *really* wanted to say yes to Tate the next time he asked. For dinner, for a kiss, for anything…

"On second thought, I *could be* ready." Hayden stirred the cream into her dark drink.

"Attagirl." Arlene pinned Emily with a meaningful look. "Now are you going to ask out Josh, or do I have to do it for you?"

# Eight

Laughing, the three ladies stumbled out of Succulence and onto the sidewalk.

Arlene curled her arm around Emily and let out a shout of triumph. "You freaking did it!"

Emily giggled, proud of herself. She should be. After round two of drinks, she'd looked up at Josh and purred, "We should go on a date sometime. My friends agree we'd look good together."

To Hayden's complete delight, Josh's lids had lowered sexily and he'd replied, "What took you so long to ask?"

"Don't get too excited." Emily belted her coat against the wind. "It's only the beginning. And beginnings are fragile."

"You mean the other F-word," Arlene said. "Fun."

"They are fun," Emily agreed.

"Well, I had a fantastic time. Goodnight, loves." Hayden kissed Emily's cheek and pulled Arlene into a hug. "Be safe!"

They'd eaten enough appetizers to soak up the alcohol and had switched to water after the drinks. Two hours of fun and laughter later, Hayden's heart was full and happy. Her walk home might not be warm, but it would be welcome. Moving her body always made her feel better.

Back home in Seattle, Hayden used to hang out with the wrong crowd. She used to drink not for recreation, but with the goal of being completely drunk. She used to wake up with hangovers and headaches and, one time, no memory of how she'd gotten home. Nothing was more sobering than realizing she was repeating a pattern that her grandmother had started. Worried that she might end up exactly like Grandma Winnie, a belligerent, controlling, bitter alcoholic, Hayden decided that maybe drinking shouldn't be her main focus in life.

Enter exercise. She'd started with running early in the morning, which kept her from staying up too late. Running didn't require special equipment or training, and she found she had a proclivity for it. She set goals to be better each week and before she knew it, she was running every day.

Bitten by the fitness bug, she left her sedentary office job, where her derriere was widening by the day, to work at a local gym. She took advantage of her employee discount to purchase yoga classes.

It was love at first warrior pose.

Yoga gave her something running didn't. *Peace.*

Rather than her heart rate ratcheting up and her feet pounding the pavement—it was hell on her knees, anyway—she spent each hour-long yoga class in an almost meditative state. Working quietly and silently on moving her body and stretching stubborn muscles.

Yoga had been the first domino to fall in her quest for self-care. She wanted to be good to herself rather than continue the abuse she'd started in her twenties. Yoga led her to Spright Island. Yoga awakened her to the unhealthy relationship she had with her family. Yoga made her want to be better *for herself.*

At her studio, she rounded the corner to enter the side door that led up to her apartment. She should hang lights this year. Every year she balked at hanging outdoor holiday lights, seeing it as a hassle and dreading taking them down after the season was over. But maybe it was time to stretch another muscle and step beyond her comfort zone. Besides, it would be worth it to see them and smile, knowing she cared enough to adorn her little porch with Christmas cheer.

Doorknob in hand, she didn't make it inside before friendly honk sounded. A white Mercedes with tinted windows pulled to her side of the street, the car belonging to the man who wouldn't leave her mind.

Tate stepped out and rounded the car, his hands in the pockets of his leather jacket. His long legs were encased in denim, ending in leather slip-ons. Even several yards away he was tempting and potent.

Totally more like ice cream than kale salad.

"I'm not stalking you, I swear." He grinned, and damned if she couldn't help returning it. "I was thinking of you tonight."

She'd been thinking of him, too, but couldn't quite bring herself to admit it.

"Can I buy you a drink? A meal?"

"I was just out with friends. I'm fed, and I've had all the drinks I'm having for one night." Tonight had been a little over-the-top for her. She rarely indulged, for obvious reasons.

Tate fell silent and Hayden wondered she was playing too hard to get. Before she could worry she'd thwarted his efforts entirely, he asked, "Can I show you my place?"

Her teeth stabbed her lip, her smile struggling to stay restrained. Emily had mentioned beginnings and how fragile they were while Arlene had argued that they were fun. Given Hayden's thundering pulse and warmth pooling in her belly, she'd have to agree with Arlene.

"Okay."

He closed the distance between them and held out a hand. Hayden slipped her palm into his. With each step, she was reassured she'd made the right decision. She'd had an amazing night already. Capping it off with a visit to Tate's house that would lead to whatever they pleased was the ultimate way to end it.

"You keep getting hotter." He shook his head as if awed.

"Yeah, well, so do you."

They stood in the street and grinned at each other like idiots for a beat, and then he helped her into the car.

When he pulled away from the curb her belly tightened in anticipation. It had been a long while since she'd felt wanted. A few years since she'd attempted to have a relationship. Her last boyfriend, Alan, had been good for her at the time. He was stable, nice and had a great job. But the more time she spent with him the less like herself she'd felt. He enjoyed staying in so she found herself staying in more. He didn't like seafood and she realized at one point that she hadn't cooked her favorite shrimp pasta in months. She'd lost herself in him, and again those old patterns she'd seen in her family became apparent. After Alan, she decided to make sure she never lost herself again.

Which made her briefly question how hard she'd fought Tate's advances. She'd resisted him in the name of maintaining her independence. Now that they were in his Mercedes gliding along the tree-lined streets, she had to question her reasoning. What could be more pro-self than indulging in the attraction pounding between them?

"I was thinking about you tonight, too," she said. She was done resisting.

His face was lit by the blue dashboard lights of his car, his grin one for the books.

He cut through Summer's Drift, one of her favorite neighborhoods in SWC. The theme was water, the palette white and sand and pale blues. Residents took the theme to heart and decorated accordingly. There were coils of rope resting on porches and miniature lighthouses standing in yards. One house even had upstairs windows that resembled ship's portals.

"Where'd you have dinner?" Tate asked.

"Succulence."

"Best sweet potato gnocchi in town."

"Not afraid of veggie fare?"

"Would a guy who built this community fear vegetables?" he joked.

"Fair point. What about you?"

"I was out with my brother. A bar called Chaz's Pub in Seattle."

"Chaz. One of the lesser-known Irishmen. How was it?"

"Good. Really good." He didn't say more but he didn't have to. She could tell by his tone and the quiet way he finished their trip that he'd had a "really good" evening. She was glad to hear he was getting along well with his newfound brother.

He turned down a long drive hooded by trees and marked by a private sign. Hayden was excited to see Tate's house. She'd always been curious what kind of house the builder of Spright Wellness Community had built for himself.

The trees ended and the house came into view. The structure was boxy but interesting thanks to the slanted roof that lent a modern, artistic quality to the home. It was big, but not as big as she was expecting. Arlene's billionaire reference had Hayden expecting an over-the-top fifty-room mansion.

"It's beautiful," she commented as he pulled into a driveway.

In the light glowing from the porch and the car's headlights she could make out the details. A sturdy stone wall climbed to the top of the house, while the rest of it was dark metal beams and wood. At the highest point of the roof, one entire side was almost nothing but windows, intersected with a set of stairs that led to an outdoor patio.

"Wait till you see the inside." He unbuckled her belt for her and they climbed out of the car.

"Living room through here." He gestured as they walked into the foyer, pausing to shrug out of his leather coat. "Kitchen's to your right. Can I take your coat?"

"Sure." Big hands moved to her shoulders. Flanked by his heat from behind, it took everything in her not to lean into his warmth.

He slipped the garment from her shoulders, leaning close to her ear to mutter, "Better?"

A tight breath was all she could manage.

She walked through the living room and admired the décor. Metal and wood and stone converged in a modern, artistic, comfortable way. Everywhere she looked, there was nature. From the petrified wood on a stand on the bookshelf to the woven rug beneath the black leather sofa and chairs.

"Mind if I powder my nose?" she asked when Tate walked into the room with her.

He pointed to the slatted-step staircase framed with an iron railing. "Top of the stairs. Take a right. Can I get you anything to drink?"

"Sparkling water? Or still, if that's too fussy."

"Lucky you. We specialize in fussy here."

In the bathroom mirror she fluffed her hair and gave herself a once-over. She looked good tonight. Thank goodness she'd worn her favorite low-heeled boots. They made her ass look amazing.

Tate had turned on music. She heard the croony voice of Michael Bublé drifting through the downstairs. Curious to see the rest of the house, she peeked down the hallway on one side and then the other. Admittedly she was being nosy, but she couldn't help it. She'd always been epically curious about how the other half lived.

At best guess Tate had spared no expense when it came to decorating and furnishing his house.

There were four bedrooms upstairs alone, and still more house to explore downstairs. One of the rooms was being used as an office, the tidy space both masculine and attractive. The enormous L-shaped desk was deep brown in color, the desk chair the same pale beige as the reading chair in the corner. A laptop was centered on the desk's surface, a square pen holder holding three pens next to it. Bookshelves lined the wall stuffed with an array of architectural books and business titles.

She bypassed a guest room, and another being used for storage. A box marked "Claire" sat on the floor, and she peeked inside. A white sweater and pair of oversize headphones were all she'd evidently left behind.

The last bedroom at the end of the hall held a model of a neighborhood in the center of a large folding table. The model had several buildings, including apartments and what looked like a retail area, as well as a a a green slab with tiny benches and a swing set.

"You found my secret project," said a voice behind her.

"Oh!" Startled, she straightened quickly and bumped the table. She turned just as quickly to steady the model, grateful she didn't knock it off and turn the impressive work of art into a pile of matchsticks.

"Sorry. I'm sorry." She backed away from the table. "I was… Um. I like how you decorate. Your house is amazing."

"Relax, Hayden. I don't think you were casing my house in search of the good silver." He handed her a champagne flute. "Your sparkling water. I added a wedge of lime. I do well with fussy."

She hummed, keeping her thoughts about Claire to herself.

"Is it really secret?" she asked of the model.

"No, but very few people know about it. This neighborhood is going to sit behind Summer's Drift. We're building around the trees. The architecture is Swedish. Row houses, a few restaurants." He pointed out the various elements.

"And a park."

"And a park." He assessed her, eyes narrowed.

"What?"

"It's just—"

"What is it?" She straightened her sweater and reached for her hair, fidgeting.

"You look ready now, Hayden Green."

Oh.

*Oh.*

"To have the hell kissed out of me?" she guessed.

He set her glass aside, his gaze zooming in on her mouth. "I'm guessing that's going to require a lot of kissing."

She rested her arms on his shoulders. "Are you up for the task?"

"Hell, *yes*," he said, his voice gravel. And then he smothered her laughter with a rough kiss.

# Nine

Kissing Hayden was like being kissed for the first time.

He moved his lips over hers, a unique thrill jolting him as she gripped the back of his head and dove in for more. Her tongue came out to play, nudging his top lip before her teeth nipped his bottom lip.

No, screw that. Kissing Hayden was like being kissed *by Hayden* for the first time. If he'd been kissed like this for his first kiss, he would've had no idea what to do next.

Thank God he knew now.

Opening to accept her tongue, he deepened the kiss, wrapping his arms around her lower back and pressing her soft body against his. She was fit, muscular and curvy, but there was give where there should be. In her breasts flattening against his chest, and her belly, which made for a perfect place to nudge the hint of his erection.

*Kissing Claire was never like this.*

He shouldn't compare, but he couldn't keep from doing it. Couldn't keep from noticing that Hayden's strength and softness were two attributes that his ex had never had. Claire was controlled, buttoned-up. Tate had mirrored those attributes, which made for some uninspired sex.

He couldn't think of a scenario where *Hayden* and *uninspired* would go together in a sentence.

"I promised myself," she whispered, tugging his hair, "the next chance I had—" she stole a quick kiss "—I'd do this."

"Kiss me?" he asked before she lit him up with another tongue lashing.

She pulled her lips away and regarded him with disbelief. "Have sex with you."

"You want to have sex with me?" he growled.

She rolled her eyes. "Oh, like you don't want to have sex with me?"

Her confidence was his favorite part about her. The second was her body. He gripped her hips and squeezed, loving the contrasting strength and give there, as well. "I do. I really, *really* do."

Something serious shadowed her eyes. The tugging she'd done earlier to his hair changing to gentle strokes. She tipped her chin and took him in, her dark eyes both earnest and vulnerable.

Leaning in slowly, he gave her the chance to change her mind, to back away and thank him for the invite and insist he drive her home. He would. He didn't want to, but he would.

She instead closed the gap between them, her lips barely brushing his as she gave him room to initiate.

Hell. Yes.

He wouldn't miss the chance to sleep with her tonight. Not when she tasted and felt this good—and he sensed she needed the physical connection as badly as he did.

Threading her hair through his fingers, he took charge of her mouth. He bent his knees to lower them to the floor and she followed, easing down with him in one fluid, graceful movement. He took a mental snapshot of her on his carpeted floor, her hair spread around her like a dark halo. She was gorgeous and, for now, *his*.

He braced his weight on his arms and hovered over her, studying her unique beauty. Until her lips spread into an uncertain smirk. "You're staring again."

"Can't help it."

"Why? Is there a problem?"

"Holding out longer than ten minutes, maybe."

"Well, forget it then." She winked, saucy, which only made him harder.

"I was admiring you. And wondering how I missed that you were this exquisite until the night you found me loitering outside your studio in the driving rain."

She stroked his hair gently. "I was admiring you that night, too."

"I was kidding about the ten minutes. Let's make this last." He covered her mouth with his own, and she returned his efforts. While her fingernails tickled his scalp, he skimmed his hand along her sweater, lifting it until he encountered a slice of soft skin. A low groan reverberated from his chest, and he reminded himself that he'd promised to make this last. As badly as he wanted her naked, he was going to take his time. He had one shot at convincing her to sleep with him more than once. After that first kiss she'd so boldly initiated, he knew *once* would not be enough.

He had to impress her.

He rucked her shirt up and exposed her taut abdomen— delicately defined, he could make out the muscles above her belly button. There was softness to the bit below, and he again admired the juxtaposition. Beauty wasn't found in the expected, but in the surprises; the imperfect.

He moved down her body to kiss her stomach and then back up to her bra. Gold and black and lace held breasts that were large and round. He was definitely going to need a moment with each of them. He helped her sit up and divested her of her sweater. Hayden shivered.

"Cold?" he asked.

"Excited," she answered. He loved her honesty.

"Flattery, Ms. Green, will get you absolutely *everywhere*."

"Sucker," she whispered.

Smacking a brief kiss onto the center of her cunning mouth, he found the hook of her bra, failed at releasing it and tried again.

"Out of practice?" She reached behind her to unhook it herself.

"Yeah. I guess I am." It'd been a while since he'd undressed Claire. He realized with stark discomfort that they'd usually undressed themselves before sex. What a waste. This was the best part.

Bra loosened, Hayden slipped it from her arms, watching his reaction as she exposed her breasts to the cooler air in the room.

Dusky rose, her nipples pebbled. He took one into his mouth and sucked gently. She reacted like he'd plugged her into an electric socket, zapping to life with an encouraging gasp as she raked her hands into his hair again.

He swirled the tender bud and then dragged his tongue over the other nipple and started on that one. She squirmed beneath him, lifting her hips to bump his. He was hard and well past ready but unwilling to rush—or so he had to keep reminding himself.

After she'd thoroughly wrecked his hair, he abandoned her breasts to undo her belt and unbutton her jeans. Halfway through unzipping, she reached for his sweater and yanked.

"Take this off."

It wasn't hard to take orders from a rosy-cheeked, topless woman on her back. Not even a little.

He whipped off the shirt and she ran her fingertips over

his pectorals and stomach, and then along the line of hair that vanished into his jeans. She bypassed the belt and zipper and molded her hand around the stiff denim hiding his cock. If he thought he was hard before, that was nothing compared to the inches of steel created by her tenderly stroking hand.

Moving her wrist, he reprimanded her with a headshake and yanked her pants from her legs. He had her short boots to contend with, so that took a second or two of struggle.

Her black and gold panties made it worth the work.

"Tell me you always wear lingerie."

"I always wear lingerie."

"Even under your yoga pants?"

"I don't wear anything under my yoga pants."

Great. He could never take a class from her again without embarrassing himself.

"Your face." She chuckled, returning her hands to his abs. "Where have you been hiding this body? I guess I wasn't looking hard enough."

"Neither of us were." He kissed her palm and pulled the sides of her panties down her thighs as he laid kisses on her belly and thighs. Once he'd stripped them from her, he lifted one of her legs and rested it on his shoulder, enjoying the way she propped herself up to watch. She opened wider to accommodate him, not the least bit shy about accepting what she wanted.

And he wasn't the least bit shy about giving it to her.

It'd been so long since a man's mouth had been between her legs she was almost too excited to concentrate. *Almost.*

Tate worked his magic until she was forced to close her eyes, lie back and give herself over to his ministrations. He paid careful attention to what she liked, doubling his efforts whenever she let out a whimper of approval.

Which she did *a lot.*

The man had skills. She had the stray thought that she'd never dump a guy who could make her come as easily as Tate Duncan. That alone would be worth the price of admission.

A gentle series of orgasms hit her like rolling waves. Arching her back, she parted her thighs. He gripped her hips and tugged her toward his mouth, continuing his delicious assault until she was moaning again. There was another orgasm waiting on the cusp. She could feel it. She reached up to tug her own nipples, and that was exactly the move that took her over. Like one of those earlier waves, she came on a cry, undulating as pleasure rocked her body and erased her mind.

Her breath sawed from her lungs, leaving her body warm and buzzing. A shadow darkened her vision behind her eyelids.

"Open your eyes, beautiful girl," Tate murmured before kissing the corner of her mouth.

She was confronted with a tender ocean-blue stare.

"Hi," he said.

"Hi." She laughed at the absurdity of the greeting, at the sheer delight of it. She'd never had this much fun having sex, and technically they hadn't had sex yet.

"Condoms are in the bathroom across the hall," he told her. "Which means I have to leave the cradle of your incredible thighs, find one and come back."

"Okay." She nodded quickly to let him know she wasn't suffering an ounce of doubt where making love to him was concerned. She was all for it.

"Okay." He stood and stepped over her, adjusting the hard ridge pushing the fly of his jeans to capacity, and then walked into the hallway.

Hayden slapped her hands over her face and smiled into her palms. She was really doing this. And it was *really* freaking incredible.

Tate returned in record time and, holding the condom wrapper between his teeth, wrestled free from his belt and jeans. She simply lay there and watched as he stripped for her, admiring the strong planes of his muscular body and the strength he exuded.

When he tugged off black boxer briefs, she felt her mouth go very dry. It was…well, it was gorgeous, was what it was. Long and thick and inviting, all brought to stark attention as he rolled the protection over his length.

"Keep looking at me like that, and we'll be done sooner than you'd like," he warned, lowering over her willing body.

"I don't believe you." She hooked her heels over his ass and tugged him forward, his heated skin warming hers. The hardness between his legs met her plush, wet folds and she gasped.

"You're far too capable, Tate Duncan—" she paused as he notched her entrance "—to finish before you're good and ready."

A feral, cocky glint lit his eyes as he seated himself deep inside her. Her mind blanked of thought as moved, slipping along the wetness he'd created with his talented mouth.

Hayden stopped teasing him and gave in to the pleasure he doled out blow by exquisite blow.

# Ten

"Mmm." Hayden hummed, pure satisfaction.

Tate smiled over at the dark-haired beauty on the floor next to him, proud of those three letters making up one truncated sound. He'd worked hard.

"We're good at that," he stated.

"We are." Her throat bobbed with a husky, sexy laugh She turned her head to face him, and he was struck momentarily speechless by the unwavering eye contact. "I had complete faith in you."

Goose bumps prickled her arms and she shivered. He rolled to the side and rubbed her biceps with his hand in an attempt to warm her.

"How about some hot cocoa or tea?"

"I'd never turn down cocoa. Do you have marshmallows?"

"What am I, a barbarian? I have *homemade* marshmallows from Blossom Bakery."

"I love those." Her expression was a lot like her last O face, which made him grin.

He offered a hand and helped her sit up.

"Wow. I'm zapped." She put a hand to her hair. "I must be a mess."

"You are a mess. A complete and utter, distracting, hot mess."

"That…was a compliment, I assume?" She narrowed one eye.

"Yes." He kissed her succinctly. "What time are you going to Thanksgiving dinner tomorrow?" He knew some families ate earlier in the day—hell, his own mother set the table at 11:00 a.m.

"I'm—" She shook her head in a rare show of discomfort. "I'm not going anywhere for Thanksgiving. My family…we're sort of distant." The arms she'd wrapped around herself tightened.

"If you don't have anywhere to be in the morning then you should stay the night here."

"You want me to stay?"

"I do. Yes. And then I want to do what we just did three or four more times."

"Four!" she said on a laugh. "Four times before tomorrow morning?"

"Preferably."

He'd hardly know himself right now if he were an outside observer. He was beyond what should be comfortable with Hayden this soon.

After he'd learned of his actual birth parents and twin brother, Tate had vowed to deal with it like he had any other moment of adversity. Just plow through with certainty and confidence that it would work out in the end. He'd underestimated the emotional toll of finding out his entire existence was a lie.

His relationship with his adoptive parents had become strained—a totally new dynamic for them—and then Claire had ended the engagement. Tate began thinking that closeness wasn't something he was meant to have on a long-term basis.

He was having trouble categorizing Hayden, though. He

liked being close to her. He liked her honesty and wit. He just plain liked her. Way more than he should.

Tate had played safe his entire life. Had laid out each step after the last in a predictable, cautious way. What good had playing it safe done him? He'd lost everything unexpectedly.

A part of him argued that he should be smart about this thing with Hayden—that he shouldn't get in too deep—and in response he raised a middle finger. He was trying a new tack. He was embracing danger and unpredictability for a change.

He needed to shake off the caution from his past. Needed to feel *alive*. And since no one made him feel more alive than Hayden Green, he needed *her*.

They both dressed, pausing to send satisfied smiles over at each other in between zipping and buckling. She tugged on her boots and pulled a hair tie from her pocket. In two seconds, and barely trying, she'd fashioned a ponytail.

"Impressive." Everything about her.

He took her hand and walked with her downstairs. Five minutes later he served her at his kitchen table, setting a mug piled high with sticky, square marshmallows in front of her.

She cradled the mug before navigating a sip of the cocoa around the melting marshmallows. "Mmm."

"When you made that sound earlier, I liked it then, too."

"Yes, well, you earned it."

Confidence straightened his shoulders at the comment and again when she looked around the room. He admired it with her—the stylish gas fireplace, the wide open windows with nothing but dark woods beyond. His carefully chosen furnishings, earthy in both materials and color.

"I'd love to have this much space." She tilted her head back to admire the overhead lighting. "Not that I don't love living above my studio. But this…" She let out a wistful sigh. "This is beautiful."

"Does that mean you're staying?"

"I didn't bring any clothes." She pressed a finger to his lips when he opened his mouth to argue. "You're going to say I don't need them."

"Damn straight." Movement outside caught his attention and he pulled her finger from his lips. "Look."

A deer poked its head from the trees, cocking its ears to listen. Hayden let out a soft gasp of surprise.

"This is why I tucked my house into the woods. So? You staying?"

"You think a deer is enough to get me to agree?"

"I was hoping that and the promise of sex four more times before morning might seal the deal."

She chuckled, but didn't answer him.

"Tell me about your twin brother." She lifted her mug.

"Not the smoothest segue."

"Go big or go home. Except I'm not going home. Not yet, anyway."

"Tease." It was easy to be with her, even when she asked questions about his newfound family.

"It has to be mind-boggling to have a twin. To have that connection with someone. Do you see aspects of yourself when you look at him?"

He had to think about how to answer that. Not because he was choosing his words, but because he hadn't really thought of Reid and himself in that way. What was it like to look at Reid, whom Tate had *shared a womb with*, for God's sake?

"We both gesture with our hands when we talk. Not wildly or anything, but subtly. We do this—" he pressed his index finger and thumb together like he was popping a balloon with a pin "—when we want to make a point. I never paid attention to that until Reid did it. And then I noticed I did it, too. That I've always done it."

"So you make the same gestures even though you haven't been around each other for decades."

"Apparently. It's surreal. I always thought I was an only child and then I meet this stranger and a few dinners later it's like I've known him my whole life."

"I guess in a way, you have." Hayden rested her hand on Tate's thigh.

"He invited me to London for Christmas." Tate took a deep breath. He wasn't sure how he felt about that invitation. "Where my parents live."

"That's exciting," she said, but there was caution in her tone.

"I didn't give him an answer yet, but Reid and Drew—his pregnant fiancée—are going."

"You're going to be an uncle." Her face brightened. "Lucky. I'm an only child. No hope of being an aunt unless I'm made honorary aunt by one of my friends."

And to think he used to be an only child, too. "It's… overwhelming to have this all happening at once."

"I'm sure it is. I bet your adoptive parents are having a hard time letting you navigate the holidays now that they have to share you."

"You have no idea." He rubbed his temple, a headache forming behind his fingers. His mother had cried when he'd told her he wouldn't be home for Thanksgiving or Christmas, and his father had demanded he consider someone other than himself. Tate hadn't argued, simply explaining that he was doing what he had to do. A breath later his father was apologizing and his mother had stopped crying. Tate still felt the sting from their reactions, though. He'd had an almost consuming need to give in to what they wanted. In the end he'd stood his ground.

"I'm sorry. Just tell me to shut up. I didn't mean to encroach on your—"

"I was kidnapped," he interrupted, and Hayden's jaw went slack. She didn't know the whole truth, and he needed her to see the full picture. If only to understand why he was making the decisions he was making "At age three. I was taken from my and my brother's birthday party in London, and our parents never found me again. My adoptive parents assumed the agency they were adopting me from was legitimate until that agency extorted money from them. They suspected something was off, but they wanted a child so badly."

His budding headache took root and throbbed like a truth bomb ready to detonate.

"The Duncans were told my birth parents were dead— they were given falsified death certificates filled out with fake names. Eventually, my real birth parents believed I was dead. They buried an empty casket five years after my disappearance."

"Oh, Tate." Sympathy flooded Hayden's dark eyes.

He continued, monotone. Might as well share it all. "My adoptive parents paid the so-called agency's exorbitant fees without asking too many questions. My mother said she never would've imagined I was kidnapped. She had an inkling that the agency was unscrupulous, but if money was the only thing standing in the way of bringing me home…"

He shook his head. It wasn't their fault. Not really. But he couldn't help blaming them for not acting on their instincts. Had Marion explored that inkling he might've been raised in London rather than California. He might've been returned to his rightful home, to his actual birth parents who were no more than strangers to him now.

*And you wouldn't have been raised by the Duncans.* Which meant never knowing the family he loved dearly.

Never setting foot on Spright Island to build a community that he treasured. Never meeting the people who lived here—Hayden included.

He wasn't sure which thought was more chill-inducing.

Spooked, the deer became suddenly alert, before turning and darting off into the trees, his white tail a visible exclamation point in the dark. Had his parents been equally afraid of digging for the truth?

"Then a month ago I was in a coffee shop in Seattle, and this guy in front of me in line starts babbling about how I was his twin brother."

Hayden's hand formed a fist and she seemed to keep herself in check. Like she wanted to touch him but didn't know if she should. "You must've been…"

"Terrified," Tate finished for her. "I called my mom after, expecting her to laugh it off. She didn't. And the next night when I had dinner with Claire, I drank a stupid amount of wine and told her everything I just told you, and…"

"She left you."

"Not that night, but eventually. Yes." He gave Hayden a sad smile. "Now's your chance."

But she didn't heed his warning, stand up and put on her coat. She gripped the back of his neck and kissed him soft and long. Achingly gentle. He returned her kiss, tasting on her lips the newfound courage she'd uncovered.

She made him feel strong, confident. All the ways he used to be that had gone missing recently. He felt as if he'd been tossed overboard into a churning sea of uncertainty and was only now clawing his way onto dry land.

"Most complicated one-night stand ever," she said, rubbing her thumb along his bottom lip.

"Is that enough for you?" God knew it was all he had to give. He couldn't rely on the future any longer. Certainty was a myth.

She tilted her head and watched him. "I'm not opposed to two nights."

He smiled. "How about we take it one night at a time?" He was already mentally undressing her, wanting more of the earlier taste she gave him.

She unbuttoned a button on his shirt and then the one under it. "One night at a time."

He covered her lips with a kiss, the sweetness from the marshmallow on her tongue. One night at a time was as unchartered as territory came for him. Completely opposite of how he'd operated before.

He had no idea where they would end up. One night at a time broke every rule he had, every guideline he'd followed previously. Which was exactly what he needed.

Different. New. Exciting.

In a word: *Hayden.*

# Eleven

One night turned into two and two into three and three into more. Hayden and Tate had been saying yes to almost three weeks' worth of nights so far.

It was December and Christmas was in full swing at SWC. Colorful lights and garland were wrapped around lampposts, retail shop doors boasted gold-and-green wreaths and holiday music was piped through speakers inside.

Hayden had decorated her small, but pretty, tree in her apartment with red and gold decorations, and the larger one in her studio with silver and blue. She even went through the trouble of hanging outdoor lights for the first time.

As loath as she was to admit it, life really *was* better when she wasn't alone during the holidays.

She'd spent a lot of time at Tate's house, in front of the fireplace and in his bed. So much time that she hadn't been at her own apartment much, save for running upstairs to change or showering after her classes. With her schedule trimmed back for the holidays, though, she had a decent amount of free time.

She'd finished up her last class of the year ten minutes ago and was just updating her planner and checking her email when the bell over the door dinged to alert her some-one was coming in.

Since she knew exactly who that someone was, she didn't bother calling out that she was closed.

Tate looked like the billionaire Arlene had accused him of being, his expensive trousers in deep charcoal gray, his shoes black and shiny. The part of him that deviated was the ever-present dark leather jacket that hung over his mus-cular, round shoulders.

"Now that's a nice scarf," she commented about the red scarf looped around his neck. She'd purchased it for him, for no reason except she'd seen it and thought of him.

His sexy grin was missing as he stalked toward her in the empty studio, however, causing her nerves to prickle, and not pleasantly.

And since that prickle came with fear that things had changed and she didn't know why or how, she didn't like it at all.

*Breathe. He's allowed to have a bad day.*

Plus, he was here. That's what mattered.

"What's up?" she asked, forcing a bright tone.

He seemed to snap out of it at the question. "Nothing. The scarf—" he lifted one side of it "—was a gift from an incredibly beautiful woman."

He was joking, that was a good sign. "Should I be jeal-ous?"

He kissed her hello, a long and lingering press of his lips that assuaged her fears some. Maybe she'd overreacted. It wasn't like she was accustomed to being happy and in a relationship. Getting used to both simultaneously would take some doing.

Hayden reminded herself not to put too much pressure on the outcome. Years ago she'd decided that being on her own was A-okay. She didn't need a family or a marriage, or even a boyfriend, to feel whole. Even so, she couldn't deny that she was happy with Tate. She was going to enjoy it, no matter how finite.

And she was *so* into Tate Duncan. More than any guy she'd ever met. It'd only been three weeks, and already he was more than a friend—way more than a sex buddy. He was just plain *more*, and she'd left it at that in her head. Labeling what they had was dangerous. Like naming it would lead to its inevitable end sooner rather than later.

"How did the meeting go?" she asked.

Tate had stopped by a planning meeting for the New Year's Eve gala, which consisted of a lush black-tie party with cocktails and dancing.

"Well. Ran into Nick there. He invited us to the Purple Rose for lunch."

Nick was, hands down, Hayden's favorite chef. He made some of freshest, most delicious meals, all using simple ingredients.

"Us?" Without her permission, her heart lifted at the reference that Tate had mentioned her to Nick.

"We're hardly under the radar, Ms. Green." But Tate's smile told her that he didn't mind they were SWC-official. "Are you available?"

"I am," she said with a smile of her own.

An hour later they were enjoying roasted vegetable–white bean salad, a quinoa bowl and a plate of crispy Brussels sprouts drenched in a sweet Thai dressing.

"As I suspected," Hayden said as she spooned another healthy portion of Brussels sprouts onto her plate. "Nick sold his soul to the devil in exchange for the recipe for this sauce."

Plus it wasn't on the menu yet. She could get used to this sort of special treatment. She hadn't been in the market for a boyfriend, if that's what Tate was, but having one that held the golden key to the city was the way to go.

Tate placed his fork on his table, swiping his mouth with a napkin. His gaze was unfocused, his demeanor shifting abruptly. She was reminded of the mood he'd been in when he stepped into her studio.

"I have something to ask you." His eyebrows compressed.

Even as her heart ka-thumped a worried staccato, Hayden said, "Okay."

"It's a big ask."

"Okay."

"Reid called me this morning, asking again if I'd consider going to London for Christmas." His Adam's apple jumped when he swallowed, and he reached for his water glass. "I've decided to go."

"That's great." She meant it. Meeting his birth parents was a huge leap for him.

"I want you to go with me."

Hayden sagged in her seat, shocked down to her toes. Everything about the way he'd been behaving would have her assuming he'd dump her not...take her to London?

She couldn't say yes to *going to London* with him. Even though she'd wanted to visit England for as long as she could remember.

Meeting his family was *huge*. And at Christmas? That was monumental.

He continued to watch her, waiting for acknowledgment, or maybe for her to shout an exuberant *yes!* Since she didn't know what to say, she sort of repeated his words. "Go with you? To London?"

"Yes. There's more."

More than inviting her to London for Christmas to meet his birth parents? She slicked damp palms on her jeans. She wasn't sure she wanted to know, but for the sake of her sanity, she *had* to know, or else the possibilities would stack themselves to the heavens before falling onto her and crushing her to death.

*Calm down. It's not like he's going to propose.*

But then he said, "The Singletons are under the assumption that I'm engaged. Because I *was* engaged. Reid knows Claire and I ended, but I asked him not to tell George and Jane that my engagement was off."

Oh, God. *Was* he going to propose?

"Why not tell them?" she croaked, her mind and heart racing like they were vying for first place.

"I'm not sure." His frown deepened. "I was concerned they'd think I wasn't doing well, I guess? That they would assume their son's life was unraveling because of the news. I guess I didn't want them to worry."

He was one of the kindest men she'd ever met. Even amidst the turmoil in his own life, he was looking out for those who loved him. Even those he had no memory of knowing.

"If you don't have a passport, I can pay to have it expedited for you."

"I have a passport," she said. "What is it, exactly, that you need from me?"

He nodded, his expression an unsure mix of dread and concern. "If they assume you're my fiancée—if they even remember I have one—all you have to do is not argue. You don't have to pretend your name is Claire, or anything."

"Good. I wouldn't." She quirked her lips and Tate's mouth shifted into a smile.

"I don't want to keep you from your plans, but it'd be a huge favor for me. Your travel and incidentals would be covered."

She started to say he didn't have to do that but with her light work schedule and shopping for the holidays she hadn't exactly stashed away a few thou for a trip to another country.

"I've always wanted to go to London."

She might be sweating the fact that Tate, who was basically a really meaningful fling, was sort of proposing to her and asking her to go to a foreign country, but she couldn't not be there for him when he needed her. Going to celebrate Christmas with a bunch of strangers might be weird for her, but she imagined for him, it'd be downright uncomfortable.

Plus, visiting London would be a dream come true. The alternative would be going home to Seattle to endure her grandmother's drunkenness, her mother's scrambling after her like a servant and her father's apathy.

Tate was still watching her carefully, as if he was deciding whether or not to sweeten the pot by offering something more. He didn't have to. She wanted to be with him, and this was a unique situation.

"I'll do it."

"Yeah?" He grinned, the agony from earlier sweeping away with that smile.

Tate deserved a win, and, dammit so did she. If pretending to be his fiancée would give them both a sense of triumph, why the hell not?

But a small voice in her head whispered, *so many reasons.*

# Twelve

Reid and Drew had flown to London two days ago. There was a reason Tate didn't sync his flight with his twin's: he wanted to keep his stay in the UK as brief as possible. With the excuse of work—partially true—he'd instead booked his and Hayden's international flight to arrive at 11:15 a.m. December 23. That gave them the day to hide away to rest, and then they could emerge for cocktail hour and dinner before ducking away again to sleep. Then all he'd have to endure was Christmas Eve and Christmas Day before flying home the next morning. Which, thanks to an eight-hour time difference, would land them in Seattle just two hours after they left England.

He'd booked first-class business tickets on the flight out, not because he was planning on working but because they were the best seats the airline had to offer. Hayden was doing him a solid by joining him—he wanted to make sure she felt special.

When Hayden sat in her seat next to a bulky armrest-slash-desk, her eyebrows were so high on her forehead it was almost comical. "Tate."

She took in the cabin around her, which consisted of thirty business-class "pods," each with its own private, wraparound seat dividers. There was a divider that could separate his and Hayden's seats as well, but he'd lowered it the second they found their seats.

"Sorry, this was the nicest seat the airline had."

"Smart-ass." Subtly, she shook her head, her smile tolerant. "I usually sit in the middle of coach with my knees smashed into the seat in front of me."

She stretched her legs out, unable to touch the pod in front of her with her toes. Then her smile faded. "It's too much."

"Let's revisit that claim five hours into a nine-and-a-half-hour flight." He lifted an eyebrow. "You'll be thanking me for copious legroom and a chair that reclines."

"And my own TV." She gestured at the screen in front of her. "And tray table, and—" She lifted a black bag labeled Amenity Kit and held it up to show him.

"Sleep mask, lavender spray and a Casper-brand pillow and fleece blanket."

She laughed, an effervescent sound, and the tightness in his chest eased. There would be a lot of people and overwhelming circumstances to deal with shortly after they landed at Heathrow, but for right now, he had it easy. With Hayden.

She'd made this trip better already and it hadn't started yet. Plus, watching her wide eyes gobble up the luxury that had become pedestrian to him was a good reminder of how far he'd come. The dose of confidence and self-assuredness would go a long way when he was a stranger in a strange land... Except it wasn't a strange land. It was his *hometown*.

Would that ever sink in?

Hayden was oohing and ahhing over the lavender spray and mentioned again how fluffy the pillow was, and he had to grin.

"You're easy to spoil, Ms. Green."

Her cheeks pinked. "I'm acting like a total country mouse, aren't I?"

"A little, but I'm enjoying it." He'd never done without. Trips he'd taken with his family had always been in first class or via private flight. Seeing this experience through fresh eyes was damned refreshing. Just like the rest of her.

"I can't help it. It's new to me." She narrowed her eyes in faux suspicion. "Are you making sure I'm not going to back out at the last second? Have you heard all sorts of horrifying secrets about your family? Am I in for the ride of my life?"

"The opposite. Reid gushes over them. And Drew hasn't met them but she says she's spent a lot of time on the phone with Reid's, um, our mother, Jane." He paused while that soaked in. "Anyway, Drew loves her already, and she hasn't met her."

"That's good news." Hayden's encouragement was careful, but Tate had a feeling they'd survive this awkward holiday regardless of what he had to face. At least he wouldn't be facing it alone.

He appreciated the hell out of her for being here.

It wasn't something he'd successfully put into words, but he hoped the first-class flight, the trip to London and every last way he planned on worshipping her in the bedroom would say what he couldn't: That there was no one he'd rather navigate this patch of his life with other than Hayden.

*One day at a time.*

Seven hours into the flight Hayden was feeling the fatigue of traveling tenfold. The longest flight she'd been on had been a five-hour flight to Toronto for a yoga conference last year. She could thank that trip for her having a passport.

She'd already been to the bathroom and had moved around to stretch her legs. Even the roomy pod, complete with seat and desk, couldn't cure her craving for movement. She struck a few poses as best she could from her chair, regardless of who watched. Though, she doubted anyone was paying attention to her or her seated warrior pose. There were only thirty seats in this section of the plane, and she assumed everyone desired privacy first and foremost. It was by far the best way to travel.

She would've liked to give Tate at least *some* money for her travel expenses, no matter how trivial. Yes, they were dating, but this went beyond their agreement to take things as they came. But each time she brought it up, he shook his head denoting the end of the discussion. An hour into their flight she'd tried again and his, "It's a gift, Hayden, stop asking," told her she had surpassed insistence and tiptoed into ungratefulness.

She couldn't help it. Financial arguments had been commonplace in her family's home especially since her grandmother drank away every dollar she wrapped her fist around, leaving her wellbeing to Hayden's parents.

Hayden hadn't grown up with a healthy view of much of anything as a kid. As an adult she'd studied her backside off trying to learn how to save and invest for her future. Since the bulk of care and concern from her mother was lavished on her father and grandmother, Hayden had been on her own.

She'd learned to care for herself, knowing no one else would take care of her. It was the harder path, but at least reliable. It was also the main reason she'd chose to stay unmarried. Trusting herself was easy. Trusting others, not so much.

Tate, reclined in his seat, arms folded over his chest, was asleep. She watched his chest lift and fall and considered how much she'd trusted him already, without realizing she was doing it.

Anyone would assume he was peacefully snoozing except for the furrow in his brow. He was worried about meeting them—his parents. She couldn't imagine how she'd feel if she'd found out she had a whole other family who lived in London.

*Relieved, probably*, she thought with a bittersweet smile.

# Thirteen

When Hayden first laid eyes on Tate's brother, Reid, she thought, *My God, there really are two of them*.

They weren't identical twins, but there was no denying the set of their mouths and—Tate was right—they both made the same gestures when they talked.

In the back seat of Reid's rental car, she sat next to his fiancée Drew while the guys carried on a conversation up front.

"They're both so attractive it's stupefying," Drew stated. "Don't you think?"

The question was asked at a near whisper, even though the guys were chattering loud enough that they likely hadn't overheard.

"It doesn't take much to stupefy me after that flight," Hayden joked. The truth, had she been forced to admit it, was that 100 percent of the attraction coming from her was aimed directly at Tate.

"No kidding." Drew snorted, and like the rest of her, it was darling. "We arrived three days ago, and my body is just now accepting that I'm supposed to be awake."

"So by the time I'm used to the time change, I'll be on my way back home."

"You're seriously leaving on Boxing Day? Criminal!" Drew clutched her nonexistent pearls. "It is sad that you're not staying longer, though."

Hayden felt similarly. She liked Drew, even having only known her for a few minutes. The other woman was both scrappy and easygoing. Hayden didn't know much about how Drew and Reid got together, except that she was the little sister of one of Reid's best friends. Hayden would bet there was a story there. She'd have to extract details from Drew over dinner.

"Hey! I heard you're engaged!" Drew exclaimed.

"Uh…"

"*Pretending* to be engaged, love," Reid corrected his fiancée, throwing a wink at her in the rearview mirror. "I told you that."

"I *know*. Mind your own business up there, Gorgeous Inc. That's his new nickname." Drew pursed her lips. "I guess though, if Reid is the CEO of Gorgeous Inc., Tate has to be, at the very least, COO." She glanced first at Reid's profile, then Tate's. "Stupefying."

Hayden giggled, but it led to a yawn. She was feeling every hour of their lengthy travel.

"Do you want coffee?" Drew offered, clearly discerning what that yawn was about. "It's easier to find tea here, but there are a few really good shops that serve both. We stopped by one when we finished Christmas shopping yesterday."

"Mum is serving tea when we arrive." Reid said as he drove past pubs and shops downtown. "Can't rob her of that."

Tate rubbed his palms down his dark jeans, and Hayden thought she saw his shoulders stiffen. No doubt the mention of his "mum" had set him on edge.

Reid, consummate entertainer, launched into his tour

guide voice and pointed out a few buildings beyond the car's window.

Drew leaned closer to Hayden, keeping her voice low. "I can't imagine how difficult this must be for Tate."

"Yes."

"And you." Sincerity swam in the other brunette's dark gaze. "If you need anyone to talk to while you're here… about family stuff or girl stuff…or *engagement* stuff."

Hayden laughed. "You're not going to give up on that, are you?"

"Nope." Drew grinned, seemingly pleased with herself, and pleased in general. She palmed her still-flat, pregnant belly. "I'm just saying, you can't predict where you'll end up with these Singleton boys. Right, Gorgeous, Inc.?"

The look Reid sent through the rearview was a smolder if Hayden had ever seen one. And when Tate peeked over his shoulder at her, that look held a certain smolder for her as well.

Those Singleton boys, indeed.


Tate took in the rows of houses they drove past, most tightly packed in next to each other. Having not been here past the age of three, he had no recollection of the area. Nothing looked familiar and the foreignness only made him long for his parents' home in California. His chest grew tight. He'd never been a homesick kid, but he felt that way now.

The cocktail of excitement and nerves over meeting the man and woman who'd created him had been shaken, stirred and then thrown into a blender for good measure. He'd had a million silent discussions with himself on the flight over about expectations, reasoning that this meeting didn't have to be anything more than cordial. But it was hard not to have expectations when Reid went on and on about their parents. He meant well, but it'd almost been too much to absorb for Tate.

"They're getting on well," Reid said. "We'll have to keep an eye on that, brother, in case they decide to team up on us."

Reid pulled into a long asphalt driveway flanked by short, decorative stone pillars. "Here we are."

The Singleton house was in Berkshire, about half an hour from the airport, and sat on three acres of land which backed up to the very wooded area Tate had been dragged to when he was a toddler.

He repressed a shudder.

"Mum's bloody gorgeous, by the way." Reid smirked, proud. "She was a fashion model in her twenties, not that she looks a day past thirty-seven." He threw the car into Park and faced Tate. "Mate. Welcome home." Then Reid lightened the heavy sentiment with, "I've already warned Mum not to smother you. You're welcome."

Tate had to hand it to his brother—Reid hadn't acted as if this was strange for a while now. Ironically, that made this entirely strange situation easier to accept.

As the four of them climbed from the car and approached the house, the dark wood front door with iron handles swung open.

He'd seen photos of Jane and George, but nothing could have prepared him for seeing his birth parents in the flesh for the first time in decades.

"Silver fox, am I right?" Drew murmured under her breath to Hayden. "His mom's hot, too."

Hayden replied, but Tate couldn't hear anything save the blood rushing past his eardrums. His poised mother was stationed at the threshold, dressed in white slacks and a cowl-necked gray sweater. She held on to Tate's father, who wore a casual suit and looked much younger than his stately name implied. Jane's hair was stylishly gray, but

George's maintained most of its dark brown with only a feathering of gray at the temples.

Tate took in every detail of the pair as he walked on stiff legs. Reid mentioned the traffic going easy before gently gripping his—*their*—mother's shoulders and guiding her inside. Before Tate stepped over the threshold, he felt Hayden's hand in his.

"Piece of cake," she whispered, looking beautiful but jet-lagged. Tate might be in unfamiliar territory but she'd become familiar. He would be here, facing this moment alone, if it wasn't for her.

He squeezed her fingers with his, unable to tell her what it meant to him that she was here, but hoping she knew anyway. Her tired wink suggested she might.

He'd make sure she had time to rest during the next few days. He pulled her to walk beside him and stole a kiss before following everyone inside. Reid led his mother into the entryway and then stood next to Drew.

George offered Tate a palm, the first to break the invisible wall between them. Looking into his father's face was like seeing someone you thought you might know but couldn't remember from where. Tate gripped George's hand.

"Good handshake, son. I'm your father, George Singleton. This is your mother, Jane." He cupped his wife's shoulder as she began to cry. Pretty at first, her high cheekbones and full lips barely shifting from their neutral positions, but a moment later, tears fell and that perfect bone structure seemed to dissolve.

Her outstretched arms shook when she reached for Tate. "Please, may I?" Her voice was broken, and Tate wasn't far behind, nodding his acceptance as tears blurred his vision.

He held his mother, expecting awkwardness, but it never came. Odd as it was to feel a connection with her, he did. The same way he'd felt it with Reid since the first moment he saw him in that coffee shop. As if a connection deep in his soul had been forged eons ago.

"Oh, my Wesley," she murmured repeatedly as she held on to him. "My sweet Wesley." She must have felt his arms go rigid, because she abruptly pulled away and corrected herself. "Tate. Tate is your name."

"They're both my names." He'd come to accept that recently. Easier now that the woman who'd carried him in her womb was standing in the circle of his arms.

Jane embraced him again, holding on for a long moment. A few other sniffs sounded in the room—from the direction of Drew and Hayden if Tate wasn't mistaken.

Jane let go of Tate, nodding with finality, her tears no longer falling. "One thing's for certain," she said as she studied his face. "You're much better looking than your brother."

"Hey!" Reid protested. The rest of them laughed and the tension that had built receded some.

It was *really* good to laugh.

"All right, then. Tea." Jane clapped her hands and led them farther into the house. Rich, caramel brown floors matched the doorframes and windowsills, and the walls were painted a soft white. The color palette was mostly burgundies and pine greens, and everywhere Tate looked was a reminder of nature. *Like my house*, he thought as he admired a piece of petrified wood in a slightly misshapen hand-thrown clay bowl.

"I made it. It's rubbish," Jane said of the bowl, bypassing it to walk to a cart in the corner of the room.

"So's what's in it," George agreed, his tone teasing. "A stick that's turned into a rock."

"Tate has petrified wood in his house," Hayden said, meeting his eyes and then Jane's. "You two have that in common." She stroked his arm with a hand as they lowered onto a jewel-toned settee, but then rose a moment later to help his mother serve.

"...lucky to have such a caring fiancée," Tate heard his mother say.

Hayden shot a quick glance to Tate, her expression no doubt matching his own. She recovered smoothly, flashing his mother a grin and offering a generic, polite response. "Thank you, Jane. I'm happy to help."

"I hear you own a nature preserve," George said, drawing Tate's attention from his fake fiancée.

Hayden handed Tate a cup of tea and sat with him and he renewed the promise he'd made to himself on the trip over. He was definitely making time to show Hayden his appreciation later.

# Fourteen

"Your parents are sort of incredible." Hayden unpacked her suitcase, stashing her clothes in the dresser in the guest bedroom.

On that count, Tate had to agree. The weirdest part about meeting them was that they no longer felt like strangers. They'd discussed Spright Island, Jane and George both eager to hear of Tate's success with the community. Jane abashedly admitted that she'd "Googled it" and was "quite impressed."

He'd always been proud of the work he'd done there. The wellness community was his passion, but also his legacy. He'd never thought much about having a family of his own, always focusing instead on work. Claire had been equally focused on her career and stated she'd never wanted to have children. After having met the members of his actual family tree, though, Tate had briefly entertained the idea of having a family of his own. He supposed that was inevitable considering the circumstances.

Hayden hid her suitcase in the closet, yawning as she shut the bedroom door. He wondered if she wanted children. She'd never mentioned it before, but given the hints that her family was rife with conflict, maybe she didn't.

It wasn't the kind of discussion two people having a day-to-day affair would have, but he couldn't stop the vision of a little boy with dark hair and his blue eyes. Or twins.

"Jesus." He pulled a hand down his face to staunch the thoughts.

"I know. I'm tired, too." Hayden yawned again and he was glad she'd assumed he was tired rather than considering her potentially bearing his children. Maybe he could blame fatigue on his thoughts. They certainly weren't par for course.

*Is any of this?*

"Why don't you stay up here and rest." The guest room was hidden away at the back of the upstairs hallway, and he knew his parents wouldn't mind Hayden not showing for cocktail hour. Besides, it'd been George that had had invited Tate and Reid for brandy. Pregnant Drew had begged off to bed and his mother told Tate she'd happily join Hayden for a nip, but only if Hayden wasn't too tired. "Jane meant what she said when she told you to do what you like."

Hayden tilted her head and studied him, a spark of interest in her eyes despite the fatigue. "Do you think you'll ever be comfortable calling her Mom? Or Mum, as Reid calls her?"

Tate sucked in a breath. He guessed it wasn't that alarming to be thinking of having a family. He was surrounded by family and piecing the relationships together as best he could.

"Maybe someday," he said, but oddly that felt like a betrayal to his adoptive mother.

"You're handling this really well." Hayden palmed his cheek.

Placing his hands on her hips, Tate pulled her closer, and she draped her forearms over his shoulders. She fit there, in his embrace. Claire hadn't fit in his arms like she was meant to be there—a detail he'd always overlooked. And now that he'd met George and Jane and Reid Singleton, he wondered if in hindsight he'd find that he never fit with his family in California, either.

"Deep thoughts?"

"How do you know where you belong? Is it with the people who are familiar, or the people who are related?"

"That's a whopper, Tate Duncan," She paused to consider. "I used to feel comfortable in chaos, but now I crave a stable environment. In your very unique case, I don't think you'll have to choose. You have room in your life for your adoptive parents and your birth parents, for Reid and Drew, and for your new niece or nephew when he or she is born."

*And you.*

Pretending to be engaged to Hayden, pretending they had a future with "forever" implied, it wasn't hard to picture her there during his brother's wedding, the birth of a niece or nephew, or even a vacation to California to meet his adoptive parents.

That, too, felt dangerous, but this was also a safe place to consider the possibility of what life would be like if he and Hayden were truly engaged.

How it'd be expected to linger in their shared bedroom...

"How tired are you?" Tate lowered his mouth to her neck.

"Mmm," she purred.

He took to her lips for a brief kiss that didn't stay that way. Sliding his tongue along hers was the foolproof cure for jet lag. He backed her toward the bed.

"Tate," she whispered, and he was sure "we can't" would follow.

"Don't tell me to stop." He needed her. Needed to ground himself in the only reality that made sense right now. If there was one component that wasn't pretend, it was their explosive chemistry.

She raised and lowered one eyebrow, suddenly alert. "I was going to say brandy with George and Reid can wait."

"Hell, yes, it can."

She'd dressed for dinner in a long-sleeved black shirt made from material that held the slightest shimmer. He slipped a hand beneath it and along her smooth skin.

She tipped her head back, her dark hair falling over her shoulders while his hands explored her full breasts over the smooth cups of her bra.

Her moan of approval spurred him on. And like that first time he was with her, he didn't want to rush. Brandy with his family be damned.

He made short work of stripping her of her shirt and bra. Cupping her breasts, he thumbed her nipples and then kissed the tips of each. Her hands explored his hair, wrecking it. He took that as encouragement and continued circling one nipple with his tongue.

He unbuttoned her dark pants, slipping his hand past the waistband of her panties to tease her smooth folds. Spreading that wetness over her clit, he guided his fingers back and forth, until Hayden's hands clutched his shoulders and her moans elevated to bleats of pleasure.

Yanking his head from her chest, she kissed him with ferocity, none of her earlier fatigue present. He tenderly stroked her into her first orgasm. Watching her mouth round in pleasure and her beautiful face contort wouldn't be a sight he'd soon forget.

She shuddered in his arms, and he supported her weight, bracing her waist and kissing a trail from her jaw to her ear.

"You're so fucking gorgeous when you do that," he rasped. "This time, do it again, but with me inside you."

"Sounds good to me." She smiled. A challenge.

He lifted her into his arms and tossed her onto the bed. She bounced, stifling her laugh with a hand over her lips while he tugged off her heeled shoes and pants.

She daintily scooted back, folding her long legs to one side and looking up at him sexily. She was like every wet dream he'd ever had, only better—because she was here. She was real. And he was *really* going to enjoy coaxing forth her next orgasm.

Tate took off his shirt, and Hayden's dark eyes flared. That she looked at him the way he looked at her—like she couldn't believe how damn lucky she was to have him naked—hardened his erection and sharpened his desire.

He finished undressing and climbed over her, tickling her lips with a series of gentle kisses before trailing his mouth down her neck to her breasts. He made a pit stop at each one—he'd never be able to resist the lure of her perfect nipples—and then made himself comfortable between her thighs.

*Ruined.*

Tate had ruined her for anyone else. Which was alarming, since she didn't spend much time considering a man permanently being around for sex, or dating, or…anything, really.

But, she wasn't above having fun.

*Which was what this is*, she reminded herself sternly.

George and Jane, and even Reid and Drew who knew the engagement was for show, had treated Hayden like family tonight. There was a part of her that had basked in that attention. At the idea of being a part of a family that genuinely seemed to want for each other, not from each other.

But Tate wasn't a permanent fixture. This was a fairy tale. One where she'd been whisked to London by a wealthy prince—one who *really* knew how to use his freaking tongue.

The sound of the condom wrapper being torn open jolted her out of her post-orgasmic bliss.

"Wait!"

Tate looked almost alarmed at her outburst, which was sort of funny.

"Let's hold off on this part." She took the condom from his hand. "There's something I wanted to do first."

Shoving him onto his back, she pressed a kiss to first one pectoral and then the other and positioned herself over him. As she kissed her way down his torso, Tate grew reverently silent. She knew he'd figured out her intentions the moment he scooped her hair into his hands and watched her work.

And oh, did she *work*.

She held his shaft at the base, flicking him a sultry glance while licking the tip of his cock. His mouth dropped open, the tendons in his neck standing out in stark relief.

He smelled of soap from their earlier—and sadly, separate—showers, and the musky smell that was his and his alone.

She alternated with teasing licks and loving kisses and then swallowed him whole, tickling his balls while the air sawed out of his lungs in uneven gasps.

Moments before she would have swallowed his release, he tugged her hair, still wrapped in his fists. "Hayden."

When she didn't stop right away, his voice grew gruff, more demanding, *"Hayden."*

She let him go with a soft pop, licking her lips. "Fine. I'll stop, but only bec—"

Without warning, he flipped her to her back and was over her in an instant. She yelped in surprise then slapped a hand over her mouth. The house was large, but not *that* large. No need to broadcast that she was upstairs shagging the Singletons' newfound son.

"Condom," she reminded him as he nudged her entrance with his very hard member.

"Right. Of course." He blinked once, then twice like he was trying to bring his brain back online. He rolled on the condom in record time and, before her next breath, entered her in one long, slow slide. Buried to the root, he paused to blow out a careful, measured breath.

"You okay, COO of Gorgeous Inc.?" She feathered his hair from his forehead, and he offered a narrow-eyed glare. "COO? Founder? Which do you prefer?"

"I prefer—" he slid out and then in again "—for you to call me by my name. Repeatedly. And with growing enthusiasm," he added as he continued moving.

*"Tate."* He seemed to gain strength as she repeated his name over and over. As if he'd needed, more than anything, that reminder of who he was. As if hearing his name had anchored him.

"Come for me, Hayden." He lifted her calf, and she stretched her leg to rest it easily on his shoulder. The angle made it easier for him to hit her G-spot, which he had a knack for finding.

"There," she said with a gasp. Damn, he was good.

"One more for me. Then I'll let you sleep for a few hours."

He grinned, and she returned it. Her smile fell when she felt the telltale building of a showstopper of an orgasm.

"Tate." She continued worshipping as she gripped the blankets with kneading fists. Her nipples pebbled in the cool bedroom air even as sweat beaded his forehead from his workout.

The fourth stroke was the charm.

She dissolved, the release hitting her so hard she squeezed her eyes shut to absorb the impact. He wasn't far behind her, growling his release. He came to a jerky stop moments before collapsing on top of her.

His weight pressed her into the mattress, a thin sheen of sweat sticking his chest to hers. "By far my favorite work out is having sex with you."

"Agreed." She swept a hand through his hair and kissed his temple.

He left to deal with the condom, but by the time he returned, her eyes refused to stay open. She was vaguely aware of the sound of him pulling on his clothes, barely awake when he feathered a kiss on her cheek.

The last words she remembered was his whispered promise of, "Rest up. You'll need your strength for later."

# Fifteen

"He had no idea who you were?" Hayden leaned closer to Drew at the tightly packed bar.

When they'd first stepped into the Churchill, she'd been agape with wonder. The outside of the building was draped with Christmas trees. "Eighty of them and eighteen thousand fairy lights," Reid had shared. From that point on, the place had fascinated her.

Hanging from the ceiling were numerous beaten-copper pots, pans and lights, and at one point she spotted a guitar case and even an accordion. As its name suggested, the Churchill was dripping with memorabilia, in memory of the man after which it was named. The walls were wooden and dotted with framed photos and paintings, the tables and chairs well worn from plenty of use.

"There's no better place to be than Church on Christmas Eve," Reid had told Tate, looping a brotherly arm around his neck as he'd dragged him inside.

Hayden was ridiculously happy for Tate. He had a fun, boisterous, lovable family. She could see clearly that his mother had wanted to accompany him out tonight only to be close to him awhile longer. And who could blame her? The woman had gone decades believing her other son was *deceased*. In the end George had wrangled Jane in, encouraging her to "let the lads and lasses have their fun."

Drew circled the straws in her club soda with lime before confirming Hayden's question. "Reid had no clue it was me."

"Then what?" Hayden was on the edge of her seat hearing how Drew and Reid had bumped into each other at a work conference. She stirred her own club soda with lime, content with the mocktail and Drew's company. She listened intently as Drew told her about the huge crush she'd had on Reid when she was sixteen years old and how running into him again was her very narrow window to properly seduce him.

"So I'm lying in his hotel room bed fast asleep and he does this—" Drew snapped her fingers in Hayden's face "—and literally *scolds* me for not telling him who I was!"

Hayden laughed. It'd be a story for the grandkids, without a doubt... An edited version, but still.

Drew was beaming, glowing. Even though half her story was shouted so as to be heard over a rowdy group of *lads* chugging down their ciders and ales.

The patrons of Churchill had worn their Christmas finery. For most of the ladies, sparkly dresses—one lass wore an elf costume—and the guys, including Reid and Tate, wore funny hats. Reid, a court jester hat and he'd talked Tate into the one shaped like a giant pint of ale.

"He's doing well, Tate," Drew pulled her eyes away from their guys to say. "I've been trying not to watch him with George and Jane, but it's so beautiful to see them together. And when Reid joins the mix..." Her eyelashes fluttered. "Sorry. Hormones."

"You don't have to explain. I've felt that same sort of emotion being around them. Tate's doing amazingly well."

"I remember the first time I had that look in my eye. It's unique to a woman falling in love."

Hayden tried not to overreact, but she was relatively certain her shocked expression rivaled the one she'd worn when she stepped into Church for the first time tonight. Except instead of awe over garland and pinecones, flickering candles in lanterns and sleigh bells strewn hither and yon, her shock was due to her inability to agree with her new friend.

"It's not love."

"Oh." Drew was uncharacteristically chagrined. "Sorry. I didn't mean to assume…"

Hayden waved a hand to cut off Drew's needless apology. "I can see how you'd draw that conclusion. We have a great time together. He asked me to come here and support him, and I couldn't turn down a friend."

Though *friend* seemed a lame word for what they had been doing together in bed every time they were alone. It sounded lame saying it out loud, too, but if Drew noticed, she was too polite to point it out.

"I'm glad he has you. No matter how you define it. And there's no need to define anything, is there? It's Christmas!" Drew lifted her glass, and Hayden tapped her own against it.

On the other side of the bar, the guys sat close to the fireplace, glasses of bourbon or some kind of brown liquid in hand. Reid tossed his head back and laughed, his throat bobbing, and Tate swiped his eyes as he laughed along with him. Hayden was hit with the oddest sense of pleasure at seeing Tate happy. And not the way she might mildly appreciate someone enjoying themselves. More like she was *invested* in him. Her assuredness about not being in love with him didn't stop her from having feelings that were, while not love, definitely love-*like*.

If there was a real fiancé in Hayden's life, Tate would be the ideal candidate.

* * *

Tate sat by the fireplace while Reid fetched refills at the bar. On the way he stopped and placed a hand on Hayden's shoulder and smiled down at her. When she replied with an eye roll, Reid winked.

They'd accepted her, his family. His parents, his brother and Drew. The same way they'd accepted him into their lives. There were rough patches, of course. Awkward moments where the air was stale and no one spoke. But ultimately someone thought of something to say, and it was always in order to help Tate feel at home.

His mother had been asking about wedding plans almost nonstop. "Let me know the date as soon as you're certain," she'd said. "I'll book a flight."

*I'll book a flight* had been Jane Singleton's mantra since Tate arrived. She was anxious to come to the States, and when Tate agreed at lunch that he'd enjoy showing her around Spright Island, she'd promptly pressed her lips together to quell more tears.

Her crying over him made him uncomfortable, but he understood. He felt as if he'd been robbed, and yet at the same time he wouldn't trade his childhood or his adoptive parents for anything in the world.

Hayden turned her head to look over at him and he waved. She smiled, demurely at first, but then her teeth stabbed her lower lip to keep away a full grin.

*My fiancée*, he thought when he returned her smile. What had he been thinking asking her to play the role? She was great at it, though. So great that it wasn't hard to imagine her in that role for real. But the timing was so off it wasn't even funny. He was scrambling to keep his life sewn together at the seams and Hayden... He kept referring back to their conversation the first night they were together. One night at a time had been the promise—a reprieve for them both.

Pretending was fine. Short-term. *Fun*. But reality came with an entirely new set of rules.

"Cheers." Reid returned and handed Tate one of the drinks. "Hayden is gorgeous and funny and you're not likely to do better." Reid's cheeks puffed as he held the liquor in them for a beat before swallowing and wincing. "Holy hellfire." He coughed.

Tate opted for a sip rather than a gulp.

"I never saw myself married or a dad, but it's about to happen for me. I'm one of those happy idiots I used to feel sorry for." Reid was more careful taking his next drink. "And before you accuse me of trying to induct you into the married people hall of fame, just know that I have no agenda other than your happiness."

Rare was the moment Reid was sincere, but he appeared so as he held his glass aloft. Even wearing the jester hat.

"I appreciate you looking out for me." Tate sat back into the stuffed chair. "What Hayden and I have now, it's working. It's easy. Simple."

Tate nodded, liking the sound of both of those words. Easy and simple wasn't something his life had been lately.

"Simple has its merits," Reid said, but it sounded like a line. Something to say to fill the air rather than the truth, which reflected in blue eyes that matched Tate's own.

Outside the Singleton home, Tate stood in the backyard, a brisk wind stinging his reddened cheeks. He'd gone to bed around 1:00 a.m., after several glasses of the burning liquid Reid kept bringing him. He'd come back here, passed out and then woke at 3:30 a.m., his heart racing like it was trying to escape his chest.

After three big glasses of water—one of them with an aspirin chaser—Tate wandered outside. The in-ground pool was draped with a black tarp, closed this time of year. He had vague thoughts of swimming in it, of losing a toy and of his mother diving in after it wearing all her clothes.

He didn't know how much of the memory was memory or how much was his mind desperately trying to connect the dots of his checkered past. Bits of information were missing and colored in with other bits from an entirely different life. He'd yet to piece himself together.

"Wesl—Tate," came his mother's voice from behind him. "Darling, what are you doing?" She bundled a thick parka around her. "It's freezing out here, you'll catch your—"

"Death?" he finished for her. "Too late."

She gave him a light shove in the arm. "Comedian like your brother. Bloody hell! It really is freezing out here."

"We can go in."

"No, no it's fine." She assessed him, something sad in her eyes before she said, "Your adoptive parents contacted us."

He felt the blood rush from his cheeks. He'd had no idea.

"Don't be angry. We contacted them first, hoping if we reached out, they'd reply. I begged Marion—ah, your mother—not to say anything to you. By the look on your face, I assume she complied."

"She didn't tell me." He felt his worlds colliding, fearing that collision and at the same time anxiously anticipating it. He couldn't be two people the rest of his life. At some point he'd have to accept that he was Tate *and* Wesley. Son of Marion and William *and* son of George and Jane.

"I wanted to...understand, I suppose," Jane said. "They're lovely. And as much as I wanted to rage at the couple who kept my son from me all those years, I realize it's not their fault they loved you so fiercely. At least that's what my therapist says I'm supposed to feel." Her mouth quirked. "But I love you, Wes—Tate. And that means I will prioritize your happiness above my own."

A surge of emotion pushed against his rib cage. After

a month of damming it up, only allowing it to release at a trickle, he was due for a tsunami.

His chin shook as another memory crawled out of the recesses of his mind. Jane jumping into the pool after his favorite stuffed toy. He hadn't imagined it. It wasn't made up. The memory was from his toddler-height point of view. And when Jane handed it back sopping wet, he'd cried more and George had helped Jane to her feet, his rumbling laughter encompassing them.

It was *real*, his life here in London. No longer a fuzzy impression he was trying to bring into focus.

"Call me Wesley, Mum," he wrapped an arm around his mother. "That's the name you gave me."

This time when she cried, he held on and cried with her. For the many years they'd lost, and the many years, God willing, they had left.

# Sixteen

Dinner was set on the Singleton table, the candles lit, tablecloth spread, and the poinsettia table markers next to embroidered cloth napkins. The Christmas tree was bedazzled with lights in the corner, though Jane mentioned to Hayden they didn't often buy a tree.

"It's a special occasion," Jane had said with a warm smile.

George and Jane sat at either end of the mahogany table while Drew and Reid took their seats side by side. Hayden settled in next to Tate, surprised that spending the holiday away from home, and in a strikingly different environment, hadn't made her feel out of place. She suspected the Singletons had something to do with that—all of them.

Her family holidays were hectic and loud, and not in the charming way. Usually her mother was arguing with her grandmother, who was pouring her third cocktail before dinner. Mom's cooking was good, though—Hayden wouldn't begrudge her that. But one look at the Singleton spread hinted that Jane knew her way around the kitchen, as well.

A whole turkey was the centerpiece, carved in neat slices and glistening with butter, its skin a crisp golden brown.

Sides of diced potatoes and onions, stuffing—though it looked more like hush puppies to Hayden—and vegetables like cabbage, parsnips and a dish of green peas filled in the gaps.

"Right, then. Let's get started." George unfurled his napkin and held out his hands on either side of him. After a beat, Drew and Hayden gathered that they should each take hold of the patriarch's hands for prayer. Hayden held Tate's hand and he in turn held his mother's, who gripped Reid's fingers as he reached for Drew's.

The prayer was brief and proper, and by the time the word *Amen* was uttered, there wasn't a dry eye in the house. Could've had something to do with George giving thanks for "Wesley" being home. "For the first time in nearly three decades," Tate's father had said, "both my sons are under this roof again."

"Gravy," Jane announced, dousing her plate of food with the stuff before passing it on. Hayden politely took the dish from Tate after he'd put some on his potatoes before handing it to George without partaking.

"No sense in watching your waistline, love," George teased with a wink. "All of the veg on this table have been cooked in duck fat." He offered the dish back as though passing on the gravy wasn't an option. She put a dollop on her potatoes. When in Rome, and all that.

Dinner was delicious, if heavy, and once the meal was finished, no one moved to scurry from the table. Typically, at her house, her mother had the food in the fridge the very moment the last plate was cleared. Here, though, Jane made no move to rush around putting food away. Instead she tossed her napkin onto the table saying, "Crackers! I nearly forgot the crackers!"

"Crackers?" Tate asked, and Hayden shared his mild alarm. After stuffing themselves with a rich, two-helpingsof-everything Christmas dinner, who could possibly have room for crackers.

"Oh! I've been wanting to do this!" Drew applauded from her seat.

Jane came out from under the tree with gift-wrapped oblong paper packages tied with ribbons on both ends. They looked like giant, festively wrapped Tootsie Rolls.

"Tradition," Reid explained to the three Americans. He took the gift his mother passed out and explained. "I hold one end, Drew holds the other." A delighted Drew gripped one end of the wrapping. "And then we pull."

A small cracking sound came and the paper tore. Out fell a bauble and a few bits of folded paper. "Looks like I've won a ring." Reid, pleased with his trinket, stuffed it onto his pinky, the purple stone set in plastic not exactly his style. He then unfolded a gold crepe-like paper crown, which he proudly perched on his head. "There, now. I'm ready for my joke."

He reached for the square of paper on the table and read, "What do Santa's little helpers learn at school?" When no one answered, he shared, "The elf-abet."

Jane, George and Reid chuckled. Drew raised an eyebrow. "These are supposed to be bad jokes, right?"

"Oh, the worst." Reid kissed her. "Now yours. Come on then." Drew's cracker held a tiny stapler that couldn't have been longer than her thumb. George's contained a bag of marbles, Jane's a puzzle game with a ball and a maze. Their included jokes were as lame as Reid's.

Tate's Christmas cracker held a small stuffed bear. One he stared at for an inordinately long time. His eyes tracked to his mother's, who blinked away tears as she shook her head.

"What a silly coincidence." She waved a hand but Hayden knew that symbol of a special moment between mother and son was anything but silly.

"Your turn," Tate told Hayden as she took the end of her cracker and he took the other. After the pop, a gaudy ring fell from her cracker. "Look at that. A matching set."

"Not quite. Mine's bigger than Reid's." Hayden eyed Tate's brother, trying to keep things light.

"Maybe you should see if it fits." Drew's winked, pure, adorable *evil*. Not at all interested in keeping the focus off Hayden's ring.

Hayden cast Tate an unsure look but he didn't waver. He took the ring from her hand and slid it onto her ring finger, admiring it in the candlelight.

The tacky plastic trinket shimmered, silver glitter swimming within the blue stone. It was gumball-machine quality, and completely ridiculous, but there was something symbolic about Tate slipping it onto her hand in front of his family that caused a lump to rise in her throat.

"The perfect placeholder while yours is being sized, then," Jane said, repeating the false story Hayden had given about why she wasn't wearing a ring.

"Right."

"My boys. Married and happy. It's all I ever wanted." Jane folded her hands at her chest and Hayden hoped it escaped notice that she and Tate were silent on the matter.

The only real part of their relationship was that she and Tate liked each other a whole hell of a lot.

"Your crown," Tate slipped the thin paper ring over Hayden's hair and, following tradition, she reached for her joke.

"Why does Santa have three gardens?" She waited a beat and then wrinkled her nose. "So he can 'ho ho ho.'" She groaned but everyone at the table erupted in laughter.

"Worst one yet." Tate leaned forward to kiss her. It occurred to her that he'd been careful about being affectionate with her in front of his family, and she him. Now he lingered over her lips, placing a second kiss there before murmuring, "Merry Christmas, Hayden."

"Jane wants us to delay our flight," Tate said as he packed away another sweater into his suitcase. They'd stayed downstairs after dinner, drinking and laughing and enjoying his their family's traditional Christmas pudding.

That brought discussion of more of his newfound family, which had led to photo albums. Turned out he had a lot of cousins, aunts, uncles and one living grandfather in the area.

"When you return, we'll have a visit," Jane had told him, hinting that she'd been careful not to overwhelm him this trip.

"It's Boxing Day tomorrow, which is a national holiday here," he continued telling Hayden, who sat on the bed. Things had gone well so far, but staying longer seemed to be pushing his luck. "They go to a restaurant and out shopping, and then there's a duck race with rubber duckies for charity in the afternoon." He raised his eyebrows. "I had no idea."

He'd booked their flights to be in and out quickly, figuring he'd be ready to retreat to the sanctity of Spright Island as soon as possible. But he wasn't as ready as he'd originally thought. He was enjoying his parents, Reid and Drew, and Hayden.

She still wore the ring he'd put on her finger at dinner. When Drew had suggested she try it on, Tate hadn't hesitated. Part of living dangerously included not overthinking moments like that one. But he couldn't deny the part of him that wanted it to be real—as real as the family who, before this trip, had been no more than a story. Would bringing Hayden deeper into his life be the same as it'd been with the Singletons? At first a vague notion, and then 3D reality come to life... Did he *want* to be in deeper?

Discomfort bubbled in his gut, and the thought of "don't push your luck" occurred again. There was fun and then there was stupid, and he'd been walking that razor's edge.

"You should take that off before it turns your finger green."

Hayden gave her finger one lingering look before agreeing, "I guess you're right." She tugged the ring from her hand and set it on the night table next to the bed.

*See? She doesn't want to go deeper either.*

"With everything going on, I hadn't so much as thought about putting a real ring on your finger for show. I should've known everyone would expect it." Not that he'd have even considered giving her the one Claire had worn. That thing was a bad omen. He hadn't gotten around to selling it yet, but he would. Another act in the one-man play he was calling *Moving On.*

"You've had a lot on your mind." Hayden came to him and traced the lines bracketing his mouth. "This will become easier, Tate. You'll see. You'll get used to having extra family, and then you'll find a way to include them all into your big, amazing life."

"You always know what to say." Always knew how to put everything into instant perspective. His lips hovered dangerously close to hers. "Thank you for coming. I couldn't have done this without you."

He meant it. Considering the depth of the emotional pitfalls he'd experienced recently, he'd tackled them with relative ease. Hayden had his back, and he didn't take that lightly.

Hayden tilted her face, her lips brushing his. "I'm glad I could help." One eyebrow lifted impishly. "You owe me, Duncan."

He gave her bottom lip a gentle nip. "Will you take payment in sexual favors?"

"My favorite kind of currency."

He kissed her, his lips sliding over hers as he settled against her in bed. He lost himself in her plush mouth, the friction from her writhing hips into his crotch giving him a damn good idea.

Her soft moans urged him on, and Tate had them out of their clothes a short while later. He was suddenly very grateful he'd stopped in the rain outside her studio that night.

Grateful for her in any capacity, even a temporary one. Maybe they were only meant to be together through this particularly difficult part of his life. Maybe once the storms cleared and the sun shined, they'd be ready to move on.

Somehow, though, he doubted it.

He took his time kissing every inch of her he exposed. Every soft, muscular, firm yet giving bit of her, until her breaths were short and fast.

She stroked his jaw with cool fingertips as she murmured her praise. And he took his time, memorizing the details of her beneath him just in case their time together ended before he was ready.

# Seventeen

"Are you sure you don't want to come along?" Tate asked his mother.

"You kids go on without us. I've had my fun."

After making love to Hayden last night, she'd convinced Tate to stay another day. She argued that she didn't have classes until after the new year, anyway, then added, "You're enjoying yourself. It'd be good for you." When he hesitated, she resorted to teasing him. "What's wrong? Can't afford to change our flight times?"

That had earned her a tickle fight that turned into slow, openmouthed kisses. When he tried to pull her under him again, she'd shoved him in the direction of his laptop. He'd reluctantly left the warm bed and made the necessary changes to their tickets.

"Listen to your mother," George warned now, beer glass raised. They'd spent the Boxing Day in downtown London for the most part, shopping and visiting a variety of booths in what was normally a concrete jungle. From there they'd gone to a pub for a beer and snacks, when Jane mentioned "you'd better see yourselves to Hyde Park before it's too late."

"Yeah, listen to your mother," Reid echoed George.

"Look at her. A woman her age probably needs to rest her weary bones."

Jane Singleton was nowhere near "weary." Her blue eyes were bright and sparkling, her smile soft and easy. No longer did she have that haunted look in her eyes like she'd seen a ghost—though Tate reasoned that he *was* a ghost in a way.

"She needs tea," Reid continued, not heeding the warning glare from Jane. "And a nap."

"Careful, son, or you'll be wearing that drink," George warned with a chuckle. "The truth of the matter is we want the house to ourselves." He wrapped his arms around his wife and kissed her neck while Jane laughed and gave his arm a halfhearted swat.

Tate smiled at the display, grateful they'd had each other while he was missing. Grateful that what had happened to him hadn't torn apart their marriage.

"What do you think?" Tate asked Hayden, but he could've guessed her thoughts given the size of her grin.

"I'd be remiss to leave London without seeing a light garden in Hyde Park." She turned to Jane. "And I'd never rob you of an evening with your very handsome husband."

"Hear, hear," Drew said with enthusiasm, holding her club soda in the air.

"But take photos!" Jane requested. "Of the light garden, the observation wheel, roller coasters and, oh! Ice skating!"

"Do you ice skate, *darling*?" Hayden asked, her syrupy tone teasing.

"You've seen me move," Tate murmured into her ear before kissing her warm cheek. "What do you think?"

Reid, ever the encourager of public displays of affection, put his fingers between his lips and whistled.

London had been culture shock for Hayden since she arrived, so she was pleasantly surprised to find the winter wonderland event in Hyde Park was similar to what she'd come to expect of carnivals and fairs back home.

Well, aside from the aged, regal architecture she'd seen driving in, which had been preserved from another era entirely.

The park itself was overdone in the best way imaginable. Gaudy, blinking bulbs decorated every stall and stand, including on the huge lit entrance sign announcing "Winter Wonderland."

Entry was free, but there were opportunities to buy everything from food to shirts and jewelry to artwork. Bars dotted the park as well as venues for live shows, a funhouse, and a Ferris wheel—which must've been what Jane meant by "observation" wheel. The ice skating rink was *enormous*, children and adults alike moving across the slick surface with various stages of skill. Some gliding, others flailing.

Hayden would probably manage something between a glide and a flail if they ventured that direction.

Tate waggled their hands. They were connected by interlocked fingers and she'd gone without gloves given the mild weather. It was chilly, but not cold and while fog threatened, it hadn't brought rain.

"Since I can't have beer, I insist upon sugar," Drew announced, pointing at a stall with candy bins filled with lollipops, candy necklaces and gummy everything.

"Done. Should we meet up at the light garden?" Reid asked.

"Yeah, one hour. We're going to try to skate," Tate called to his brother. Reid nodded his acknowledgment.

Tate, bracketing Hayden's hips with his hands, pulled her ass against his crotch. "Let's see what you're made of, gorgeous."

Snow machines blew flaked ice into the air as they laced up, Hayden unsure what she was getting herself into.

"I'm sure it's like riding a bike," she'd famously said before falling onto her backside. They made their way clumsily around the rink once, and by round two, while they hadn't exactly glided, they had swept across the ice in a way that was at least semicompetent.

Skates off, boots on, she and Tate made their way to the closest booth that sold beverages and sat on a nearby bench with their drinks.

"Thank God for my core strength," she said with a laugh over her paper cup of wassail.

"I enjoyed watching you wobbling across the ice."

She nudged him, careful not to spill his drink into his lap. "You actually did better than me. I'm impressed." She poked him in the belly, and his abdomen clenched into a wall of muscle beneath her finger. Which reminded her of what he looked like without any clothes, and that in turn reminded her of what they did together best. "It's kind of a turn-on."

"Ice skating turns you on?" Tate lifted a dubious eyebrow.

"Pretty sure you doing anything turn me on." She said it with an almost disappointed lilt. This fantasy of being fake engaged, the fairy tale of Christmas in London, was about to come to an end. She'd been tempering her reactions, trying to monitor the way she responded to him, but she wasn't always able to keep her true feelings from surfacing.

She issued a reminder that it was smart not to grow accustomed to flying business class to London at Christmas, or having a Hallmark-style scene on ice skates...

Hayden had become independent out of necessity. Since the moment she'd invited Tate into her apartment—into her *life*—he'd been chipping away at the wall she safely hid behind. She felt a pull toward him that was simply undeniable.

"I could say the same to you, Ms. Green." She was rewarded with a kiss that reminded her of the wassail. Sweet, clovey, cinnamony…*temporary.*

"You freak me out a little," she admitted. "I'm not used to…so much lavish treatment."

"Excuse me? Lavish? We hopped on a plane. We're at a park."

"You flew us to London in our own private pods! We're at *Hyde Park*. You own an entire community, meanwhile I'm leasing my studio and my apartment."

"And my treating you to what you deserve is making you uncomfortable?"

"I…" But her pending argument died on her tongue. She was stuck on the "deserve" part. Tate had no problem filling the silence.

"You do deserve it, Hayden. The good life. It's not reserved to people who were lucky enough to be born into it. Or adopted into it," he added softly.

"My grandmother's an alcoholic," she blurted out, as if the secret of her own parentage refused to be stuffed down any longer. "And my mother is a master of guilt. Both at absorbing it and doling it out."

Tate's eyebrows knitted, but he stayed quiet. She hadn't opened up to him about just how wide the gap was between his life and hers, and it seemed wrong not to share at this point. She knew his secrets.

"When I moved out on my own for the first time, they didn't let a day go by without reminding me that I was betraying them in the worst way possible. And when I moved to the refuge of Spright Island, they were jealous. Enormously jealous." She rolled her eyes as she replayed her mother's words about Hayden being *too good for them.* "I saved and saved and saved. And I work hard. I earned the right to live there. I made that decision on my own. It didn't come without a price, though. I'm not sure I have what I deserve."

She smiled sadly as she remembered another conversation with her mom, this one before she left for London. Patti Green hadn't been supportive of her daughter choosing to "flit around the globe" over spending time with family.

"Sometimes the healthiest choice for you isn't the popular one," Tate said. "I love my adoptive parents but when I found out about the Singletons visiting them became hard. I drew boundary lines around them even though I knew it would hurt my mother's feelings."

She heaved a sigh. "Adulting is hard."

"The worst," he agreed, but his smile was light, and she felt the weight lift from her shoulders having admitted some family conflict of her own.

"After the new year, life will return to normal," she reminded both of them. "But getting lost in this—" she gestured to the gazebo with a decorated tree in the center and the many, many ropes of lights strung in every direction "—is worth it."

"Good."

"Thank you, Tate. I really appreciate you—this. You've been generous."

"Stop making this sound like goodbye." A little lean forward would be all it took to kiss him. A tiny nudge all it would take for him to mean so, so much more to her.

But it was Christmastime, and Tate smelled like wassail and leather, so Hayden lost herself in the heat of his mouth, and postponed worrying about the consequences for a little while longer.

# Eighteen

Recovering from jet lag took a lot longer than Hayden anticipated.

The flight back from London was unremarkable and a lot less comfortable than the flight there. Despite Tate's insistence they change airlines to book first class or charter a private jet to go home, Hayden refused. She'd assured him that any seat was fine. He'd finally let her convince him and they'd ended up crammed in a middle aisle in a tight seat for the incredibly long flight home.

She'd needed the reminder that life wasn't all champagne and caviar. Halfway through the flight, however, as she was trying to stretch in the pitiful space between her seat and the one in front of her she realized she was being ridiculous. Why was it so hard for her to indulge?

As part of her new year's resolutions next year, she was just going to enjoy her damn self. Tate had been a good sport, sending her a weary "I told you so" glance, but never bothering with the sentiment. She'd ended up apologizing once they were back in SWC, but he'd only kissed her forehead and sent her up to her apartment before returning home himself.

Now that she'd been home for a few days and was well

rested, she was having what might be the most productive day of her life. She'd finished her laundry, planned her meals for the week, *and* finalized her class schedule for January as well as posting it on her website.

A knock at her door came earlier than she expected. Tate had made dinner plans for them to eat at the Brass Pony. She was wearing one of two new dresses she'd purchased since she'd returned home. One in black for the New Year's Eve party, which was much fancier than the red one she wore now.

"You weren't supposed to be here until six," she said as she pulled open the door. He was dressed handsomely in a suit sans tie, the collar open on a crisp white shirt. But his face was drawn, his mouth downturned.

"Wow. Rough day?"

"You could say that." He handed her a tall white cup from EterniTea. "They haven't opened yet, but I know a guy. Thought you might like to try the green tea latte."

"Thanks."

He leaned in and kissed her, lingering over her lips as he pulled in a breath. "Ready to go?"

"Are you sure you *want* to go?"

"Of course." He made a half-assed attempt at a smile but it didn't reach his eyes.

"Do you want to talk about it?" The second she asked her phone beeped—her mother's ringtone, which was as dooming as Darth Vader's theme song.

She staunchly ignored it, sipping her tea instead. "This is delicious."

"Don't you want to get that?" He frowned.

"No." Hayden had tried to call her mother to let her know she'd returned from London. She hadn't heard back and had counted herself lucky. "It's my mom."

"We have time."

"Trust me. Answering that call isn't about *time*. My family's...not like yours."

"British?" he teased.

*"Normal."*

"No family is normal. Answer it. If you do and find it's more drama with no real point, then mention we are headed to dinner and hang up. It's just that easy."

"And if it's an actual emergency?"

"Then we'll deal with it."

*We.*

She realized upon hearing that word that she'd never had support when it came to her family. It'd always been more of an "us versus them" situation.

"I'm sure your day was rough enough without dealing with—" the phone beeped again "—whatever this is."

Tate remained resolutely silent, even when the chime of her voice mail sounded.

"Fine," she told him, lifting her cell phone and turning on the speaker. "Here we go."

The recording started with a frantic "Oh, Hayden" that chilled her blood. Hayden's mother spoke between nervous breaths.

"Your grandmother is in the ER." Her mother's recorded voice shook. "This is worse than usual, Hayden. Much worse." Patti went on dispensing one horrific detail after the last, which made Hayden worry all the more. Patti ended the call with the name of the hospital.

Hayden crossed the living room to grab her keys and purse but was confronted by Tate, who plucked the keys from her hand.

"I'll drive."

Her head was already shaking. "I can't ask you to do that."

"You didn't ask. I told you we'd deal with it. Let's deal with it."

After years of independence and relying on herself, Tate, even after hearing that voice mail, was willing to go with her. It was hard to accept.

"Yes, but…"

"You met my family."

As if that was the same? But then she thought about how he'd been brave enough to ask for her help. Was she brave enough to accept his?

"Hayden." He held her hand. That was all it took to convince her. She let him lead her to the door and the uncertainty that waited for them at Seattle Memorial Hospital.

A hard, bitter line was the best description of Hayden's mouth as she navigated the hospital's hallways. She was a woman on a mission, and reminded Tate more of a woman who was walking into a courtroom to hear a verdict than someone visiting her sick grandmother.

He'd dealt with his own bullshit today in the form of Casey Huxley. Tate had spent an hour arguing with the jackass head contractor who was spearheading the new neighborhood in SWC—that "secret" project model Hayden had stumbled upon in Tate's upstairs bedroom.

Casey had been amenable to the design until recently. Now they were arguing over bulldozing more trees to expand. It wasn't happening. Tate wouldn't compromise nature simply because Casey was too lazy to find a work-around.

At the nurse's desk, they learned that Hayden's grandmother had been downgraded from ICU to a room of her own, which only firmed the bitter line of Hayden's lips, causing them to vanish altogether.

He didn't have a lot of experience with true dysfunction and had zero experience with alcoholism, but he knew stressful situations which was clearly what she was involved in here.

"When's the last time you took a deep breath?" he asked, catching her wrist before she could march in the direction of her grandmother's room.

Hayden glared up at him, unwilling to let go and let God.

"Wouldn't it be better to walk into that room calm and collected?" he tried again. Advice he could've taken from himself earlier when he'd been in a screaming match with Casey in the trailer at the worksite. Tate would have some backpedaling to do if he hoped to quell the gossip train. Destroying land was a hot button for him. He refused to compromise his integrity, or his island's.

She didn't look happy about it, but Hayden took one breath, then another. "You don't have to go in with me. My family is… They're…" She shook her head, giving up.

"Family," he answered. "Not serial killers. Family. Messy, complicated, unpredictable."

"The student becomes the teacher." Her smile was faint.

"I'm a fast learner."

In the hospital room, there was an empty bed by the door and a frail, pale woman in a bed by the window. He guessed the woman at her side holding her hand to be Hayden's mother. She had the same dark brown hair, but shot through with gray. She carried more weight than Hayden and her face was lined.

A man in jeans and a long-sleeved sweater approached from the corridor, limping like he had a bum knee. He didn't seem very old, but his beer belly and the dark circles beneath his eyes aged him.

"Hayd. You made it." His voice was bright, almost cheery. Odd considering the situation.

"Hi, Dad." Hayden's smile was cautious as she held herself in check. No warm family greetings here.

"Went to grab a coffee. Guess we'll be here awhile." He sipped from his cup before turning to Tate. "Hello."

"Dad, this is Tate Duncan. He drove me here. Tate, my father, Glenn."

"Nice to see you, Tate. Can I grab either of you a cup of coffee?"

"No, thank you," Hayden told him.

Tate tried not to take her "he drove me here" comment personally, as if he was a chauffer and not the man who'd taken her to London over the holidays.

"Okey-doke. Well, I'll let you go in and visit, then. I'll wander around." In place of goodbye, he said, "Tate," and then turned and walked away from them.

"He's mellow." It might've been the strangest interaction Tate had ever had with a parent, and that was saying something.

"It's a coping mechanism," she said.

"Hayden? Oh, Hayden!" Her mother, having just noticed them at the threshold, frantically waved her deeper into the room. Hayden's grandmother lifted her head, her eyelids narrowing. Tate could've sworn the temperature of the room went down a few degrees.

"Hi, Mom." Hayden gave her mother a side hug and then dipped her chin to acknowledge her grandmother. "Grandma Winnie. How are you feeling?"

"Wellllll, if it isn't the princess from the high tower," came Winnie's barbed reply, her voice dripping with sarcasm. "So nice of you to deign to come visit us common folk." She turned stony eyes on Tate and barked, "Who the hell are you?"

# Nineteen

*Here we go.*

Hayden shot Tate an apologetic smile, feeling instantly guilty that she hadn't warned him. Anyone she'd dated as an adult had no reason to meet *the fam*, and the guys she dated when she was living at home weren't exactly the kinds of guys to bring home to mom.

"Mother, your heart," Patti warned Winnie.

"Don't worry about my heart," Winnie snapped. "Worry about smuggling in a cocktail. It's long past five o'clock. Keeping an old woman from one of her only pleasures in life is criminal."

*What's her other pleasure in life? Bossing around my mother?* Hayden wisely kept the snide thought to herself.

"Well?" Winnie speared Tate with a glare. "Introduce yourself."

"Tate Duncan," he replied coolly, hands tucked into his pants pockets. "I'm also Wesley Singleton, but that's a long, complicated story."

Hayden gaped at him before turning back to her grandmother.

"Never heard of you." Winnie's frown pulled the corners of her mouth lower.

Hayden looked up to tell Tate they could leave—no one should be subjected to her grandmother's abuse, but he chuckled good-naturedly.

"I'm not surprised," he said. "My reality show airs late at night, and I keep my celebrity appearances to a minimum."

"Smart-ass." But Winnie's mouth curled at the edge. Was it possible that Tate was winning over the world's biggest critic? It'd been a long while since Hayden's grandmother had regarded anyone with respect, so the experience was unique.

Patti, meanwhile, didn't catch the joke. "You have a reality television show?"

"Not yet," Tate's smile remained. Amazing.

Hayden gestured toward the hallway. "Can I talk to you in private, Mom?"

"What's wrong with in here?" Winnie demanded.

"Nothing's wrong, ma'am," Tate answered for them.

"Ma'am," Winnie barked, amused.

Had Hayden ever heard that sound come from her most embittered family member?

"I'll be right back, Mother," Patti told Winnie as she walked for the corridor. Winnie's call of "and bring me a cocktail on your way back!" followed her out and then the volume on the television skyrocketed.

"She's really very sweet," Hayden's mother explained to Tate once they were outside of the room.

Hayden barely banked an eye roll.

"No judgment from me," he said easily. When Hayden looked up at him she was surprised to see the sincerity on his face. He meant it. He wasn't standing in judgment of her or her family tonight.

Hand around her waist, he tucked her close, and Patti didn't miss it.

"You two seem close. Hayden and I used to be that

close." She sent a woe-is-me look at her only daughter. "I'm glad for her though."

Hayden hated that she was skeptical, but her mother had accused her of "flitting" to London instead of spending time with her family.

"Are you the one who took her to London?"

"Mom—"

"Yes. To meet my birth parents."

"Oh." Patti's ears pricked at the barest whiff of gossip. But then she faced Hayden, guns blazing. "You met his parents. And *this* is how you choose to introduce him to us?"

"That's not… We're not…" Hayden closed her eyes and pulled in another deep breath, staunching her knee-jerk reaction. She didn't owe Patti an explanation about why she did anything. "Why is she really here, Mom?"

"What's that supposed to mean?"

"It means you should look into rehab if Grandma Winnie's drinking so much she's blacking out."

"Blacking out? Who told you that?" Patti's eyes widened, flicking to Tate first as she offered a shaky smile of embarrassment. "This is hardly the place to air family grievances, Hayden. Your grandmother is ill."

"Yes, very." Hayden couldn't help agreeing. "She has been sick with this illness for as long as I can remember. You can't stop her. I can't stop her. I came as a courtesy…"

"A courtesy!" Patti let out a sharp, humorless laugh. "Well, my, my. Excuse us for interrupting your glamorous life. By all means, go and enjoy a *fabulous* night with your *celebrity* boyfriend. If you'll excuse me." She saved one last disingenuous smile for Tate before stomping back into the hospital room.

Drained and exhausted from that brief interaction, Hayden shook her head at Tate, at a loss for what to say.

He suffered no such loss.

"I don't remember if I told you…" His arm still looped

at her waist, he walked with her toward the exit. "You couldn't look more beautiful if you tried. I like you in red."

She shook her head. He was too much.

"Did you also know that your *celebrity boyfriend* knows the chef at the Brass Pony personally?"

"I did not." She was grinning, a feat in and of itself.

"It's true. Any special requests you have for your *glamorous* dinner are well within reach."

Warm browns, golds, and greens made up the décor at the Brass Pony, along with gilded frames holding mirrors and paintings of horses and landscapes. The tables were lit by low candles on crisp, white tablecloths, the silverware was gold and the glassware copious.

Upon entering, Hayden took her first full breath in hours, embarrassed more by her own behavior than her family's. What must Tate think of her? That she's completely intolerant?

"Mr. Duncan." A man in a smart blue suit, his hair dusky blond, regarded Tate with both surprise what could've been a borderline nervous smile. "I haven't seen you in a while."

"Jared." Tate's hand on her back, he ushered her forward, then offered that hand in greeting to the manager of the Pony. "Apologies for my behavior last time I was in here. You caught me on one of my worst days. This is Hayden Green, she owns the yoga studio down the street."

"A pleasure, Hayden." Jared nodded his greeting then said to Tate, "Glad to have you back. Your usual table?"

"If it's available."

"Right this way."

Hayden had been to the Brass Pony once since she moved here. The food was exquisite; the atmosphere on the stuffy side, but it had its merits. For one, it was quiet. It was also tidy. Bussers, waitstaff and hosts were dressed in black pants, long black aprons and white shirts with the restaurant's green logo on them.

Tate's "usual table" was located in a back corner, the C-shaped booth tall and private. From her spot in the center of the C, the restaurant's patrons were visible, but Hayden and Tate were shielded from prying eyes.

In short order they were served a bottle of wine, goblets of water and a special made by the chef that Tate requested.

*All part of dating a billionaire*, Hayden thought with a wry smile.

Fiddling with her gold fork, Hayden tried to think of a way to explain her behavior tonight. Explain that she'd endured years and years of neglect and verbal abuse from her grandmother and mother. Explain that while Hayden loved them, they were complicated to know and even more complicated to like.

Before she could arrive at any arrangement of those words, though, Tate spoke.

"My parents—the Duncans—aren't perfect, either, you know." His blue eyes sparkled in the candlelight.

"Yes, but are they manipulative?"

"They can be." He lifted his wine. "They're parents."

"I don't want you think that I'm this uncaring, selfish—"

He reached for her hand, shaking his head to stay her words. "Don't. You already know what I think about you."

Did she? He must've seen the question on her face.

"Giving. Caring. Selfless. Beautiful. Strong. Patient. Enduring. Really, *really* amazing in bed." He grinned and she pulled her hand away to shove his arm.

"Do you see where we are? Behave yourself."

"I'm tired of behaving myself. You should know that better than anyone."

"Are you a rule breaker now?" she teased.

"More like the rules I put stock into were broken for me. I'm enjoying not heeding them. And so should you."

She sipped her wine, both rich and complex, like the man who ordered it. "I'm not heeding any rules."

Not her mother's rule that Hayden should be involved in every family emergency. Not her own warning her not to get serious with a guy, or allow herself to be spoiled unnecessarily. And dining "off" the menu and letting her date treat her to a trip to another country definitely counted as her being spoiled.

No, she wasn't following any rules, which she knew damn well could lead to breaking even more of them. But as she met Tate's eyes over their appetizer of crisp calamari, she couldn't dredge up any motivation to change.

Although…maybe he'd changed her already.

# Twenty

Hayden had dreamed of attending the swanky New Year's Eve party in SWC since she moved here.

As a business owner, she'd received a coveted vellum invitation to the event last year. Knee-deep in doing two million things business owners *without personal assistants* did during the week of Christmas, she hadn't been able to attend. By the time last year's party rolled around, she was full-on Cinderella minus the Fairy Godmother. She'd been overworked, exhausted, and in need of a mani, pedi, haircut *and* eyebrow wax. Readying herself for a fancy party where she'd be expected to present her best self was as far-off a fantasy as waiting for a prince to knock on her door with a glass slipper on a silk pillow.

So. She'd stayed home.

The FOMO had been epic.

This year, though, she was going. She had an invitation in hand, a gorgeous date chauffeuring her to the event, and a dress she'd picked up on the clearance rack of Basic Black Boutique in town. The dress was black and low-cut in the front, formfitting to show her curves, and sparkled no matter which way she turned thanks to a zillion small silver "diamonds" sewn into the fabric. She'd swept her hair up for the night and pulled on a silver cuff bracelet and chandelier earrings, forgoing the necklace. The plunging neckline drew enough attention without one.

Tate had offered to buy her a gown for tonight, but she'd declined. After the night of the hospital drama, he'd been everything she needed, and she didn't feel right expecting more. He'd taken her to the Brass Pony—where they ate an incredible gourmet meal that wasn't on the menu—and he didn't ask her to explain or talk about it. She'd opted to do neither. For too long her mother and grandmother had dictated her moods. Being in that hospital had cemented the reason she'd left Seattle in the first place: She wanted be her own woman—independent and self-reliant. And yes, that, too, was part of the driving force that led her to buying her own dress.

Excited, she waited in her yoga studio rather than outside, watching out the wide windows for Tate's Mercedes to show. She'd insisted on meeting him there, but he wouldn't allow it, even though the event was closer to his house than hers. It seemed no matter how much distance she tried to put between them he closed the gap.

She fingered the lacy material of her shoulder wrap as she paced along the scuffed studio floor. She'd shown up for him in London, and he'd shown up for her at the hospital. Originally she'd believed it was tit for tat, a simple exchange of favors. But that wasn't all this was, was it?

She'd erected that independence wall, building it as tall as she could. Ever since she'd said yes to Tate, he'd been chipping away at it and now that wall was crumbling. Through the holes she was seeing a future she'd never imagined.

Tate was in that future.

Not temporarily, not as means to goods and services, or favors. He was there, bold and exciting, for one simple reason.

She'd fallen for him.

Like Buttercup for Westley in *The Princess Bride*, Hayden had tumbled ass over teakettle down the hill, with her heart bouncing ahead of her.

Not her brightest move to date, but what was she supposed to do about it? Tate was giving, and kind, and great in bed and hot—*don't forget hot*. Puttying in the holes in that crumbling wall of hers was no longer an option. What used to be her protection was now starting to resemble a prison. She didn't *want* to hide behind a wall any longer.

Her ride pulled to the curb, and she drew her wrap over her shoulders and stepped outside. Gripping her clutch, she shuddered as sharp, icy wind cut through the thin garment. Nevertheless, she'd worn a sleeveless dress and had slipped her feet into sparkly peep-toe black heels to show off her new pedicure. No detail went unnoticed when she readied herself for tonight.

It wasn't every day she told the man of her dreams she'd fallen for him.

Stupid? Maybe. She had no idea how he'd react. But she couldn't think of a better time than midnight on New Year's Eve to tell him. That would blow up her wall completely.

Tate stepped out of the car in a black tuxedo and bow tie that weakened her knees. How…*how* could this man look good in literally any style of clothing?

He stopped short of opening her door for her, his eyes roaming over her dress, his mouth slightly open like he was going to say something but forgot what it was.

"I guess you can 'buy your own damn dress,'" he joked, throwing her words back to her. She hadn't been angry when she said it, just exasperated. She wouldn't allow him to cater to her *constantly*.

"I couldn't figure out how else to make you stop offering." She grinned.

"Fair enough." He opened her door and she walked to

him, tall enough in her heels to place a cold kiss on his warm mouth. He swatted her ass, reminding her that as gentlemanly as he was, he couldn't be defined him by only that word.

He was much more layered, and meant more to her than she'd previously imagined. All because she'd met him outside in the rain and offered him a cup of tea.

The Common, a rentable space for parties and where SWC held most of their meetings and sponsored parties, was a sea of Edison lights dangling from the ceiling.

Hayden couldn't suppress a gasp when she stepped through the double doors and was met with those glowing bulbs hanging from black wires and tied with a lush black bow at the base.

"Tate." She clutched the arm of his tuxedo, admiring the many guests in their finery. The black tie affair was dripping with luxury, from the gold and black and white decorations to the five-piece jazz band playing softly onstage.

The fairy tale, it seemed, was real.

"I like that smile." He brushed her lips with his. "Don't want to ruin your lipstick."

"Ruin away. I have more."

As they walked through the room, the guests parted like the Red Sea for Moses. All eyes were on Tate. In this community, he really was a celebrity.

He shook a few hands and introduced her to a few new people, though she spotted a lot of people she knew, too. She might not be as iconic as the *great and powerful Tate Duncan*, but seeing so many familiar faces reminded her that she'd built a life here as well.

She released Tate's arm to accept the glass of champagne, and he raised his own.

"To your first NYE at SWC." They *cheersed* and sipped,

and wow, even the champagne was expensive. Tate wouldn't have had it any other way.

"This is incredible. I feel like Cinderella."

"Good." Arm locked around her waist, he leaned in to kiss her, pausing a breath from her lips to mutter a very unromantic *"Son of a bitch."*

"Duncan." The gruff voice belonged to guy nearly seven feet tall, with arms the size of 55-gallon drums. His hair was buzzed close to his head, his mustache thick and walrus-like. He turned stony eyes to Hayden for a brief moment before glaring at Tate.

"Hayden Green," Tate said after a long, and awkward, pause. "Casey Huxley. I've mentioned him before. The contractor partnering with me to build a group of houses on the eastern side of the island."

"Oh. *Oh.*" The top-secret project that wasn't really secret, she remembered. Also, she'd learned at their dinner at the Brass Pony, the same contractor who Tate had argued with over taking down quite a few trees in SWC.

She hadn't wanted to talk about her drama, but she'd needled Tate about his. He'd shared, and she let him, until it was obvious from his copious swearing she shouldn't have pried.

She had hoped Tate and Casey would work out their differences. Since they stood positioned like they were about to have Wild West style shoot-out, it was safe to assume that hadn't happened yet.

Casey took a champagne flute, delicate in his wide, meaty palm, and with a final eye slice to Tate, stalked off in the opposite direction.

"That was intense," she told Tate after Casey was out of earshot. "The way you made it sound, you two nearly went to fisticuffs the other day."

"Nearly," he grated, then, "Don't look so concerned. I can take him."

"I wasn't thinking that." She palmed the front of his tux and smoothed her hands over his built chest. He wasn't a slouch by anyone's definition. "I was hoping you two would have worked things out."

"He cares about control, I care about my island. We're nowhere near being on the same page."

"Tate!" A cheery man with dark olive skin, dark hair approached.

"Terry Guerrero." Tate pumped the other man's hand and then introduced Hayden.

"Nice to meet you." Terry's accent hinted at Spanish descent. He was so friendly it was almost jarring after the tense run-in with Casey.

"I promised Terry I'd talk to him about the development tonight, but that was before I made plans with you." Tate narrowed his eyes jovially at Terry. "I'm guessing you're holding me to it."

"Much as I hate to sully your evening with business, I'm going to on vacation tomorrow for two weeks. I'm not working from the Bahamas—Ana would kill me."

"Good man," Tate said.

"I'll have to introduce you to my wife," Terry told Hayden, "when she's finished chatting up the interior designer—the woman who designed this party. What is her name? No doubt Ana wants to hit her up to do our daughter's engagement party."

"Lois Sherwood," Tate answered. "And congratulations."

Hayden knew Lois. The chatty gray-haired woman was waving her arms in the air, excitement reigning supreme as she spoke with Terry's wife. She was an energetic, busy little thing. And flexible. Lois attended yoga classes three times a week.

Tate and Terry spoke for another minute before Terry excused himself. "I'll be at the bar. Hayden, a pleasure."

Once he was gone, Tate let out a sigh.

"Go. I should probably be hobnobbing with business folk, too. This event is meant to bring business owners together after all, right?" She smiled, quoting the wording on the invitation.

"I guess." His mouth quirked playfully before he leaned in to kiss her. He didn't make it this time, either. Sherry interrupted next.

"Look at you two! You two are the cutest ever!" Sherry shuffled in place like she couldn't contain her joy, but lowered her voice conspiratorially when she spoke again. "I knew it! I knew it! Even in that class we took together, I *knew* Tate had a thing for you."

Hayden stole a glance up at Tate to find him wearing a patient smile.

"Your timing is perfect," Hayden told the other woman. "Tate was about to talk business at the bar and leave me standing here alone. Should we grab you a refill?"

Sherry glanced down at her empty glass. "Oh, goodness. Must be a hole in my glass. I'll grab another and meet you right back here." She pointed at Tate and then Hayden before moving to the nearest waiter to pluck a flute from a tray.

"I see her caffeine addiction hasn't gone anywhere," he muttered.

"*You're welcome* for letting you off the hook."

"I'll be brief," he promised.

"You'd better." Hayden gripped his lapels and kissed him solidly before someone else came along to interrupt.

After he met with Terry to discuss the new SWC neighborhood, Tate spotted Hayden in a conversation with a cluster of women. He decided to hang back and give her time to work her magic. By the delighted smile on her face he could tell she was enjoying her first SWC New Year's gala. He watched her a beat longer, wondering if he'd have noticed her if she'd come to last year's soiree. Yes. He would have. Even if she hadn't worn the sparkling black dress— an absolute showstopper. Her lethal curves and dark hair, full mouth and elegant way she handled herself in a pair of tall shoes would have been impossible to overlook.

She *glowed* with life.

Then again, he'd had a girlfriend last year at this time, so noticing Hayden would have been moot. He couldn't have acted on any passing attraction no matter how tempting she would've been.

He polished off his drink and relinquished the empty glass to the bar. Shoving his hands in his pockets, he strolled along the back of the room only to freeze in place a moment later when he spotted a familiar golden-haired, slim woman on the arm of Casey Huxley.

What the hell? Had he summoned her with his mind? And what was she doing attached to Casey, of all people? Especially now that the bigger man had cemented himself into the role of Tate's nemesis.

How had Claire and Casey ended up in the same *room* together let alone found anything in common once they were there?

It was definitely his ex-fiancée, though. There was no mistaking her slightly upturned nose and the rigid way she held her shoulders. As if she felt eyes on her, she turned to face Tate fully, giving him a demure finger wave before standing on tiptoes to whisper into Casey's ear.

Casey murmured something to her, his coal black eyes on Tate. And then they parted, Claire heading unmistakably in Tate's direction.

*Son of a bitch.*

# Twenty-One

Tate, with no other choice than to acknowledge Claire, crossed the distance to meet her halfway. Casey continued staring, but he wasn't Tate's problem tonight, or ever after Tate ended this deal.

"Hi, Tate." Claire stood before him, poised, wearing a no-nonsense black dress. No glitter, no shine, no light. Nothing like Hayden. The only sparkles on Claire were coming from the ring on her—

*What the hell?*

"Is that…" He hadn't meant to react, but there was no ignoring the giant diamond ring…on her left hand. She'd returned his engagement ring and, then what, run out to get engaged? *To Casey?*

She glanced down at her finger, almost like she'd forgotten the ring was there. "Oh, yes. I'm engaged."

"To Casey Huxley?"

"What? No. God, no. We're business partners, Casey and I. He invited me as his plus-one to introduce me around. *We're* not engaged. I'm engaged to…someone else."

That was a lot to ingest. Tate didn't know what to ask about first. He'd offered to introduce Claire around plenty when they'd dated, but she never would come with him anywhere. He'd start there.

"You hate Spright Island."

"As a residence, yes. As a business opportunity, no."

"Since when are you interested in land development?"

"Guess you rubbed off on me." She tipped her head. "It's my new side gig."

Tate's livelihood—no, *life's purpose*—was Claire's *side gig*? He was certain anger was turning his face a deep shade of pink.

"Are you getting back at me for something?" It was the only explanation that made sense. That or he was having his own private *Twilight Zone* moment.

"Always about you, isn't it Tate?" She rolled her eyes. "You're not the only one who knows what people want."

He had to let out a dry laugh at that. "And you do?"

"Casey and I do. People want wide open spaces. Room for lawns and yards. Fences."

"Suburbia." Tate's lip curled.

"People want lawns to mow, Tate."

The neighborhoods at SWC were designed to look as if they were tucked into the trees. There were no "lawns." Each plot fostered native vegetation—low growing plants interspersed with rocks and mulch. "I'd never compromise SWC's unique design. You know that. After our last meeting, Casey sure as hell knows that."

"People don't want to be buried in the woods."

"What the hell would you know about mowing a lawn or the woods? Aren't you a self-proclaimed city girl?"

"I like my space."

"No kidding." She'd taken plenty of it when it came to him. "You made it clear you didn't want to be married," he said through clenched teeth. Hayden hadn't noticed him missing yet. Maybe he could get her out of here before she laid eyes on Claire. He didn't want Hayden's evening to be ruined, too.

"Your family…confusion wasn't what I signed up for." Tate opened his mouth to say it wasn't what he'd signed up for, either, but before he could, Claire added, "I saw you with her earlier. Your date. She's—"

"Amazing," he interrupted, unwilling to let his ex-fiancée fill in the adjective. "*Amazing* is the word you're looking for, and even if it isn't, you can spare me your opinion."

His voice was hollow.

Like his chest.

Running into Claire had stolen the oxygen from his lungs and robbed him of reason. Probably there were some unexamined emotions revolving around their breakup he hadn't dealt with, but when would he have had the time?

Between winter holidays, and recovering from being in a couple, to trying to reacquaint himself with his brother and then Hayden… There hadn't been time to process much of anything. His head felt like a knotted ball of Christmas lights.

"Did you meet *him*—" Tate gestured to her engagement ring "—before or after ending it with me?"

Her mouth opened, then closed, but she didn't answer. At least she had the decency not to lie to him.

"Jesus, Claire."

"Don't judge me."

He took a deep breath and willed himself to stay calm. The last thing he needed was to make a scene and have this unfortunate run-in with his ex go down in the annals of Spright Wellness Community history.

"When you know you know." She offered a shrug.

More platitudes.

"Listen, I don't want to fight." She held up a hand, calling a stop to the conversation he should've called quits to first. "I came over to say hello, and I wanted to come clean about my involvement in the new project. Personally, and before someone else told you."

"How magnanimous of you."

Her expression was sharp, unfriendly. "I'll keep my distance for the rest of the party. Casey's not interested in talking business tonight, anyway."

"What business? Casey's fired. Especially if you're involved in the design." So much for being the better person, but he couldn't help himself. He'd been ready to throw Casey off his island after that last meeting, but learning of Claire's involvement had sealed the other man's fate.

"Don't make threats. He won't refund your *very* large deposit, some of which was my seed money."

"Keep it," he grated, hating that he'd unknowingly accepted money from Claire. Hating that he'd thought Casey might eventually come around to Tate's way of thinking.

With a shake of her blond head, she started back to the party.

"Who's the lucky guy?" he called after her.

"You don't know him." She blew him a kiss on her way out.

Thank God for small favors.

A blur of black caught Hayden's attention as she was resting her empty glass on a nearby tray. Tate's shoulders were beneath his ears, his fists balled at his sides.

He looked furious. Until she caught his eye and then he smiled, though it was a touch disingenuous.

"There you are." A few beads of sweat had broken out on his forehead.

"What happened to you?" She turned her head in the direction he'd come from but he pulled her close, one hand pressing her lower back, his other hand cradling her jaw. He gave her a lengthy kiss and she wobbled from the force of it, practically melting into him. Tate was an exceptional kisser.

"Wow, thank you," she said when he pulled away. He brushed her cheek with his thumb. "Was it that Neanderthal, Casey?"

He gave her a jerky nod.

"What did he do?" She searched the party, having half a mind to walk over to the idiot and give him a piece of her mind.

"He left." Tate turned Hayden's chin to face him. "Can we get out of here?"

She understood he was angry and processing an obviously loaded conversation, but… "Before midnight? I wanted to stay for the countdown."

She'd planned for a kiss at midnight under the chandelier in her beautiful dress. She'd planned on telling him she loved him.

"It's a lot to ask, I know." His frown faded, his lips softening some. "I have something better to do tonight."

Anticipation like warm honey trickled down her spine.

*"You."* He nuzzled her nose, charm dialed to eleven. "Ever since I saw you wearing that dress, I've been preoccupied with the idea of taking you out of it." His voice was a low murmur of appreciation, the flattery gaining him a lot of ground. She'd never been able to resist him when he couldn't resist her.

"Champagne at midnight here is special, but I have champagne at my house." He leaned close, his warm breath tickling her ear, his voice wickedly sexy. "When the clock strikes midnight, I'll drench you in champagne and kiss you everywhere the bubbles touch. Come home with me, Hayden, you won't regret it."

"That…is a compelling argument, Mr. Duncan," she practically purred. Tate offering private kisses at the stroke of midnight was more tempting than champagne toasts on New Year's, but she'd dreamed of counting down, kissing him, and offering up an *I love you.* "Can't we go home after? Midnight is a little over an hour away and—"

Blue eyes drilled into her. "It would mean *the world* to me if you and I could ring in the New Year alone."

Tonight she had very special plans for announcing how she felt about Tate, and by the look in his eyes, he had a similar announcement in mind. That was worth skipping the toast at the party. That was worth skipping a lifetime of toasts.

"Okay."

"Yeah?" He looked relieved as he cast another quick, maybe even nervous glance around.

"Yes. I'd love to go home with you."

His grin was heady and gorgeous, the attractive smile lines around his mouth and at the corners of his eyes in full force. She loved seeing him happy. She loved making him happy. Who cared about a silly toast when they had memories to make?

"Shall we?" He offered his arm, his relaxed features showing no signs of the turmoil she thought she'd seen earlier. Business rarely mixed with pleasure, but she was glad he hadn't allowed it to put a damper on the evening ahead of them. Not when he had so many delicious things in store for her.

"We shall," she said and then threaded her arm into his.

# Twenty-Two

Flames in the gas fireplace bloomed to life and Tate tossed the remote onto the coffee table. Exactly how quickly he could turn her on, Hayden thought, eyeing her handsome date.

She admired the broad set of his shoulders in the tuxedo jacket, his perfectly even bow tie. His hair, playfully falling over his forehead, and his enviably thick eyelashes shielding those gemstone eyes from view.

She still wore her dress and shoes, the wrap covering her bare shoulders, but she'd discarded her purse on the kitchen counter.

A golden glow came from a floor lamp, the only other illumination in the room from the flickering fire. The woods beyond the living room windows were dark and quiet, no wildlife peeking through the trees tonight.

"You're right. Your house is a much better venue for a New Year's Eve party."

Tate approached her with the slow, intentional steps of a predator hunting its prey. "Sorry, I'm only available for private parties."

He lifted one of her hands and with his palm cupped

her hip, moving close to rest his cheek on hers. Then he began to sway.

"Are you dancing with me? To no music at all?" she asked, moving with him.

He continued the steps and smoothly spun with her in a slow circle before bringing her flush with his chest. "How's my driving?"

"You're doing great," she whispered into his ear, pleased when a shake ran down his arms. It was nice to know she affected him the same way he affected her—to the *marrow*.

"I owe you for leaving. It wasn't fair of me to ask."

She stopped their silent dance and pulled her cheek from his. "I had to talk to a few people I don't particularly like. I can imagine it'd be upsetting to deal with someone you loathe."

His eyebrows jumped. "You have no idea."

"As long as you reserved plenty of energy for me—" she smoothed the crease above the bridge of his nose "—then I'll overlook you whisking me out of there."

A hint of challenge tightened his jaw. "Are you questioning if I'd keep my word about the champagne kisses and fireside romance?"

"Of course not." She feigned innocence. "I'm simply reminding you that you made promises and that there's no room for waning energy."

He tilted his hips, a hardening part of his anatomy nestling gently into her belly. "Does that feel *waning* to you, Ms. Green?"

She rested her top teeth on her bottom lip, going for her most demure and sex kitten–ish expression.

Then she decided, *screw* demure.

She stroked his erection over his tuxedo pants. He grunted, and she rubbed him again. "Feels positively *mouthwatering* to me," she said against his lips. "But there's only one way to truly test that theory."

He crushed his mouth into hers, pulling away after she was breathless.

"Then test it," he commanded.

Fisting her wrap, he yanked it from her shoulders, sending chills along her back as the lacy material tickled its way down her arms. His grin was slow and sensual and enough to make her drop to her knees right then and there. He stopped her from sinking to the floor, though, his hands cupping her elbows. "Hang on."

On the other side of the room he opened a trunk, pulling from it a rug of faux deer pelts. He spread the blanket in front of the fireplace—large enough that if it *had been* a real deer, it'd have been the size of an elephant—and then threw a few pillows on top of their makeshift bed.

"I don't want you to be cold or uncomfortable." He returned to her embrace.

"Such a gentleman," she cooed.

"Not always."

"Do show me, Mr. Duncan, how ungentlemanly you can be." She loved the take-charge part of him whenever it came out, and tonight she wanted to play.

He reached into her hair and felt for the pins holding it back, and one by one tossed them to the floor. One, two, three… Her hair spilled from its updo, and then he swept it off her face and gathered it into a ponytail at the back of her head. Tightening his hold, he pulled her head back and lowered his lips to her neck. Teasing and suckling, he worked his way from her throat to her jaw to the sensitive skin behind her ear. "On your knees, gorgeous."

But when he backed away, there was a tickle of a smile on his lips and a question in his eyes, asking if she was okay with this. And since she was very much okay with him being in charge of her—heart and body—she replied, "Yes, sir," and then did as she was told.

Against Tate's chest, Hayden let out a satisfied hum, her breath coasting over his body as she snuggled against him.

After she'd blown his mind and he'd in return happily blown hers, he discarded the condom in the nearest bathroom and grabbed a shearling throw off the couch to cover them. They'd been lying here ever since, the fire warming them—as if they'd needed any help after the amazing sex they'd had.

"Ten point oh" were the first words out of her mouth.

"What's that?"

"The score on your stellar performance." She grinned up at him with sheer sexual satisfaction.

He put an arm behind his head, proud. "You were keeping score?"

"Not really, but I can't deny you any less than perfect, considering it's all I've thought about since we stopped."

He loved satisfying her. Loved more that she was open and forthright about complimenting him.

After the night he'd had, the unpleasant run-ins with both Casey—*the prick*—and Claire, Tate hadn't wanted to ruin Hayden's night, too. Bringing her back to his place was the best decision he could've made.

"What about me?" she asked, raising her eyebrows. "What's my score?"

He pretended to think about it, turning his eyes up to the ceiling. "Eleven million." Her husky laughter drifted over him and he added, "Point eleven."

Her eyes were soft, dreamy.

"Happy new year, Hayden." He was about to apologize for missing the countdown…and forgetting his own promise of champagne, but what she said next stole the remaining oxygen from his lungs.

"I love you, Tate."

He blinked, stunned to his core.

*Love.*

She loved him. That took living dangerously to an entirely new level.

"I've been in love with you since London. I think." Her nose scrunched in a cute look of consideration. "Probably sooner."

The throw, Hayden's body heat and the fire were suddenly making him overly warm. He threw the blanket off himself, but she only snuggled closer.

"It's hard to know how to tell you've *completely* fallen for someone," she said conversationally as sweat pricked Tate's armpits. "I wasn't planning on falling for you. But I did. So, here we are."

*Here we are.*

Her tone was playful and light and questioning at the same time. For good reason. When someone told you they loved you, the expected response was to say it back. That was the deal.

That's how it'd been with his and Claire's relationship. Hell, he didn't even remember who'd said it first, only that one of them had and the other had followed suit. Tate had been the one to propose. At a fancy restaurant while wearing a suit, with a ring in a velvet box. He'd done everything by the letter, exactly the way tradition insisted he should, and she'd walked away anyway. Walked away and become someone else's fiancée, before finding an interest in the very part of his life she'd been ambivalent about the entire time she and Tate were together.

In life he'd assumed the next step would naturally appear above the last. That he'd climb one and then ascend to the next. One step up after the last was how he'd built this community on Spright Island, how he'd handled his business dealings. How he'd acted every day of his life…up until the day he bumped into Reid Singleton at that coffee shop.

Life had no rulebook.

What he'd thought was firm footing leading to the next step up had instead been a chute spiraling him down into the darkness, where he'd felt as lost as if he'd worn a permanent blindfold.

Discovering his twin brother.

Finding out he was kidnapped.

Learning about his biological parents in London.

Realizing that his adoptive parents had been wary of the agency from which he was adopted…

Then there was Hayden.

Beautiful, strong, trusting, giving Hayden.

She'd been his confidante and true friend, the woman of his sexual fantasies come true.

*And now she loves me.*

In what might be the worst timing in the world, Hayden Green had fallen for him, and he had nothing to offer her except metaphors for what he thought life was…and wasn't.

Given enough space he could easily fall in love with Hayden. Hell, if he did a deep-dive into his emotions, he might find he already had. But in no way was he ready for a next step—not with anyone. Claire had reminded him of that tonight.

Hayden deserved a man who knew he loved her without pause or breaking into a cold-hot sweat. After meeting the family who'd put her second her entire life, Tate knew Hayden deserved a man who could put her first.

He wasn't that man.

Not with a hundred other things fighting for first place. His community. Two sets of parents and extended family. His own sense of identity.

Tate had a loose idea about where he was headed and a

truckload of physical affection to shower upon her. But an engagement ring and a future?

He swiped the sweat now beading on his brow. He wasn't ready. Not yet.

At the start of this evening, he'd been sure how tonight would go. He'd planned on kissing Hayden at midnight, drinking champagne as gold and silver confetti fluttered to the floor, and then bringing her back here and having sex in front of the fireplace. But only half that plan had come to fruition. He hadn't prepared for bumping into Casey or Claire, or learning that the two of them were business partners.

He'd been building a mountain out of surprise molehills lately, so it shouldn't come as a shock that Hayden had blindsided him with a proclamation of love.

His heart sank.

This was his fault. He'd leaned on her and let her take on his emotional baggage—he'd lavished her with physical love and flew her first-class. Tonight was a Cinderella story right down to the clock striking midnight.

He moved her gently from his chest, ignoring her when she asked where he was going. He reached for his pants and checked his phone. 12:15 a.m. Close enough.

He turned to face Hayden. Beautiful Hayden, with her mussed hair, holding the blanket over her naked body. She was ethereal and perfect and the most sensually attractive woman he'd ever spent time with.

And Tate?

He was the asshole about to break her heart.

# Twenty-Three

It didn't take long for Hayden realize that the "I love you" she'd thrown out after Tate's innocent "Happy new year" hadn't gone over well. She didn't know what she expected, but she knew what she'd hoped for.

She'd hoped for one of his easy smiles. She'd hoped he'd thread his fingers into her hair and look deeply into her eyes. She'd hoped for those coveted words—"I love you, too."

She wouldn't have minded if his "I love you" had also included a lengthy explanation of how gobsmacked he was by her announcement.

But this…he looked like he'd witnessed an accident. Panic had surfaced on his features, and he'd become instantly fidgety.

So, yeah, it hadn't gone over well.

"Oh-kay, so that was awkward," she said with an uneasy laugh. "What I *meant* to say was 'Happy new year to you, too!'"

Her heart beat out a clumsy, erratic rhythm. She hadn't fallen in love with someone in a really, really freaking long time. And this time felt more real, more grounded. She knew who she was and what she wanted. She knew who she loved.

"Claire was at the party tonight." He stood and stuffed his legs into his tuxedo pants.

"Pardon?" Surely she hadn't heard that correctly.

"Claire Waterson. My ex-fiancée."

"I know who Claire is." What she hadn't wrapped her head around yet was that Claire was…at the party?

"She's engaged. And for some reason in a business partnership with Casey." Tate's teeth were all but gnashing.

If Hayden understood what he was saying, his evening had gone south not because of a run-in with Casey, but a visit from Claire…who was *engaged*.

"You didn't tell me she was there," Hayden said.

Hands on his hips, Tate looked down at where she sat on the blanket. "I didn't want to ruin your evening."

"But we left," she reminded him. "*She's* why we didn't stay?"

"It doesn't matter why we left."

But oh, it so did. She'd said I love you and instead of "I love you, too," Tate had told her that his ex-fiancée was engaged to someone else. As if that was the takeaway for the evening. The highlight of tonight!

"We had a special night planned," he explained. "I knew if you saw her it would derail those plans."

*Wow.*

So Claire had been at the party, had walked over to tell him she was engaged and instead of Tate coming to Hayden and telling her his screwy ex-fiancée was in the building and had apparently moved way, *way* on, he hadn't told Hayden anything. He let her believe that he'd been rankled by that Casey guy, then Tate had swept her up with his handsome smile and wooed her with promises of champagne and making love…

He'd lied by omission. And Hayden was the most honest she'd ever been.

"Let me get this straight…" Hayden heard the shake in

her voice. "You thought if I saw Claire tonight, that your chances of getting laid would go way down."

"What? No."

Hayden didn't wait for another of his explanations. She riffled through her discarded clothes and clumsily pulled on her bra and panties.

"Hayden, wait. Don't get dressed."

"I'm not arguing with you naked." She jerked on her sparkly dress, angry that she had nothing else to wear. This was hardly a time for celebrating.

"We're not arguing." When he noticed she was fumbling with her zipper, he offered to help, but she swung away from him.

She raced into the kitchen for her purse, but only when she lifted her coat off the chair did she realize she was stranded. She didn't drive herself tonight.

"Can we talk about this, please?" He snatched his shirt off the couch and pulled it over his shoulders, leaving it open in the front. She admired him, dammit, even while angry with him. He was handsome with his hair a disaster and his shirt open, revealing flat washboard abs, the legs of his pants falling to bare feet that were as attractive as the rest of him.

"There's nothing to talk about. You're still clearly in love with Claire if the news of her engagement hit you so hard you had to leave the party. I'm the moron who thought your heart would be as available as the rest of your body parts!"

"That's not true!" Tate actually shouted, the sound bouncing off the high ceilings and ringing off the light fixture over the dining room table where they stood on opposite sides in a faceoff. "Can we please talk about this?"

"There's nothing to say. I shouldn't have told you…what I told you." She couldn't say those three words to him— even in reference. She should've known better. "I'd been planning on telling you this evening and I thought—"

"You'd been planning this?" But he didn't sound flattered or even appreciative. He sounded *distraught*. "For how long?"

"It doesn't matter. It's clear you don't feel the same way about me." Try as she might, she wasn't able to keep her chin from trembling. This was a nightmare. A waking, living, breathing nightmare. She was in love with him, and not only didn't he know how to tell her he didn't feel the same way, but he'd sort of lied to her tonight, too.

"It's not that. I could... Given enough time. I think." His eyebrows arched sympathetically. Meanwhile, she'd be over here dying of humiliation.

Never had she been this hurt. This disappointed. Not even when her parents had skipped her high school graduation to rescue her grandmother from yet another midday bender.

"The timing is off," Tate said. "That's all this is."

"Oh, is that *all*?" She bit down hard and willed the tears currently tingling behind her eyes not to come. "Tell me, Tate, when is the perfect time for your girlfriend to tell you she loves you? For that matter, when's the perfect time for you to find out you have a secret brother? Or an entire family, for that matter!"

Anger brought forth the tears she'd been swallowing down. Angry at herself for so many reasons, she swept them away with her fingers.

"We can still—"

"Sleep together?" she interrupted before letting out a humorless laugh. "I bet you'd love that. Oh, sorry. I bet you'd *enjoy* that. Let's not use the L-word."

He stalked toward her, his face reddening with anger of his own. A muscle in his jaw ticked, and she felt that win all the way down to her toes. She'd rather him be mad at her than frozen with panic like he'd been earlier.

"I'm not saying the timing has to be perfect," he said. "I just need things to slow down for one goddamn second!"

He pulled his hands over his face like he was startled that he'd yelled, and then calmer, tried again. "I tried to live dangerously. I tried my life being in complete disarray. It didn't work."

Disarray? Danger? Was he referring to their relationship, or was he blaming Hayden for bringing disorder to his life? Was he longing for Claire? The perfect Stepford wife?

"I've worked hard my entire life to keep things steady," he said. "To achieve incrementally and move my life toward the finish line. The...*situation* with my family has made me question everything I thought I knew about myself. Learning that Claire was engaged threw me, but not because I want her for myself. She was another in a line of failures I couldn't prevent."

Hayden blinked, finally understanding. "And you don't want to be responsible for failing where I'm concerned. So you're not taking the chance? You tried to live dangerously, to give yourself over to the experience that was me, and now I'm not worth the risk."

"You don't understand."

"I understand perfectly. You're too scared to take the chance to love me. I thought you were lost. I didn't know you were a coward."

It was like his blue eyes went up in flames. His complexion darkened, his voice the low warning of a lion.

"I can't meditate and make my problems go away! I *am* Spright Wellness Community." He jabbed his breastbone with one finger. "I'm responsible for an entire community of people. I have to focus. I have to implement actual decisions and strategies that affect others. Even when my life was falling down around me, I kept this place going. Everything I do is in service to the legacy I built. This place will house generations to come. Throughout every bit of adversity I've faced, SWC has thrived. Casey Huxley was a warning that my island could be on shaky ground. I have to be responsible, Hayden. I have to live up to the unbelievable pressures of being the perfect environmental oasis for the families who live here. I'm not a coward. I'm a goddamn saint."

"A saint who is putting work before me!" Hayden shouted, her exposed heart burning with the realization. Another person she loved putting her in second place.

"Yes, exactly!" Tate threw his arms wide before ramming his hands into his hair. "I *can't* put you first! You deserve it and I can't do it."

"It's not like you're housing the homeless, Tate. This is a luxury community. You dwell in a mansion on top of a hill! And who cares what others expect from you? Your 'community' doesn't need you to survive. It can go on without you, you know. You're the asshole with a god complex."

His upper lip curled, the silence stretching between them like a band about to snap. Had she pushed him too far?

"Tell me, Hayden, all the ways you've sacrificed your own needs to take care of the people who need you."

Her ears rang like an explosion had gone off next to her. The words were like a sharp, stinging slap to the cheek. More tears fell, but she didn't feel them. She only knew they were there when they splashed onto her folded arms.

Realization dawned on his face so fast it was dizzying.

"I'm sorry." He stepped closer, and she skirted him and collected her shoes. "I didn't mean—"

"Take me home. *Now.*" She slipped on her shoes and pulled her wrap over her shoulders protectively. If only it were an invisible cape.

"Hayden, give me a chance to…" He followed her to the front door. "That was… I'm angry, okay? I spoke without thinking."

"Now, please." She wouldn't allow Tate to make her

feel guilty over a situation he'd never understand. She'd worked hard to untangle herself from her family's codependent strings.

Besides, she was beginning to believe that she and Tate weren't good together. This argument had proven that they had a knack for exposing the other's soft underbelly.

She'd been open and honest with him. Now he was using that honesty against her, which made her feel as if she were slowly suffocating.

"Hayden—"

"I have some meditating to do, and I'd prefer to be at home when I do it." Their gazes locked, and she tried not to see the human part of him. Tried to hate him for being cruel and elusive. But she couldn't. She loved him too damn much.

She couldn't stay and continue loving him, not when he didn't love her. With sex in the mix, it would border masochism.

And she refused to linger and hope that one day the timing would be right. That he'd return her feelings when life settled down. Life didn't settle down. Life *was* change—it was a series of bumps and hills, not flat, even plains.

With a tight nod of acquiescence, Tate finished dressing and put on his coat. He shut off the fireplace and scraped his keys from the kitchen counter, walking past Hayden without a second look.

"I'll warm up the car. Come out when you're ready," he said over his shoulder.

Once the door was shut, she looked out the wide picture window into the dark woods beyond.

Like the cold, still landscape, she was empty and alone. As if she'd traded places with that earlier version of Tate who'd stood outside her studio lost, and soaking in the rain.

# Twenty-Four

$A$t her front door, her hand resting on the knob, Hayden read the black-and-silver frosting on the sheet cake. "'Happy retirement, Roger'?"

"A mistake," Arlene said, her normally huge blond waves pulled neatly into a ponytail at the back of her head. "Rodger's name is actually spelled with a *D*, or so the lady at Blossom Bakery told me. This was the only cake available on such short notice."

"Why are you bringing me cake?" Hayden stepped aside and Arlene bustled in, a tote and her purse slung over her shoulder.

She'd called Arlene the morning after the New Year's Eve debacle at Tate's house, and Arlene had promised to be right over with "reinforcements."

"I assumed you'd show up with Emily and a few tubs of ice cream." Hayden shut her front door.

"Emily is with *Josh*," Arlene paused for a meaningful eyebrow waggle. "And ice cream is cliché." She pulled a bottle of sparkling wine out of the tote. "I also have hummus, pretzel chips, brie, salmon and lots of those really fattening buttery crackers we love but know are bad for us."

Hayden offered a wan, though grateful, smile. "Don't ruin your resolutions on my account."

"Pfft. Please. It's not too early to crack this open, right?" Arlene asked rhetorically as she tore the foil from the neck of the wine.

"Three o'clock is well within the day-drinking window."

"I'm so sorry I wasn't closer, or I'd have been here sooner." Arlene had been in Seattle when Hayden called her and had promised to come ASAP.

"It's fine. What were you doing, anyway?"

"I was doing a *very* fine younger bodybuilder type named Mike."

Hayden's eyebrows rose.

"I snapped a pic in the shower when he wasn't looking. Want to see?" But her friend's smile fell when Hayden's eyes filled with tears. Arlene quickly put down the bottle and ran to hug her. "I'm sorry. Sorry, sorry," she soothed as she rubbed Hayden's back. "It's too soon for me to be bragging about my hot hookup. And forget about Emily and Josh."

Hayden let out a watery laugh. "It's not too soon. I want you both to be happy."

Arlene leveled her with a look. "I wore my yoga gear so you could torture me in the studio. Whatever makes you feel better."

That did make Hayden laugh. "Yoga's about being kind to yourself, not about torture."

"Whatever you say. Cake first, though. I insist."

Half a sheet cake later, Hayden and Arlene sagged on the sofa, their champagne glasses in hand.

"After that much sugar, you'd think I'd have more energy." Hayden stabbed her plastic fork into the remaining cake. They hadn't bothered with plates. Arlene found two plastic forks left over from takeout and brought them to the couch with the wine and the cake.

It'd been therapeutic to eat her way through half of Rodger's retirement cake, but Hayden still felt the hum of loss in her bones. Arlene knew, though, and like any good best friend did, offered practical advice.

"In Tate's defense, I can imagine his life feels like it's been shaken vigorously and then tumbled out like Yahtzee dice. Can you imagine the combination of joy and disappointment and terror and… I don't know, weirdly, probably peace, he must feel at knowing he has a brother and an entirely new family?"

"His whole life changed. In a blink." Like hers. She hadn't expected to ring in the new year with a breakup *or* a relationship. A few months ago she assumed she'd be working round the clock to accommodate January visitors who'd made resolutions to get fit for the new year.

"Regardless—" Arlene pulled her chin down and gave Hayden a stern stare "—you can't keep your love on ice and wait for Tate to come around. If he has stuff to work through, that's on him. Nobody puts Baby in a corner." She smiled at the *Dirty Dancing* reference, but Hayden couldn't smile just yet. She'd already used up her one for the day.

"I made a commitment before I moved here that I wasn't going to accept half measures in any relationship—from my family, friends or whoever I happened to date."

"I commend you on that." Arlene raised her glass.

"I also committed to listening to my gut. Which is why I called the woman I leased this building from right after I called you."

"*Why* did you do that?" Arlene winced. "Don't say you're leaving me!"

"I'm not going far. I don't think. I might get a job at a gym rather than have the overhead of a new studio right away. I need to not be *here*. Where I'll run into Tate or read about him in the *Spright Times*," she said of the local printed newsletter that was in the café every month.

"But this is your refuge!" Arlene argued, throwing Hayden's words back at her. "I know you're upset, but are you sure you want to give this place up? We love it here. It's peaceful."

"Not if I'm walking through town panicking over the possibility of running into him."

Arlene nodded in what looked like reluctant agreement. "What did the woman say? About your lease?"

"I don't know. I left her a voice mail. The problem is it's a five-year lease. I can't commit to that any longer. I need to cut that tie first. And figure out the rest as I go. I have a nest egg. I'll be fine." Even though Hayden knew that was true—she would be fine—she didn't want to start over. She didn't want to move. She didn't want to look for a job. But with her heart filleted and lying on a cutting board, she didn't see another option.

"You might feel differently in a few days. Don't do anything rash. What if he calls to talk—"

"I don't want to talk to him."

"Do you think he's in love with that Claire chick?"

"No. I don't. That was the spark that started an argument, not the reason for the argument. The only part that matters is that I love him and he can't love me back. His work means more to him than me, and while I want to tell him that's a crock, there was also a time that I put my work before my family, too."

"That's different and you know it." Arlene leveled her with a firm look. "Your family is detrimental, and you're nothing but good for Tate."

Hayden agreed, but... "I don't want to be here. I wish I could... I don't know. Just disappear for a while."

Arlene sat up. She set down her flute of sparkling wine—they hadn't drunk even half a glass apiece since they'd been eagerly wolfing down sheet cake—and stood from the sofa. "Let's go then."

"Let's?"

"Yes! I have frequent flyer miles and some vouchers from work for a free stay at Caesars Palace. You want to get away, and lucky for you, since I went in for the last holiday, my boss owes me. She even said, 'You can have a few extra days off whenever you need. Just let me know.'"

"Caesars Palace? In Vegas?"

Arlene was already tapping the screen of her iPhone. "Well, I ain't talking about going to Rome, honey." Then into the speaker she said, "Amy, hi. It's Arlene..."

While Arlene paced the width of Hayden's living room explaining to her boss that she'd be out for a few days, a smile Hayden didn't know she had hidden away pulled her cheeks.

Maybe this was what she needed in order to think straight. A few days of being somewhere that was the total antithesis to Spright Island. A loud, smoky, hectic environment where she couldn't sit still and lick her wounds. What had Tate said? That he'd tried living dangerously for a while? Well maybe it was time for her to do the same.

Leaving for a few days was only a matter of packing a bag and rescheduling a few classes. Tate might've convinced himself that this community couldn't survive without him, but she knew they could live without yoga classes for a couple of days.

She was in no shape to be teaching anyone this week, anyway—especially if she spotted Tate walking by or, heaven forbid, if he came in. No one needed to witness her screaming at him, or worse, *blubbering* in the middle of king dancer pose.

"Done." Arlene swiped her phone's screen. "Now for the flight. How soon do you want to leave?"

Hayden crushed Arlene into a hug. A vacation was exactly what she needed. Time to recoup and think about her choices. Maybe Arlene was right and a few days later she wouldn't leave her beloved home. Only time would tell. "Thank you."

"Oh, honey. You know I have your back." All business, Arlene disentangled Hayden from her neck and tapped her phone again. "How soon?"

"As soon as humanly possible."

"That's my girl," Arlene said with a grin.

Tate had promised to entertain his adoptive parents when they came in on January 2, so in spite of not being up to having company, he was resigned to keep his word. Especially since he had skipped Christmas with them to fly to London and spend it with the Singletons.

His mother, Marion, hadn't acted as if it'd bothered her but his father, William, mentioned she'd been sad over the holidays without their normal traditions. Tate loved his parents, and he hadn't been the most receptive son since finding out the news that he was *someone else's* son, too, so he decided to keep his chin up for their sakes—regardless of his tumultuous emotional state.

Which he was determined to compartmentalize.

After dinner at Brass Pony, Tate drove by Hayden's yoga studio, taking note of the closed sign. Her upstairs windows were dark, but it was after nine, so maybe she'd turned in early.

After their argument on New Year's Eve, he'd given her space the next day. It'd nearly killed him not to text or call and apologize or ask that she forgive him—though *begging* might not be out of the question. But he'd been where she was before—angry, bewildered, confused. She had expectations and he'd failed her miserably.

This morning he'd keyed in two texts. One: I'm sorry and another: Let's talk. Both had gone unanswered, and he supposed he deserved that. She was angry. She had a right to be. She'd professed her love for him, and he'd sat there like a dope.

After Claire's pop-up appearance, his only thought was to get Hayden the hell out of there. His ex showing up at the café had nearly ruined his and Hayden's beginning, and he'd be damned if she'd trumpet in the end.

As much as he wanted to blame his ex for ruining his relationship, though, he couldn't. The fault lay squarely on him. The problem was his inability to be honest with himself, or Hayden. He'd been trying to compartmentalize and control different facets of his life. His head over here in this box, his heart in that one. He was beginning to see it wasn't working. There were no "compartments." There was only him—the whole him.

Marion chattered away about how stuffed she was and how delicious dinner was. "The cheesecake wasn't necessary, Tate." She cradled a plastic takeaway box on her lap in the front seat of his car.

"You mentioned that turtle cheesecake was on the menu fourteen times, Mom." From the corner of his eye, he watched her smile.

"Yes, but my diet..."

"You're beautiful," William said to his wife, squeezing her shoulder. "I tell her that every day," he explained to Tate. "She doesn't believe me. I don't know how many times I have to say 'I love you' and 'you're beautiful' for her believe me."

"Only about a million more times," she answered, patting William's hand.

Dread settled over Tate like a dark cloud. The five-star cuisine in his stomach churned. He reached into his pocket for a red-and-white-striped peppermint candy, unwrapped one end using his teeth and popped the candy into his mouth.

"Are you okay?" his mother asked.

"Ate too much," he told her, but it wasn't true. His throat was full like there was a lump in it and it wasn't from the ahi tuna bowl he'd enjoyed for dinner. He hadn't even had a cocktail, choosing water with a slice of lemon instead. No, he wasn't okay. He was negotiating with grief...or maybe worry was more accurate. He reminded himself for the millionth time that just because they'd argued didn't mean Hayden was gone forever. She was just unreachable at the moment.

In his driveway, he slowed to open the garage door and parked inside. Once his family was in the house, his mother stowed her cheesecake in the fridge "for later," and his father went for the whiskey cabinet to see what was available.

Tate watched them interact with easy smiles and the playful elbow to the ribs he'd often seen his mother give his father. They were in love. It was painfully obvious and not exactly the sort of behavior he'd welcomed as a teenager. He remembered when he was a teenager, rushing his friends off to another part of the house when William and Marion started making out in the kitchen.

"Here you go, son." His dad handed over Tate's drink. "I'm going to watch football. You coming?"

"Yeah. Let me just... In a minute."

William bypassed the dining room and the fireplace where Tate had laid Hayden down two nights ago. In the attached family room, the television clicked on, the sounds of cheering and announcers infiltrating the space.

"Okay." Marion climbed onto one of the bar stools at the breakfast bar and folded her hands. "Why don't you pour me a glass of wine to go with your cocktail and we'll talk about it."

Marion and William Duncan were well into their fifties. Both shorter than Tate, he remembered noting how obvious it was that he was adopted when he'd shot up to six two at age seventeen. Marion's dark hair was cut medium and circling her face. Her cheeks were rosy and round and, despite her suggestion that she needed to lose ten pounds, was on the slim side.

William had a belly, suggesting he liked to eat, and was losing his hair, something that Tate wouldn't have to worry about given George Singleton's full head of hair. But that was a simple matter of DNA and genes passed down—scientific markers of who he was.

Whether or not he was taller than Marion and William, or didn't share their body types didn't matter. Marion and William knew her son. Tate had been living with them from age three and a half until he flew the nest.

In short, they were his parents. They loved him. And his mother could help him through this if he would let her.

"Her name is Hayden" was where he started the story. And since it was a long one, he rounded the bar and sat down before sharing the whole sordid tale.

# Twenty-Five

Tate's parents stayed for breakfast and then they were off to catch their plane to San Francisco. The second they were out the door, Tate told himself he needed coffee, but he knew once he left his house and pointed in the direction of the café, he'd drive by Hayden's once more.

*Damn.*

The closed sign was still hanging on the door of the yoga studio. This was the third day in a row.

At the risk of being accused of being a stalker, or at the very least a heartsick moron, he decided to park and try knocking on her front door.

Last night he'd told Marion everything about Claire. About Hayden. About the trip to London. As the old black-and-white gangster movies his dad liked to watch were known for saying, Tate had sung like a canary.

It bubbled out of him in one messy, winding story, and by the end he was mortified to find himself hunkered over his drink, his eyes burning with unshed tears and his liquor untouched.

But his mother had never expected him to ignore his emotions, so he didn't.

"It's too much to handle. I just need time," he'd said in

frustration, finally taking a burning swallow of the whiskey his father had poured for him.

His mother's hand rubbed his back as she hummed thoughtfully to herself.

"That's what you've got for me?" he asked. "A thoughtful hum?"

Knowing he was teasing her, Marion's mouth curved at the edge. "I'm not sure if you want me to tell you you're wrong or not. Should I agree instead?"

He'd had to admit he could use some female insight, so he answered his mother's question with one of his own.

"How am I wrong?" The question came out with a frustrated edge, so he took another swallow from his glass. "What the hell was I supposed to do when everything was thrown at me in rapid succession?"

Another thoughtful hum came from Marion. "Be honest with yourself, and then be honest with Hayden."

"I was!"

"You *weren't*. You acted as if you don't know how to feel." Marion shook her head. "That's bull, Tate. You know. You're afraid to admit it, but you know."

He'd opened his mouth to argue, but he couldn't.

She was right.

Last night he'd gone to bed and had slept three, maybe four hours on and off. He'd tossed and turned and rationalized and thought through, around and over everything he and his mother had talked about.

He was in love with Hayden. Of course he was. She'd taken as much of him as she'd given of herself, and when she'd been vulnerable, he'd offered a lame excuse about *timing*.

He woke with a panicky feeling, an unease unlike any he'd felt before. He knew what he had to do, and for once, making the decision to confess how badly he'd fucked up seemed easy.

Upstairs, at Hayden's apartment door, Tate ignored the fullness of his heart, now lodged in his throat, and knocked. He waited. Knocked again. No answer.

"Hayden? If you're in there, I just need a few seconds." He braced his palms on the doorframe and waited. Nothing. "I have something to say and it has to be in person. Sixty seconds, tops."

He needed her to listen to what he had to say. He couldn't let another moment pass with her believing that he'd prioritized everyone and everything in his life over her—over the woman he loved.

"How about thirty seconds?" He could work with thirty. He just needed her to open the damn door.

Pulling his phone from his pocket, he called her and heard the distinct jingle of her ringtone inside the apartment about one second before he heard the outside door close and the sound of someone coming up the stairs.

"She left her phone at home. She's not here." One of Hayden's friends, the one with the short hair, not the bawdy blonde one, regarded him coolly. "I'm here to water her plants."

"Where is she?" He stepped aside so she could unlock the door and let herself in.

"I'm sure if she wanted you to know that, she would have told you."

She started to shut the door but he stopped it with one hand. "Is she safe?"

"She's safe." Her eyes warmed slightly. "She's with Arlene."

"Arlene. The blonde one." Tate offered a smile, but the brunette only scowled. "Thank you..."

"Emily." She sighed.

"Emily. Thank you. Can you tell me when she'll be back?"

She pressed her lips together.

"Ballpark?" he tried.

"Tomorrow, unless they decide to stay in...*wherever* they went."

"You know though. Where they went."

"Of course I know where they went." She frowned. "I also know that she's seriously considering buying herself out of the lease and leaving Spright Island because of *you*. Do you know how much she loves it here? Can you even fathom what she did to move here? What she gave up? She doesn't own a car, Tate. Not because she's trying to save the planet but because she sunk every dollar she had into her yoga studio. When Hayden goes in, she goes *all in*. Her friends are lifers."

Her lips twisted in consideration as she considered him, and his position in Hayden's life.

"I know I screwed up," he said, still wrapping his head around the idea that Hayden might leave Spright Island because of him.

"You think?" Emily propped her fist on her hip, not ready to let him off the hook.

"I *know*. I'll do whatever it takes for her to stay."

"Like what? Buy the building?" she snapped.

He smiled, not denying that buying the building was his first instinct. But he wouldn't trap her into staying. He wouldn't trick her into sticking around. She deserved to have the life she built, and he'd honor that.

"No. I'm not going to buy the building. But I promise, I won't be the reason she leaves."

Some of Emily's skepticism fled from her face, compassion replacing it. "This community is better because of her."

Emily was right. He'd seen residents interact with Hayden, the smiles at the café or the restaurant whenever she was around. She was contagious and beautiful. Incredible, really. How had been so obtuse not to see what was right in front of him. Of course Spright Wellness Community was better because of Hayden.

"We all are," he told Emily. And then he turned to leave.

# Twenty-Six

Vegas was exactly what Hayden needed, which was surprising to say the least. Normally she focused on being quiet and listening to her inner voice to clear her mind.

In this case a few days of drinks, gambling and a male strip show had cleared her mind just fine.

Arlene dropped Hayden off at her studio, a large pair of dark sunglasses hiding the evidence of a killer hangover. Hayden, while she'd enjoyed a few cocktails, hadn't abused her liver while she was in Vegas. Her drug of choice had been the craps table. She left up forty dollars, which she considered a win since she'd been down over two hundred bucks before that. She knew when to cut and run.

*Apparently.*

"I'm going to go home and die," Arlene said, droll.

"I have detox tea upstairs if you think it would help."

"Not sure anything would help except maybe a time machine. Then I could undrink those last four margaritas."

Hayden had been swamped with regret during the flight home to Washington, which made Arlene's next question easy to answer.

"Are you seriously moving off Spright Island?" Arlene

looked sad to ask it, which warmed Hayden's heart. She truly loved her friends.

"Of course not."

"Yes!" Arlene shouted before clutching her head with both hands. "Ow, my skull."

"Go home. Get some sleep. And thank you for a fantastic trip."

She stepped out of the car and Arlene drove away. It was cool, but sunny, and Hayden paused to take in the market across the street, waving at Sherry who'd just pulled open the door to walk in.

All around her there were smiling faces, and beautiful trees. Homes and retail establishments that were cared for and well-loved.

Spright Island and the people who lived here were Hayden's salvation. No matter what happened between her and Tate in the future, she wouldn't rob herself of the joy of living here. She was a better person here and this community—a place that Tate had envisioned into all its glory—was special. She sucked in a lungful of crisp air and turned, alarmed to see the man of her thoughts standing on the sidewalk outside her studio.

That speech had sounded fine inside her head. Faced with him, however, her instincts told her to protect herself. Build that wall as high and strong as she could.

"Hayden."

*That voice.*

Tate had said her name in every way imaginable. During the throes of heated sexual contact, in jest, when he was angry or happy. She heard compassion in his voice now; saw it on his face, too. He regretted their argument, that much was clear. But if he didn't love her—when she still loved him with everything she was—then nothing had changed except the date.

"Hi."

"Can I talk to you?" he asked.

She didn't want to talk to him. Not yet. Not until… Until what? Until she fell out of love with him? Who knew how long that would take.

Willing herself to be brave, she called up the very strength of character that brought her to Spright Wellness Community in the first place. "Sure."

"May I?" He gestured to her carry-on and she nodded, letting him take the luggage as she unlocked her studio door. She tried to ignore the brush of his hand on hers and the soft scent of leather coming off his coat. She tried, but failed.

Mere days ago she could've greeted him with a kiss. A hug. Maybe more. It was hard to believe after all they'd experienced together—with his family and hers—that this was over.

Stepping into her yoga studio, she focused instead on its pale wood floors and salt lamps. The padded blocks and yoga mats and water bottles for sale.

No way would she abandon her dream any more than Tate would abandon his. She hadn't run away from her family or her responsibility when she left Seattle. She'd run *toward* a dream—a vision that burned in her heart. There was a difference.

"I heard you were considering leaving," he said, flipping the lock behind him.

So they were doing this here.

"Where'd you hear that?"

"Emily. But don't be upset with her. She told me that so I'd know where her loyalty lies. With you. She doesn't want you to leave." He took a long, slow look around her studio. "No one at Spright Island wants you to leave. *I* don't want you to leave."

It was great to hear that. She wanted to shout with joy!

But just because he didn't want her to leave didn't mean he was suddenly and madly in love with her, did it?

"I'm not leaving," she said cautiously.

"Good." His smile caused an ache in her heart she was sure would drop her to her knees. So she flexed her core to keep her standing and folded her arms to protect herself. It wasn't a wall, but it was all she had. She wanted to believe that everything had changed. That he'd recalled their fight with the regret she felt whenever she thought about it. That he wished as much as she did that they had stopped and put their egos on hold long enough to have a conversation about what it meant to be together—and just how much they meant to each other.

It might not have salvaged what they had—she wasn't accepting less than she deserved from anyone—but they could've ended things amicably.

He stepped deeper into the room and came as close as he could without touching her. So close she had to tilt her head back to look up at him.

"I love you, Hayden. I fell in love with you probably before you fell for me, but I was too busy compartmentalizing and trying to sort out everything to realize it. I *should've* realized it. Nothing has ever been clearer than the fact that you belong with me and I already belong to you. I handled that night by the fireplace so badly. I messed up."

She felt her mouth drop open and she stood there in stunned silence combing over everything he'd said. He'd... fallen in love with her?

"I'm sorry," he continued. "For everything I said that night that was unfair and untrue. For making you think for one second you mattered less to me than anything on this planet."

She still couldn't speak so she stood there, mute as a mime as Tate reached into his jacket pocket and came out with his phone.

"You were thinking of leaving so that you didn't have to run into me, weren't you? So we could avoid each other at the market. Not cross paths while dining in the same restaurant." He tilted his head. "Not bump into each other in the park in the spring."

Yes to all of those things, but that was juvenile, wasn't it? Trying to avoid him. Tate Duncan *was* Spright Island.

"We'll work it out," she said carefully, still unraveling what he'd said to her. Her heart was grasping to his "I love you," desperate to be healed, but her mind... Her mind was more skeptical.

"I have a proposition for you. If you still love me, I want to be with you without barriers. Without compartments. Without playing it safe. Safe is for pussies."

Half her mouth lifted, hope filling her heart against her will.

He swiped the screen of his phone. "But if you've stopped loving me, or you can't trust me to make good on my promise to love you back, well..."

He offered the cell phone and she took it with shaking hands.

"It's a deed," he explained. "To my new house in San Francisco." He tapped the screen of the phone and brought up a text message with a timestamp from yesterday. "Which means I can sell my house here."

It was from Sherry, the real estate agent. Hayden read it, her eyes heating with tears. *I'm sure we can find the perfect buyer for your house, and fast!*

"You're...leaving?" Spright Island without Tate was as wrong as Hayden's life without Tate. "You love that house."

"I do," he admitted.

"You love it here," she said, emotion tightening her throat.

"I do." He put a hand on her arm and gave her a gentle squeeze. "But not more than I love you. I won't put anything before that."

He plucked the phone from her trembling fingers and pocketed it. "I know you can't see it, but I'm falling apart, Hayden. I miss you every moment you're not here, and hearing that you were considering uprooting what you've built because of—because I was too afraid to be honest with you… It's not right for you to compromise. So I will. For you. You deserve everything you've worked so hard to gain."

He waited while she stared, tears trembling on the edges of her eyelids. His every word had sealed up the crack he'd put in her heart.

He loved her. He *loved* her.

And he wanted her to stay. He was willing to walk away from his legacy and move back to California. He was giving her the community that needed him as much as he'd originally stated.

*Silly billionaire.*

"If I could rewind that night, we'd stay at the party, and drink champagne at midnight, and I'd kiss you so that everyone there would know what you meant to me. We'd still make love at my house by the fire—" he blew out a breath "—I don't see how that could get any better."

She bit her lip to hide a smile. Neither did she. It'd been everything.

"But you wouldn't have had the chance to tell me you love me, Hayden. Not before I said I loved you first." His eyes shimmered, as if the emotions he'd refused to share with her had pushed their way past his defenses.

"I followed rules my entire life. None of them kept me safe from drama or a broken relationship. When I broke those rules with you, though, I was more whole than I've ever been. My identity was mixed up in parents I'd never met and a twin brother I was getting to know. What I didn't know was that with you, I was becoming someone else. Someone better. I hope…the right man for you." His smile broke through, but nervous like he had no idea how she'd react. She knew, though. She knew. "I love you so much. I don't know where you went, but I know why, and I deserved it. I deserve whatever it is you say next."

He swallowed thickly, straightening his shoulders for the blows that would come. Ready to accept whatever she had to say—ready, if she said the word, to walk away from everything he cared about.

But she loved him. She'd never ask him to do that.

"When I left Seattle behind, when I parted ways from my family, it was to become a better version of myself. The reason I'm not leaving Spright Island isn't because of my yoga studio, or my apartment, or even this amazing community. I'm staying because of who I am when I'm here. I'm better. More caring. More giving. And that has a lot to do with you, Tate Duncan. You're more than this community. You're more than a legacy for generations to come. You're the man I love more than anything." A tear tumbled from her eye. "I'm better when I'm with *you*."

Before she finished speaking, Tate was crushing her against him.

"Thank God," he said into her hair, before lifting her face and seeking her lips with his. One kiss, perfect and sweet, and then he looked down at her with sheer awe.

"You, Hayden, are my legacy. Not this community. I'll never let work, or exes, or family come between us again. Whatever comes up we'll handle it. Together. Forever."

"I like the sound of forever." She wrapped her fingers around his and stood on her tiptoes. "But first, you have to make up for the last few days."

He smiled against her lips. "Name your price."

"Well, there was this strip show I saw…shirtless guys covered in oil…" She ran her hands over his button-down shirt. "How do you look in a g-string?"

He laughed, but frowned when he saw that she was serious. "Really?"

"Maybe. But I definitely will need you to call Sherry and tell her you're not selling your house in the woods."

"Done."

She brushed a lock of dark hair from his forehead. "I see no harm in keeping the house in San Francisco, though. We have to stay somewhere when we visit your parents in California."

He scooped her up against him and kissed away her grin, his mouth exploring hers in a movie-worthy, happy-ever-after kiss before setting her on her feet.

"I love you, Hayden Green."

"I love you, too, Tate Duncan." She tapped her chin. "Or is it Wesley Singleton?"

"Something else for you to decide."

"Me? Why me?"

"I'd like to give you one of those last names soon, along with a wedding ring. And a coveted house in the woods on an island."

Her head spun with possibility, with a future she hadn't dared imagine before this moment.

"What do you think?" he asked.

"I think…that fairy tales do come true."

"Except in this case, you're the one who saved me." Tate gestured to the sidewalk outside her studio. "You pulled me out of the rain, and then you kissed me. And I was never the same."

"Me neither."

"Well, then maybe we saved each other."

"Yeah." She smiled. "Maybe we did."

# Epilogue

*3 years later*

The Duncan-Green wedding had happened last summer. The Commons were transformed for the lavish ceremony, decorated in, lavender and cream.

Hayden's family—the Greens—had attended, on their best behavior without Grandma Winnie in tow. She'd passed away eight months ago now, her suffering meeting its end. Quite a bit of Hayden's and her mother's had died along with Winnie. Both of Tate's families had shown as well—the Duncans and the Singletons—and as a result the Singletons hadn't returned to Spright Island that winter for Christmas.

This year, they had. Christmas dinner had been served in their home—Hayden and Tate's mansion in the woods. They'd proudly stepped Marion and William through the tradition of Christmas crackers, and Jane and George had gotten their first taste of American holiday cuisine.

Reid and Drew had come to celebrate with them as well and were currently sitting on the floor with their two-year-old son, Roland. Drew cooed over her baby boy, who was tearing apart a box—a box that had previously contained an outfit that Roland was ignoring.

Aunt Hayden understood his lack of excitement.

Tate came into the room with a tray of mugs as Jane followed with their family's specialty: bread pudding. Hayden had thought she was too stuffed for another bite, but now that she saw the rich dessert she knew she wouldn't be able to deny herself a taste.

"We have one more gift," Tate said after everyone had settled into the sofas and chairs with their desserts.

"A surprise actually," Hayden said, pulling one last paper-wrapped Christmas cracker from its hiding place on the tree.

"Another cracker?" Jane asked.

"A *very special* cracker." Tate took the wrapped gift from Hayden and handed it to Jane, then gestured to his Marion. "Mom, why don't you take the other end and give it a tug."

"Okay, but I'm not reading another silly joke." Marion warned. Her Christmas cracker contained a dirty joke about Rudolph and his "sleigh balls." Hayden wasn't sure how it got there, but she thought Reid might have had something to do with it.

"I promise there is no joke." Hayden tucked her palms around her protruding belly, excited for the grandparents to learn what she and Tate now knew.

The pair of moms tugged and the cracker popped, spraying out paper confetti and a rolled photo. Jane reached for it first, gasping as she studied the blurry black-and-white ultrasound.

"You know the sex!" Jane exclaimed, squinting at the blurs and bumps on the photo.

"Let me see!" Marion sat close to Jane and leaned in also.

It took only a few seconds for Jane to recognize what had so obviously been there all along.

"Twins!" Jane exclaimed.

"Twins?" Marion repeated and both women burst into tears.

William and George shook hands and then claimed it was time for celebrating with cigars. Drew left Roland in Reid's arms to see the photo for herself.

"Twins?" Reid frowned at his own son and then to Tate. "Show-off."

Soon after, the bread pudding and coffee were gone. The men went to light cigars in celebration of twin baby boys coming soon to a wellness community near them.

Before Tate went outside with his brother and fathers he made sure to stop and place a kiss on Hayden's lips.

"Merry Christmas, Tate."

"Merry Christmas, Hayden." He bent to press his lips to her tummy then stood and gave her a wink. "And family."

\* \* \* \* \*

# READY FOR
# THE RANCHER

ZURI DAY

At home on the range or a night on the town
Whether funky line dancing or lazing around.
This book is for the reader who likes to enjoy
A ride around Sin City and a sexy cowboy!

# One

The same sounds that helped build the Breedlove empire worked Adam Breedlove's nerves, especially after putting in a twelve-hour day. Spinning wheels. Jangly music. Bells. Beeps. Chimes. Sounds that could be heard in any casino everywhere, even the virtual ones now online and accessible by almost anybody with a computer and an internet connection. Yet he took his time as he strolled through the loud, spacious area, two floors down and away from the CANN Casino Hotel and Spa's opulent, upscale and quiet main lobby. He was "keeping his feet in the grass," as his father would tell him. Staying close to the source of their great wealth was to always be reminded of who was really important—the CANN customer.

Before leaving the executive offices where Adam served as vice president of research and development for CANN International, he'd removed his suit jacket and tie and had rolled up the sleeves of his stark white shirt. It was a move to leave the position behind and appear casual, blending in with the patrons. He took in the vast Friday-night crowd, noted with satisfaction that a majority of the machines were occupied. He smiled and offered discreet waves to employees who recognized him. Eyes all across the room charted his progress. Some women offered flirty smiles. Others just stared. Men, too. Adam took it all in stride.

"Yo, Adam!"

Adam stopped and turned in the direction of the yell. A

stocky man of average height waved as he walked toward him. The face looked familiar but…

"It's Dennis, man. Dennis Washington."

"Washboard?" Adam laughed and shook the hand Dennis extended.

Dennis patted his beer gut. "Not anymore."

"That's why I didn't recognize you! What's going on, man? I haven't seen you in forever."

"Since high school, no doubt."

"Where have you been? Still living here, in Las Vegas?" Adam began walking toward an exit leading from the casino into a quieter hallway, a small seating area and a bank of elevators. Dennis fell into step beside him.

He shook his head. "Bakersfield. The family moved there shortly after I graduated, and just before I left for the military. When I came back, I settled there. Felt it was as good a place as any."

"You were in the service?" Adam asked, his look one of teasing surprise. "I can't imagine anyone telling you what to do."

Dennis smiled. "It was an adjustment."

"How long were you in?"

"Four years." A pained expression flickered across his face. "That was enough."

"That's awesome, Dennis. Thank you for your service."

Dennis's response fit somewhere between a grunt and a snort. Adam didn't know what the sound meant, but he knew to leave it alone.

"Are you staying here, at the hotel?"

"No, this place is too rich for my blood." He took a long admiring glance around. "It's something else, though. You Breedloves always were a cut above the competition. But this place is cuts, plural."

Adam couldn't disagree. His family had made history when their company, CANN International, had built the first seven-star hotel in North America. It had become the hotel of choice for anyone who had money or clout. But he'd been at the hotel since early that morning. Right now he couldn't wait to get away from the place.

"An army buddy of mine has a place in Henderson. I'm crashing there," Dennis said.

They reached the elevators. Adam went to the one on the end, slid open a panel discreetly tucked next to the doors and placed his thumb on the scanner. "How long are you going to be here? It would be cool to catch up."

"I'd love that, bro, and would especially like to talk about your other business, Breedlove Ranch. I read that you breed cattle and are building your own processing plant."

Adam nodded. "You read correctly. It's almost completed."

"That's the industry I'm in."

"Oh, yeah?"

"Yep. I manage a slaughterhouse in Bakersfield, one of the largest in the state."

The elevator arrived. Its doors opened without a sound. Adam waved a hand over the door panel. The elevator doors remained open.

"No kidding. How long have you been doing that?" Adam asked.

"Been working at the plant since returning from the military eight years ago, managing it for the last four years."

"We should definitely talk. How long will you be here?"

"I'm flying back tomorrow night."

Adam pulled out his phone. "Give me your number." Dennis complied. "I'll give you a call. Maybe we can do lunch."

"Sounds like a plan."

After a hand grip and shoulder bump, the men parted ways.

The next morning, after confirming a meeting with Dennis via text, downing a quick breakfast and enjoying a ride on his prize stallion, Thunder, Adam jumped into his brand-spanking-new limited-edition pickup and headed into the downtown of Breedlove, Nevada. The unincorporated town of just over two thousand residents was founded more than twenty years ago by Adam's father, Nicholas, and a group of like-minded businessmen. It was about twenty-five miles northeast of the Las Vegas Strip, surrounded by mountains, with planned communities and a number of businesses in and around the quaint downtown square. Anchoring one corner of that square was a restaurant Adam owned called BBs, which stood for Breedlove Burgers, purchased specifically to showcase the beef raised at his ranch.

He reached the place and pulled into a crowded parking lot. An affordable menu, comfortable decor and stiff drinks had made the spot a favorite among the residents, especially the younger crowd. Adam drove around to the reserved parking at the back of the building and entered through the employee entrance.

"Hey, Adam!"

"*Hola*, Miguel." Adam gave a shoulder bump to the restaurant's head chef. *"Qué pasa, hombre?"*

"Nada, man." Miguel shook his head at what he jokingly called Adam's "gringo Spanish."

"You come here to work or what?"

"I came here to eat a good burger. Think I can get a table?"

"I don't know, boss. You might have to wait in line."

Adam spoke to and joked with other employees as he continued past the building's offices, through the kitchen and into the main dining room, where he spotted Dennis sitting at one of the tables by the window. What made Adam almost stop midstride and have to catch his breath was that his former high school friend wasn't alone. If heaven was missing an angel, Adam knew where God could find her. Sitting at his burger joint—BBs.

* * *

Ryan Washington felt nauseous, and not just her stomach was upset. When inviting her to lunch, Dennis knew the last place his vegetarian sister would want to eat was a burger joint. He wasn't the only one at fault. She should have known that Dennis's inviting her anywhere held an ulterior motive, came with strings attached. She'd grown up adoring her older sibling and while she'd wished otherwise, they'd never been super close. Heck, before his call that morning she hadn't even known he was in Las Vegas. At first she'd flat-out refused. For many reasons. She'd had a full day planned, a practice about to open. Then there was the very personal matter that she hadn't shared with her family. But as was often the case, Dennis had persuasively changed her mind. After admitting there was a little more to his request than just having lunch, he'd told her about meeting an old friend who was now very successful. That he hoped to do business with him and that her presence might help. When she asked why, he'd very politically incorrectly said, "Because my friend likes pretty girls."

That should have been enough to reinstate her refusal. Dennis wasn't generous with compliments. For her brother to call her pretty meant he really felt he needed her help. And hinting to set her up with one of his friends? Not in a million years. What kind of business was this? And what if said business meant he'd spend more time in Las Vegas?

So there she sat, handling what work she could by way of her cell phone, mentally blocking out odors and wanting the meeting to be over.

"There he is!"

Ryan looked up when her brother spoke, and momentarily froze. The man—or was it the brother of Adonis?—who returned Dennis's greeting was gorgeous, as though he'd stepped right out of a Wild West billboard ad and walked in for a meal. Everything about him screamed cowboy—Stetson hat, plaid shirt, snug-fitting denims and

Western boots—all on a body for which it looked as though the clothes had been designed. *But a cowboy with clean, manicured nails?* That observation didn't fit with her assumption at all. That could never happen. Tall, dark and handsome was way too common a statement to use for the hunk in front of her. But it fit. He was toned and fine with close-cropped curls, dark, intense eyes and lips made for kissing. He smiled and revealed the knockout punch, a dimple. Ryan had always been a sucker for those.

For once, a temporarily speechless Ryan was grateful for her older brother's big mouth. She dropped her eyes down to her cell phone to call up composure and pull reasonable bits of calm and collected back from whatever part of her mind they'd fled.

"Good to see you," Dennis continued, as Hunkalicious sat down in one of two remaining wooden seats around the square table. "Couldn't believe when the waiter told us this was your place. Guess I shouldn't have been surprised, you running a cattle ranch and all. The server who seated us swore the burgers here were the best in the West. Didn't she, Ryan?"

Ryan meant to look at her brother, but of their own accord her eyes were drawn to the ones now boring into her with a casual intensity, deep chocolate orbs that fairly twinkled, framed by slightly arched eyebrows and long curly lashes.

She refocused on Dennis. "Yes, she did."

Actually Ryan hadn't been paying attention while Dennis flirted with the server. But since this guy her brother was trying to impress owned the establishment, she felt a little creative conversation was justified.

"You remember me talking about the Breedloves, right? The family who owns the CANN hotel on the Strip? This is one of the brothers, Adam. He and I went to high school together."

"Hello." Adam's smile was warm and genuine.

"Hi." Ryan suddenly felt shy, a rare occurrence. But she maintained eye contact.

"I don't think you ever met Ryan," Dennis continued. "She's my kid sister. Growing up she was a nuisance. I rarely allowed her around."

Ryan's brow raised at her brother's comment. Not that it wasn't true. As a precocious eight-year-old with a new-found love for board games and sports, she'd followed her fearless, then-fourteen-year-old athletic big brother around like a puppy, wanted to be where he was and to do what he did. For him, it was so not cool.

"I can't imagine you being a nuisance." Adam held out his hand. "It's a pleasure to meet you."

His voice reminded her of how a good brandy tasted—earthy, spicy, with a warmth that burned gently on its way down. She took his hand and noted its softness. He may own a ranch, but this definitely wasn't a man who spent his days herding cattle or baling hay.

"Likewise," she replied.

It was the merest caress, just a light squeeze of the hand she placed in his. But for Ryan it transmitted all sorts of messages. That he was thoughtful and gentle, yet strong and secure. He was probably a fabulous lover. Ryan had no idea why the thought crossed her mind. She couldn't have cared less, but there was something about him...

Ryan wasn't the only one smitten. *Am I smitten? Surely not!* At least half a dozen other females within her line of vision were, and definitely their cute server with perfectly coiffed twists, who bounced up to their table wearing a smile as bright as her starched white shirt.

"Hey, Adam!"

"Hello, Zoe, a ray of sunshine, as always. Zoe is our top server," Adam said to Dennis and Ryan. "When she heads off to college next year, it'll be our loss."

"Mine, too," she lamented. "I'm going to miss eating here almost every day and seeing...everybody."

Ryan felt anyone looking at the lovestruck teen would assume that "everybody" was Adam.

Zoe turned to Ryan. "What can I get for you today?"

"Why don't you start us out with drinks and an appetizer trio tray?" Adam interjected. "I'll run down the menu so they can make informed choices."

"Great idea." Zoe pulled out a small electronic tablet and recorded their drink orders. "For the trio, how about beer balls, fried pickles and onion strings? Those are the most popular items on the starter list."

"Beer balls?" Ryan asked.

"It does sound a bit weird," Zoe replied with a laugh. "They're meatballs, made with Breedlove beef and spicy pork, then coated with a beer batter and deep-fried."

"Sounds delicious," Dennis said.

"Ryan?" Adam looked at her.

A slight hesitation and then, "That's fine."

"Are you sure?" he asked.

"Don't mind her," Dennis said. "She's one of those funny eaters…a vegetarian."

"Really?" Adam perched his Stetson on a wall hook, then reared back in his chair and observed her. "You don't eat beef or pork?"

"Nothing with a face," Ryan responded.

"Not chicken, either, or fish?"

The incredulity in his voice made Ryan laugh out loud. "None of the above."

Adam shook his head. "I'm a meat-and-potatoes man to the bone. For me, living that way would be like dying a slow and painful death." He picked up the restaurant menu, a simple two-sided sheet covered in plastic, and placed it back down with hardly a glance. "We have a couple salads on the menu," he suggested. "They're fairly straightforward but I've eaten them a time or two. Honestly, they don't get ordered much. But we wanted a few healthier options along with all the fried stuff. We also have a turkey burger but that won't help you, either."

"No, but it's okay. I'm not that hungry."

"But if you were, your choices would be limited. Honestly, with all the time we spent on the menu we didn't give vegetarians much consideration. This is a huge meat-eating town, everything with a face."

Ryan laughed. This guy was delightful.

"How long has it been since you've eaten meat?" Adam asked.

"About five years."

"Why'd you stop?"

"Because a screw came loose," Dennis joked. "Anyone who'd turn down a good burger can't be right in the head."

Adam looked at Dennis but didn't laugh. Ryan appreciated his nonresponse to her brother's barb. For as much as she loved Dennis, he could be a bully and often made her uneasy. Hurtful, disparaging comments in the guise of teasing were something she'd endured from him for much of her life.

"Do you work with your brother?" Adam asked in her silence.

Ryan glanced at Dennis. His eyes conveyed a message that she couldn't read. Her answer was noncommittal. "Not really."

"She doesn't butcher cows," Dennis said. "But she does work for me from time to time, typing and other things that can be done online. She's really good at stuff like that."

*What?* Updating Dennis's résumé and typing up a couple reports hardly qualified her as being Dennis's employee, especially when she did those things for free. Again Ryan assumed this was part of why she'd been brought here. To contradict him outright wouldn't look good. Dennis wouldn't like it. Ryan's mother had taught her a long time ago that Dennis was the golden child and image was everything. Even so, she barely concealed the question from being broadcast on her face.

"You live here?" Adam asked.

"Yes," Ryan answered.

Dennis turned to Ryan. "Adam works with his family but he has his own company, too, Breedlove Ranch, where they raise cows for market.

"You guys hiring?" he asked Adam. "If you have any openings in the office, Ryan here would make a great employee."

This time the message in Dennis's glance was clearly conveyed. *Play along.*

Ryan gripped her fingers together beneath the table. Otherwise she could imagine them around her brother's neck! To say that she worked with Dennis was ludicrous, and that she'd have anything to do with a company that bred animals for food was an outright lie.

But then Adam looked at her with those bedroom eyes and said, "I'm intrigued. Tell me more."

And Ryan felt that appearing to go along with her pushy brother, at least through lunch, couldn't hurt. She didn't see herself seriously dating a sexy meat-and-potatoes stallion like Adam. But she could certainly ride him for a night or two.

# Two

Adam was surprised at how Dennis teased his sister, and didn't like it at all. He'd been on the receiving end of such treatment. That's how he and Dennis had become friends. The guy he remembered from high school was one who defended people who were being treated badly. That he'd been rude to his sister bothered Adam, maybe more than it should. He sensed Ryan wasn't comfortable with the situation, either. So he decided to let the matter go…for now.

Zoe returned with their drinks and to take their entrée order. Dennis and Adam opted for the house specialty and the most popular menu item—a half pound of Breedlove beef on a toasted bun topped with onion strings, dill pickle slices, and a homemade condiment blend of spicy mustard and creamy aioli.

Adam looked at Ryan. "Would you like a salad, possibly with smashed potatoes or fries?"

"What type of oil is used to cook them?" Ryan asked.

"Good question," Adam said. "I have no idea."

Ryan's query led to a visit from the chef. Once schooled in the preparation of her limited choices, her order was taken.

Dennis took a large swig of beer and then set down the bottle. "So, Adam…how'd you go from casinos to cows?"

Adam shrugged. "Wasn't planned, although if you'll remember, I always had a little bit of cowboy in me."

Dennis grinned. "That I do recall."

"Me and Christian had accompanied my father on a trip

to Tokyo, where we'd just opened a second hotel. For dinner our host served us Kobe beef. It was hands down the best bite of meat I'd ever put in my mouth. I asked the host about its origins and basically became obsessed with finding out everything I could about how it was processed. When a family meeting led to a large tract of unused land being up for grabs, I jumped at the chance to come as close as I could to producing that taste in America. It's been five years in the making, but we're confident that Breedlove Ranch is about to deliver that product. Not Kobe, of course—that type can only come from the region that bears its name—but the best Wagyu beef ever produced in this country."

"Is that what's served here?" Dennis asked.

Adam shook his head. "Not yet. We've had customers sample the Wagyu, but here we'll continue to offer the less expensive prime Black Angus."

He looked over as Ryan made a face. "Sorry about that."

"No problem," Ryan responded.

"Tell that to your face," Adam drawled. "You just scrunched up your nose like you got a whiff of poo."

The comment caused Ryan to burst out laughing yet again. From a woman who Adam felt was somewhat guarded, the sound was as carefree as it was unexpected. It was a sound he decided he quite liked. A lot.

"Where is your meat processed?" Dennis asked.

Adam glanced at Ryan before answering. "Until now we've sold the bulk of cattle wholesale, keeping back a supply for the hotel, a few restaurants and stores in this area, that are processed by a small, family-owned business in Henderson. But we're four to eight weeks away from completing our own facility."

"Having your own processing plant has got to be exciting."

"It is," Adam replied. "Four thousand square feet, state of the art."

Adam saw Ryan reach for her purse. "Excuse me," she said, standing up.

"Don't go," Adam responded. "We can talk shop another time."

"No, really. It's okay. I want to wash my hands."

Adam watched her walk away. He was struck by her beauty to be sure—curvy figure, curly hair, skin the color of hot cocoa and he imagined just as sweet. But there was something else about her, an aura of calm assuredness, a peacefulness that somehow calmed him, too. These days, as he balanced his responsibilities at CANN International with the expanded growth and heightening profile of Breedlove Ranch and the beef it produced, moments of true tranquility were in short supply.

"I see you," Dennis said with a smile in his voice. "Checking out my sister."

Until then Adam didn't realize he'd been staring. "I never knew you had a sister. I remember your brother Charles, but not her."

"Everyone thought Charles and I were brothers. He's my cousin."

"You're right, I didn't know that. We became close rather quickly in high school but you were a senior when we met. It was only that one year."

"Makes sense about Ryan," Dennis replied. "That you never met her. She was several years behind us in school and I don't think you ever came to my home."

"That's because you guys were always wanting to come over to mine!"

"Heck, yeah. Who wouldn't? Swimming pools. Horses. A full basketball court. Dinners made to order from a personal chef. Going to your house was like going to Hollywood! I couldn't believe people really lived like that. You're one lucky dude."

"I'll admit to luck in being born a Breedlove. After that, everything was hard work."

"I know all about hard work," Dennis said.

"At the meatpacking plant, right?" Dennis nodded. "How does Ryan fit into your operation?"

Adam ignored Dennis's knowing smile, one that suggested the sister had been brought along to help seal the deal. It was a good move and a smart one, but Adam figured Dennis didn't have to know that.

"Like I said, she's helped out here and there. But she doesn't live in Bakersfield, hasn't in a while. She went to school in San Diego and lived there after graduation. Until about three months ago when she moved here."

"Why'd she move?"

Dennis shrugged. "She got a degree in some kind of natural medicine or something. I don't know much about it. But I know she isn't working anywhere yet. She probably needs a job."

"And you think she'd be comfortable working on a ranch?"

Ryan returned to the table. "Talking about me?"

Adam stood but he was too late. Ryan had already pulled out her chair. He waited until she'd sat down before returning to his seat.

"Dennis thinks you'd be a good fit for my operation. He says your administrative skills are impressive."

*And if they are half as impressive as the view of your backside as you walked away from the table...*

Adam shut down the inappropriate thought, gave himself a mental chastisement, forgave himself because his thought was the truth, then refocused his attention on Ryan.

"I handled a few items for him in the past, but that was a long time ago. I'm focused on developing my own business right now."

"Which is?"

"Naturopathy," Ryan said after a pause.

"What's that?" Adam asked as he watched Ryan stiffen as though expecting a verbal blow. Dennis didn't disappoint.

"A hobby," Dennis said.

"My career," Ryan countered, a cool breeze skittering over the previously warm and calm demeanor Adam had earlier observed.

"Lunch is served!" Zoe announced as she arrived at their table, moving a few items before expertly setting down a circular tray. "Both the pickles and onion strings are vegan," she said to Ryan, having obviously spoken with the chef. "The barbecue sauce is also vegan but the buttermilk ranch contains dairy. Your entrées will be up in about ten minutes. Bon appétit!"

"These are cool," Ryan said, using the tongs hooked to the bowl to pull out a wad of thinly cut and battered onion slices. "Onion strings, huh? I've had onion rings and a flowering onion but never ones quite like this."

"That's Miguel's handiwork. He puts a unique spin on any dish he touches."

"I like the beer balls," Dennis said around the food he'd picked up with his fingers and plopped into his mouth. "That big old juicy burger will be even better. Good old cow meat," he continued, smacking loudly and reaching for another meatball.

"Older brothers can be a pain in the butt," he said to Ryan. "I know, I've got one, too."

Ryan smiled. Adam immediately wanted to think of something else witty to make her smile again.

"Good to know someone else understands my pain."

"He's not all bad, though," Adam continued. "Standing up to bullies is how I met your brother."

"You mean he wasn't one of them?"

Adam laughed. "Not that time."

"What happened?" Ryan asked.

Adam and Dennis exchanged a look.

Adam thought back to the day as a freshman in high school where he had fought an admirable but losing battle against four students who'd ganged up against him—at first verbally, then physically. Dennis had come to Adam's defense. The two had quickly regained the upper hand before school administrators rushed into the melee and broke up the fight. It was Adam's last physical fight. That summer his muscles filled out and he grew six inches. Once his dyslexia was properly diagnosed, his popularity grew along with his confidence. But still, scars remained. There were traces of the disability that lingered to this day.

"Kids were always teasing me. One day, I found myself in a fight where I was outnumbered," Adam said. "Your brother jumped in and helped me out. That's how we became friends."

"Interesting," Ryan said, giving her brother a look that Adam couldn't quite read.

"I always appreciated how you took up for me," Adam finished. "Just like one of my brothers would, had they been there. It showed character, which is very important to me. That along with loyalty, honesty and respect are the principle virtues I look for in people I work with. Which is why I wanted to have lunch with you today, Dennis. You mentioned your sister working for me but actually the opening I'm trying to fill ASAP requires a different skill set. The person we'd hired to manage my processing facility was involved in a serious automobile accident. He's alive, but his recovery isn't going to allow for the type of rigor required for that position. Are you interested?"

Dennis sat back. "Wow, really, Adam? You're offering me the job of managing your meat-processing operation?"

"I'm asking if you're interested. We'd still need to go through the application process, but if everything from there is in order then yes, I'd feel good in you having that job."

"Thanks, man. I appreciate it and yes, I'm very interested. I've always loved your family's land. Working on it would be my pleasure."

"I might come up to Bakersfield," Adam said. "Get a look at your operation and see how it compares to ours."

"Okay," Dennis said, after a beat.

Adam found the hesitation odd but didn't dwell on it. Now that he'd potentially solved a huge dilemma, a delay that would have put a serious wrench in their scheduled plant launch, he was ready to find out more about Ryan. Whether or not he ended up working with Dennis, he wanted to see more of her. Before parting ways he asked Dennis to send him a proposal, and asked Ryan for her number.

"Why?" Ryan asked, her expression suggesting she couldn't think of a reason why he'd need to talk to her.

Adam smiled slightly, impressed. Most women were all too eager to give him their number. He was appreciative of one who hesitated. "To talk about food," he replied, "and what types of vegetarian options might work with our current menu."

She seemed relieved that his reason was work related. It wasn't the only one, of course, but it was as good of an excuse as any.

# Three

Ryan hadn't been surprised yesterday when Dennis ran off before she could confront him. He hadn't returned her calls from last night or yesterday, either. Blindsiding her with a job she'd never heard of in front of the man wanting to hire him was pretty low, even for a brother known for sometimes being underhanded. But honestly, Ryan couldn't be totally mad. Adam Breedlove was one hot man. She had no intention of working at Breedlove Ranch but she could put in a personal shift or two with the boss. She'd been in the city for three months without dating. One day after the other had been all work, no play. Dennis's friend could prove a nice lightweight diversion. A little sin in Sin City every now and again.

The prospect of a rendezvous with the cowboy was totally titillating, but Ryan forced her mind back to where it belonged this Monday morning—on her practice, and building it up. After years of sharing "her hobby" as Dennis had called it with friends, classmates and coworkers, she'd gotten serious about her love for alternative healing and obtained a bachelor's degree in naturopathy, specializing in plant medicine, biophysics, massage therapy and nutrition. She'd simultaneously pursued and received certificates in energetic healing and emotional frequency technique from the prestigious Institute of Higher Holistic Learning in La Jolla, California. From her childhood until her early-adult years as she came into her own, she'd sought to please others and be what they thought she should be. After learning of her passion, her parents had suggested traditional medicine, had thought she should pursue a nursing degree. But Ryan had finally followed her heart and become submerged in Eastern medicine and alternative forms of healing. Those three years of expedited learning were the best ones of her life. This was also when she'd met her ex, which had added some worst moments to those educational years.

While attending an expo during her senior year she'd met Brooklyn, a woman named for where she'd been born, who'd moved cross-country to Las Vegas, a place Ryan had doubted she'd ever return to live. But their long conversations on the alternative and holistic landscape evolved into others on working in complementary fields. Their shared interests and similar personalities led to them being best friends, the sister Ryan had always wanted. Brooklyn suggested they open a practice together. Ryan jumped at the chance to have her own business. That's why she'd moved back to Las Vegas. Not the only one, but the one she felt most comfortable admitting. The other reasons were complicated, both hopeful and painful. There were secrets she hadn't unearthed and couldn't share…yet.

Ryan's ringing landline startled her out of daydreaming. A blessed interruption, she inwardly noted, while crossing the airy living room of her Summerlin townhome. No doubt it was Brooklyn, calling to make sure Ryan was on schedule and that she'd make it to their appointment on time.

"Yes, I'm ready. Five minutes and I'm out the door."

"Um, okay, but where are we going?"

Ryan's heart raced. "Adam?"

He chuckled, a sound that sent goose bumps dancing over her skin.

"I hope it's okay that Dennis gave me your home number. I tried your cell phone a couple times but didn't hear back, and the question I have is time-sensitive so I called your brother."

Halfway through his explanation, Ryan had begun

searching for her cell. She'd checked the living room and master bedroom. Now she headed toward the garage.

"Ryan, are you there? If this is a bad time—"

"No, it isn't," Ryan said, while lying on her belly and searching her car's back seat. "I'm looking for my cell phone that I now realize I haven't heard ring all morning."

"When is the last time you remember having it?"

"Definitely this morning before leaving the house. I tried calling Dennis in fact and…aw!"

"Whoa, are you okay?"

"Yes!" Ryan laughed. "I just remembered where it was." She headed into her house and the bedroom. "I forgot I placed it in my yoga bag before going into the studio."

She found the bag in her closet, opened it up and retrieved the phone. "Listen, Adam, if you're calling about what Dennis is doing—"

"I'm not."

"Oh." Ryan glanced at the clock on the wall. It was almost time to head out for her meeting. But she had five minutes. She sat down. Adam's voice was better than a massage. It made her feel all noodly, if that was even a word.

"What's up?"

"Magic, if you're into that sort of thing."

*If you're doing the tricks, I very well could be.* "What kind of magic?"

"What kind do you like?"

His voice had lowered just enough for Ryan to imagine a double entendre. If his bedroom moves were half as sexy as that raspy tenor…

"All kinds, I guess. I find fantasy entertaining. The ability to conjure another type of world within this one is an incredible skill."

"I agree. Our hotel is hosting a private premiere that we feel is going to be very special. It is a show that blends illusion with dance, great music and scenes. Rather than separate tricks, an entire story is told. The guy is from Denmark. His name is Valdemar."

"Never heard of him."

"Few have, in America. At least not yet. And no one in the way he'll be presented at CANN. The show is tomorrow night and I'd like very much for you to join me."

"It sounds interesting. What time?" Ryan asked, as though it mattered. Mentally, she was already going through her closet for what to wear, but a girl couldn't appear too hasty.

"The show starts at nine but I was hoping you'd also join me for dinner. I spoke with hotel management, who recommended a couple of our restaurants with stellar vegan and vegetarian choices."

"That's very thoughtful of you." *Or presumptive.*

"I wanted to be prepared, just in case you said yes."

Ryan hesitated.

"I know it's late notice. I wasn't planning to go until, well, I caught a bit of the rehearsal and what I saw blew me away."

"It sounds incredible, Adam. I'd love to join you."

"May I pick you up around…six thirty?"

"Are you sure? I could meet you there."

"No way. I'll come to you. What's your address?"

Ryan rattled off her address while gathering her tablet and a couple folders and placing them in a stylish hemp tote. She ended the call, exchanged house shoes for a pair of wooden throwback clogs that she adored, placed her clutch inside the tote and walked to the car with her cell phone in hand. There was one more call she needed to make.

As soon as her Bluetooth engaged, Ryan called Dennis, at the office this time. "I need to speak to my brother, Katy. I know he's there so tell him to pick up or I'm coming over."

"Um, Dennis isn't here," Katy said.

"You sound uncertain. Are you sure?"

"Let me check and call you back."

"I've been waiting for callbacks, Katy. I hate to put you in the middle of this, but I really need to talk to Dennis, now."

"I'll find him for you and either he'll call back or I will, promise."

Ten minutes later, her phone rang.

"Hey, sis!"

"Don't 'sis' me. You owe me an explanation regarding lunch this weekend. What was that about?"

"What do you mean?"

"You know full well what I mean. I never worked for you, have zero interest in being a secretary and am not looking for a job. Of course you don't know this because you never asked me. We haven't talked in weeks."

"Ah, Ryan, don't be upset. I could tell Adam liked you and played on it is all, hoping his interest in you would give me an advantage when I asked him for a job. Turns out that didn't happen because he asked me!"

Ryan sighed. "I'm glad it worked out for you, Dennis. But from here on out, don't put me in the middle of your business, okay?"

"That's fair, sis. I just have one more request."

"What?"

"You're coming home next week, right?"

"How do you know about that?"

"Mom told me."

"Yes, I'm going home. Why?"

"Adam wants to visit my, um, facility and I thought it would be cool if I schedule his visit at the same time you're here so we can all have dinner together."

"What'd I just say about involving me in your meat-factory business? I don't want to take part in it."

"I know, and after this, you won't. It's just that Adam is big on family, huge. Mom likes that and wants to have him over for dinner. Your being here could be a buffer. Mom isn't always the most gracious person, you know."

"Yes, I know." She had a son who was just like her.

Ryan reached the block where her business rental was located. She pulled into the parking lot, found a space and parked.

"I get a feeling there's more to this. What aren't you telling me?"

"That's it, I swear! Mom says you'll be here Friday. I'll ask Adam to come up then, and Mom will do dinner that night. Cool?" Ryan's eyes narrowed as she tried to get a feel for what was really going on.

"It's all about family, Ryan. I'm asking you to help me the way we've helped you, all right?"

*Of course he'd pull that card.* "I guess, but after this I'm out. Are we clear?"

Dennis laughed. "Don't get all huffy just because you've got a billionaire interested in you. I could tell him a few things to make him change his mind."

Ryan ended the call more conflicted than ever. Going on the date with Adam now felt like a bad idea. She found him super good-looking and was madly attracted, but did she really want to go on a date and maybe sleep with a guy that her brother might end up working with? Someone she might have to see after a fling?

No, she didn't. She couldn't, especially now, just as she was about to open her business. Few people knew what Dennis threatened to share with Adam, details of a painful past she'd worked hard to overcome. One that for twenty years her adoptive mother, Ida, had encouraged her to keep secret. She'd demanded that her "embarrassing" birth mother, Phyllis, be left in the past. That Ryan had been in contact with Phyllis off and on for the past five years would definitely anger her. As would the latest secret, that for the first time in Ryan's life, she was going to try and find her birth father.

Dennis was right. There were things Adam didn't know, facts hidden beneath a carefully crafted facade of perfectly placed secrets. Even without her dysfunctional history, a man like Adam was clearly out of her league. For a while, though, she'd forgotten, had allowed herself to believe that she could have the fairy-tale life of her childhood dreams. Happily-ever-after came only in books, something Ryan would do well to remember.

# Four

Adam strolled out of the hotel's private entrance, eased into the roomy back seat of the car that awaited and clipped the hanger holding his suit jacket over the bar. He hoped Ryan wouldn't consider his transportation choice bougie, although that was a fairly apt description for an executive limousine. Any other woman and he wouldn't have given it a second thought, knew that picking up most dates in the company's brand-new four-seater SUV limo would impress them right out of their undies. Not that he was thinking about Ryan's lingerie. He'd be lying to say that since meeting her such thoughts hadn't crossed his mind from time to time.

Ryan lived in Summerlin, just over ten miles from the Strip. Adam thought of a few things he could do in the twenty-five or so minutes it would take to reach her, longer if traffic didn't cooperate. There were emails to answer, phone calls to return. But instead of returning calls or checking texts or browsing emails he dropped his head, closed his eyes and thought about how Ryan had tried to get out of attending the show with him tonight. He couldn't remember ever having a woman try to break a date. Why had Ryan? And for a man who could go out with just about anyone he wanted, especially when only interested in a casual good time, maybe a bedroom rodeo, why had her canceling their date not been an option?

"Something came up," she'd said. He'd told her she couldn't cancel. When asked why he'd calmly replied, "This is a major event with huge implications for the continued success of this particular hotel venue. Every RSVP has already been tabulated into the report for our board. I can't show up alone and there is no time to call in a replacement. You've given your word. I'll be there in an hour." Five minutes later, he'd walked to the car.

What Ryan didn't know was that what Breedloves wanted, Breedloves got. Period, point-blank, end of story.

They pulled into one of Summerlin's planned communities and onto a street ending in a cul-de-sac framed by townhome-styled condos. One had a red door with earthen pots on each side, brimming with flowers and greenery.

"A hundred bucks that's Ryan's home," he said to the driver, who checked the address and nodded at Adam.

"Good thing I didn't take you up on that bet."

Adam got out of the car and strolled up to the door. A burst of excitement spread from his core to his groin. With a smorgasbord of women to choose from any given night of the week, he'd grown jaded to the art of wining and dining. It felt good to be excited. He rang the bell.

*"Un momento,"* she sang out. *Gringo Spanish.* He thought about Miguel and smiled.

In less than a minute, she opened the door. Adam turned, but wasn't ready for the woman he saw. Not this Ryan—part innocent femininity, part femme fatale. The dress, long and flowing, following her curves like water followed the falls. The color almost matched her tawny skin, making him imagine her nude. At the restaurant her curls had been tamed by a band on top of her head but tonight they bounced wild and free, framing her face and brushing her shoulders. They teased his senses; he wanted to touch. He liked that she wore little makeup yet still looked flawless. Her lips kissed with a color of gloss that reminded him of a fine wine. He wanted a taste. How was it that with most of her body covered she managed to look so sexy?

"Hello" was all he said at first because it was all he could manage.

"Hi."

"I'm sorry for earlier, and sounding so forceful. It's just that I couldn't take no for an answer."

"It's okay. Everything…worked out." Ryan turned and locked the door. Adam offered his arm. Her touch was light, yet a thunderbolt of desire shot through his heart, ricocheted off a vein and zoomed into his groin.

He helped her enter the vehicle, then got in on the other side.

"You look…stunning."

The smile that she gave him could have cured a disease. "I hoped it would be appropriate. I wasn't sure."

"It's perfect."

"Thank you."

Adam's brow furrowed. "Are you sure you're okay?"

"It's just that… Yes. Really, I'm fine."

The SUV pulled away from the curb. Ryan took in the roomy interior. "This is nice."

She sat perched on the seat, taking in the swank decor. "I've never been in something like this before. From the outside it looked like an SUV but in here…"

He watched as she ran her hand across the lambskin seat. Her eyes, initially reticent, now sparkled while examining the console, with its built-in bottle chiller, various openers and glass rack. She stopped suddenly, as if becoming aware of her innocent wonder. She may have thought he'd find it amusing. He thought it endearing, and with a trail of showgirls, sycophants and rich chicks in his wake, a breath of fresh air.

"So this is a limo?"

He nodded. "It's called an executive SUV."

"I like it."

A brow raised. "You don't mind that it has leather seats?"

"I'm not a member of the PETA police, Adam, you can relax."

He made a big show of taking a breath, which made her laugh as he'd intended.

"While I don't own a gun or a hunting license, my choice to be vegetarian is for nutritional reasons, mostly. I am cognizant of the earth's precarious state and do what I can to try to protect the planet. I believe our bodies are our temples so I make an effort to be kind to mine. But I try not to be a holistic zealot trying to win everyone over to my point of view.

"That said…" She paused dramatically. "There are faux materials that work just as well or even better than cowhide, and mushroom dishes that would make you throw away your steak."

"Baby," Adam drawled, "unless that mushroom had hooves and could moo, trust me, there'd be no competition."

She was funny and natural and easy to talk to, yet emanated a vulnerability that brought out his chivalrous side. He wanted to protect her. From what, he had no idea. By the time they'd rounded back to the hotel, the stress of Adam's day had faded, the questions he'd had about her demeanor forgotten for now.

They entered the hotel through the private entrance and once inside the elevator, Adam accessed the panel to bypass all floors and take them straight to Zest, CANN Casino Hotel and Spa's premier restaurant, located on the building's one hundredth floor. As the elevator zoomed to the top, Ryan stepped closer to Adam and gripped his arm.

"Afraid of heights?"

"No, but I'm not fond of rockets masquerading as elevators."

"I've got you, girl." He placed an arm around her, grateful for a reason to brush a hand across her soft skin. "Stay close to me and don't worry about a thing."

The elevator doors opened, and as the host led them around the corner, Adam was rewarded with the gasp of awe that escaped every newcomer's lips to the wonder that was the hotel's crowning architectural and culinary masterpiece.

With exquisite attention to detail, the main dining room, with a seating capacity for 140 guests, still afforded many booths semiprivacy, space between tables and an unobstructed view of the world beyond through floor-to-ceiling paneless windows that brought the outdoors inside. Classical music delicately played provided a subtle melody for the low murmur of conversation heard as Adam and Ryan were led to a booth. Its back created a wall between them and the other guests, while before them lay the whole of the Vegas Strip.

"Do you want to go for a closer look?"

Ryan shook her head as he finished the question. "It's the most phenomenal view of this city I've ever seen, but believe me, I'm good."

They sat down to a table set with linen and china, a bottle of sparkling water cooling on ice.

"This is so pretty," Ryan said wistfully. "To think that this is everyday life for some people is a bit unbelievable. I feel like Cinderella."

"Does that mean I'm your prince?"

"Until the clock strikes midnight," Ryan said, her voice low as her eyes sparkled with seduction. Then, in an instant, the vulnerability reappeared. "Then I'll have to run away before the carriage becomes a pumpkin and my clothes turn back to rags."

"Have I told you how much I like rags?" Asked so earnestly that not only did Ryan laugh but Adam cracked himself up as well. "In fact I think I'm going to start a clothing line. Rags by Adam."

"All cotton, no leather," Ryan teased.

"Not cotton," Adam responded, "leaves."

Adam loved to hear Ryan laugh. While far from being a comedian, he'd turned the mood funny so that a certain body part straining to stand at attention would return to its at-ease position. The next few minutes was a parade of perfection as the sommelier, the maître d' and their personal server ensured them the best of dining experiences.

After toasting to the belief in magic, the two newfound friends settled against their seats and looked at each other, comfortable in the silence, each in their own thoughts of what the night was and all it could become.

Ryan cocked her head. "What?"

"You don't like me looking at you?"

"Worse could happen. But you're frowning."

"I guess I'm trying to figure you out. You're as different from Dennis as night is from day. I only met your dad a time or two but I remember him as a quiet man. I'd say you were more like him."

"I can be quiet," Ryan replied. "I guess we have that in common."

"So Dennis must be more like your mom."

"They are almost exactly alike."

"It will be good to see them again after all these years. And you'll be there, too, Dennis says."

Ryan nodded.

"Do you get back often to visit?"

"A few times a year, holidays mostly. But since my dad's diagnosis, I've tried to go more frequently, and with the business about to open I thought that now, before that happened, would be a good time."

"What's going on with your father, if you don't mind me asking?"

"He has chronic kidney disease."

"I'm so sorry."

"Me, too."

"How long has he had it?"

"Apparently much longer than anyone realized. He battled diabetes and high blood pressure for years. No one knew how much havoc was being wreaked on his kidneys. The symptoms were always attributed to what we already knew."

Adam observed the hurt reflected in Ryan's face as she nervously bit her lip. Clearly, she loved her father. For a Breedlove, that kind of family devotion was a very endearing trait.

"Is that what made you want to study…"

"Naturopathy? That was part of it. But I've always had compassion for anyone hurting. I watched people struggle and wanted to help them, especially as a little girl."

Adam watched as another flicker of pain flitted across her face. He wondered who caused it even as he felt an urge to protect her from it ever happening again.

"My parents thought I'd be a nurse. But I can't stand the sight of blood, which in the field of nursing is a bit problematic."

"Then you'd definitely not fare well at a meat-processing plant."

"Definitely not. During my senior year of high school I went to a job fair and discovered alternative-based medicine. It's where I first heard the word *naturopathy*. Before the hour was over I knew what I wanted to do. Now, I'm here."

"About to open your own business?"

"Yes. Me and a partner are opening our own practice in a strip mall not far from here."

"What services will you offer?"

"My specialties include whole food nutrition, that's a plant-centered diet, and energy healing that includes therapeutic massage."

"Hmm." Adam's eyes brightened. "I've got a few kinks. Can you work them out?"

"Kinks I can get rid of, but your eyes are sending a more kinky vibe. I'm not sure I can take care of that."

"But you could try." He reached for Ryan's hand. It was soft and delicate, engulfed in his much larger one. Her nails were manicured and squared. She wore no rings. "Yes, I think you should try. These feel like magic hands."

"They're healing hands," Ryan corrected, slowly pulling her hand out of his while looking in his eyes.

It was as though Adam felt every cell on her delicate skin. He wanted the time to touch more of it, all of it, everywhere. "For someone who's sick, healing is magical. And I get the feeling that for any number of ailments that I might encounter, your...magic...could be the cure."

The teasing continued, flirting increased and lust heightened through six incredible courses. Just as they finished up a decadent concoction of sweetness that gave dates, coconut, gelato and cacao nibs new meaning, Adam checked his watch. The timing was perfect. The show was set to begin in the Jewel, a two-thousand-seat state-of-the-art arena named for Adam's grandmother. Between the two of them a bottle of Krug had disappeared. Alcohol always stirred Adam's libido and it appeared to stoke Ryan's fire as well.

The arm that held Ryan's slid to her waist as they neared the elevator. She wasn't petite exactly, and her body felt toned, but her five foot five was overshadowed by his six foot two, even with her sexy stilettos. He felt protective and probably wouldn't have been able to keep his hands off her even if he hadn't remembered her aversion to the fast-moving car.

"Are you ready for magic?" he asked as they descended.

She turned to him, her eyes sincere. "I thought it had already begun."

Adam squeezed her waist gently and then dropped his hand. It wasn't Ryan's fault that she'd lit him up like a match soaked in gasoline. His body was burning with desire. He hoped in time the enchanter beside him could help douse the flame.

# Five

Her birthday wasn't for another two weeks, but Ryan knew that no celebration she could dream up or afford would top what was happening tonight. Since this was the only date she'd have with Adam, she intended to make the most of it. The champagne helped her push thoughts of possible repercussions or regrets to the back of her mind. As they ascended the stairs to enter the Jewel arena, she was aware of both admiring and envious eyes. Adam cut a suave figure as he walked next to her in a suit tailored to the perfection of his lean frame. The finely spun black wool matched his close-cropped curls, soft, she knew, because her hand had brushed across them in the elevator when she'd picked an imaginary piece of lint from his suit jacket collar, just to be able to touch them. The white shirt he'd paired it with emphasized his bronze skin and dark brown eyes. He walked with assurance and purpose, seemingly comfortable with all of the attention afforded him. For Ryan, this was a whole new world, one in which she wondered if she could ever be comfortable. Adam had called her beautiful but her dress, as much as she liked it and as pretty as it was, paled in comparison to the diamonds, beaded gowns and designer everything that surrounded her. She saw more than one woman sweep her from head to toe and decide she was hardly worthy of Adam's attention, much less his arm. The devil on her shoulder told her they were right. She tried to ignore them by going within as Brooklyn would tell her, to summon an inner angel to counter those negative voices with the truth, that she was enough, just the way she was.

It also helped still feelings of inadequacy by looking past judgmental faces and focusing on the elaborate entryway. It was, in a word, magnificent, and the interior, too. She thought it impossible for any space to outdo Zest but that feat had been accomplished. When it came to glitz and glam, Las Vegas was known for its gaudy, sometimes garish displays. But in this room the theme of jewels was understated and sophisticated. The ceiling twinkled with them, like stars in the sky, a 3-D effect allowing one to believe they could reach out and touch them, while in actuality they were more than thirty feet away. They reached a center aisle dividing the orchestra section from the lower tier. Adam led them down that center aisle toward a curtained entry.

"I probably should have warned you sooner," he said softly as they passed through the curtain and mounted a short flight of stairs. "But you're about to meet my parents."

She stopped their movement. "What?"

"They won't bite you," he said, and the dazzling smile he shared with her chased the initial panic away. "But just so you know, my mom's a matchmaker who'll try to learn your life between acts. You're under no obligation to allow her to pry, or to answer questions, no matter how skillful her attempted extraction. Are we good?"

"I guess so," she responded. They continued around the corner and up another short flight. "Though had I known I was going to be meeting your family I may not have drunk that last glass of champagne."

"Don't worry, Ryan Washington. Just be yourself."

They entered a private box to the right of the aisle. It contained ten chairs, of which six were occupied. A beautiful couple sat in the two front left chairs. They turned and smiled. At once Ryan knew they were Adam's parents. He had his dad's eyes and his mother's smile. There was another couple beside them of similar age and a handsome young man behind them stamped with the Breedlove beauty that the girl beside him clearly adored. She took in this tableau within the seconds it took to cross the wide aisle and enter the booth.

Both older men stood. "Mr. Chapman!" Adam returned the middle-aged gentleman's hearty greeting and kissed the hand of the woman smiling at them from her seat. "Sherry, you look lovely as always.

"Greg, Sherry, this is Ryan Washington. Ryan, the Chapmans. Greg works at CANN and both are longtime friends."

Ryan shook their hands. "It's a pleasure to meet both of you. Sherry, I love your necklace."

"I was just going to say the same about yours. I've never seen a design quite like it. So...bohemian chic!"

Ryan's hand went to the chakra necklace she'd purchased during a visit to Taos, New Mexico. Made with crystals ranging from amethyst to yellow topaz to trapiche emeralds, the jewelry had cost a small fortune, a graduation present to herself. "It's one of my favorite pieces."

"Dear, you wear it very well."

They continued to where the woman Ryan assumed was Adam's mother stood with his father, a thought that was confirmed when he gave both a warm embrace.

"About time you got here," the man said. "The doors will lock once the show starts and this is one you don't want to miss."

"We were here," Adam responded. "Just finishing dinner at Zest."

Ryan noted a suddenly raised brow above the kind eyes that viewed her. "You had dinner at Zest?" she asked. She looked from Adam to Ryan. "The lovely woman on your arm must be special indeed!"

"Ryan had never been there," Adam answered. "Mom, Dad, this is Ryan Washington. She's Dennis Washington's sister. Remember the guy who used to beg for Gabe's cinnamon rolls every time he came to the house?"

"The young man who that one summer practically lived in our pool?" Mrs. Breedlove asked.

"That was Dennis," Adam responded with a laugh. "Ryan, these are two of the greatest parents in the world, my mom, Victoria, and my dad, Nicholas."

Victoria stepped forward and pulled Ryan into a light embrace. "It's wonderful to meet you, Ryan. You look lovely tonight."

"It is my pleasure," Ryan responded. "I'm looking forward to the show."

She offered a hand to Adam's father but he brushed it away. "Handshakes are for business deals," he said, giving her shoulders an affectionate squeeze. "Hugs are for friends of the family."

"It's nice to meet you, Mr. Breedlove."

"Please, call me Nicholas."

"Okay, Nicholas. Thank you."

"And I'm Victoria."

"All right."

"Had I known you were bringing a guest," Victoria said to Adam, "I would have rearranged the seating. It would have been great for your date and me to get to know each other better."

"Exactly what I was afraid of," Adam retorted, which earned him a frown from Ryan, a laugh from Nicholas and a slap on his forearm from Victoria. "Looks like the show will be starting soon. We'd better take our seats."

After a quick introduction to one of Adam's younger brothers, Noah, and his date, the two settled into comfortable, spacious seating where Ryan proceeded to be mesmerized by the best and most beautiful show she'd ever seen in her life. Valdemar was more than a magician; he was a creative genius who transported the audience to imaginary worlds.

A magnificently performed trick left Adam's eyes bright with wonder, and Ryan even more thrilled to have been invited, to be the woman sitting beside him enjoying the show. When in the finale everything on the stage seemed to disappear, Ryan joined Adam and everyone around her in an enthusiastic standing ovation. The handsome Valdemar had almost convinced her that magic was real and dreams did come true. Ryan allowed herself to enjoy the moment but knew from experience that magic was for arenas like this and dreams were for sleeping. No matter how beautiful, eventually one woke up and the dream came to an end.

"Was that not the most spectacular show ever?" Victoria beamed, squeezing Ryan's hands in her own.

"I'm speechless," Ryan responded. "I've never seen anything like it."

Victoria turned to Adam. "Are you two joining us backstage? There's going to be a brief meet and greet and reception for the cast and special guests."

Ryan looked at Adam. She could have drowned in the depth of desire she saw in his eyes. They'd rarely spoken throughout the magical performance but she knew he'd felt the energy emanating from the stage as deeply as she, and was fully prepared for him to turn down his mother's invitation for a romp in the nearest hotel suite.

Instead he placed an arm around Ryan. "Would you like to meet Valdemar?"

"Of course."

He looked at his parents. "After you," he said.

Valdemar was as quietly introspective in person as he was gregarious and commanding onstage. They met other people, too, familiar faces Ryan had seen on television or in magazines. People were gracious, but Ryan couldn't help feeling that she didn't belong. She was glad when they left the Jewel and arrived at the car, where the driver stood at an open door. Happy that the trek through the hotel was over, Ryan climbed inside. Once seated, she immediately leaned forward and removed her shoes.

"Oh my goodness, my feet are killing me!"

Adam settled in beside her. "May I?"

Desire, already pooled at the base of her core, splashed and bubbled over, sprinkling her feminine flower with dew. "Sure."

He hit a button. The privacy partition raised. His eyes bored into hers as he pulled her feet into his lap and ran a large hand over the sole of her foot. His gaze dropped then as strong, sure fingers began massaging her heel, pressing against the ball of her foot and caressing her toes one by one.

"Am I doing it correctly?" he asked.

Ryan closed her eyes and leaned into the limo's cushiness. "That feels so good."

He finished one foot and reached for the other. Ryan was vaguely aware that music had been turned on, barely recognizable because so was she! Who cared that he was out of her orbit? At the moment she wanted nothing more than for this man, Adam Breedlove, to make hot and passionate love to her, to send her to another world. Would he think her too easy if she asked for what she wanted, nothing deep or serious, but a night filled with mind-blowing pleasure, the kind she would have bet money that Adam could provide? He was Dennis's friend, something that would have normally been problematic, except one, she'd never been attracted to any of his other friends, and two, what happened between her and Adam was something that Dennis didn't need to know. She and Adam had flirted all evening. Had he been dropping real hints about how he wanted the evening to end, or just testing the waters? When she felt his fingers leave her heel and proceed up her ankle and gently squeeze her shin, she threw caution to the wind and decided to find out.

She lowered her foot so that it touched his leg, slowly ran it up his muscled thigh until it rested near his crotch. Her eyes flittered open to find his narrowing as he sucked in a breath. It was all the encouragement she needed. That single simple intake of air unleashed a torrent of physical craving from inside her, brought out a boldness not normally possessed. She brought her feet to the floor and shifted her body closer to him, placed a hand on his chest and leaned in.

"May I?" she asked in a whisper, catching his answer with her lips.

Adam responded by opening his mouth and swiping his tongue in a manner that suggested that she do the same. She did; their tongues touched and danced and mimicked each other, even as she felt Adam's arm slide around to her waist and down to her butt. Having expected a kiss that was hard and demanding, as powerful as Adam's long-legged strides, she was surprised at the softness with which he approached her, how he nibbled her lower lip and kissed her cheek before sliding his tongue back into her mouth. He kissed her slowly, thoroughly, as if savoring the taste of her. His leisurely kiss, deep and hot, drove Ryan crazy. She moved closer, her hands finally able to play in the curls the way she wanted before sliding down and over broad shoulders and back to the nape of his neck. Adam's hands moved in time with hers, one sliding beneath the silky fabric of her dress and tickling her thighs. She moaned, her hips moving of their own accord, to a rhythm she wanted to dance with the partner beside her. Then something happened.

The car stopped.

Ryan opened her eyes and took in the red door of her condo, softly lit by the porch light she'd turned on when they left.

"We're here already?" She sat back, straightening her dress. "That was fast."

"Too fast," Adam said.

She looked into his eyes, wondering if she should voice her desire. With this next question there'd be no turning back.

"Would you like to come inside?"

Adam's smile was slight as he shook his head. "No. I want to go home."

Her heart fell. A man like Adam? She should have known. She gathered her purse and made a move for the door.

Strong fingers clamped around her arm, holding her fast. "Wait! I want you to come with me so that we can…finish what we've started. Would you like that?"

Ryan laid her head on his shoulder. "I'd love that."

She watched Adam push a button and tell the driver, "Elvis, change of plans. Take me home."

Ryan closed her eyes as she felt Adam's lips against her temple, his hand stroking her hair. Those blasted whispers tried to push through the haze of happiness and warn her that she was just being used and would then be tossed away. She shut her mind and refused to listen. She was a twenty-first-century woman who knew what she wanted. If in fact Adam was using her, so be it. Because tonight she planned to put his hard, strong body to good use, too.

# Six

Adam relished the feel of Ryan in his arms. They needed to talk before…whatever…to establish what this night was and, more important, what it was not. He'd faced uncomfortable situations more than once when a woman's inability to remain emotionally detached had turned one night of pleasure into months of pain. There were those who had ulterior motives, who'd used various means to try to trap him or begin a relationship with him as a way to increase their social status or bank account. He could spot women like that a mile away before he turned twenty-one, thanks in large part to a caring older brother who used his own experiences as lessons for Adam. He'd had his own teachers, too, and the hard knocks as proof. He didn't feel any of that energy coming from Ryan. From her, all he felt was sensual heat.

But they still needed to talk.

"I'm really feeling you, beautiful," he began, pulling his arms more tightly around her. "But we need to make sure we're on the same page so that later there will be no hurt feelings or misunderstandings."

Ryan sat up and away from him. "Well, that's a first."

"What?"

"A man trying to kick me out of his bed before I ever get in it."

Adam groaned. "That's not it at all." He tried to pull Ryan back into him but she resisted.

"I'm teasing, but I get it. Before we get all caught up in

the throes of passion you're wanting to make sure I'm not some crazy stalker type who will see tonight as anything more than it is—two mutually consenting adults coming together to give each other what we both want."

"I would have worded it differently, but when it comes to dealing with people in general, and especially the opposite sex, I've learned the benefit of being up-front. Even when the cards are placed squarely on the table there is still no guarantee against hard feelings. But at least I know I've been as honest as possible, without anyone being purposely misled."

Ryan nodded. "Thank you."

"You're upset."

"No, really, I'm not. I appreciate your honesty. It's all too rare these days." She turned more fully toward him. "To be clear, you and I are on the exact same page where tonight is concerned. I think you're hot. You said I was, too. We're attracted to each other and want to have fun. I'm not looking for anything else, including more physical encounters beyond tonight. I'm not looking for a relationship, a sugar daddy, a baby daddy or a husband. I've just started a business, and will have very little focus to place elsewhere. If you don't have condoms, we'll need to make a pit stop. After we've…enjoyed the evening, I'd like a ride home. I'd also like whatever happens to remain between us. Dennis especially doesn't need to know about it. Does that just about cover it?"

"Harshly, but yes."

"You wanted all the cards to be put on the table."

"I would have placed them down gently, maybe added a flashy little spin to the ace or the joker."

"And here I come and slap 'em down like we're playing bid whist and I'm headed to Boston. Then again, you probably don't even know that card game."

"I'm familiar." He smiled, briefly, before turning serious

again. "As for your brother or anyone else for that matter, I'm a very private person. I don't kiss and tell."

"Good to know."

Adam eyed her for a long moment. "You're a different kind of woman, Ryan. I like it. It feels good to speak plainly, like we're doing. There's too much time spent in life playing games."

"Depends on what kind of game." Ryan had just begun to lean back into him when they reached the gates of the Breedlove estate. The car stopped, its headlights illuminating the opening of the majestic wrought iron wonders.

"You live here?"

"My entire family lives here."

"Oh." Adam heard trepidation.

"But not in the same house."

"Oh!" He heard relief.

The car drove through the gates and down the wide, winding road. Even in semidarkness the landscape looked grand, lanterns attached to the poles of white picket fences, trees creating dancing shadows as they bent with the wind. Adam watched as Ryan once again displayed a sort of vulnerable wonder that tapped on an unknown place inside his heart. She was quiet as he joked with the driver before they said goodbye and walked up the steps. He opened the door and stood back.

"After you, my lady. Welcome to my home."

Ryan walked inside and stopped just inside the foyer. "You're the only one who lives here?"

Adam nodded. "I have help that comes and goes. But tonight, it's just you and me."

He took her hand, walked them through the house and into the master suite. After hours of flirting and teasing and mental foreplay, it was time to get down to business.

"Your place is beautiful," she said, looking around.

Still holding her hand, Adam walked to the bed and sat down. "I'll give you the tour tomorrow," he whispered as he gently pulled her to his lap. "But I need something else tonight."

The kisses, already hot, wet, deep and searching, quickly gave way to more in-depth pursuits. Adam lay on the bed and pulled Ryan with him, tongues twirling in lips still locked together. He pushed away silky material to caress silkier thighs. His hand moved from there to squeeze the plump cheeks that he adored and back to the triangular patch of lace covering her paradise. When he ran a finger over the material and down her folds, she groaned, tightened her arms and deepened the kiss. Clearly, he was headed in the right direction, a fact further sealed when he slipped a finger beneath the fabric and felt her dewy lips. His sex thickened and lengthened. Any clothes at all was too much of a barrier.

"Hold on, baby." He sat up. "Let me help you out of that."

He gathered the hem of her dress. She raised her arms. He pulled the material over her head, cupped the weighty globes that greeted him and brushed his fingers across breasts that were barely concealed. He reached for the thin piece of fabric adhered to her skin, gently pulled and revealed a nipple that put the most scrumptious blackberry to shame. He kissed it, pulled off the other cover, and kissed that nipple, too. His shaft was fully engorged now, his control paper-thin. He rolled off the bed, removed his clothes, reached inside the nightstand drawer and put a box of condoms on the table.

Ryan pulled off her undies as she cocked a brow. "Think you have enough?" she asked.

He sheathed himself, then crawled back on the bed and between her legs. "If not, I'll buy more tomorrow."

When it came to making love to Ryan there was so much more that he wanted to do, intended to do, needed to do. He wanted to draw out the foreplay, lick every inch of her skin. But his body had a mind of its own. Ryan spreading her legs beneath him didn't help. He rubbed his sex against her softness before touching his tip to her door. She swiveled her hips beneath him. He sank farther down. Pulling out to the tip, he kissed her, slowly thrusting forward and back. He pulled and plunged, repeating the move until fully engulfed, deeply and completely, until all of him belonged to Ryan. He felt her muscles clench and her body expand as he placed his hands beneath her booty to go deeper still. She clasped her legs around him, brought out goose bumps by lightly running her nails over his flesh. He set up a rhythm—swirling, grinding, pumping—that took them to a magical heaven, over and again.

"That was amazing," Adam said, once his breathing returned to normal. "Even better than I imagined. Was it good for you, too?"

Ryan turned fully toward him, wiped away a bead of sweat. "So much so that I want seconds."

Adam said nothing, just reached for the condoms and prepared for another round. Somewhere from the back of his mind came Ryan's words about no further physical encounters after tonight. Of course she was right. This shouldn't go further. As the sister of a potential employee it couldn't go on. He looked into her eyes while idly flicking her nipple with his finger, and realized just how difficult it would be to not have any more physical contact with Ryan. Maybe impossible, even. But keeping his distance was the right thing to do. So he would try.

# Seven

In the days that followed her night with Adam, keeping her feelings toward him casual was easier said than done. One errant thought, and Ryan's body would tingle as it had when he'd touched her. At night, her muscles remembered and clenched like he was still inside her. There was nothing blasé or inconsequential about what they'd shared. From the time he'd picked her up in that fancy limo until he'd dropped her off in an even cooler sports car, every moment had been special. There was nothing casual about that evening, or about Adam Breedlove. It's the reason why even though they hadn't spoken since then, he was still on her mind. Why she had mixed emotions about going to Bakersfield the coming Friday, when she'd see him again.

Having a business to open helped. It kept her busy and focused, thinking about others instead of herself. People who were hurting and needed the type of healing that she could provide. As she pulled into the parking lot of their newly updated establishment, Ryan was determined to keep the reason she'd come back to Las Vegas in the first place front and center in her mind.

Ryan parked in a space near the new office and let out a yelp. Brooklyn had called last night saying the signage was finished, but she didn't know it had been mounted. A smile of satisfaction clung to her face as she exited her car, her eyes never leaving the window. Once in front of the classy artwork of white-and-gold lettering against a backdrop of deep blue, she stopped and took it in:

THE INTEGRATIVE HEALING GROUP
FOR MIND, BODY, SOUL
Brooklyn Chase, CSP, CHT * Ryan Washington, ND

Whole Food Nutrition,
Energy Healing–Prana, Reiki
Massage Therapy, Hypnotherapy, Acupuncture
Intuitive/Angel Reading, EFT Calibration

The sound of a blaring car horn caused Ryan to jump. She turned and waved as Brooklyn pulled up in her canary yellow Kia Sportage complete with airbrushed angel wings. What a woo-woo chick! Ryan loved her like the sister she'd always wanted but never had.

Brooklyn jumped out of the car and ran up to Ryan. "Isn't it beautiful?" she exclaimed, pulling her sister/friend/business partner into an enthusiastic hug. The women danced around like little girls before Ryan pulled out the brand-new, sparkly gold office key.

"Let's take this party inside," she murmured, "before we scare away our clients."

The women stopped just inside the door and took in the foyer/waiting room specifically designed to bring immediate peace and calm to all who entered. The soothing shades of blue, warm lighting and gently flowing fountain created the desired effect. Abstract pictures, a table containing magazines and pamphlets, and three chairs completed the look.

"What do you think?" Ryan asked.

"Hmm…" Brooklyn did a slow turn around the room. "I think we need one more thing."

"What?"

"Some type of aromatherapy."

"An essential oil diffuser!"

"Exactly," Brooklyn said with a nod.

The women high-fived and continued down the short hall with rooms on both sides.

Ryan stopped at the second door on the left and opened it. "I'm glad we decided to rent out these two extra rooms," she said.

Brooklyn followed her into the room. "I agree. I'm still thanking the angels that Suyin replied so quickly."

"I think her acupuncture practice will do really well. But do you think this room will be big enough for her table?"

Brooklyn nodded. "I think so. She'll have that, maybe a chair and a place to set her equipment. What else will she need?"

"I don't know." Ryan pulled out her phone to type notes. "But I'll set up a time for her to come check it out so she'll know exactly what's needed."

They left the small office and continued viewing the rest of the space, taking notes on what decorating items were left to be purchased.

"How's your love life?" Brooklyn asked her as they reached what they'd planned as a break room, in an abrupt segue from a conversation involving bamboo plants.

"What love life?"

"With Hollywood, that guy who took you to the show at CANN."

"Oh, Adam," Ryan replied, a yawn the only prop missing from her attempt at sounding bored. "That was one date. He isn't my love life."

"I googled him."

"You what?"

"Yep." Brooklyn crossed her arms and calmly leaned against the counter. "Sure did. Put his name in the search engine. Picture came right up. That man is fifty-two kinds of gorgeous, darlin'. His family owns the CANN Casino Hotel and Spa. He's freakin' rich!"

"And?"

"And when are you seeing him again?"

"Friday."

"My girl!" Brooklyn held up her hand.

"But just as friends. We're not going to date."

"Please. Tell that to someone who hasn't seen how good he looks. Talk about balancing your kundalini with a little tantra…"

"Shut up!"

"Why?" Brooklyn asked.

Ryan laughed. Brooklyn didn't. "I'm happy for you, okay?"

"This isn't what you think. Adam's a casual acquaintance, my brother's friend. Neither he nor I are interested in anything serious. We've both got way more important things on our plates."

"There's nothing more important than love, Ryan."

Ryan gave her best friend a patient look, as one might a child. "That sounds good, but love isn't going to pay the lease on this office."

"And this business, no matter how successful, will never hug you, love you, or keep you warm at night. One needs balance to be truly happy—work, play and love."

Ryan didn't respond. She headed back down the hall toward the foyer.

Brooklyn walked alongside. "Hey, maybe you guys can come to Johnny's concert on Friday. It's a battle of the bands. Should be fun."

"Sounds like it, but we'll be in Bakersfield."

"Meeting the family already! Wow, that is huge!"

"No, this is business! Adam might give my brother a job. He'll be in Bakersfield to tour the plant where Dennis currently works. I'll be there to see Mom and Dad."

Mentioning her adoptive father tempered the mood. "How is he, Ryan?"

"About the same, I guess."

"He's agreed to your treatments, right?" Ryan nodded. Brooklyn reached out and placed a compassionate hand on Ryan's arm. "I'll be sending love and light as well. I hope that they help."

"Me, too."

"And I hope that your brother gets the job. Just remember that contrary to popular belief, business can be mixed with pleasure. A soul mate can show up anytime, anywhere. If it knocks, Ryan, answer it. Take a chance on love."

Adam had offered to book Ryan on a flight to Bakersfield. Tempting, but she'd declined. It didn't feel right to have him spending money on her, even if he was a billionaire. Besides, the drive from Vegas to Bakersfield was just over four hours. She enjoyed short road trips. They helped her relax, gave her time to think and get her head right. For a weekend in the Washington household that included dinner with her lover, a healing session with her father and the first time seeing her mom since a visit with her birth mom, the woman that Ida had forbidden her to see, she'd need it.

That Friday she filled up her tank and left Vegas just after rush hour, arriving at her parents' home around two. She pulled luggage and her laptop out of the car and headed toward the front door. She hadn't always gotten along with the people who'd adopted her, but they were her parents and it had been a while since she'd seen them. Even with the turmoil that surrounded each visit, in the moment, it felt good to be home.

Ryan rang the bell, and then bent down to search for the spare key always hidden beneath the welcome rug. The door opened.

"Oh, hi, Mom."

"Ryan, your hair!" Ida exclaimed, before turning abruptly to walk back down the hall.

Ryan hid an eye roll as she followed her mother, Ida Marie, inside. She'd traded perms for her natural curls her first year of college. But every greeting was as though her mom saw them for the first time.

Ida Marie Washington was a formidable woman, more in comportment than appearance though she was plus-size. Ida wasn't particularly attractive but she worked with what she had. Ryan could count the times on both hands and maybe a foot that she'd seen her mother without makeup or properly dressed in more than twenty years, usually in a color scheme involving black, navy or tan. Outside, she wore low-heeled pumps. Inside, black ballet-type house shoes. No exceptions. Ryan often wondered about the rigidity, what her adoptive mother held on to so tightly. What nurturing or healing needed to happen with Ida's inner child.

"Baby girl!"

Ryan left her luggage at the living room entrance and hurried over to hug her dad. Where Ida was cold and icy, Joe Washington was warmth and comfort. An introspective man with a quiet demeanor and ready smile, he'd often been the salve soothing Ida's barbs and Dennis's taunts. When Ida would get angry and question why she'd bothered to adopt Ryan, Joe would pull her to the side and say, "You are this home's sunshine. Don't let nobody dim that light." She'd loved him every day that she'd known him, and would love him into forever.

"How are you, Dad?" Ryan perched on the arm of the recliner her father occupied, keeping her smile bright despite the shock of noticing her dad's continued weight loss.

"Better now!"

Ida entered the room and sat on the couch. "Don't sit on the arm of the chair like that. Have you forgotten how you were raised?"

*Much of it, yes, thankfully.* "Sorry, Mom."

Still holding her father's hand, she sat cross-legged on the floor beside him and began inconspicuously doing energy work, as they talked.

"How's Vegas working out for you, Ryan?"

"Things are going well. My business partner and I found a space for our practice and will open in two weeks."

Ryan hung on to her father's "That's great, baby," while trying to ignore Ida's "Practice? Please."

"We've been marketing for clients for well over a month now and already have an almost full first week on the schedule. The final push begins when I get back on Monday. It's a lot of work but…fingers crossed!"

"Had you gone into nursing, a sensible profession, you wouldn't have to beat the pavement for clients. They'd come to you right through the hospital's front door."

"When the Raiders get there in a year or so, you'll have all kinds of injuries to heal," Joe offered.

"Absolutely, Dad! Don't think I haven't already put together a proposal. You know I've always been a Chargers fan but my favorite color is green so…"

The two laughed as Ryan repeated a statement Joe often used in discussing one of their favorite subjects. Dennis preferred basketball. Ida didn't do sports. Joe and Ryan had bonded on long-ago Sundays, watching football and eating popcorn sprinkled with hot sauce, another shared love.

"Give me your other hand, Dad."

"What are you doing?" Ida asked. "And why is your luggage still in the entryway?"

"I forgot all about that," Ryan said, getting up off the floor. And to her dad, "Be right back."

She crossed where her mother sat on the couch, then stopped and turned around. "Maneuvering that bulky luggage inside I didn't even get a hug," she said, bending down to place her arms around her mom's neck. "Are those new earrings? I like them."

"You won't see me in much of anything new anymore," Ida said, after a light pat on Ryan's back. "With Joe on disability, money is tight."

"I'm so sorry for what you and Dad are going through, Mom. It must be a very difficult adjustment."

"Hmph."

Ryan grabbed the handle of her luggage and headed toward the stairs. She reached the second floor of the place she'd called home from the time she was nine until two weeks after turning eighteen. She tried the knob on her old bedroom door and was surprised to find it locked. Moving on to the smaller room, she opened the door. A daybed had replaced the double that Dennis used when he'd returned there after leaving the military. The bedding was cream-colored, giving the room a lighter feel. Dennis preferred black, so the change was stark. Ryan liked it. She pulled her luggage into the room, placed her computer bag on the bed and then in a reversion back to the curious child she'd always been, she grabbed a bobby pin from the hallway bathroom and opened the other room's locked door.

One step inside and Ryan stopped short. The place was a mess. Boxes were everywhere, along with clothes she assumed belonged to Dennis strewn all over the place. Had he moved back home? She walked into the room, trying to figure out the mystery as she looked around. She lifted the lids of a couple boxes. One contained files and other loose paper. With just the slightest twinge of little-sister guilt, she knelt and began flipping through files, all from Ba-kersfield Meat Packing. Further, intrigued, Ryan looked through the folders more closely and pulled out one labeled H&R. On top of the pile was a formal-looking letter dated three weeks ago.

*Dear Mr. Washington:*

*This letter shall serve as official notice that you have been terminated from…effective immediately…*

Ryan sat back on her haunches. WTH? How was Dennis giving Adam a tour of a plant where he no longer worked? Hearing feet on the staircase, she hurriedly returned the folder to the box, slapped on the lid and exited the room, careful to lock the door behind her, just as Ida reached the top of the stairs.

"What are you doing?" she asked.

Ryan had a question, too. "Has Dennis moved back home? That bedroom door is locked."

Ida walked to the door and tried unsuccessfully to open

it. "As it happens, your brother will soon be joining you in Las Vegas. He's been recruited for a high-level management job with CANN International, a billion-dollar company."

*Is that what he told you?*

"You need to get yourself a real job, Ryan. When this project you're working on fails to make money, your dad and I won't be able to help you."

Ida continued on to the master bedroom at the end of the hall. It was just as well. Far be it from Ryan to correct whatever information Dennis had told her. Of more interest to Ryan was what Dennis had told Adam, and why he'd been terminated from his job. Ryan tried to tell herself it was none of her business. Then she remembered tonight and Adam coming for dinner, and knew that as much as she wanted to wash her hands of what felt like sneaky shenanigans, Dennis had her all up in the mix.

# Eight

Adam felt it as soon as the door opened, an air of tension and discomfort despite the bright smile from the woman who opened the door.

"Hello, son." The woman gave Dennis an enthusiastic hug while eyeing Adam appreciatively. She released him and held out her hand. "Hello, I'm Ida Washington, Dennis's mom. You must be Adam."

"Yes, ma'am." Adam offered a firm grip and a smile as he shook her hand. "It's very nice to meet you."

"Come on in, you two."

Dennis lifted his nose. "Something smells good."

They entered the living room. "It sure does. Mrs. Washington, I told Dennis that your cooking dinner was totally unnecessary, but I appreciate it."

"It was no bother and, please, call me Ida."

"Thank you."

Adam took in the stately woman who escorted them into the room. Ryan didn't look like her mother at all. He looked for her features in the neatly dressed man sitting in a recliner. Both had smooth cocoa skin and high cheekbones. But the big doe-like eyes, pert nose, full lips and sweet curves seemed to be uniquely Ryan's, one of a kind.

"Hey, Dad." Dennis gave his dad a pat on the shoulder. "You remember Adam, a friend from high school? His family owns CANN International."

Adam shook the older man's hand. "Nice to see you again, Joe."

"He owns a cattle ranch, too. That's why he's in Bakersfield, to take a look at the plant that I run. He's looking for a manager for the one he's building. Looks like I might be joining Ryan back in Vegas."

Dennis looked around. "Is she here? I saw her car."

"She'll be down momentarily," Ida said. "Have a seat, you two. Dinner is almost ready."

As Adam walked over to sit on the couch, he felt her before he saw her. A subtle change in the atmosphere, like a ray of sun breaking through clouds, before Ryan walked into the room. He looked up as she entered wearing a colorful oversize sweater with bright red leggings, her bouncy curls wild and free, and felt comfortable for the first time since entering the home.

"Ryan." He quickly stood, an instinctive move, and given the reactions it elicited, one he instantly regretted. Dennis's eyes traveling between them as his expression grew smug. Ida stopping midstride, a slight frown on her face before she realized it and took her look neutral. The only one who had a reaction he understood was Joe. He beamed, as though Ryan was the beat of his heart.

He pushed his hands into his pockets, tried to look nonchalant. "Hey."

"Hey, Adam!" Her hug was brief, but he felt a shakiness to the hand that squeezed his arm after. She turned to Dennis, clapped him on the shoulder. "What's up, brother?"

"You, I guess, the way Adam jumped up to greet you."

"No, man, that's just how I was raised, to get up when a woman enters the room."

"They're called manners," Ryan teased. "Those practiced by gentlemen, which is probably why you didn't recognize them."

"Whatever," Dennis replied, without further comeback to the rare and nicely placed barb.

He looked unconvinced, but Ida, who hadn't moved from

where she'd stopped on her way to the kitchen, finally continued around the corner.

"I'm going to help Mom set the table," Ryan said.

She left and Adam would swear that just a bit of his air left the room. He'd hoped that the intense feelings he'd experienced since their night together would have abated. It was one reason why he hadn't called her until yesterday, and then only to offer the plane ticket. He'd been with women more beautiful, more successful, and with Ryan being a vegetarian while he butchered what most Americans ate for dinner, more evenly matched as well. After how his body had reacted just now Ryan clearly had him under a spell. Unfortunately it would have to be broken. She was too beautiful to be hidden, too special to be treated as a casual friend. But dalliances were all he had time for right now. He was focused on helping to run a family empire while building another successful business that was all his own.

It wasn't long before the men were called to dinner. As they sat and Ida and Ryan brought in the rest of the dishes, the doorbell rang.

"Who's that?" Ryan asked, taking the seat across from Adam.

Ida entered with the last covered dish and placed it on the remaining trivet. "Probably Luke." She took a seat at the head of the table. "He has a sixth sense when it comes to my cooking and showing up just in time to eat."

Dennis returned to the table with Luke, whom Adam had met while at the plant. Dennis had introduced him as a friend and colleague he'd known practically all of his life. Luke was a nice-looking guy who cleaned up well. The dirty jeans and stained T-shirt from earlier had been replaced with a casual tan-colored suit and a black V-neck pullover. Adam could tell that the clothing he wore was of a high quality and didn't miss the diamond stud that winked from his ear.

"Miss Ida! Papa Joe!" Luke walked over and shook hands

with Joe, then moved on to give Ida a hug. Joe's greeting to Luke was enthusiastic but Adam noted Ida's was fairly cool, but then again given her personality, maybe not.

He looked at Ryan, stopped and took a step back. "Ryan, wow," he said, slowly shaking his head as he ogled her in a way that to Adam skirted precariously close to disrespect, although Adam knew his observation might be biased. He had no claim to Ryan but in the moment could imagine how Tarzan felt if someone hit on Jane.

"It's been a long time."

"Yes, it has."

Über observant by nature, Adam didn't miss how before Luke got anywhere close, Ryan held out a stiff arm for a handshake instead of a hug. Her lips smiled. Her eyes didn't. She looked most uncomfortable. Adam made a note to find out why.

"I didn't think you could get any prettier," Luke said, "but I was wrong. Don't you have a birthday coming up soon?"

"In a week," Dennis responded, with a frown that was only partially mocking. "And no, you can't buy her a present, or be her present."

Luke laughed. To Adam, it sounded forced. He didn't think Luke found the comment funny. It was the first time he'd heard Dennis actually defend his sister. He had no way of knowing it, but that boded well for Dennis potentially being hired to work at Breedlove Beef.

Luke took the seat beside Adam. Dinner service began. Ida lifted the lid from the main dish, smothered chicken and gravy. "It's not the fancy food you're used to, Adam," she said, spinning the utensils on the rotating serving dish toward him. "But I hope you enjoy it."

"Oh, I like good food, Mrs. Washington, Ida, fancy or not." He placed a hearty serving on his plate. "And this smells super good."

"Mom can burn," Dennis said, taking the ladle Adam offered.

"She is an excellent cook," Ryan said.

"How do you know?" Ida asked. "You don't eat my cooking."

"I don't eat the dishes you fix that contain meat," Ryan replied. "But my mouth watered as I brought those candied yams to the table, and your mac and cheese will probably keep me eating dairy for life!"

"You always did like that dish," Ida said with a smile that suggested Ryan's compliment pleased her. "Dennis will eat anything I put in front of him, including the plate I imagine, if he were hungry enough. I can say there's less fried foods and fat in our diet. We are trying to eat healthier now."

Luke and Dennis led the bulk of conversation as other lids were lifted and plates filled. Adam noticed that other than the chicken, which was some of the best he'd ever put in his mouth, the other dishes seemed to be ones that Ryan could eat.

"Is this your first time in Bakersfield?" Joe asked as he reached for a glass of sweet tea.

"On the way up that's something I was trying to remember," Adam said. "As a young kid I traveled all over California with my dad, so it's highly likely that I was here, but a long time ago."

"Bakersfield isn't the most memorable city in the Golden State," Joe continued. "But it's an agricultural hub. So you're raising cattle now?"

"I thought your family owned a hotel." Ida looked from Adam to Dennis, clearly confused.

"They do, Mom," Dennis said. "In fact, they own several, all over the world. But Adam has other interests, ones that will complement the hotel business. He's an entrepreneur. Right, Adam?"

"A component of Breedlove Ranch is complementary to the hotel enterprise. The cattle I raise will be used in many of our restaurants."

"Oh," Ida said. "That's nice."

"More than nice, Mom," Dennis said. "He's raising the highest-quality beef one can get in this country. Have you heard of Kobe beef?"

"Of course."

"His will be high quality like that."

"And Dennis will be working with you?" Ida asked.

"I hope so," Dennis interjected. "Both me and Luke."

Adam set down his fork and wiped his mouth with a napkin. "We're in the final phases of constructing a plant on the ranch and are looking for the right person to manage it. Running into Dennis and finding out that's his niche definitely put him in the running, and after touring the plant he manages here, I'm even more impressed. But the decision isn't solely up to me. The choice will be made by the team."

"You own the company," Dennis said. "The buck is supposed to stop with you!"

"The buck does," Adam replied, smiling. "But not this decision. Whoever takes this job will have a ton of responsibility on their shoulders, and will work closely with the ranch manager and department supervisors. Running a ranch is complex, definitely a group effort. Experience, education, skill, that all counts. But so does making sure the fit of one is right for the whole."

Dennis made a show of puffing his chest and bulging his arms like Superman. "I can handle it."

Everyone laughed except Ryan, but Adam did see the glimpse of a smile.

"I told him that Ryan was looking for a job. She wasn't interested, though, being that she doesn't eat meat and all."

"Is that true?" Ida asked. Her voice was pleasant, but Adam noticed a slight change in her demeanor, a difference between her interactions with her daughter compared to how she treated her son. "I would think that working for someone affiliated with a corporation as large as the CANN hotels would be a huge opportunity."

"I'm more impressed with what Ryan is doing," Adam

said, "using her education and training to help people heal. I never paid much attention to the connection between what we eat and how we feel, but it makes total sense."

Luke cleaned a chicken bone and unashamedly licked his fingers. "Then I must be 100 percent healthy because this chicken is making me feel good!"

"You seem to know quite a bit about Ryan," Joe said to Adam. "The two of you know each other from high school, too?"

"No, sir. I didn't even know Dennis had a sister."

"She tagged along the day I met Adam for lunch," Dennis said. "Some things never change," he said, shaking his head. "The next day he called and asked for her home number, so..."

"It was business," Ryan quickly interjected. "Adam wants to offer healthy alternatives on his menu, a conversation that came up at the lunch Dennis mentioned. Remember, Denny?"

"Yep, I remember."

"That's why he wanted to contact me."

Adam felt something soft, tickly, slowly moving up his leg. He was seconds away from slapping away what he could only think was an insect when the "bug" tapped him, and he realized it was Ryan's big toe.

"We've talked, a couple times at length, about ways we can prepare food that is nourishing and still completely delicious," she said.

The little minx! Had she any idea how long it had taken for him to get a handle on his hormones after she'd walked into the room? And here now, with every word from that sweet little mouth, the testosterone was buzzing again. Still, he enjoyed the subtle flirting. It reminded him of the wonderful time they'd had Tuesday night. The trip to Bakersfield had been interesting, to say the least. There would be a lot to process when he went home. But when it came to Ryan there was nothing to think about. His feelings were clear. He needed to see her again, to wrap his arms around her softness, feel her breath in his ear and hear her breathy whimpers as he gave her pleasure. One more time. One more night into the morning. After that she'd be Dennis's sister, a platonic friend, maybe a consultant to his restaurant…nothing more.

# Nine

Ryan got the first text on Friday night, less than an hour after the guys had left her parents' home—Adam headed to the airport, Dennis and Luke no doubt went to the nearest bar for the most accommodating women. For Ryan, Luke couldn't leave her sight soon enough, but she missed Adam already. She'd volunteered to do dinner cleanup to keep herself busy and her mind distracted, and was loading the dishwasher when her phone vibrated.

You looked beautiful tonight.

She'd hurriedly replied. You looked good, too.

You looked good, smelled good, felt good. Running your toe up my leg like that? You were being a very bad girl.

The message made her giggle. The look in Adam's eyes after she'd done it made her think he might be feeling what she was feeling, but with the other company present she couldn't be sure. Until now. The attraction continued to be mutual. She sent a smiley face.

When are you back in Vegas?

Monday.

Why not Sunday? I want to see you.

It wasn't what they'd planned. But getting together again is what they both wanted. Even so, her reply was noncommittal. Maybe.

When Ryan saw Dennis in his room the next morning, Adam's text and their plans for the following day were still on her mind. So was his suggestion that Luke be hired, too. She could understand Dennis wanting to help out a friend but nothing she knew about Luke made her think that hiring him would be a good idea. She'd stayed quiet at dinner but today was different. She and Dennis needed to talk.

"What a mess," she said, her mood deceptively light as she entered his room. "I thought military guys were neat freaks."

"I thought you knew about manners but I didn't hear you knock."

"That's because the door was open." She plopped down on the unmade bed. "When did you move back home?"

"A little while ago."

The tone of his answer conveyed his annoyance, but Ryan plowed on undeterred. "Why?" No answer. She needed to push, so she slid off the bed and walked over to where the boxes she'd rummaged through were stacked against the wall. "Is it because you're no longer working at the plant?"

Dennis turned around with a scowl on his face. "Who says I'm not working there?"

"Mom did. She thought you were already hired in Vegas." Ryan closed the bedroom door and leaned against it. "But I saw the paperwork in one of those boxes. You didn't quit, either. You got fired."

Though her statement was explosive, her voice remained low and calm. Dennis's did not.

"What the hell were you doing snooping in my things?"

"It wasn't intentional. I came back to my old room and

found all of this crap in it. Opened a couple boxes to see what was in there."

Dennis shrugged. "Big deal."

"Does Adam know you were fired?"

"Get out of my room!"

"Shh! You'll wake Mom and Dad." Ryan felt her brother's anger but still needed answers. "I just wondered how you gave him a tour of a place where you no longer worked."

"What's it to you? Mind your own business!"

"This became my business the day you invited me to lunch!" Ryan stopped and took a breath. Getting angry, or loud, would not be productive. "Look, I don't want to fight with you. I just don't want to be a part of whatever you're scheming."

"I'm not scheming."

"You're trying to get Luke a job with Adam. I don't like him."

"Who asked you?"

"Nobody. But if Adam asks for my opinion, I'll tell him the truth."

"You'll keep your mouth shut," Dennis snarled, his volume rising with every word. "Now…get out of my room!"

The door opened as Ryan turned to leave. It was Ida. Her eyes zeroed in on Ryan. She didn't look happy.

"What is all of this yelling about?" she demanded, glaring at Ryan even though Dennis had yelled. "Why are you bothering him?"

"She's trying to sabotage my opportunity with Adam," Dennis answered. "I think she wants him all to herself."

Ryan couldn't help but laugh. "That's ridiculous."

"It sure is," Ida said. "I saw you trying to impress him last night. But that boy's way above your pay grade."

"She's upset that I'm moving to Vegas and that Luke might come with me. If Adam asks her about Luke she said her answer won't be good."

"I said if asked I would give my opinion."

"He knows Luke and I are tight. If you bad-mouth him, what would that say about me?"

"What would it say about me if I lied about how I feel about Luke?"

"You've never cared for that boy," Ida said, her eyes narrowing as she glared at Ryan. "I never understood why."

"That's because you can't know what it's like to be teased about being adopted."

"I told you then to pay him no mind, yet what he said all those years ago is still on yours? So, you were adopted. So what? We gave you a family and this is how you thank us? By being upset that someone pointed it out a time or two, a kid who was known for teasing? Yet here you are playing the victim. Do you think you're the only one who suffered?"

Ryan clamped her mouth shut. If she opened it to answer, she might not be able to control what else flowed out.

"I tell you what. You weren't. I suffered plenty more than you. And I'll tell you another thing. You'd better not mess things up for Dennis. Because when it comes to opinions, there are some that can be shared that would mess up your life, too."

Soon after, Dennis stormed out of the house. Her mother wasn't far behind him. Since her father's diagnosis Ida had taken on more hours, often working at the Postal Service's processing plant on Saturday afternoons. Neither spoke another word to her before they left, though she heard mumbling that included her name. With a skill honed over a lifetime of verbal abuse, Ryan locked away what happened to be processed later and went in search of her father. She wanted to do a session of energy healing while the house was quiet and knew that helping to ease or take away some of his discomfort would lessen her emotional pain.

Ryan's dad rarely got involved in their mother-daughter arguments, but he was often her refuge once they were done. He had a way of comforting the adopted daughter without bashing his wife. Today was no exception.

"Ida is like a mama bear when it comes to Dennis," he began, after lying facedown on the portable table that Ryan had covered with a thick memory foam pad. "It's always been that way. She lashes out, but she doesn't mean it."

"The words hurt just the same."

Ryan began the treatment. The fluid Reiki movements over her adoptive dad's body brought calm to her spirit. She allowed the prior conversation to float back into her mind. She listened to the mental replay dispassionately, hearing the pain beneath Ida's caustic words.

"I wonder why Mom adopted me," she softly mused.

"Because she loves you," Joe answered.

"Maybe so, but she doesn't like me very much."

"Sometimes she doesn't like me, either, and I've been married to the woman for more than thirty years." He winked and lay back down on the table. It was Ryan's first smile all day.

Ryan finished the intensive healing session with Joe. Afterward, they enjoyed a leisurely brunch. Ryan was by no means a cook, but her veggie-filled omelet was cheesy and spicy, and one-on-one time with her father was better than any meal. She didn't spend the night though as originally planned, but headed back to Las Vegas before Ida returned home. Ryan felt conflicted on so many levels. She needed time to process everything from the past twenty-four hours—her Adam attraction, the Dennis dilemma, her loathing for Luke and the Ida enigma. Those problems were ones she'd have to figure out on her own. But there was someone who could help with a piece missing from her life—her birth father. She left Bakersfield for Las Vegas and a visit with her birth mom, Phyllis Moore.

The visit didn't go as planned. They'd met in person only a handful of times, awkward prison visits. Scant emails and short phone calls were hardly building blocks for a mother-daughter relationship. Ryan realized she'd expected too much.

"Can you tell me anything about my father?"

"Not really."

"You don't have anything, not even a name?"

"I've got several names, none that you need. Why learn something about a man you've never met?"

"Because he's my dad."

"He's the man who knocked me up and kept on walking. Let the past stay there!"

"I have a right to know where I come from," Ryan replied, near tears.

Phyllis seemed moved, but the brief moment passed.

"Who it was doesn't matter. Nothing you find out now can change what happened back then."

"It will change me," Ryan had countered. "Learning of your addiction helped me understand why I was abandoned. Hearing about your back problem and the prolonged use of prescription medication that led to the opioid addiction provided a reason I was put in foster care, one that replaced the one believed until then—that I wasn't a person worth loving."

"You knew how I felt. Loving you is why I let the Washingtons adopt you. I knew they could give you what I couldn't."

Ryan had asked her mother about the relationship with Ida, whether she'd known her beforehand and why they didn't get along.

"She discouraged me from looking for you," Ryan explained. "Why would she do that?"

"Because you already had a mother," Phyllis replied. "One is all you need. Leave the past alone, Ryan, and live in the moment."

The visit ended with Ryan feeling almost as though she'd been abandoned again. Yet after a good night's sleep and some leisurely shopping, she'd decided to take Phyllis's advice and live in the moment by having one more romp with Adam before breaking off all romantic contact. Out of the market and back in her car, she engaged her Bluetooth, then merged into the light Sunday-morning traffic.

"Where are you?" was his greeting.

"Hello to you, too." His voice warmed her heart.

Adam laughed. "Hello, gorgeous. Where are you?"

"Near Red Rock."

"Cool, you're not far from the hotel. Can you meet me there?"

"Why?"

"I've got something for you."

"Really? What?"

"It's a surprise."

The sexiness in his voice was as thick as molasses that she could imagine oozing wet and sticky down her bare skin, much as Adam's tongue had the one time they'd been together. The slow way he spoke, raspy and low, should have been illegal. At the very least he should have been required to register a voice like that as a lethal weapon. But if that happened, Ryan thought, she needed to be arrested, too. Because becoming that aroused by nothing more than consonants and vowels should be against the law.

"I just spent an hour at the farmer's market. Maybe I should go home and shower first."

"I know you've never stayed there but we have showers in every suite. I'll text you the room number and leave a special card key for you at the front desk. See you soon?"

"Yes."

"I can't wait."

Ryan reached the CANN Casino Hotel and Spa and as Adam had instructed in the text he'd sent, she stopped at the valet booth. From there until she arrived at the elevator, the service she received was stellar, the best she'd ever experienced at a hotel or anywhere. Was this what it felt like to be wealthy? Knowing this was the first and last time she'd experience such luxury was bittersweet.

Adam had directed her to a penthouse suite. She got on the elevator and closed her eyes, tried to ignore the pang of fear in her stomach as the car sped upward. Her discomfort with elevators was only part of the reason for her anxiety. She'd bet the money from her first fifty clients that Adam would have questions about his visit to Bakersfield in general and Dennis in particular. He was considering her brother for a very important position and was obviously an excellent businessman. Why wouldn't he ask what she thought about it? And how could she answer without lying, yet not quite tell the truth?

The elevator opened to a small landing with doors on each wall. She went to penthouse A and slid in the card.

"Hello?"

Ryan paused and stepped inside. A beautiful foyer led into a short hall. Soothing music wafted toward her, along with wonderful scents she recognized including jasmine and vanilla. Adam came around the corner, arms outstretched. He was barefoot, and wore gray drawstring pants and a black tank top. Perfect.

"There you are." He pulled Ryan into his body, squeezed her as though she was something exquisite and rare. There was no need for words because their bodies were talking. Ryan's arms slid around his neck as their lips came together. He palmed her butt, pressed her against his already hardening shaft. For several minutes they got no farther than that hallway. By the time he gently took her hand and pulled her into the main living space, her dress had already been removed and left behind on the floor. The room took her breath away.

"This is incredible! Adam, oh my God!"

Ryan had never been overly modest, and something about standing in front of floor-to-ceiling windows in nothing but a thong made her feel powerful, sexy and a little bit naughty. Being over a hundred stories in the air helped, too, she imagined. Adam came up behind her, teasing her nipples into pert attention. His other hand snaked down to her heat between her legs.

"Can anyone see us?" Ryan asked. Posing naked was one thing. Being the unwitting subject of a potential sex tape was something else altogether.

"No, babe. These are one-way windows. We can see out but no one can see in."

She turned in his arms. "Let's take a shower."

They did, and soap and water wasn't the only thing felt on skin. Fingers skimmed. Tongues glided. Ryan's eyes turned mischievous as her knees met the polished stone floor. She encircled Adam's dick with her fingers, flicked her tongue on and around its mushroomed tip. His fingers stroked her hair. She slid wet lips up and down his generous package, slowly at first, then faster, harder, until a strained hiss escaped his mouth and he pulled away. Before Ryan could rise on her own Adam lifted her up, perched her on the bench and placed her legs over his shoulders. She didn't have to wonder what came next because mere seconds passed before her back was against the shower walls and his face was buried in the juncture of her thighs. Had his oral feats been filmed, the video would have definitely gone viral. His tongue was masterful, his fingers relentless, creating an orgasm that shook Ryan from head to toe. He gently lowered her to the bench, stepped out of the shower and returned with a familiar square foil. After making delicious love under the rain forest showerhead, they washed each other's satisfied bodies and tumbled into bed.

"Even better than last time," Ryan murmured, stretching like a satisfied feline. "I think between that tongue—" she kissed his lips "—and those fingers—" she wrapped hers in his "—every muscle in my body was rubbed."

"What can I say? You bring out the beast in me."

There was a knock at the door. Ryan started. "Who's that?"

"Room service." Adam slid off the bed, stepped into a walk-in closet and, once robed, strolled to the front door. Seconds later, he returned wheeling a tray loaded with covered dishes.

"Brunch in bed," he told her. "And guess what? It's all vegetarian."

After retrieving her dress, Ryan rejoined Adam on the bed. If asked she wouldn't have said she was hungry, but one bite of the veggie-filled omelet topped with cashew cheese and she was all in. Adam enjoyed a pecan pie pancake topped with caramelized bananas, dripping with spiced maple syrup.

Ryan took a few bites, then reached for the pitcher of orange juice and poured two glasses. "When it comes to your restaurant and vegetarian options, I don't think you need my help. Just get with the chef who fixed all this."

"Emilio is talented but you're way cuter," Adam teased. He reached for the glass of juice Ryan had poured for him. "Thanks."

"You're welcome."

Adam took a long swig of the juice, then picked up his fork and resumed eating. "I enjoyed meeting your family on Friday," he said after a few bites.

"Even with Dennis trying to stir things up by suggesting there's something between us?"

"It's natural that he'd be curious to see whether or not his plan worked."

"So you picked that up, huh? That he was trying to set us up."

"Bringing a vegetarian to a burger joint made that move fairly obvious. Maybe he'd planned to ask for a job all along and thought bringing along his very pretty sister might improve his chances of getting hired."

"Since we're keeping our rendezvous a secret, he'll never

know." Ryan reached for one of the intricately folded linen napkins. "It's funny that you were onto him from the start. I love my brother but sometimes he can be a cad."

"I noticed that. I also got the feeling that he's your mom's favorite while you seem closer to your dad. Am I right?"

"Yes."

"You look more like him, too, although some of your features don't resemble either of them. But I get that. My older brother, Christian, is clearly a Breedlove but looks more like our grandfather than our dad."

Ryan nodded but became very interested in eating. The longer her mouth stayed full the less she'd have to talk.

For a while they ate in silence. "I'm surprised at how delicious this food tastes," he said after finishing off his omelet. "I liked your mom's cooking," he added.

"I used to," Ryan admitted. "Nothing like comfort food." Then because she couldn't stand the feeling of waiting for a hammer to drop, she asked him, "How was your visit to where Dennis works?"

"Interesting," Adam said. He shifted and sat up against the headboard. "The guy who came to dinner, Luke, works there, too. He said the two were as close as brothers and that if there were more openings at the plant, I should give him serious consideration."

Again, Ryan kept silent. The best thing she could say about Luke Johnson was nothing at all.

"What do you think?"

Adam had done the very thing she'd been afraid of— sought out her opinion. "I'm probably not the best person to ask," she finally said.

"You don't like him." His accuracy surprised her. It showed on her face. "I saw your reaction to him the other night."

"No, but it's for personal reasons."

Adam's countenance darkened quickly. "Did he do something to hurt you?"

"No."

"Something unethical?"

Ryan shook her head. "It all happened a long time ago, before I left for college. I hadn't seen him for years."

"I get the feeling you were fine with that, not seeing him."

"I never knew him very well and what I did know…yeah, not impressed."

"The way he eyed you as though you were a barbecued rib made me want to punch him."

Ryan smiled. She knew the statement was made because guys were naturally territorial, not because of any special feelings that he had for her. But it sounded good anyway.

"Dennis knows his way around a slaughterhouse, that's for sure. Their facility is larger than the one we've designed, and handles more livestock. So when it comes to general overall experience, I believe he'd be a good fit."

Ryan nodded.

"What do you think about my hiring him? Is he someone you'd recommend?"

Ryan couldn't tell him what she really thought. So she made light of the moment. "Seriously, you're asking me about someone's qualifications to work in meatpacking?"

"Well, stated that way it does sound crazy." Adam finished his juice, put down the glass and looked beyond her, and it seemed beyond anything he could see from the tall, paneless windows.

"I've always liked your brother, you know?"

"Because he defended you, right?"

"He did."

"Why were the guys teasing you?"

The question was simple but from the subtle yet unmistakable change in Adam's demeanor, the answer was not.

He pinned her with a hard look and said, "Growing up, I suffered from dyslexia. I was almost seventeen years old when it was finally diagnosed."

Ryan saw that it wasn't the man but a little boy that answered, the one that her brother had protected. The pain in his voice hurt her heart. "You have dyslexia," she gently corrected. "But you don't have to suffer from it."

"Why? Do you think you can heal me? Will it go away if I eat the right foods?"

"I don't know," Ryan said. "But I can try to help you."

Adam placed the containers they'd set on the bed back on the tray and pulled the tie on his robe. "I know a way you can help me," he said, once again reaching for the hem of her dress. "And this requires no reading at all."

Ryan had planned to have another conversation, the one where she said this was it and they couldn't see each other romantically anymore. But she followed his lead and allowed the distraction. She understood the need he felt to run away from what shamed him. She'd been forced to do the same. If he discovered her secrets, who knew? Maybe he'd want to get away again…from her.

# Ten

Adam stanched a yawn as he entered the barn that contained the offices of Breedlove Ranch. Ryan hadn't left his private hotel suite until Monday dawned. Halfway through forty winks he had to get up to attend a 7:00 a.m. business breakfast, fortunately located in the hotel, followed by one meeting after the next. His late lunch had been a sandwich at his desk while on a conference call with the architects and construction company handling the CANN Island build in Djibouti, an ambitious project dreamed up by his brother Christian and on track to be completed within the next twelve months. He'd handled a slew of correspondence with his secretary before dashing out to not be late for his own meeting. Hiring a manager for the processing plant was top of the agenda. He'd spoken with Stan, the ranch manager, on Friday and sent over Dennis's résumé to be reviewed. He knew there were at least two other well-qualified candidates in the running. The sooner the decision was made on who to hire, the better he'd feel about meeting their projection of shipping out the first orders of Breedlove Wagyu at the first of the year.

While clearly qualified and Adam's first pick, Dennis wasn't quite the man that Adam remembered. Life seemed to have hardened the guy he used to call Washboard. A cloud of cynicism hung over his life. Adam would have liked the opportunity to speak with people Dennis worked with other than Luke. He didn't doubt that his old friend was good at his job, but Breedlove Beef would be no ordinary slaughterhouse. The same care and attention given to raising the cattle would be demanded in how the facility was run and how the meat was processed. A bad batch of beef could ruin a farm. Quality was everything. Loyalty to the Breedlove brand, paramount. The Dennis from back in the day had stood up for him and had his back. Would he have the same devotion to Adam's company and Breedlove Beef? Could he be trusted with the most important position Adam had to fill since starting the company five years ago?

Adam took the steps two at a time and entered the room at the top of the landing. Stan was already there, along with a few of the company's board members including Wally Martin, Henry Tolliver and his grandmother Jewel's husband, Adam's Native American stepgrandfather who knew land, cows and horses better than almost anyone, Will Yazzie Breedlove.

Stan, who ran the ranch the way he used to run his military platoon, made a show of checking his watch.

"You're late."

"I'm a minute early."

"That's what happens when you keep time with a foreigner's watch. You need one of these." Stan held up his arm to show off a chunky black watch with a thick band. "Something made in America."

"Sure thing," Adam replied, not giving his manager the chance to sing the praises of his country the way he knew Stan wanted to do. The guy was a patriot to his soul, one whom Adam highly respected. It was men like him who filled the forces that helped keep the country safe.

Adam sat down, crossed a leg over his knee and looked around the table. "Okay, let's get right to it. We all know why we're here. We need to hire a plant manager ASAP. On Friday, I visited Bakersfield Meat Packing, managed by an old friend of mine. It's a big operation, larger than ours. I think he'd work well for us. Stan, what were you able to find out on Dennis Washington?"

Stan picked up the paper in front of him. "Looks good on paper, for sure. I appreciate that he's a military man. Nothing too serious came up on his background check. He likes speed and has a number of traffic violations to prove it. His credit isn't the best, which tells us he manages a plant better than he does his bank account. Speaking of the plant, did you know that he no longer works there?"

"No, I didn't. When did he leave, and why?"

"I'm not sure," Stan answered. "HR could confirm that he'd worked there as the manager but for legal reasons wouldn't tell me how or why he left. Luke Johnson, a co-worker at the plant and one of his references, says he recently resigned but another source said he was fired."

This information blindsided Adam. Just the Friday before, Dennis had given the tour of Bakersfield Meat as though he owned the place. Had something happened over the weekend? Did Dennis believe the job at Breedlove was a fait accompli?

"What's your overall impression?" he asked Stan.

"I'm leaning toward the guy from North Dakota. He's older, more seasoned, a solid cattle rancher. But there's no denying that when it comes to meatpacking plants, Dennis Washington knows his stuff."

Discussion continued. Adam listened to everyone's opinion and then made his decision. They hired Dennis Washington. He told himself that it was because he knew Dennis, because his old friend was highly qualified and the position must be filled quickly. That he had a very attractive sister who was never far from his thoughts had nothing to do with it. That's what he told himself. But it did.

By the eve of her birthday, Ryan was exhausted. She'd spent the week traversing one end of Las Vegas to the other, handing out flyers and setting up her portable massage chair in malls, stores and casinos to perform various types of hands-on healing to drum up business for Integrative

Healing. Earlier today she and Brooklyn had attended an Oktoberfest event. Much of the crowd had drinking and celebrating on their mind, but Brooklyn's angel readings were popular and Ryan had rubbed more necks and shoulders than she cared to count. She turned down an invite from Brooklyn to Johnny's concert, and when Adam texted not long after, said no to him, too. But now, two hours later, full, showered and relaxed, she wished she hadn't turned him down so quickly. Having had a tiring day was only part of it. The other part of it was feeling the walls closing in on her. Dennis got the job and was moving to Vegas. Her mother had left a message to not muck it up for him. If her adopted mom only knew. Her "mucking" probably helped him get the job! Would his being so close impact her personal decisions of trying to build a relationship with Phyllis and find her birth father?

Ryan decided not to call Adam. Instead, after tossing the phone on the couch, she punched a pillow to put behind her head and grabbed the remote with the hopes of getting lost in someone else's story. The next thing she knew she woke up to find the movie over and the TV watching her. Guess she hadn't needed company after all. She shed her clothes, crawled between the covers and was quickly back asleep.

Hours later, when the doorbell rang, Ryan didn't move immediately. She thought she was dreaming. It rang again. Her eyes blinked open. She looked toward the window, where dim shards of light eased from the space around the edges of the blinds. It was almost still dark outside.

*What time is it?*

"Just a minute!" Throwing back the covers, Ryan snatched a robe from the foot of the bed and hurried toward the door. One look out the peephole and her heart melted. Someone had sent her flowers!

She opened the door, wondering who could they be from. No one from her family, she knew for sure. Dennis rarely remembered her birthday and she'd received a card from her parents earlier in the week. Brooklyn, maybe?

"Hi."

"Ryan Washington?"

"Yeah, that's me."

"These are for you."

"Wow!" The bouquet was even bigger and more beautiful than it appeared through the peephole. The vase alone was huge.

"Do you need help getting it inside?"

"No, I think I've got it. Hold on, though, and I'll get you a tip."

"That's already taken care of. Enjoy your day."

Ryan set the arrangement down on the first available table and looked for an envelope. It was hidden within the abundance of greenery. She opened it up and pulled out the card inside it.

*Flowers pale in comparison to your beauty, but I hope these will brighten your morning. If you have a couple of hours today, I'd love to spoil you with a little R&R. Call me. Adam.*

Ryan took another look at the flowers, bent over and inhaled their heavenly scent. It would be really easy to fall for Adam, she decided. But she couldn't, especially now that Dennis was moving here and they'd be working together so closely. For the best, she decided, returning to her room and flopping on the bed. Getting Integrative Healing off the ground would and should be her singular focus. When trying to build one's own empire, who had time for cowboys?

She fluffed up the pillows behind her, lay back and tapped her cell phone screen. Said cowboy answered at once.

"Good morning, birthday girl!"

"Good morning."

"Or maybe *girl* isn't the right choice. Maybe I should have said birthday woman, or lady."

"I prefer birthday goddess."

"Ha! You are that," Adam replied, his voice slipping an octave, making Ryan feel all girlie inside.

"Thank you for the flowers. They're amazing."

"You're welcome."

"Even if you had them delivered earlier than the bird that got the worm."

"Ha!"

"Just kidding. It was very thoughtful of you. I appreciate it."

"There were two reasons why I had them delivered now. One, in case you had plans they could arrive before you left home. Two, if you don't have plans, you could join me here, at the ranch. I'm going riding in an hour and would love for you to join me."

"What kind of riding?" Ryan purposely asked the question in a way that could hold many meanings, as though she hadn't told herself just moments ago that the two had no future together. Her willpower had been strong, her decision firm. And then she'd heard that sexy voice. Dammit.

"There's certain types of riding I welcome at any time." Ryan smiled at the inflections in Adam's voice, leaving no doubt as to what kind of riding he meant. "But right now," he continued, "I meant horse riding. It occurred to me that I'd never invited you out for one of my favorite pastimes."

"Horse riding. That sounds so…highbrow."

"That's probably because of the cost of maintaining horses, which can be expensive. But spending time with, taking care of and bonding with horses is one of the best experiences any human being could have, and there are ways for anyone to enjoy that, no matter their social or economic status."

"They're beautiful animals."

"Have you never ridden a horse before?"

"Never."

"I'll send a car over and you'll see that it's the perfect way to start the day."

"Just text the address instead. I'd rather have my car to run errands afterward."

An hour later, Ryan pulled her car up to the grand wrought iron entrance. A friendly-looking gentleman came out of the guardhouse located just outside the gate. She looked around at the picturesque scene and tried to imagine actually living here. She couldn't.

"Good afternoon, Ms. Washington," the guard said.

Ryan didn't try to hide her surprise. "How do you know my name?"

"Adam informed me of your imminent arrival and my need to provide directions for you to get to his ranch."

He handed her a square white card that contained a map of the estate. She could see where a pen had been taken to highlight the route to Adam's house.

"It's a lot of land and can feel intimidating, but if you head straight down this road, all the way, then take a left here, and a right by the pond, you'll see the arch for Breedlove Ranch. Can't miss it from there."

"Thank you."

Ryan entered the estate, her eyes widening as they took in the sheer beauty of the land. The grass was the most uniform shade of green she'd seen outside of Astroturf. *Pristine* didn't begin to describe her surroundings. She didn't see a speck of dirt out of place, an errant leaf on the ground. And were those peacocks? Her jaw dropped.

Ryan was emotional by nature and by the time she reached Adam's spread, the estate's beauty had almost brought tears. She drove under the arch and down to where she saw Adam looking like a cowboy ad again, his booted foot on a plank of fence, a kerchief around his neck. Beyond him, two horses trotted in a corral. Farther away, cows dotted the landscape. Seeing them sobered her a bit. They were leisurely grazing when she knew how their story would end.

As she pulled in, Adam walked over. "Hello."

"This place is amazing," Ryan said, as they hugged. "The

other night I could feel that the area was vast, but to see it in the daytime? Wow."

"Did you have any trouble finding me?"

"No, but only because I had a map, the first time needing one after arriving at my destination."

Adam smiled, stepped back and whistled. "Whoa, girl. Look at you wearing those jeans!"

He reached out and felt the denim. "The material is a bit thin, though. I hope they'll be okay."

"We're riding horses, right, not bucking broncos?"

"Ha! I guess you've got a point." He checked out her sneakers. "These will do for today but we're going to have to get you a pair of boots."

"Anything else, fashion stylist?"

He gave her a once-over that warmed her blood. "That's all for now. Come on, so I can introduce you to Biscuit."

The horse was beautiful, the landscape breathtaking, the riding easy. Ryan enjoyed it more than she'd imagined. Back at the house Adam's actions made it clear that he was interested in a different kind of ride. An afternoon of lovemaking was tempting. Adam's sexual prowess would have been the perfect birthday present. But doing so would have only prolonged the inevitable.

She eased herself from Adam's embrace and took a few steps to put distance between them before turning around.

"There's no denying our sexual compatibility. You are totally intoxicating."

Adam walked over to a chair and sat down. "I think I hear a 'but' coming."

"But…" Ryan smiled as she sat on an opposite chair. "This is a very busy time for both of us. I'm getting my practice ready to open and next week you'll be orienting a new employee—my brother."

"Does his moving here bother you? Or is it that he'll be working for me?"

"A little bit of both, but mainly it's that you and I agreed that our getting together would be fun, casual and uncomplicated. I'm not sure that by continuing to see you it can stay that way."

As the words left Ryan's mouth she felt her heart ache. The slight narrowing of Adam's eyes showed they'd affected him, too. But when he spoke, his tone was casual.

"Are you starting to have feelings for me?"

"You're a good man, Adam, very easy to like, and yes, I could probably fall in love with you. Right guy, wrong timing, for many reasons. None of them personal. Maybe later on we can hook up again, after both our new ventures are off the ground and life has calmed down. I'd like that... very much."

He looked at her a long moment, then walked over and tugged her out of the chair. "I don't think I've ever been dumped so eloquently," he said, pulling her into an embrace. "But you've got to do what you've got to do, baby. It sounds as though you've already made your decision so of course I'll support it, and you. Good luck with your business."

"Thanks, you too," Ryan said, swallowing the cry that clawed at her throat, blinking back the tears that threatened. She ended their embrace and tried to lighten the moment. "With my brother working for you I'm sure I'll see you around. When that happens, behave yourself," she playfully chided. "No undressing me with your eyes or giving me that sexy look that will have me wanting to take my own clothes off."

"I promise nothing," he said, punctuating the statement with a look that was as sexy as hell.

"You're incorrigible," she said, gathering her things.

"Thank you." They laughed. "You sure you don't want to stay for a late lunch or early dinner?"

"Positive. I need to leave before this very tenuous resolve I feel totally melts away. Oh, I'll send you some information on handling dyslexia. I did a bit of research and think you'll find it as interesting as I did."

"Sure, send it over. I've overcome it for the most part, except when I'm frustrated or rattled. But I'm open to reading what you found."

"For frustration and anxieties, deep breathing works wonders. It's something few people do, fill the lungs with air that expands the stomach so that the oxygen can circulate, stimulate the organs and the body."

"I can think of an organ and how it can be used for stimulation."

"On that note…" Said with a smile as she shouldered her tote and walked outside.

Adam walked her to her car, opened the door and placed a light kiss on her forehead.

"Stay gorgeous," he said.

"Stay handsome," she replied. "I'll see you around."

She kept the smile in place until she'd exited the estate's wrought iron gates. Then her eyes teared up again. She missed Adam already.

# Eleven

Adam hadn't wanted to stop seeing Ryan romantically, but he didn't dwell on it. There was simply no time. With the construction for CANN Island underway, he had the freedom to focus more fully on Breedlove Beef Processing Center. The state-of-the-art facility had been erected near the far north end of Breedlove property, downwind from the closest residents and miles away from where the cattle were bred and raised. The exterior of the four-thousand-square-foot building was made of brick, wood and aluminum. The interior was a wonder in those elements combined with stainless steel. Adam knew architecture and construction. Dennis knew meat-processing plants. It had made for a winning combination in creating a facility that at best rivaled and would likely far exceed any other facility in the country.

The first Wagyu shipments were scheduled for the second week in December. Dennis suggested the meat be allowed to age for three to four weeks. So the first butchering had been scheduled to happen next week. Adam was both excited and nervous. It would be his ranch's first time handling the process from beginning to end. For the past half hour he and Dennis had been in the field, marking cattle for market. Now Adam headed back to meet the workers Dennis had hired and make sure his precise instructions had been conveyed and would be followed.

He pulled a rugged Jeep into a temporary gravel-strewn parking lot. Adam exited on one side while Dennis hopped out of the other. Dozens of men milled around outside, finishing stalls, walkways and other tasks. Adam saw the foreman talking with a group. Rather than interrupt him he simply waved before he and Dennis stepped inside the space.

Dennis placed his hands on his hips and took in the vast interior. "Man, I tell you what. This is a long way from the geodesic dome I built in the backyard."

Adam looked at him. "The what?"

"You never saw my dome? Oh, that's right. You never came over."

"I don't remember ever being invited. Had that happened, I probably would have accepted and come over. Especially if I'd known you were building something. That's been a passion of mine from the time I was a little boy. That and horses, or anything to do with a ranch."

"I remember that side of you well, your love for horses and horsepower, like that souped-up '65 Chevy you owned."

Adam laughed. "Ah, that was my baby. Belonged to my grandfather. We still have it."

"I'd love to see it again. That was a pretty ride. A rich kid who had everything. To me, that was you."

"Maybe, but life wasn't perfect, remember? That's how we met."

Dennis clapped Adam on the back. "Nobody's perfect, brother. At least you have an excuse for difficulty reading. I can read fine, just hate to do it."

"Why?"

Dennis shrugged. "Never was into the books much. Even now, I only read when necessary. Otherwise I'd rather be doing something with my hands or outside."

"I can understand that."

They stopped in front of a large enclosed space. Dennis stood next to Adam. "Does Ryan know about your... problem?"

Adam frowned, remembering he'd told her and wishing he hadn't, even though there wasn't another human on the planet who could have been more understanding, and even though he'd largely conquered the condition. "Yes."

"Just asking," Dennis said, his hands raised in apology.

"Don't worry about it. Defense mechanism." Adam began walking the periphery of the main floor. Dennis followed suit. "After being properly diagnosed, I was given tools to counteract the effects of dyslexia—the use of phonics, color codes, exercises in how to focus. Ryan emailed me a few natural remedies. Kinda cool what she does, healing various ailments through natural means."

"A bunch of hocus-pocus if you ask me," Dennis said. Then after a beat, "Are you and my sister dating?"

"We're friends," Adam said.

"With benefits?"

Adam's pause in movement and barely raised eyebrow was the only physical reaction to Dennis's inappropriate question. "Friends, period."

They stepped onto a rectangular-shaped area of the concrete floor. Dennis wisely changed the subject.

"This holding pen came out real nice," he said.

"It's called a lairage," Adam corrected.

"Maybe," Dennis responded. "But in lay terms it's a pen that holds animals, so that's what I call it—a holding pen."

The humor melted the frostiness that Dennis's comment had created. "Where are the guys?" Adam asked.

"In the main conference room, boss, waiting for you."

"Let's get this party started." Adam headed toward the stairs, confident that he'd chosen the right man to bring his dreams into reality.

Today was a big one for Adam. In mid-November, after five years of planning, three years of implementing those plans and almost a year of working with a PR and marketing team to brand the company as one dealing with only the most exclusive members of the hospitality industry, Breedlove Wagyu was being unveiled. It had been a long and hard road with a steep learning curve. But in the process of acting as both boss and eager student, the makings of an empire had come together—assembling a meatpacking industry dream team, acquiring livestock, monitoring intake for maximum quality, building the processing plant, and securing national and international customers to enjoy the fruits of their labor.

The black-tie event he'd planned would take place at the CANN Casino Hotel and Spa and give two hundred people from all over the world a taste of the meticulously prepared meat. As often happened when attending an event there, Adam was staying in one of three deluxe suites that were used almost exclusively by the Breedlove family. Ryan had spent the previous night there, too. They hadn't seen each other since that day at the ranch, but they'd kept in touch. Without the physical distraction, each had learned greater aspects of the other. Their friendship deepened. When he asked if she'd escort him to the dinner, she'd said yes without hesitation. When he shared plans to spend a few days at the hotel in his private suite and asked if she'd join him, she'd hesitated only briefly before saying yes to that, too.

"I've missed your stimulating organ," she'd told him.

"I've missed everything about you," he'd honestly replied.

Adam had surprised Ryan by having a gown delivered, one he said had been customized just for her. Again, she'd been moved by his attention to detail. Meticulous not only in business, but in his personal life as well. She'd argued the gift was too extravagant, had thought the chiffon dress she'd purchased from a designer outlet store had been a steal of a deal. But once she'd stepped into Adam's gift there was no comparison. The stretchy silk fabric caressed her body, had structure while at the same time being flowy and light. The color was that of a deep burgundy wine with colorful crystals—the name of which Ryan didn't remember and couldn't pronounce—splashed as though tossed across the bodice and down a skirt that draped into a short train. When she looked in the mirror, she hardly recognized the woman who looked back at her.

Adam had gone for simple and classic. A tailored black tuxedo had been paired with a white shirt, striped vest and black tie, his black suede shoes the only nod to his understated fashion sense. As he looked in the mirror, he felt hands run up his back and squeeze his shoulders before Ryan came from behind him and looked at his mirror image.

"You look hot, guy."

"Thank you, gorgeous." He ran a hand over soft curls that glistened slightly thanks to the hairdresser who'd styled him less than an hour ago. He turned to face her, admiring the Grecian-styled burgundy number with crystals haphazardly splashed from head to toe. "You…look amazing. I love your hair like that."

"Yes, well, take a picture, because any style that takes longer than ten minutes is one I won't wear much."

Adam fingered the thick tresses that had been flat-ironed and now flowed over her shoulders.

"So…what's our story?" she asked.

"Story?"

"We're attending a high-profile dinner together, one that I imagine will be covered by the press. Dennis will be there and he already suspects we're seeing each other. So when people ask, what is our story?"

"You are a beautiful woman, a vegetarian friend who graciously accepted my invitation to a dinner serving tons of meat. To me, that makes you a very accommodating friend and a superspecial date."

"People will assume we're dating."

Adam placed a gentle kiss on Ryan's temple and whispered in her ear. "Take a deep breath, darling, and don't worry about it. Worse assumptions could be made."

He placed his hand at the small of her back, letting it

slide to the low vee cut of the dress, then lower, to her butt. They exited the suite and crossed the hall to the elevator. "You sure you'll be all right surrounded by plates of premium beef?"

The elevator doors opened. They stepped in. Ryan moved close to Adam and pressed her body to his. "This will be enough premium beef to distract me," she cooed, squeezing his Grade A rump. Adam lowered his lips to hers, searing her with a kiss that lasted one hundred floors.

Even before reaching one of the hotel's smaller ballrooms, a buzz of excitement was heard. Ryan watched as Adam squared his shoulders—unconsciously, she thought—and entered the room with a confident swagger that seemed etched into a Breedlove's DNA. Immediately, they were the center of attention. Or Adam was, to be more precise. Reporters, clients, well-wishers, women, all moved toward him as if drawn by a magnet. The more assertive females seemed to have little regard for Ryan as they tried to maneuver past her to be by his side. Ever aware, Adam reached for Ryan's hand and held it tightly as he engaged those close enough to speak or ask questions while navigating his way to the front of the room and the Breedlove table. The gesture made her feel protected. Clearly, of all of the men in the room, she was with the prize.

They slowed as they reached the table directly behind the one where Adam's family sat. Ryan saw Dennis, looking fresh and clean-shaven, all gussied up for the occasion. He stood to speak to them. Ryan didn't see her brother dressed up often. She thought he looked quite the executive in a double-breasted navy suit. She couldn't say the same for the snake beside him. Of all the people who could have been his plus-one, why'd her brother bring Luke?

Dennis had barely finished speaking before Luke thrust out his hand. He spoke to Adam but was drinking in Ryan as though she was the last glass of water in the Mojave Desert.

"Good to see you again, Adam. You, too, Ryan. You're

looking good." He held out his arm for a handshake. Adam shifted Ryan away from him. If that move didn't tell Luke that she was off-limits, his barely concealed scowl surely did.

Ryan remained quiet and suppressed a smile. *Oh those alpha males!*

Luke dropped his hand and cleared this throat. "Um, Dennis has been bragging about the beef you raised. Wish I could have been a part of that process but... I'm looking forward to dinner."

"Dennis spoke very highly of you," Adam said. Ryan felt Adam was leery of Luke and thought his was a diplomatic answer that allowed his opinions to be kept to himself.

"Rusty, there—" He nodded at an older gentleman whose tanned, weathered face told a story that included years in the sun. "He's been with the family a long time, is an expert on animals and already worked at the ranch. Whenever possible, we like to promote from within. So that's what we did."

"That's an excellent thing to do for your employees," Luke replied. "I just met Mr. O'Brien. Great guy. But I told Dennis to let me know if an opening comes up. I could use a change of scenery and I think the Vegas lifestyle might work."

*Or not*, thought Ryan.

Adam said nothing, just gave a slight head nod and continued to the next table, where his family sat. His chagrin with Luke was palpable. Ryan gave his forearm an affectionate squeeze and heard him exhale. *Relax.*

"There's the man of the hour!" Christian stood and gave his brother a hearty hug while Nick and Noah chatted with Ryan.

"Babe." Adam pulled her closer to him. "This is my older brother, Christian, and his wife, Lauren. She's the good taste behind that dress you love."

"Oh my goodness, you picked this out?" Ryan leaned down to give Lauren a hug. "It's beautiful."

"Looks like it was made for you," Lauren said. "The way that color highlights your skin...fabulous!"

"Thank you. That's a wonderful color you're wearing. Are you a model?"

Lauren laughed. "Hardly."

Christian heard the comment as he sat down beside her. "See, babe, I told you. You could be."

Lauren shook her head.

"You really could be. That color is very complementary. What is it, like a…"

"Emerald green," Lauren said. "Christian's favorite color for me to wear, right, babe?"

"No," Christian said, lowering his voice so that only Lauren and Ryan could hear. "My favorite color on you is nude."

Lauren gave him a playful swat. "You're so bad."

Christian kissed her cheek. "That's why you love me."

Adam introduced Ryan to the others at the table she'd not yet met. When meeting his grandmother Jewel and step-grandfather Will Breedlove, he reminded her that while out horseback riding, their home was the one they had seen with the imposing cedar arch whose inscription announced La Hacienda Breedlove. He introduced Lauren's parents and told her that Lauren's father also worked for CANN International. Once they sat down, Adam explained that he would have introduced Noah's and Nick's dates, had he known their names.

"Until those two," Adam continued in a whisper, "I thought Christian was the ultimate playboy. These guys took playing the field to a whole other level. They built a whole new stadium for their game."

The evening began. Ryan found herself enjoying what she thought would be a drudge to get through. Though identical, she quickly learned one way the twins were different. Noah was quiet. Nick was a hoot. Five minutes in and it felt as though she'd known him forever and easily imagined him the irksome younger brother that Adam described.

A venerable army of waiters began serving courses with an equally proficient group of bussers quickly clearing the used china after each one. Ryan watched the orchestration in awe. The first course, a chilled vegan soup, was exquisite.

The table made quick work of the second course. The bussers appeared from several entrances to do their thing. She picked up her glass of tea and sat back to watch them, to admire their efficiency and ability to move around bone china while hardly making a sound. As a group neared her table she locked eyes with a woman who was…no…it couldn't be…her birth mother, Phyllis.

"Are you all right?"

Adam's voice pierced through Ryan's shock. Only then did she realize her hand gripped his forearm. The woman faced her fully, her features better lit under the table's light. She could have been her mother's twin, but it wasn't her.

"Oh, sorry. I, um…" She eased her hand from Adam's arm, her voice trailing off as well. "It's nothing," she finally managed.

"Are you sure, baby?" Ryan's eyes pierced her, filled with concern. "You look like you've seen a ghost."

Ryan shook her head, further rattled by the accurate assessment Adam's common phrase delivered.

"It was work, something I thought I forgot," she said, giving him the first answer she thought he'd find plausible. "But I didn't. It's okay."

Finally assuaged, Adam's attention turned elsewhere.

The evening continued. So did the queasy feeling in the pit of her stomach, along with the questions her reaction brought up. Why had the thought of seeing her mother caused so much angst? If discovered, how would Adam and his family respond to her past, the drug addiction and jail time? Ryan had wanted nothing more than to get to know her birth mother. She hadn't considered how that relationship might impact other parts of her life. Ryan felt burdened by the weight of her secrets, and the fear that Sin City wasn't big enough to hold them all.

# Twelve

That Sunday, the day after the Breedlove Beef official unveiling, Ryan pulled up a website on her computer, one that she hoped might help her find her birth dad. Her reaction last night to seeing the woman who looked like Phyllis had been surprising and left her shaken. She'd always longed for a relationship with her mother, but had never given much thought to what that would look like, how Phyllis's presence might impact other areas of her life. She was, after all, basically a stranger. Who was she beyond the woman who'd given her life? And equally as important, who was her father?

Ryan had nothing, not even a name, to begin the search. That week, while working with Brooklyn to put the final touches on their office, Ryan shared "a client's" frustration of not being able to trace her ancestry. Brooklyn told her about a show she'd seen on television where birth parents of adopted children were found through matching DNA that had been placed in a national database. The odds weren't in Ryan's favor. Any potential blood relative out there would have to be in that system, also looking for lost family. It was a long shot but the only one that Ryan had. She pulled out a credit card and ordered the kit. That done, she switched her focus from personal to business. The day she and Brooklyn had dreamed of had almost arrived. The next day Integrative Healing opened for business. The whirlwind began.

The first week wasn't jam-packed with clients but Ryan and Brooklyn were busy. If either had free time during the day, they'd market online, network with other practitioners through cross-promotions and referrals, and one day hit the Strip and Fremont Street downtown with their mobile chairs, offering neck and shoulder massages. By the end of that first week both women were stressed, and asking each other what the heck had they been thinking, to which Brooklyn's spiritual adviser said, "Awesome! Sounds like you're exactly where you need to be!"

Ryan left her office and went to the break room. Brooklyn was pouring herself a drink from a glass pitcher.

"Sit down, girl, relax for a minute. I'm serving us up some celebratory kombucha."

Ryan leaned on the counter where Brooklyn worked. "I've been sitting for the past two hours. Think I'm going to hit a yoga class before I go home."

She took the tumbler that Brooklyn offered, and clinked the thick glass against the other. "What are we toasting exactly?"

"One week in business, and neither one of us died."

"Ha! And we're still friends," Ryan added.

"And Johnny still loves me even though all week I've been too tired to make love. Heck, I couldn't even make like."

Ryan and Brooklyn cracked up laughing. "We're delirious," Brooklyn finally decided.

Ryan nodded. "Yeah, it feels good to laugh."

"Your energy definitely feels better now than it did on Monday. I knew something was going on but I didn't want to ask—figured you'd tell me when you're ready."

Ryan nodded. "I will."

"I was kind of hoping the good mood had to do with Adam."

Ryan's smile disappeared.

"Did something happen?"

"Not really," she said finally. "And nothing ever will.

He's a fun date, but it's about time to pull the plug on that fantasy."

"It's obvious how much you like him. Why would you end something making you happy?"

"Why prolong the inevitable? It's only a matter of time before he ditches the person he likes to sleep around with for someone he can marry."

"Don't underestimate your value, Ryan Washington. If anything serious happens between you and Adam, he will be the lucky one."

Thanksgiving arrived, giving Ryan a much-needed break from work. Word of mouth helped the clientele grow quickly for her, Brooklyn and the acupuncturist Suyin. The personal front wasn't running as smoothly. Feeling her life was already filled with too many secrets, she finally told Ida that she'd reconnected with Phyllis and that she hoped to find her birth father, too.

Ida called it a betrayal. Her usually supportive father had sided with Ida and told Ryan she shouldn't have "done this behind your mother's back." Though their reaction was painful, Ryan was glad to have her search out in the open. Now all she could do was wait for the DNA results that would hopefully lead to information on her father's family.

The only bright spot was Adam. Their called-off liaison was on again. They'd only seen each other a couple more times, but oh those memorable nights. She was falling in love with him. A problem, but right now his touch wasn't a luxury. It was a necessity that helped keep her sane. When he suggested she spend Thanksgiving at the estate, and to invite her family, Ryan initially said no. But asking her mother what she thought about the prospect of spending the holiday in Vegas with the owners of CANN melted the chill and got them talking again. Ryan was optimistic that this visit would go well. Ugly attitudes had no place in a setting as beautiful as that of the Breedlove estate.

On Thursday, the weather couldn't have been more perfect. A bit chilly, but as Ryan reached the tents that had been erected for today's dinner, she saw the strategically placed heaters that would keep everyone toasty and warm. She knew her family was already there and she spotted them right away. She waved and headed over. Everyone was all smiles. Her father's deteriorating health was a continuing concern but today he managed to look dapper in dress slacks and a sweater over a shirt and tie. For the first time since Ryan could remember lately, her mom had curls! Dennis's look was more casual but Ryan saw that he'd still not regrown his beard. She didn't know the woman sitting beside him.

"Hey, everybody!" Starting with her father, she greeted everyone.

Soon, Victoria joined them. "Hello, Ryan!" They shared a warm embrace.

"You've met my mom and dad?"

"I have and it's such a pleasure. Adam believes that Dennis is a solid addition to the team. You remember Lauren, of course."

"Of course! Hi, Lauren."

"Hey, Ryan." The women shared a brief hug. "It's good seeing you again. I heard about your new business for holistic health. Congratulations."

"Thanks, Lauren."

"I'd love to know more about it. In fact, I have a quick question. Never mind. It's a holiday and listen to me putting you right to work."

Ryan laughed. "I don't mind."

Lauren and Ryan stepped away from the others. The conversation began with Lauren's interest in acupuncture, then turned to Ryan and Adam.

"You guys look like you belong together. You make a nice couple."

"Me and Adam?" Ryan asked. "We're just friends."

Lauren laughed as though Ryan had just told a joke. "I saw how that man looks at you, with love in his eyes. The way yours lit up at that statement, I'd say the feeling was mutual."

"I might be falling in love a little," Ryan admitted. It felt good to say it out loud. The more time she spent with Adam, the more she found to love about him. Perhaps it was time for another conversation, for what they shared to be redefined.

"I'll admit to being surprised when he told me about you. I love your vibe, but never thought I'd see any of the brothers with someone with such an earthiness and realness about them. Of course," she continued, "I never thought they'd have looked twice at someone like me, either. So I hope you don't take what I'm saying the wrong way."

"Not at all. I would totally put them with a model/celebrity type." Ryan nodded toward the twins. "Like the women Noah and Nick brought with them."

Lauren eyed their dates. "Those guys are having so much fun right now. They love being with women who are drop-dead gorgeous, and who fawn all over them as though they're God's gift to heaven. But trust me, those feelings don't run too deep. They've been well-schooled by their older brothers on what type of women to watch out for, and the myriad of ways a woman can scheme to get into their wallet."

Ryan and Lauren continued to watch the women with the twins. They were stunningly gorgeous, no doubt about that, with bodies that could have been bought and paid for. If so, it was money well spent. She smiled, but inside couldn't help feeling that if Adam knew about her background he might believe that she was on the "come up," too.

The day was lovely. Ryan appreciated the attention Victoria paid to her family, making sure they felt welcomed. Common ground was found between Victoria and Ida when she mentioned the CANN Foundation, and the fund-raising done for various charities. Victoria promised to invite her to a future event. Ryan could tell that made her mom happy. Both she and her mom were surprised to learn that the delicious meal—turkey, Wagyu beef and tons of sides—had all been prepared by the family's matriarch, Adam's grandmother Jewel, with assistance from several family members. Adam joined her at the table with her mother and dad, while Dennis sat with guys from the processing plant and his date, a woman Ida told Ryan he'd met online.

Just before dessert was set to be served, Ryan made a quick trip to the restroom. She returned and was surprised to see Dennis halfway up the walk assisting their father, and Ida making apologies for their unexpected and abrupt departure.

"What's happening, Mom?"

"Your father's not feeling well. We're going to take him back to the hotel where he can rest."

"I'll meet you there."

"There's no need for that, Ryan. Dennis will be close by if we need him, and all your father is going to do is sleep."

Adam came up then and placed an arm around Ryan's shoulders. "Is everything okay?"

"It's my dad. I could tell how much he enjoyed himself today but I think he may have overdone it a bit." She turned to Ida. "I'm going to meet you at the hotel, Mom."

"Okay."

After talking Adam out of coming with her, and taking the containers filled with desserts as Victoria insisted, Ryan left the estate and headed toward downtown Las Vegas and Fremont Street, where her parents were staying. She worked a variety of healing modalities on her dad and left him sleeping peacefully, with Dennis and his girlfriend in a room down the hall. She spent the night with Adam. Her parents had planned to stay the weekend but her father continued to feel bad so they left the next day.

Two days later, her father passed out and was rushed to

the hospital by ambulance. Tests were run. The news was not good. His kidneys were no longer functioning. Only intense dialysis or a kidney transplant would keep him alive.

## Thirteen

# Thirteen

For the past several days, Ryan had been Adam's priority. Hearing her father's prognosis had been understandably upsetting. He'd offered his many resources to help. Walking into the boardroom at CANN International, Adam was prepared to provide updates on the various stages of design and construction happening with half a dozen new CANN hotels going up in the next eighteen months. Along with CANN Island, an ambitious string of über-luxurious properties on islands near Djibouti, plans were underway for hotels in Geneva, Sydney, Fiji, Oslo and Macao.

No one was talking about that. The chatter was all about Wagyu.

As soon as Adam reached the table his dad, Nicholas, exclaimed, "Breedlove Beef is king!"

"Oh, here we go," Adam said, though he couldn't help but for his chest to puff out just a bit. He accepted several handshakes before sitting down.

Greg Chapman, VP of international sales, agreed with Nicholas. "You're all the industry is talking about."

"The money spent on public relations paid off, and it was a boatload. No doubt the column written by one of America's top food critics—"

"And published in the Sunday edition of every major city—"

"Right," Adam said. "There really isn't a dollar amount that can be put on that."

"I bet they tried, though," Christian added, holding up a fist for Adam to bump.

"No doubt. The retainer is hefty, plus expenses. But the phone has been ringing off the hook. We might have to cut back some of those orders for..."

Nicholas sat up. "Orders for who? I know you're not going to say the orders for CANN International, the other company you work for, the reason you even have your little enterprise." Nicholas's dismissive wave of the hand elicited laughter around the table. "I know that's not the company you're planning to put on the end of that sentence. The first shipments of that prime, in-demand Wagyu need to be addressed to CANN International, and that's after you've come up the road and filled up my and your mama's fridge."

The jokes continued for a bit before Christian took charge and returned their attention to CANN business. It was like each brother had been born with a specific talent that together could create one's empire of choice, all overseen by their father, the ultimate dreamer. Christian was company president. Adam handled expansion as the R&D VP. Noah worked in finance. Numbers came to him the way music came to Mozart. His family teased that instead of asking for video games, Noah wanted calculators. He was quiet, introspective and smart as a whip. Which left Nick, the patriarch's namesake. The most charismatic and carefree one of the bunch, he was officially a member of the sales force, but someone with Nick's personality could basically be successful doing whatever he wanted.

Once everyone had their say the meeting ended. The brothers hung back while the others returned to their offices. The next thing anyone knew, Adam was being hit in the head with a Nerf football that Nick found God knows where.

"Hey!" Adam reached for the ball and aimed for the brother now using the table as a shield. Adam fired as hard as one could a Nerf ball, missing his brother's head by inches. "Fool."

"When am I going to get some of that good beef?" Nick asked.

"What do you mean? You've tasted it several times."

"I'm talking about a stash for the house, like Dad was saying."

"Nick's right," Noah chimed in. "A couple rib eyes would be nice."

"Y'all are a trip," Adam said, laughing along with his brothers as they left the conference room and went back to their offices while he headed out of the building. With the meetings over for the day, it was time to go to the ranch. On the way he remembered something Noah had said after being introduced to Ryan's family.

"I hope that guy Dennis works out for you, bro. If you fire her brother, I'm not sure Ryan will stick around."

He'd been joking, of course. But when Noah asked, Adam hadn't denied that Dennis's relationship to Ryan had given him an edge over the competition. Still, there was a matter Adam wanted to revisit.

He rounded the corner to find the new manager standing just outside the small meeting room, looking over the balustrade that allowed a full view of the barn floor below, where long rectangular tables held a variety of equipment and devices used on the ranch. Rows of grain, also cow feed, went on for several acres. A pond could be seen from the second floor, along with cows roaming freely over the hills. Adam frowned, not because Dennis was standing around not working, but because of who was beside him, someone who as far as Adam was concerned had no business here.

Dennis heard Adam's boots on the floor and turned. "Adam! Hey, buddy. We were just talking about you."

Adam reached him. He and Dennis shook hands.

"Man, this place is awesome," Luke said, his arm outstretched.

Adam was slow to shake it.

"I hope you don't mind that I'm showing Luke the building. He was in town and asked for a tour, was curious about how operating an organic process differed from how it's done at Bakersfield."

"That's part of it," Luke added. "The other is that I'd really like to work here. Everything's fine at Bakersfield Meat and I never thought the word *beautiful* could describe a slaughterhouse, but this place is amazing. Working for Breedlove Beef would definitely be a step up." He added a chuckle as though he were joking, but Adam got the feeling that he meant every word.

"I told Luke about coming over here back in the day. Even then, being at the estate felt like I was visiting royalty—"

"Yeah, right."

"You know it was like that. Saturday mornings, Sunday afternoon, this was the place to be! It was cool then, but the way you've turned this side of the estate into a cow ranch beyond the best I've ever seen…well, it's impressive."

"I appreciate that," Adam said. "Especially with the hands-on experience you have in the industry. Luke, Dennis and I need to meet. Is there anything Olivia could get for you? Coffee, soda, a beer, before you're on your way?"

"No, I'm fine. I need to get downtown and handle a few things myself." Luke craned his neck before his eyes settled on the petite older woman sitting at a desk at the end of the hall. "That your full-time secretary?"

"Olivia? Secretary, teacher, mother figure, boss. I've known her my whole life. Her husband, Clarence, passed at about the same time I started building this place. I thought taking care of things around here would give her something else to focus on besides how lonely life was without him."

"You're a good man, Adam," Dennis said.

"I try." When he saw Luke still standing beside them, he looked over to where one of the workers was cleaning a stall. "Hey, Bobby. Do me a favor and escort our visitor to the gate."

Dennis mumbled a goodbye and followed Adam toward the meeting room. Luke walked outside with the worker, clearly dismissed.

"Hope you don't mind that I showed Luke around," Dennis said as they settled into chairs in the meeting room with a large window through which cows could be seen grazing at their leisure.

"For someone who says he's fine at his present job, he seems eager to try out a new one."

"That's probably my fault," Dennis said. "I've bragged about this operation since day one. He's seen all of the positive write-ups about the company. Heck, everybody has seen them. He knows what a fun town Vegas can be. Housing prices beat those in California hands down. There's no state tax. Lots of beautiful women. Luke's a bit of a hardhead but overall a good dude."

"Would Ryan agree with you?" Adam paid close attention to Dennis's reaction, saw a flash of annoyance before Dennis schooled his features.

"Probably not," Dennis said with a bit of a chuckle. "Luke used to tease Ryan. She didn't like it. Too sensitive. He used to flirt with her, even though it was clear she didn't like bad boys, which is what she considered him back then."

"Was he?"

Dennis shrugged. "He got into a little trouble, a run-in or two with the law. But that was a long time ago, Adam. Like me, Luke's changed. We've all grown up."

Dennis's frank answer was unexpected and basically lined up with what Ryan had alluded to when he'd asked her about Luke.

"One more thing. You resigned in Bakersfield before I hired you. Why?"

"It was foolhardy, I know. But I was beginning to have problems with one of the owners, issues about safety, and pay. I should have told you, Adam, but I wanted the job and knew I could do it."

"You're proving that and yes, resigning is something you should have disclosed. Thanks for being honest." Adam stood, satisfied that he'd made the right choice. "I have to go to a meeting."

He headed home, where Ryan would meet him for a trip to BBs and a sampling of the new vegetarian options. Later that night, despite their resolve, they spent a leisurely hour sampling each other.

# Fourteen

The Christmas season was Ryan's favorite time of the year. She loved everything about the holiday—crisp winter weather, colorful decorations, shopping, singing, everyone filled with cheer. As she headed to Bakersfield, her thoughts were on Joe, her adoptive dad. The dialysis wasn't working. He needed a kidney transplant. The immediate family was being tested, along with Joe's brother and nephew. Because being a blood relative wasn't a mandatory requirement when seeking a potential donor, Ryan would be tested, too. Joe had always treated her the same as he treated Dennis. Like his very own child. For him to live, she'd give up her kidney in a heartbeat.

Holiday traffic was heavy. Ryan arrived at her parents' just after dark. Christmas lights outlined the house. The same artificial tree with white lights and gold bulbs that had graced the living room for at least the past decade could be seen through the window. Ryan pulled her luggage from the trunk and reached into the back seat for her Christmas gifts. As she started up the walk the door opened. Her mother came out, not quite smiling, but with a look that came close.

"Hi, Ryan."

"Hey, Mom. Merry Christmas!"

"Not for another few hours. Do you need help?"

Ida met her halfway and took the shopping bag filled with presents. At Thanksgiving dinner, Ryan had told Ida what happened with her birth mother and didn't miss the irony that her falling-out with Phyllis had further thawed

Ida's demeanor. She stepped inside, stopped, inhaled and was transported to her preteen years. The smell of mulled tea blended with that of the crispy sugar cookies. During the twelve days of Christmas and Kwanzaa the cookie jar would be kept full, guaranteed. When she turned the corner, took in the familiar tree with the kente-clothed angel topper, the dining room centerpiece she'd helped pick out, and other decorations she used to help hang with family and some of the neighborhood friends, Ryan was surprised to feel love swell up inside. It had been a while since she'd felt this way but tonight, it felt good to be home.

Ryan greeted her father, then made a beeline for the cookie jar. "Where's Dennis? I thought he'd be here by now."

"Oh, he's here. So is April."

"April? Where's Ginny, the girl from Thanksgiving?"

Ida shrugged. "Turned out to be a turkey, I guess."

Ryan laughed out loud, both shocked and delighted at Ida's joke. She didn't make them often.

April had lived next door with her parents and siblings when the Washingtons moved there. She was a cute girl, on the thick side, with expressive eyes and a hearty laugh. Dennis always denied they were in a relationship, but Ryan had seen him tiptoe across the backyard more than once. He'd gone into the service and when he came back April was married. But Ida had never been convinced that the two stopped hooking up.

"Divorced and back home with two kids. She was real happy to see your brother." Ida stopped and looked over her reading glasses with an expression that conveyed "you know what I mean."

The neighbors came over. One of her dad's good friends and former postal coworkers stopped by with another type of cheer, a brown liquor in a blue pouch that made the men jolly, and after mixing theirs with cola had the women's spirits bright, too. When a random scrolling through the channels revealed a harried Jimmy Stewart feeling trapped in his life, the room settled into watching the black-and-white classic. Perfect entertainment and a feel-good finish. Even with the challenges ahead, it felt like a wonderful life!

Ryan went to bed when the movie ended. She woke up hours later to a dark room, a quiet house, a mouth filled with cotton and a vow to never drink strong liquor again. She headed downstairs for a glass of water, added a smaller glass of juice and a bag of chips to the mix, and tiptoed back upstairs.

Passing Dennis's room, she heard voices. Ryan's eyes widened. April? No! Ryan hurried to her room, deposited her midnight kitchen run and tiptoed back ever so quietly to her brother's door. What was happening in Dennis's room was none of her business. But Ryan couldn't resist. Cupping her hand, she placed it against the door with her ear firm against it. She heard Dennis's voice first.

"The money is rolling in like water, man, two hundred and fifty a pound."

Ryan thought her brother could use a brushup on his pillow talk but maybe April was a meat lover. Could be sexy.

"I'm telling you, man. We could get in on that."

Not April's voice…at all.

"I just started working there, dude. I'm not trying to risk my job like that."

"It wouldn't be a risk. You're in charge! I've got the substitute."

Dennis was talking on his cell phone, with Luke's voice coming through the speaker loud and clear. The conversation was making her stomach roil again.

"You said it yourself—there are thousands of pounds. You think with all that shipping going on they'll catch a few swapped-out steaks here and there? Going all over the world?"

"I don't know, man."

"Even if we run it for just a few months, now, while business is booming, we could do at least twenty or thirty

apiece. I have a connection in LA who can probably un-
load every ounce we get. He caters for the A-list crowd. We
could get top dollar. And you could finally pay back what
you've been owing me for years."

Ryan slowly backed away from the door and returned to
her room. She tried to tell herself she hadn't heard correctly.
Dennis and Adam were friends in high school. Simply being
connected to a powerful family like that opened wide the
door of possibilities. Her brother wouldn't be stupid enough
to steal from Adam and get that door slammed in his face,
and possibly another one clanked shut, one with bars and
concrete and neighbors called inmates. Ryan slipped back
into bed and pulled the covers over her head, not wanting to
believe what she'd heard. Tomorrow would be soon enough
to question her brother and learn the last ten minutes had
been a dream.

The next morning, Ryan woke up early. She wanted to
speak with Dennis while their parents were still sleeping.
She didn't want an argument. But she wanted and would
get the answers to explain what she heard last night. She
knocked lightly, then checked the knob. The door was unlocked.

"Denny," she whispered, approaching his bed. She gently
shook his shoulder. "Hey, wake up. It's important."

"What the heck time is it?" Dennis asked, his eyes
squinting in Ryan's direction. "What's going on? Is it Dad?"

"No, Dad's fine." Ryan sat on the bed. "I want to ask
you about something that I heard but I don't want to argue,
okay?"

"If you think the question might start an argument, then
maybe you'd better not ask it."

"I have to, but I don't want us to start yelling again and
wake up Dad."

Dennis was wide-awake now. His eyes were hard as he
glared at her. "What, you heard me talking to Luke about
a new enterprise?"

Ryan hadn't expected Dennis to admit they'd had a conversation. Maybe what she thought she heard was a big misunderstanding.

"Yes, and it sounded as though you were going to swap out the more expensive meat that Adam raises for a lesser quality and make a huge profit."

"And?"

"Are you kidding me?" Ryan screeched, forgetting about the need to keep her voice low. "You've got a great thing going at Breedlove Beef. Why ruin a great job with someone like Adam to make a quick, illegal buck with Luke?"

"Exactly." Dennis laughed as his head flopped back on the pillow. "You know Luke is always scheming. We were running the numbers, talking what-ifs. I think Adam could have paid me more. He's definitely got the money. But I like working at the estate. Plus, I'm not going to steal from my sister's boyfriend. So stop worrying, girl. Luke's just talking. And I'm just humoring him by going along."

It was a civil exchange, pleasant even. Ryan made herself comfortable on the bed, chatting with Dennis for almost an hour. She admitted how much she liked Adam, but denied being ready to become his missus as Dennis suggested. They talked about being back in Las Vegas, both admitting it being better the second time around. But mostly they talked about Joe, and finding a kidney. Ryan enjoyed spending the evening with her brother and hoped the camaraderie would continue. Returning to Vegas she thought about Adam, the sexual attraction and deepening feelings, and admitted that however uncomfortable and inconvenient, she hoped their spending time together would continue, too.

# Fifteen

The year was winding down and, after today, so too would Adam's workload. The first shipments of Wagyu had been delivered. Business owners were thrilled, customers were satisfied, positive product reviews continued, and orders were brisk. That's why he was still in the office well after the sun had gone down, and after putting in almost a full day at CANN International. His body felt every hour he'd worked, and every long day for the past two months. That's why with operations running smoothly, he was taking a week off. The barn would see him next year.

Even being tired, Adam bypassed his truck parked in the lot and began walking the short distance to his house. After being cooped up in offices for most of the day, the cool night air was refreshing and there wasn't anything quite so beautiful as a midnight-blue Nevada sky.

Tapping his Bluetooth earphone, he pulled out his phone and called Ryan.

"Hey, baby."

"Hey."

"How is the woman with the healing hands?"

"Would you stop with that?" she asked him.

But he heard the smile in her voice. "I'm only saying what's true. And check this out. I'm booking my appointment soon and when I do, I get a discount."

"You will?"

"Absolutely. I told Mom and my assistant, Olivia, about

Integrative Healing. If they haven't already, both will be calling soon. They've also promised to spread the word."

"Wow, Adam, thank you! The best marketing for services is word of mouth, so I really appreciate you telling others about the business. You'll absolutely get a discount."

"Any news on your dad, and finding a donor?"

"Not yet, but it might be me. My blood type and Dad's is the same."

While a fairly common procedure with relatively low risks, removing a kidney was still major surgery. Ryan would be left with only one. What if somehow it was damaged? Would she then be in search of a donor? Knowing how Ryan felt about her father, Adam didn't voice his concerns. If Nicholas needed anything donated, the brothers would be in line to help him get well.

"Two more tests are needed to see if I'm a true candidate."

"You almost sound excited."

"I'm hopeful. So far, no one else has been a match. His name has already been placed on the donor list, but the wait through that avenue can be anywhere from six months to a year. I'm not sure Dad… We want him to get the transplant as soon as possible."

Adam heard what sounded like the beep of doors unlocked with a car fob. "Where are you?"

"Just leaving the office."

"This late?" Said even while remembering he'd just left, too.

"Yeah. I had a walk-in right as we were about to close up, then did some paperwork. Plus I'm still catching up from all the time spent helping to take care of Dad."

"Are you headed home?"

"Yes."

"Want some company?"

A slight pause and then, "Sure."

"I'm on my way." Adam spun on his boot and headed back to his pickup. He was suddenly not tired at all.

Just outside of Breedlove's city limits, his phone rang.

"Hey, Miguel, what's up?"

"Hey, boss. I'm not sure. Are you in town where you can come by real quick?"

"I'm just outside of town on my way to Vegas. What's going on?"

"I just opened a package of beef marked Wagyu instead of Black Angus. I'm not an expert on the new beef, but it didn't look like either of the stock we raise. Didn't cook up like it, either."

Adam let out a long, slow breath. How could this mix-up happen, especially since the restaurant wasn't serving Wagyu? Minutes into the weeklong vacation he'd planned, it was the last thing he wanted to hear. But quality was where Breedlove Beef hung its hat. There was no way he could leave errors to chance. So he checked the mirrors, made a U-turn and headed to BBs.

He pulled into the parking lot a short time later. Since it was the holidays and many were out of town, the restaurant wasn't as crowded as usual. He pulled out a key and entered through the side door, then headed straight to the kitchen, where he found Miguel sweating over a grill full of meat.

"Hey, boss."

"Miguel." Adam stepped closer to the grill, examining its contents. "Where's the meat you called about?"

"Hang on a sec. I put it up so it wouldn't get mixed up with these orders."

Adam watched as Miguel worked the grill like a maestro, delivering to-order doneness from rare to well in choices from burgers to steaks. To be admired, even in Adam's state of chagrin. After finishing the orders, Miguel pulled the towel from around his neck and wiped his face. He turned to the other stainless steel counter and uncovered a patty on a saucer.

"This is the burger from the package," he said, handing it to Adam, before continuing to the fridge.

Adam eyed the burger, smelled it, then broke off a piece to taste.

Miguel walked back to where Adam stood. "This is the package."

It wasn't discernible to Adam's eye, but one whiff and his suspicions were as heightened as Miguel's were, and one bite was all he needed to drop the saucer back onto the counter. That wasn't Breedlove anything, Wagyu or otherwise. He opened the packet to inspect the raw meat, then the packaging itself, which was definitely from his facility.

"Do me a favor. Put this back in the fridge, but when you leave tonight, take it with you, okay? I don't want any chance for that to be served, but we need to keep it so I can find out its origins and how it ended up with our label."

"Because it isn't Black Angus, either, huh?"

Adam shook his head.

"I wonder what it is?"

Adam placed the Stetson he'd removed when entering back on his head. "I don't know, but I'm going to find out. On second thought, hand me that package. I've got to figure out where this meat came from and how it was mislabeled. Have the wrong customer get a lower-quality product than was ordered, one who takes their complaint to the media, and our reputation could be damaged. It's too early in the game for us to take that chance."

Back in his truck, Adam called Ryan. "Sorry, baby, change in plans."

"Is everything okay?"

"Probably, but I got a call regarding something at the plant and need to head back there. I probably should have Dennis meet me there, too. Call you later?"

"Sure."

"Rain check on keeping you company?"

"Anytime."

Adam's call to Dennis went to voice mail. He made a couple others. By the time Adam reached the plant, Stan and Will were waiting for him. They followed Adam into a break room.

"What's going on, boss?" Stan asked.

"Whatever it was sounded important," Will said.

Adam pulled out the package of meat from Miguel. "Take a look at this, guys, and tell me what you think."

Will gave Adam a look. "You pulled me away from a warm fireplace to look at ground round?"

Adam watched as Will pulled off a chunk of the meat and brought it up to his nose. He made a face and examined it closer.

"Where did you get this?" he asked.

"It was in a package boasting a Wagyu label delivered to the restaurant this morning."

"This sure as hell isn't Wagyu," Stan said.

"It isn't Black Angus, either," Will replied. "Not our stock, anyway."

"The package has our label," Adam said. "It had to have come from this plant."

"Where's Dennis?" Stan asked.

"I called but he didn't answer, left a message about a fire that needed to be quickly put out."

The sound of the outer door opening cut off further conversation. All three men looked toward the door.

Dennis hurried into the room rubbing his hands together for warmth. His hair was tousled and his eyes were bloodshot. Adam figured he'd been drinking, or keeping company with a woman, or both.

"I just got your message, Adam. What's going on?"

"A mystery," Adam said, nodding for Stan to give the cellophane-wrapped meat he held to Dennis. "We need to understand how that meat got in packaging labeled Wagyu."

"Likely human error," Dennis said.

He took the package from Stan, examined the contents

and placed the meat to his nose. "Perhaps the package got mislabeled."

Will slowly shook his head. "I don't know where that meat came from, but it's not from our breeds."

"That's impossible," Dennis said, looking between the three men. "Unless a stray cow wandered into the herd somehow. Don't worry, Adam. I'll get to the bottom of it."

"Stan, Will, I need you to work with Dennis. I'll be here first thing tomorrow, too. We have to make sure this is a onetime error. It cannot happen again."

# Sixteen

Ryan's hands slowly glided just above the woman lying facedown on her table. Her eyes were closed as she worked, fingers hovering over the areas where she felt energy blocked, or strains of the body lacking ease, being ill at ease, dis-eased. She completed the procedure and after a moment, gently placed her hand on the client's back.

"We're finished," she said softly.

"Are you sure?"

Ryan chuckled. Her work often relaxed clients to the point of falling asleep. The peaceful, healing atmosphere was an addictive one that people often didn't want to leave.

Ryan chuckled. "Yes, Miss Olivia, I'm quite sure. Would you like me to help you? Here." Ryan stepped forward as the older woman turned and used her arms to raise off the table. "That's it, go slowly. All of that energy is still settling. Some get light-headed if they move too quickly."

Miss Olivia sat up, turned her head one way and then the other.

"How do you feel?"

"Why, it's the most interesting thing. It feels as though I just had a massage but you barely touched me at all!"

Ryan reiterated what she'd told Miss Olivia before starting the process, how blocked, nervous and other negative energies affected the body and how the practice of Reiki helped bring the flow back into balance. "I felt quite a bit of tension around your neck and shoulders," she finished.

"That's where you seem to hold a lot of stress. So try to relax, okay?"

"That's easier said than done these days. We're so busy at the office that I finally told Adam, look, I'm an old lady. I can't do all of this by myself."

She eased down from the table and walked over to where her shoes rested in front of a chair.

"So we're going to hire somebody and I told him the sooner the better."

"I'm glad to hear that, Miss Olivia. It sounds like everyone is a bit surprised at how successful everything turned out."

"Oh, not me. I've known Adam for many years and one thing I can tell you. When he makes up his mind about something, know that it will get done and better than anyone else could do it. He's a driven man, but a good one." She lowered her voice as her cornflower blue eyes twinkled. "And he's single. But you know that."

"Yes, I do." Ryan looked at her watch. While Olivia put on her shoes, Ryan retrieved her personal items from off the credenza. "Just as Adam referred you, if you tell someone and they come in for an appointment, you'll receive 20 percent off on your next visit."

"Whether or not I get the discount, sign me up."

Ryan walked Olivia to the door and gave her a hug. For a woman who'd turned seventy last year, she was in great health, stress and all. It had been a pleasure to treat her. With another appointment scheduled for a half hour later, she rushed back to ready the room. As she reached her office, the phone rang. She rushed in to grab it, tapped the speaker button and sat down at her desk.

"Integrative Healing, Ryan speaking."

"Hello, Ryan, it's Victoria Breedlove."

Ryan stopped, surprised at the call. She quickly recovered. "Hi, Victoria."

"I know it's the middle of a workday. Is this a good time?"

"My next client is in a half hour. Your timing is interesting as I just finished up with Adam's assistant, Miss Olivia."

"She told me that she was going to come see you. Adam was very impressed with all you've shared with him about your business, and recommended you to several of us."

In the moment Adam sounded like such a great guy and considering her brother's conversation that she'd overheard, Ryan felt like a jerk.

"Are you calling to make an appointment?"

"No, and I'd love to go into detail when you have more time but I'm calling with an invitation. You might recall the Thanksgiving conversation I had with your mom discussing the CANN Foundation and the various events held to raise funding for any number of charitable causes."

"Yes, I remember."

"In February, we're hosting an event called Loving You. Contributors have paid handsomely for a two-hour pampering at the hotel, followed by a private lunch. Would you be open to have one of your services included as part of that package, perhaps the energetic work that you've done on Adam and now Olivia? You'd be compensated, of course," she hurriedly added. "And have the opportunity to market your services to high-end clientele, and they'd have an opportunity to learn about different ways to feel better. It could be a win-win for both of us."

"Wow, Victoria, this was totally unexpected and a wonderful opportunity."

"I was hoping you'd think so, and would like to set up a meeting for later this week. Is there a time that works for you, for either lunch or dinner?"

"Dinner would definitely be preferable. But can we meet next week instead?"

"Sure, sweetheart, either Monday or Tuesday if possible. I'll look forward to hearing from you."

Ryan ended the call and looked at the clock on her desk. She had a little free time before her next appointment. She headed down the hall and passed Brooklyn's office. The door opened suddenly. Both women jumped. "Oh! Crap, you scared me," Brooklyn said.

"Me, too."

They continued into the break area.

"How's your morning?" Brooklyn asked.

"Okay. I have a nutrition consultation in about twenty minutes. What about you?"

"Nothing for about an hour. I'm thankful for the break." Brooklyn pulled a powdered product from the cabinet. "Want a protein smoothie?"

Ryan shook her head.

"You probably need one."

"Okay, Mom."

Brooklyn smiled. Ryan managed one, too. Her business partner's mother-henning was legendary.

Brooklyn whipped up the drinks, poured a glass and handed one to Ryan. "This is delicious," Ryan said after a drink of the creamy concoction. "And you're right. I did need it. Thank you."

The doorbell buzzed. The women looked at each other.

"Walk-in?" Brooklyn queried.

Ryan headed for the door. "We'll soon see."

She reached the foyer and looked at the security camera video screen placed discreetly behind a large potted plant. The pensive-looking face on the other side of the door was the last one that she expected. She hurried to open it.

"Adam?"

Upon seeing her, Adam's face broke into a smile. "I need a massage, badly," he said, giving her a hug. "Can you fit me in?"

"My next appointment is in about fifteen minutes but sure, we'll work something out. Come on back."

Ryan saw that Brooklyn's office was empty and continued down the hall to the break room. "Before we get started, I'd like you to meet my partner."

They entered the break room. Brooklyn had taken a seat at the table and was thumbing through a magazine. Seeing Adam, she jumped up.

"Hi!"

Ryan chuckled. "Obviously you already know, this is Adam. Adam, meet my business partner and best friend, Brooklyn Chase."

"It's a pleasure to meet you, Adam," Brooklyn gushed. "You're even more handsome in person."

"You've been researched," Ryan explained.

"Thoroughly," Brooklyn added, completely unapologetic. "Spending time with my bestie, you had to be checked out."

"I guess you found all in order since I'm not getting kicked out."

"So far, so good," Brooklyn said.

While Brooklyn chatted with Adam, Ryan went for her phone. She texted her nutrition client and was able to push that appointment to later that day. She returned to the break room, where Adam waited, alone. They hugged. Ryan learned her man hadn't been joking about needing a massage. His strong back and broad shoulders felt as tight as a drum.

"All right, guy," Ryan said, after checking to make sure the massage room was ready. "We now have a full forty minutes. Let's get started."

She handled Adam as she would any client, giving him a moment of privacy to undress before reentering the room. There were none of Adam's usual flirtations and innuendos. He was quiet and remained so as she began her work.

After doing a quick energy scan, she started on his shoulders. "What happened?" she asked, her voice as soothing as the light New Age music wafting from hidden speakers. "You are as tense as I've ever felt you. What has you so stressed?"

"I was up most of the night dealing with a problem at the plant," he explained after a pause. "We believe it's handled but can't be totally sure. Because we weren't able to determine how the problem occurred, we can't guarantee it won't be repeated."

"What was the problem?"

Adam began explaining what had happened after talking with her, the call he'd gotten from Miguel and what was discovered.

"Dennis believes a stray cow from another farm somehow ended up in our pasture. There are other cows in the area but there are miles between properties. It's a far-fetched explanation at best, but the only one we had."

With every sentence Ryan heard, her heart sank further and further into despair. She believed she immediately knew how the foreign product got into Adam's plant. She had to remove her hands from his skin, they began to shake so badly. "I need to get a special oil from the storeroom," she whispered. "Be right back."

Ryan ran to her office, closed the door and took several deep, calming breaths to prevent what felt like an oncoming panic attack. She felt nauseous. Dennis had sworn that she'd misinterpreted what she heard. She so wanted to believe that was true, but could what Adam have told her be coincidence? Was there really another explanation to how foreign beef ended up in his plant's freezer? Every option to remedy her dilemma led to a headache. She felt one coming on right now and headed toward the herbs in the break room cabinet.

She reentered the massage room as quietly as possible. Adam looked up. "Where's the oil?"

"Oh, we were out. It's okay." Ryan walked over to a tray filled with various tubes and bottles. "I have something else that will work just as well."

"Are you all right?" he asked, his eyes narrowing as he continued to observe her.

"Lie down and relax, Mr. Breedlove. Don't worry about me. It's my job to make sure you feel better, and that's exactly what I'm going to do."

She concentrated and placed all of her focus into what she was doing. She felt the knots began to loosen as Adam finally relaxed. When she finished, he was almost sleeping. He turned over and pulled her to him.

"There's one more muscle you need to massage," he murmured, guiding her hand toward his groin.

She playfully pulled her hand away. "Later, I promise," she said. "Right now I need to prepare for my next client. How do you feel?"

"Like I've been touched by an angel," he said, sliding off the table and reaching for his clothes. "And totally cured."

Back-to-back clients kept Ryan busy for the next two hours but she found enough time to send Dennis a text, short and to the point.

You. Lied.

She didn't receive a reply from him. She wasn't expecting any.

"So here's a scenario," Ryan began after walking into Brooklyn's office and plopping down in a visitor chair. "It involves three friends. Friend number one overhears friend number two plotting something against friend number three. Friend number one loves both of them in different ways and knows that if she tells friend number three what she heard number two say about them, it could be very problematic. Should friend number one say anything?"

"Let me think about that." Brooklyn picked up a beautiful amethyst crystal and rolled it around in her hand. After a few seconds, she set it down and walked around her desk to where Ryan sat.

"I think you, I mean friend number one, should follow

this." Brooklyn placed a hand over Ryan's heart. "It will never steer her wrong."

Later that afternoon, as Ryan worked with her nutrition client toward a natural solution that would reduce her high blood pressure, eliminate type 2 diabetes and balance her cholesterol, a possible next step for Ryan's situation began to form. After finishing the consultation and walking her client to the door, she returned to her office and opened her tablet. She clicked on a search engine. Ryan's hands hovered over the tablet keys as she thought of the right way to phrase the search. After beginning and deleting several possibilities, she typed *listening devices* and clicked Enter, and a whole new world appeared on her screen.

Thirty minutes later she'd ordered a product that she didn't know existed thirty-one minutes ago. There were mixed emotions about using it, teetering on all kinds of ethical and moral fine lines. Soon, she'd be able to listen in on Dennis's conversations and read his texts. If Breedlove Beef was mentioned, she wasn't sure how she'd handle it. But at least she'd know the truth.

# Seventeen

An old year went out. A new year came in. But the problem with the mystery meat did not go away. It became worse, which caused Adam to take drastic action. He wearily looked up as someone tapped on his office door. "Everyone rounded up?"

Olivia nodded. "They're ready, boss."

"Okay." Adam rose from his chair and reached for the suit jacket hanging on a hook. Most days he came to the plant dressed in flannel and denim. Today wasn't like the others. In fact, life at Breedlove Beef Processing Center hadn't been the same since he'd gotten the call from Miguel. There'd been more calls regarding inferior product, and meetings with Dennis, Rusty and the supervisors over each detail. A plan had been devised and was ready to be implemented. He slid on a finely spun wool suit jacket, ran a hand through his curls and headed to where the employees had gathered for this mandatory meeting. Many didn't know why it had been called, but one look at their boss's dress and demeanor, and chatter rapidly diminished before disappearing altogether. By the time Adam reached the front of the room you could hear a fly land on a cow's tail.

"We have a problem," he began, as his gaze slowly took in every face in the room. "Somehow meat from cows not raised at Breedlove ranch has found its way into this plant. It didn't walk in, didn't amble into the building on four hooves. So that can only mean that someone working here is mishandling product.

"Recently, a very astute chef called me, gravely concerned about a packet of meat that was supposed to be Wagyu but was in fact a type of beef not bred on this ranch. Since then we've received several more calls from the high-end restaurants clamoring for our product, but we also received a couple of calls from Black Angus customers who said the meat wasn't the same. I believe whoever is behind this switching up of product felt it was okay to throw in a few pounds of average meat and sell the Wagyu for a nice little profit. I believe that person most likely can hear me right now."

Adam took in the various reactions. His eyes narrowed as he observed those he felt might be culprits. He'd gotten Dennis's and Rusty's input on who they thought might be behind the problem, and he had a couple ideas of his own. But no one would be called into question right now. Adam would strike, but only when the time was right.

"I'm implementing a few changes effective Monday, three days from now. Each employee will be issued a badge that will be required for entry. The floor is being reconfigured, with the Wagyu operation completely separate from the Black Angus in a room that will be locked at all times.

"No one is being looked at to be fired, yet. But some of you will be questioned and all of you will be monitored. If you're guilty and come forth voluntarily, come to my office and talk face-to-face, there may be a chance that any criminal charges that we're considering might be taken off the table. Sometimes there are extenuating circumstances, a right reason for something done wrong. If you come to me, admit what you did and tell me why, and agree to the terms I'll require regarding your termination, you'll still be fired. But you might remain free."

The meeting ended with the employees somberly filing out of the office. Finally only Adam and Dennis remained.

"This is all my fault," Dennis said with a heavy sigh.

"More than forty people help to run this operation. If one person is at fault, it's me."

"I manage the operation. It happened on my watch!"

"Have you ever seen a situation anywhere similar to this?"

"No, but I haven't worked at a plant with this quality of meat, either." He placed a hand on Adam's shoulder. "I had your back in high school. I've got it now. We'll get to the bottom of this, bro. Hang in there."

Adam nodded and walked out of the room with Dennis, heading to his car and a meeting at CANN. But his mind stayed on Breedlove Beef Processing, and the person trying to ruin what he'd built.

# Eighteen

As had become her practice, Ryan walked her latest client to the door and gave her a hug. This time she continued outside.

"Are you leaving?" the client asked.

Ryan shook her head. "Just getting a breath of fresh air."

"I don't know how fresh it is, but...see you next time!"

"Okay," Ryan said, while laughing. "Have a beautiful rest of your day."

Ryan watched the tall, gorgeous redhead walk to her car. She closed her eyes, stretched and performed exercises that allowed her to release the energy absorbed when working on others, especially important when the client was troubled and shared with her aspects of their dark lives. Practitioners such as Ryan often became pseudo-counselors and therapists as well. Ryan hoped she'd gain the courage to leave a man who was verbally abusive and make room for one who deserved her.

That wasn't the only conversation that required another deep breath, but that would come later. Ryan walked back inside. Her next appointment was for a massage, a new client named Fred. He'd booked through the phone app so his first name was all she knew about him. That was fine, because once he was on the table his body would tell her everything else she needed to know.

Ryan stopped by the restroom, then entered her room and began preparing it for the appointment. She changed the music from the Asian-influenced sounds currently playing to a list with more classical tones. She switched out the sheets, sprayed them with lavender and had just picked up oil for the diffuser when the door buzzed. She walked over and pushed the intercom button.

"Fred?"

"Yes," he mumbled.

"When you hear the buzzer, turn the knob and have a seat in the foyer. I'll be right out."

Ryan lit the diffuser, raised the dim lights a notch and went to greet her client. She opened the door and turned toward the chairs. They were empty.

*Where is he?*

She turned to the other side of the room. "Adam?"

"Um," he said in that same muffled voice. "Call me Fred."

"Oh my God, are you..." She burst out laughing and ran into his arms. They kissed, softly at first and then another, longer exchange.

Ryan ended it and led the way down the hall. "You nut!" she said after they'd entered the room and she'd closed the door. "I can't believe you're back so soon. And what's with this Fred act?"

Adam shrugged. "The unexpected makes life more fun."

"Sometimes..."

"Right. Sometimes."

Ryan chuckled again. "So, Fred, I will leave the room as you get undressed, and comfortable on the table, and return in two minutes."

Adam began unbuttoning his shirt. "I wouldn't think of it. In fact, why don't you take off your clothes, too. We can massage each other."

"That sounds incredibly tempting. You surprising me like this is a definite turn-on. But these walls are thin and the rooms are full. Suyin is performing acupuncture next door. Hearing grunts and moans from the other room could have her poking needles in the wrong place."

Having sat to remove his shoes and socks, Adam stood to take off his pants and boxers. "Fine," he said, strolling over in all of his naked glory and pulling Ryan into an embrace. "I wouldn't want anyone getting poked in the wrong place. But will you let me poke something later?"

Ryan hugged him, choking back a laugh as her hands skimmed his bare skin. "I can't with you," she whispered. "Get that fine ass up on my table."

He smiled, got on the table and tried to pull her on with him. She jerked her arm away. "Will you behave?" she asked through clenched teeth. "Now, over on your stomach, please."

He huffed, and Ryan caught a childlike expression that had probably gotten him out of trouble more than once. "You're no fun."

"Perhaps, but you'll feel better."

"Does that mean this appointment has a happy ending?" Ryan smacked his butt, then kissed it, before covering the firm gift of nature with a thin sheet and beginning her work.

For several minutes she worked in silence, starting with his feet and moving methodically upward. She was a naturopathic doctor who worked on bodies for a living. Being dispassionate should come naturally but with this particular client, being a woman came first, followed closely by being a lover of fine male specimens. Still, she worked with quiet efficiency, paying attention to physical knots and energetic blocks and clearing both before moving on. When she reached his thigh and massaged out a particularly tight muscle, he groaned aloud.

"Having fun yet?" she asked.

"Best time of my life."

She chuckled. "Which business is all of this stress, tension and nervousness from, the ranch or the hotel?"

"Yes." They both laughed. "Remember me telling you about that weird incident when Miguel received a package of beef with our label that was not from my ranch?"

Ryan's hand slowed, but for only a second. "Yes."

"I was hoping it was a onetime fluke. It wasn't."

"He got another package of the same meat?"

"Not Miguel. Another customer received it. This time it wasn't the ground Wagyu but a steak."

"How is that happening? I don't understand."

"Someone is stealing the prime Wagyu and replacing it with cheap stock. As to how it's happening, I don't understand that, either. Not yet. But we're working on it."

"We?"

"Me and management. Your brother, Dennis, and Rusty, the assistant manager. Changes were made that are going to make it very difficult for more thefts to occur. If the culprits get past all of the security we've set up, then I'll personally give them the same amount that they stole."

Later that day, Ryan called Dennis on his office line. He hadn't answered calls from her cell phone but now he picked up.

"Breedlove Beef, Dennis Washington."

"Is it Breedlove Beef?" Ryan asked, her voice deadly calm. "Or is it the beef you and Luke somehow switched out to make big bucks on the black market?"

"You don't know what you're talking about. Look, I'm busy and can't talk right now."

"What was the figure I overheard that night? A couple hundred thou—"

Dennis hung up on her. Ryan was livid. She was barely able to make it through the rest of the day. After her last appointment she got into her car and pulled out of the parking lot with one destination in mind, the Breedlove estate. She needed to have a conversation with Dennis, have him prove that he was not behind what was happening at the plant. She couldn't know what was going on and stay quiet. It just wasn't right.

Ryan reached the gates to the Breedlove property with no clear plan. She didn't want Adam to know she was there,

but knew the guard might call and announce her arrival.
Fortunately, the guard had been there on one of her previous visits. He opened the gate and waved her through. What she hoped was her biggest hurdle had just been jumped. Now all she had to do was get through to her brother. Ryan pulled into the plant parking lot. She kept an eye out for either Adam's sports car or truck as she hurried up the walk and reached for the door. If she saw Adam, she'd tell him the truth. That she was there to speak with her brother. Hopefully he wouldn't ask what about.

It wasn't until finding out the door was locked that Ryan noticed the bell on the door frame. She rang it. A young man came to the door.

"Yes, may I help you?"

Ryan poured on the charm. "Hi, I'm Ryan, Dennis's sister. I need to speak to him."

The man hesitated before opening the door wider. "Sure, come in." He led her to where a security guard leaned against a stand. "This lady says she's here to see Dennis."

Ryan introduced herself, then remembered her client, Olivia. "If you'll let her know I'm here she can help me if he's preoccupied."

Mentioning Olivia did the trick. Her client was surprised to see her but brought her up to the offices on the second floor. When told Ryan was there to see her, Dennis said he was busy. That if she wanted to speak to him, she'd be waiting awhile.

She waited. By the time Dennis finally opened his door, Olivia and most of the other workers had gone home. A good thing, since Ryan's patience had ticked away with the time. She saw Dennis and lit into him.

"You've made me wait an hour, so I'll tell you what. You've got five minutes to convince me that you're not guilty."

"You've got five seconds to get out of here before I call security."

"Fine, call security. They'd be very interested to hear what I overheard, the scheme to make big money on high-priced beef."

"You're crazy, kid. Making stuff up."

"I can't keep quiet, Dennis," Ryan said, working to calm down. She tried another tactic, hoping to find an ounce of compassion in her brother's cold heart. "Adam and I are dating. I'm falling for him. Things might get serious. How can I know what's going on and not say anything about it?"

"Because I know things I haven't shared with him about you," Dennis said. "You're standing there in your moral dress, as if your life is perfect. Have you told Adam your secrets, little sister? About how you're adopted? And how your birth mother ended up in jail after committing fraud to get drugs?"

He went on about how lucky she was to have been raised in a "normal" household, and how different it could have been.

"I'm not ashamed of my past and in time will tell Adam everything, including what I know about—"

"What?" Dennis interrupted. "What exactly do you think you know? I'd really like to hear it."

"So would I."

Ryan whirled around to see Adam standing in the doorway. Dennis had obviously seen him first. That's why she was interrupted.

"Is there something either of you need to tell me?" he asked.

"It's a sibling squabble, Adam," Dennis said. "Nothing to do with you."

"The fight sounded pretty serious. I heard the yelling from downstairs." He looked at Ryan. "Are you okay?"

Ryan fought to hold it together. "I will be," she answered. "Sorry to bring this kind of drama to your business."

She pushed past him, ran out the door and wondered what all Adam had heard.

# Nineteen

A week had passed since the confrontation, since he'd gone back to the office and found Dennis and Ryan locked in a heated argument, had overheard talk about family and keeping secrets. Dennis had sworn it was about Ryan. Later, Ryan said it involved Luke. But she wouldn't say anything else, and that bothered him. What had Luke done to her and why wouldn't she share it? At the mere thought that he could have hurt her, Adam's hands balled into fists. That following Monday Adam had met with Dennis outside the office, had first invited him to go riding (Dennis didn't do horses), then to a round of golf (he didn't do clubs, not iron ones, anyway), then finally settled on drinks on the bar side of BBs restaurant. When asked the reason for them getting together, Adam had been purposely vague.

"There's been a lot going on," he'd casually replied. "Between CANN and the ranch I've spent too much time in offices. Plus, you and I haven't had a chance to just hang out since work started. Thought it would be good to kick back for a minute, off the clock."

Of course, there'd been more to it. The more relaxed the environment and in turn, Dennis, the better the chances he'd slip up and say something Adam needed to know. Unlike Rusty, he didn't think his old high school friend was the one stealing the Wagyu. But he believed Dennis knew more than he'd shared. Adam couldn't figure out what that was, which was why in addition to hiring a private investigator, he'd called an impromptu meeting with his brothers to beat their brains about it.

"I think he's lying," Nick said, after Adam had caught them up with what had happened since last Friday. He cracked another peanut, tossed the shells on the concrete, before throwing up the nut and catching it in his mouth.

The brothers were out on Adam's massive patio, their chairs haphazardly placed around the roaring firepit. Shells littered the floor around Nick and Christian, a stainless steel bowl filled with peanuts on a table between them. Bottles of beer were scattered about. Adam carefully snipped a cigar.

Noah stood and leaned against a thick wooden beam anchoring the pergola. "I do, too. I think he's in on it."

"So does Rusty," Adam replied. "He spent the weekend and a lot of hours this week glued to a split screen running back surveillance video, hours and hours of tape from cameras mounted inside and outside. He was looking for Dennis specifically."

"What did he find?" Christian asked.

"Nothing." Adam reached for a lighter on the table in front of him and began toasting the cigar from a box he'd recently received as a Christmas gift.

"It's frustrating because until the renovation last weekend our focus regarding theft was for the actual cows. Heck, when it comes to the pastures, especially West Wagyu, there are probably more cameras than birds."

The brothers laughed.

"I remember you telling me about the company's humor at your request," Christian said. "What was the line you said the owner kept saying?"

Adam placed the cigar in an ashtray and stroked his chin. "Oh, man, don't make me hear it again."

"He said Adam was after bird-gulars."

Nick burst out laughing. In stark contrast, Noah slowly shook his head. "That was so bad."

Adam finally gave in and smiled. At the time, it had been funny. Not now.

"We put cameras by the doors to catch anyone walking out with large boxes or packages. If anyone were to steal, which I honestly doubted would happen, we thought it would be a steak or two here, or maybe a slab of ribs there. We didn't have cameras in the cooling room, or in the chop area right outside. So far, no one I've questioned has raised a red flag. They are good, honest, hardworking employees. That's what their résumés and references showed. That's why I hired them."

"Obviously there's a bad apple," Christian said.

"Obviously," Adam agreed. He pulled on the cigar, the circles he blew dissipating in the night air. "But we'll find him and we'll cut him out...before he spoils the whole bunch."

One by one the brothers dispersed and headed home. Adam walked into the house and turned on his big-screen TV, looking for sports. He found a tennis match but was too restless to watch it. He decided to head over to BBs, and had just reached for his jacket when the phone rang.

"Ryan."

"Hey, Adam."

"Babe, what's going on? I'm giving you the space it seems you need but we've got to talk, and soon."

"You're right, Adam. We do need to talk. I'm sorry for how I've been acting lately, about the argument at your office and that I've been pretty much silent since then. There is a lot that I need to share with you, especially now."

Adam perched on a barstool. "What's going on now?"

"All of the tests have come back. I'm a perfect match. Six weeks from now, I'm going to give my dad a kidney."

"You were hoping to help him. I'm so glad things turned out as you wanted."

"Me, too. And with the surgery scheduled, I don't want any secrets between us."

"Are you at home, Ryan? I can come over now."

"Not tonight. I'm working on a time-sensitive project. But soon, okay?"

"Okay."

"Adam?"

"Yes."

"I... I'll see you soon."

Adam ended the call, placing the phone in his pocket as he reached for his jacket and headed to his truck. He was glad that Ryan called him, but what she'd shared had him very concerned. The research he'd done on kidney transplants and donors had left him feeling better about that operation. But what else did Ryan have to tell him? What were the secrets that she needed to share? Did they involve Luke or Dennis? Were his brothers right that Dennis was lying? Was one of Ryan's secrets that she was lying, too?

# Twenty

Ryan sat cross-legged in her bed, staring at her cell phone. She'd already picked it up and placed it back down several times. Somehow she felt these moments, right now, were the last of the world as she knew it. Once she opened the application, accessed the information and printed it out, her life would not be the same. She couldn't say all of the different ways that it might change, but it could not return to the way it was now.

She reached for the small instruction booklet that had come with the cell tracking and listening device. There was really no need for her to read it again. It was straightforward, easy. She'd been shocked and appalled at how the tracker worked, what all it could do, how easy it had been to install and how for over a week she'd had complete access to her brother's cell phone without him having a clue. For all that time she refused to dial the number, would ignore the buzz on her phone indicating that her brother was either making or receiving a call. After last Friday night's blowup had been the first time. She'd just arrived home and was sitting in her car, trying to process what had happened and forget the look of confusion on Adam's face, the questions in his eyes. That's when the phone had buzzed and she'd picked it up and tapped the key to listen in. Within seconds, Dennis's voice came through so loud and clear Ryan had held her breath, certain he could hear her, half thinking he could see her, too. Pangs of guilt assailed her for being a lurker but once she heard what was being discussed, she couldn't hang up.

*"...I'm telling you, Luke, this is serious! I don't know how much of our conversation he heard."*

*"And I'm telling you that you need to chill out."*

Ryan's jaw dropped. Luke was in on it. Then again, she should have known.

*"There's no chilling out. Pandora is out of the box with cameras rolling!"*

Ryan could feel the panic in her brother's voice.

*"But he doesn't suspect you, man, he trusts you. Didn't you tell me that you were the only one with the key to the good stuff?"*

Ryan eased out of her car and gently closed the door. The instructions had assured her that there was no way she was being detected, that her spying was not noticeable in any way and could not be traced. Didn't matter. Only sheer force of will kept her from tiptoeing once she'd opened the door.

*"No, man,"* her brother was saying when she'd refocused on the call from that night. *"You're not hearing me. This stuff is over. The gig is up. That plant is locked down worse than prison. They're gunning for who jacked up those orders, who switched that meat, and I'm square in their crosshairs. Getting away with this will take a miracle."*

*"You owe me too much money to try calling shots. This was the way you came up with to pay me back, so you need to keep making it happen."*

*"There's no way, man, too risky."*

*"What about Ryan?"*

Ryan gasped and quickly slapped her hand over her mouth.

*"What about Ryan?"* Dennis repeated back to Luke.

Ryan listened intently. Yeah, what about her?

*"Didn't you say they were dating?"* Luke asked.

*"Yes, and?"*

*"Bring her into it. She already knows and according to you won't say anything about it."*

*"No, she's won't say anything. She's got secrets, too."*

*"Then she'd be the perfect middleman to drive the product off the property. Since they're dating, seeing her car would be normal. It's actually perfect, man. I can't believe you didn't think of it."*

Ryan waited, her heart beating out of her chest.

*"Ryan would never agree to do it. And I can't force her."*

Her relief had been palpable. It felt good to know that her brother wouldn't sell her all the way out. What he said made her decision more painful. But it didn't change her mind. She'd checked her brother's texts and as she figured, incriminating conversations had occurred between her brother and Luke, proof of exactly what they'd been doing and possibly even information on where some of the beef had been sold. She'd give Dennis one more chance to tell Adam himself. If he didn't, she would. So after taking a deep breath she sent Dennis a text, relayed that information and attached a screenshot of one of his damning texts to prove she wasn't bluffing. Adam needed to know the extent of the damage that had been done to his stock and reputation. The more he knew, the better he could divert a scandal and the potential loss of millions of dollars.

An hour later, Ryan was emotionally exhausted. Dennis had called, as angry as she'd ever heard him, shouting threats about exposing her past and having her cut off from the family. He said everything but what she needed to hear, that he'd speak with Adam. He'd made his decision. She'd made hers—to expose the truth. Doing so may be the end of her family, but she had to do the right thing. She printed out the messages for Adam, then sent a text for them to meet ASAP about something important. She slipped on a pair of jeans, locked her door and had just pulled out of the garage when her cell phone rang. It was Bakersfield Medical.

She tapped the Bluetooth. "Hello?"

"Hi, may I speak to Ryan Washington?"

"This is Ryan."

"This is Kathy, a nurse at Bakersfield Medical. I'm working with the doctors who will be performing the transplant for your dad."

"Is something going on with Dad? Is he okay?"

"Your father's fine. I was rechecking your charts and noticed a trait that is genetic in nature. It won't impact the procedure. The surgery will go on as scheduled. But the doctor wondered if anyone had ever talked to you two about a specific gene, PCSK9?"

Ryan pulled over and put the car in Park. "What type of gene?"

"PCSK9. It manages the amount of cholesterol in the bloodstream. Those who do not have this gene or have a mutation of it usually experience a lower cholesterol level and therefore are at less risk of heart disease. Total absence of the gene is quite rare, especially in African Americans. The gene is not present in you nor your father—"

"Wait, how can that be? I'm adopted."

There was a long pause on the other end of the line.

"I'm not sure what to tell you," the nurse finally said. "This trait is passed along genetically, present in either your mother or father. Are you in contact with your birth parents, or do you have their medical records?"

"I need to make a phone call and get back with you."

Ryan hung up without saying goodbye, thoughts of Adam and what she planned to share forgotten. Her fingers were shaky as she punched another number. When Ida answered, Ryan worked to find her voice.

"Is Joe Washington my birth father?" she managed.

Ida's hesitation was Ryan's answer. She walked into the house as though through a fog, having learned the biggest secret of all.

# Twenty-One

"Hey, Chris." Adam stepped fully into Christian's office. "Do you have a minute?"

"I might." Christian was engrossed in something on the computer. He didn't look up. "Depends on what you need."

"A witness." That got Christian's attention. "The detective called me, says he has some information. He's in my office."

Christian was up before Adam finished his sentence. "Say no more. Let me close this out." A few taps on the keyboard, then he walked toward Adam. They left his office. "I'll be back in a bit," he told his secretary as they passed by her desk. "Unless it's an emergency, I'm unavailable."

Christian gave his brother a comforting pat on the shoulder. "Do you have any idea what you might hear?"

"Not a clue. But he's been on this for a month and it's the first time he requested a meeting."

"Then it must be something significant."

"I hope so. He's the top PI in the area and his rates reflect it."

Christian laughed. "I don't think he'll break your piggy bank."

Adam was appreciative of his brother's lightheartedness. Hearing from the detective had put a knot in his stomach. It felt more loose already. A look at his vibrating phone caused another smile. It was Ryan with a message about important, incredible news.

What happened last night? I was expecting you. Worried. Calls went to voice mail.

Sorry. Long story, need to tell you in person.

Headed to a meeting. Come by in an hour.

They walked into Adam's office. A guy of average height and medium build had been looking out the window. He turned when the two men walked in.

"Christian, this is Owen Haynes. Owen, this is my brother, Chris Breedlove."

They exchanged greetings.

"Let's sit over here, guys." Adam motioned toward a sitting area just around the corner of the large L-shaped corner office. Christian took a seat on a gray leather sofa. Owen chose one of two top-grain leather club chairs.

"Are you sure I can't get anything for you, Owen?"

"No, I'm good."

"All right, then." Adam sat on the other end of the couch. "What do you have for me?"

"Do you remember the commercial that asked, 'Where's the beef?'" At the confused look on both brothers' faces, he waved a dismissive hand. "Never mind. Too young. I can't answer the question of where the beef is, but I just might be onto who took it."

A slight ripple along the jaw Adam clinched was the only indicator of how tense he felt. His eyes slid to Christian, whose look was one of silent support.

Adam leaned forward. "I'm listening."

Owen pulled out a cell phone, tapped the face a few times then held it toward Adam.

"Do you recognize this guy?"

Adam took the phone and studied the picture on the screen. "This is out by the back gate."

Owen nodded. "It's time-stamped two thirty a.m."

Adam enlarged the picture, and saw boxes stacked up next to the gate and a man bent over them. A second guy carried a box to the truck, prime Wagyu no doubt. A baggy jumpsuit made it impossible to accurately guess the man's build and a baseball cap obscured his face.

"Ring any bells?" Owen asked.

"No," Adam said. "What about the guy by the fence? Did you get any of him?"

"Yes, but his whole face is covered, even the eyes. Swipe the screen. He's in the next couple pictures."

Adam's eyes narrowed as he studied the next few images. The second guy wore a baseball cap, sunglasses and a bandanna over his face. Totally unrecognizable, as Owen had said. *And likely the employee who's stealing.*

He scrolled back to the first picture and passed the phone to his brother. "Any idea who this is?"

Christian gazed at the screen for a moment, then shook his head. "I've never seen him before."

"What about the truck?" Owen asked.

"It doesn't look familiar. Send me those pictures. I'll have the parking lot cameras checked to see if it's ever been on the property."

"Dammit." Adam held out the cell phone. "I so want to catch whoever this is."

Owen forwarded the images to Adam, then pocketed the phone and stood. "Don't worry, there's a lot more video to study. These pictures are from the first one I downloaded and since one of the faces was fairly clear, I thought it was worth a shot to see if you recognized him. But I've got footage from here to the main highway in both directions. Learning who owns that truck and IDing the driver is just a matter of time."

"I appreciate the hard work," Adam said, standing up to shake Owen's hand.

"No problem, buddy. I'll be in touch." Owen tipped a

well-worn cowboy hat to Christian before putting it on and walked out the door.

Christian placed a hand on Adam's shoulder. "Hang in there, bro."

Adam watched his brother exit, then crossed over to his desk. He downloaded the images from Owen and attached them to an email addressed to the head of security. He cc'd Stan, the ranch manager, then returned to the image of the truck with the boxes in the background, thieves in the very act of stealing the Wagyu that his men had so meticulously raised.

He sat back with the calm of a snake just before striking, confidently believing that it wasn't a matter of if he'd catch these guys, but when. His thoughts turned to Ryan, brightening his mood. After Owen's visit he could use a dose of her sunshine, and hoped whatever she had to share with him was good news.

Ryan pulled up to the valet counter, dread piercing the cloak of shock she'd worn since the fight with her brother and then, like a one-two punch, learning that Joe was her birth father. Ida had finally confirmed it. Dennis had texted more threats. Joe had called but Ryan hadn't answered. There was still too much to process. Plus, this wasn't a talk to have over the phone. She was headed to Bakersfield to see him in person, with one very important stop to make along the way. Everything about her life would change after that. Dennis would hate her. Adam would be angry. Ida might just kick her out of the clan. Her decision was risky but this was Vegas. Time to take a gamble and let the chips fall where they may.

It was Ryan's first visit to CANN's executive offices. Walking off the elevators was like entering another world, all gleaming and polished with the feel of wealth in the air. A deep, rich carpet soaked up any sound that her sandals may have caused as she crossed over to the receptionist desk. The perfectly coiffed woman on the other side made Ryan feel totally inadequate but the smile she offered helped to settle Ryan's nerves.

After the receptionist phoned Adam, they walked to a set of double doors at the end of a hallway. The receptionist motioned for Ryan to enter the office before quietly shutting the door.

Ryan stepped into what looked like a miniature lobby. "Adam?"

Hearing nothing, she ventured down an L-shaped hallway that opened into a room with a wall of glass, offering a breathtaking view of the strip to the north and the mountains to the west. Adam stood facing the mountains. He turned to her with a smile.

"There you are! I was on the phone. Hello, beautiful."

"Hey."

She walked into his outstretched arms and relished the warm embrace that he gave her. He kissed her. She allowed that, too, tried to return the fervor. The attempt was half-hearted. Her mind was too preoccupied.

Adam released her and stepped back. "Is everything okay? Are there problems with your father, with the transplant?"

"No, well, there has been a new development but Dad's okay. Everything is on course for the surgery to happen as scheduled."

"Then what's with the sadness that I detect in your voice?"

Ryan went to the window where Adam had stood. The view he had was picture-perfect. She was about to ruin it.

"Ryan," he softly coaxed. "What is it?"

"I know who's been stealing your product," she said, still taking in the view. Then she turned and faced him. "It's Dennis."

"Your brother?" She nodded. "Are you sure?"

"Positive."

Ryan watched Adam's face as he took in this information, saw the light dim from his eyes, the smile disappear from his face.

"Is that what you and Dennis were arguing about the other night at the plant?"

A slight pause and then, "Yes."

"Really?" Adam folded his arms across his chest. "How long have you known about this? Were you in on it, too?"

Ryan's shock was genuine, anger replacing fear of what she was disclosing and regret for not doing so sooner.

"How dare you! I come here to prove that my brother is stealing and you accuse me of betraying you? Fine." Ryan whirled around, then threw over her shoulder, "Get the proof on your own!"

She heard footsteps, then felt a strong hand on her arm.

"I'm sorry," Adam said. "But you lied to me, Ryan. I don't know what to believe."

"I never lied to you!"

"You did. That night when I walked in on you and Dennis arguing, I asked point-blank if either of you had anything you wanted to tell me. You could have shared this then, but you didn't."

"I still had no proof. It was my suspicions against his denials. He's my brother, Adam. I desperately wanted to believe what he told me, that he wasn't involved with what happened, that there was no fire behind the smoke. Not sharing my suspicions with you felt awful but the thought of accusing Dennis without being sure felt even worse."

"How long have you suspected him?"

"It started before the holidays, but—"

"The holidays?" Adam crossed over to where she stood by the window. "You've listened to my frustrations, rubbed away the kinks from the stress I've been under, and all this time knew who was behind it?"

"No! Aren't you listening? I had suspicions, a gut feeling, but nothing concrete. I questioned Dennis, told him how

I felt. He repeatedly denied everything, said I was being paranoid. He even accused me of being jealous and wanting you all to myself."

Adam's eyes bore into her like lasers, almost black, the way they became in the throes of passion, now, with an emotion she couldn't comprehend.

"That night at my practice, when you shared what was happening, all of the suspicions I had flared up again. I became determined to find out the truth. And I did."

She reached into her purse. "This is what proved to me what Dennis is doing, text messages between him and Luke."

Adam exploded. "Luke was in on this, too? His so-called best friend was his partner in crime?"

He turned his back without taking the papers. Ryan's heart dropped. She placed a hand on his shoulder to offer comfort. He flinched, and shook it off.

"I'm sorry," she said, taking a step back to put space between them. "I don't blame you for being angry. Maybe I should have said something sooner."

He didn't turn around. She set the text message copies on a nearby table. "I'm telling you now because it's the right thing to do."

"You had suspicions this whole time but chose to remain silent, while I pulled out all the stops to catch this thief—more surveillance equipment, ID badges, security clearances, office renovations. All that, and I could have had the answer from you with just one phone call."

"He's my brother, Adam. I had to be sure. Can you forgive me?"

Adam crossed over to his desk and picked up his cell phone.

"Wait," Ryan said, closing the distance between them. "Aren't you going to say anything?"

"Yes," he said, slowly meeting her eyes. "Get out."

The command was low, raspy. Ryan hoped she'd misunderstood.

"What?" A whisper, barely pushed past the lump in her throat.

"You heard me."

"Okay, but have you heard me? Can't you understand how hard this was, the way going against my brother, my family, makes me feel?"

"Awful, I'm sure, the way I feel now, knowing I've spent time with a woman that I cannot trust."

Again he walked away from her, putting his massive oak desk between them. He sat down, his cell phone still in hand.

"Leave, Ryan, before I say something that can't be taken back. As for your question, in time, I might be able to forgive you. Until then, whenever that is, I don't want to hear from you again."

"You're angry, but, Adam, you can't mean that. I'm headed to—"

"I mean it." Adam's eyes blazed. "Do I need to call security or will you leave on your own?"

Ryan took one step back, then another. She turned, fleeing from his office. Outrunning her thoughts wasn't as easy. They chased her, taunting, as she hurried down the hallway.

*Were you in on it, too?*

Past the smiling receptionist.

*The gene is not present in you nor your father, father, father...*

To the elevator and through the lobby.

*In time, I might be able to forgive you.*

At the valet stand manned by the perky attendant.

*Are you in contact with your birth parents?*

In her car and a block away was the first time she became cognizant of breathing.

*I don't want to hear from you.*

Two blocks later the first tear fell. Before long there was

a torrent sliding down her cheeks. It matched her flood of emotions—surprise, regret, sadness, disappointment and the merest, almost intangible feeling of joy. How could one of her best days also be one of her worst? She'd found one man, her birth father, but lost Adam Breedlove, the love of her life.

# Twenty-Two

If you wronged one Breedlove, you wronged them all. So it was no surprise that a few days after Ryan's visit to Adam's office, Christian, Nick, Noah and their father had converged on the ranch to support Adam through the crisis. Detective Haynes was there, too, along with Clifford Dixon, the company's attorney, and Sasha Buchanan, a powerful and successful public relations fixer who'd been brought on board to handle damage control for Breedlove Beef's image, reputation and bottom line, as well as by association any spillover to CANN International. Owen had pored over extensive video footage and found pictures that pointed to Dennis being the masked man squatting near the boxes by the black truck, including one from a gas station with a clear image of Dennis getting into the truck, sans bandanna. Interestingly enough, though, it was Ryan's evidence that had given Adam the irrefutable proof needed to place the blame for what happened squarely on her brother. The legal team had acted swiftly and decisively, presenting a host of felony charges set to be filed. Dennis had one choice—cooperate fully or risk a long stint in jail, with his friend Luke likely there to keep him company. Dennis hadn't liked it, but the evidence was overwhelming. His attorney urged him to work out a deal before the courts got involved.

"Well, son," Nicholas asked once arrangements were finalized. "How do you feel?"

"Hopeful. I think the words coming directly from the culprit's mouth will help to clear mine and the company name.

I'll know better after meeting with each affected customer face-to-face, to truly feel that I've regained their trust."

"I'm still concerned about one of the ways you're doing that, bro," Noah said. "Refunding 100 percent of all purchases to date, across the board, no questions asked, will cost you into the millions."

Typical Noah, Adam thought. Often considered aloof and impersonal, his brother was quiet, introspective, with an A-type personality that kept him focused, determined and single-minded. It's what made him a perfect team player in the financial arm of CANN International. But Noah could cut a person off as easily as breathing, could detach in a heartbeat. These traits contributed to his shrewd business dealings, but Adam thought it would make Noah a lifetime bachelor.

"Restoring one's reputation has no price," Adam finally told him.

"What about Ryan?" Christian asked.

"What about her?" Adam retorted.

"Come on, bro," Nick said. "Without those text messages, this thing might have dragged out in court for a very long time."

"I'll talk to Olivia," Adam said. "Have her send over something from the company."

Every Breedlove present gave him the eye before Nicholas spoke. "Whatever that young lady receives doesn't need to be prepared by your assistant or sent from the company. It needs to come from you."

Largely due to the respect Nevada and the food and service industry had for the Nicholas Breedlove, Sr., but also due to Adam's hard work and Sasha's top-notch PR, even in the face of some negative national coverage, the damage from the scandal was quickly contained. There was still a good two weeks between Adam and a full night's sleep, even longer for true peace of mind. But in at least one area of his life, things were turning back around. Adam had taken his daily horseback ride and had just stepped out of a long, hot shower when he heard the knocker. *Ryan.* He'd thought of her all week. It irked him that she was the first person who came to mind. After quickly slipping into a pair of jeans and pulling on a tee, walking down the hall and looking through the paned glass, he chided himself for feeling disappointed. He'd told Ryan to get out of his life. She'd done exactly as he'd asked.

He opened the door. "Hey, Mom."

"I was in the neighborhood and thought I'd drop by," Victoria said, a smile breaking through the concern on her face. "May I come in?"

"Of course." He stepped back so that she could enter, and noticed the ceramic pot she carried. "What's that?"

"Food," she said over her shoulder as she continued to the kitchen. "Which given how low those jeans are riding is clearly needed."

"I'm eating," he sullenly replied, though truth be told he couldn't remember the last meal.

Victoria set the pot on the stove, then turned to envelop him in a hug.

"I'm worried about you," she whispered as she stepped back and placed a hand on his cheek. "Though I must say, that beard makes you look rather debonair."

"Why are you worried?" Adam rounded the counter and slid onto a barstool. "I'm fine."

Victoria looked skeptical as she turned on the burner. "Not according to your brothers."

"My brothers have big mouths."

"And bigger hearts when it comes to their love for you. Christian was right. You haven't been sleeping. Those dark circles under your eyes are not cute."

Adam brushed a hand over his face as he slouched against the chair's back. "Yeah, trying to save a company, my reputation and the family name left little time for shut-eye."

"And little time for Ryan, from what I hear."

"Since the rest of the fam has kept you updated about the goings-on in my life, they had to have told you that Dennis's wasn't the only betrayal. That Ryan knew about what was going on and didn't say a word."

"They said she waited until she had proof." Victoria slowly stirred the creamy chicken and vegetable concoction. "And then passed that on to you."

"It was too little too late," Adam snapped.

"It was her brother," Victoria softly replied. "Did you thank her?"

Surely his mother was joking now. "For what?"

Victoria reached into the cabinet and pulled down a bowl, her voice gentle as she ladled soup into it.

"I cannot imagine the agony of knowing two men, being related to one of them and very fond of the other, and having to make the hard choice of doing what's right, and noble, at great cost to that brother, and no doubt herself."

She placed the bowl in front of Adam. "Eat, son. You need your strength."

"You're not going to join me?"

"No, the soup smells delicious but my appetite seems to have scurried away." She walked around the counter, gave Adam a huge hug and a kiss on the cheek.

"You're a thoughtful man, Adam, a good man. I believe Ryan is a good woman. Whether or not you continue seeing her is none of my business. But I have a feeling she's had a pretty hard week, too, and probably without the type of support that you've enjoyed."

She squeezed his shoulder and turned to leave. Adam slid off the stool.

"Oh, no, sit and eat. I'll see myself out. Love you."

Adam watched the proud carriage of his mother until she turned the corner. He listened, heard the door gently shut. He took the spoon and stirred the soup, which indeed smelled delicious. But Victoria's words settled like a weight in his stomach. He couldn't eat a thing.

* * *

There was magic in Ryan's hands. Adam felt it all the way to the bone as she pulled and squeezed and worked the tension out of his body. She ran her fingers down the length of his spine before jiggling her bare bottom on his, and demanding he turn over. He did and beheld a goddess—gloriously naked—her breasts pert, nipples hard, hair wild and free.

She leaned down teasingly, her nipples brushing against his chest as she rained down light kisses. "I'm finished, lover," she purred. "Feel better?"

"Infinitely."

"Good. Now it's time for you to make me feel better, too."

She rose up then, her legs on each side of him, lovingly grasping his manhood, lining it up with the portal to paradise and sliding oh…so…slowly down.

Umm.

"Adam!"

"Yo, what?"

"You're over there snoring like a steam locomotive. You need to head to one of the bedrooms and get some real sleep."

Adam straightened and looked around, his mind dazed as he pulled himself from dream to reality. He was on the company plane, halfway through the list of customers to be visited. Instead of Ryan, it was his brother Nick beside him. Life wasn't fair.

"I'm good," he said, yawning, as he looked at his watch. "I've got a conference call with Earl soon, and need to prepare for it."

"That's not for another four hours, bro. You can't keep running on caffeine and conviction. You need real sleep. In a bed. For more than two hours."

"You're right." Adam motioned to the attendant and requested a double espresso.

Nick shook his head, tapping away on his satellite phone. "Fool."

Adam laughed, shamelessly peering over to view the profile pic on Nick's screen. "Is that Sasha?"

"Yes, why?"

"You're texting her?"

"Looks that way, doesn't it?"

"Is she back in Vegas?"

"Yes."

"Are you seeing her again?"

"No."

Adam peered at his brother. "Liar. I can't believe it. She dumped you, Nick. How could you let that woman back into your life?"

"How could you chase Ryan from yours?"

Adam didn't have a quick comeback for that.

"It's wrong how you're treating her," Nick added.

"There is no treating her one way or another. We broke up."

"That's the problem."

"No, the problem was her brother stealing and Ryan remaining quiet about it."

"With good reason. She had to be sure. That dude is her brother, man. Family first. You're tripping."

"No, you are, along with the rest of the fam. Ryan isn't the first woman I've stopped dating. If it doesn't bother me, it shouldn't bother you."

"That's why we keep bringing it up, Adam. Because the situation is bothering you, man. We all see it, we feel your unhappiness, and know it's not just about Breedlove Beef."

"Ryan was special, I'll admit that. But like you said, family first. Unfortunately, Dennis is a part of hers. How can there be a future with someone whose brother was stealing right under my nose?"

"Maybe there isn't one," Nick said, closing his eyes as

he settled against the cushy seat. "But since you two are no longer dating, I guess we'll never know."

Adam sipped his espresso, bothered by Nick's uninvited opinions. Had Ryan spoken up sooner, the public scandal could have been avoided. He continued the internal argument but finally admitted the truth in the rebuttals his family presented. He and Ryan had unfinished business. It was time to give her a call.

# Twenty-Three

Ryan had taken a few days off from her practice to try and recover from the secrets that had rocked her world—that the man she'd known for most of her life as her adopted father was her real dad, and that the brother she'd adored from childhood had stolen from the love of her life. She'd known all along that what she'd had with Adam was temporary, a fantasy. Still, the reality check hurt like hell.

Ryan's mother was still not speaking to her but she and her father texted every day. He kept her apprised of what was happening with Dennis, including news of an upcoming press conference that would be covered by local stations. Ryan idly surfed the channels looking for a distraction. But her mind kept returning to what happened a week ago when an innocent call and a firm rejection had changed her life.

Too upset to travel after meeting with Adam, Ryan had returned home and gone to bed, hoping a good night's rest would make life feel less awful. Sleep eluded her. At three forty-five she gave up trying, packed her car and hit the road. Four hours later she arrived in Bakersfield, shortly after her mother would have left for work. She reached her parents' home. April's mother helped to look after her dad and answered the door. Ryan told the kind neighbor that she'd take over watching her father. April's mother walked out the door. It was just Ryan and Joe now, alone. She walked up the stairs and knocked on the master bedroom door. There was no answer. She peeked in and saw her father, asleep. For a long moment, she stood at the end of the bed staring at him. Seeing his face as though for the first time, and traces of herself in it. He opened his eyes.

"I'm sorry, baby," he said, his voice raspy with sleep and emotion. "For years, I wanted to tell you but I gave Ida my word. I had you in my home. She had the secret. That was the deal."

Ryan sat on the bed and placed a hand on her father's arm. "You and Phyllis..."

"...had an affair. It shouldn't have happened but I'm not totally sorry because that's how we got you."

Joe talked for the next hour, almost nonstop. About how he, Phyllis, Ida and a group of others all used to be friends. He'd always been attracted to Phyllis but Ryan's birth mother wasn't into anything serious. She liked to party, liked adventure. Joe preferred a steady life and wanted a family. He married Ida, but Phyllis was still in his system. The affair was short, just a few weeks. But it only took one night to make a baby. The affair ended, but a new life had begun.

"Ida was livid," Joe continued. "And had every right. It was a betrayal of two friends, worse for me because I was also her husband. I didn't want to break up my family and did everything that Ida demanded. I cut all contact with Phyllis. Stayed true to my wife. It hurt to know about a child in the world, that I'd never seen, never touched. But I kept my word."

"But you found me, in foster care."

"That was Ida. The tough exterior she presents covers a heart of gold. As hurt as she was over what happened, she kept up with your whereabouts through mutual friends. Phyllis hurt her back and got hooked on pain pills. You went in the system. It took Ida a while to locate you and, while looking, she became a foster parent. When she found you, we took you in and gave you my name. It was Ida who did that, because a child needs her father. And while I never said anything to her about it, she knew this father needed his child."

It was an emotional discussion, one that taxed Joe's strength. He went to sleep and Ryan went to work on her father, hoping the energy healing provided some comfort or helped his rest. When Ida returned home, one look at Ryan's face and she knew that Joe had told her.

"Thank you," Ryan said simply, then walked to the woman she'd called Mom since being adopted and gave her the biggest hug. Ida stood there and slowly returned the embrace. When the hug ended, there were tears in both of their eyes. They sat at the table and had a long conversation, for Ryan, the best one ever. They cooked and cared for Joe, talked to the doctors, made plans for the transplant. She'd lost Adam but still had her family. The hope that they'd survive this ordeal grew with each passing hour.

Then Dennis came home. The peace was shattered. He blamed Ryan for everything. Ida took Dennis's side. Joe was too weak to weigh in. Ryan returned to Las Vegas ready for the surgery, but unsure of everything else.

"There is breaking news this hour regarding Breedlove Beef and the controversy surrounding the low grades of meat some customers received instead of the high-quality Wagyu they'd ordered. Let's go live to a press conference happening now."

The voice from the television drew Ryan's attention back to the screen, where her brother stood at a podium. He looked terse and uncomfortable, as he read from a prepared statement.

"My name is Dennis Washington. A few months ago I was hired as the manager for the Breedlove Beef Processing Center in Breedlove, Nevada, by the owner, Adam Breedlove. I abused the authority and access I had to the facility to engage in practices that were unethical and caused great damage to the Breedlove name and the company brand. I take full responsibility for any product delivered to any person or company that was not what they ordered, or expected. I exploited our prior friendship and Adam's good name for personal gain. He knew nothing of what I was doing. For that, as well as the harm done to him and his family, I apologize."

Ryan had seen enough. She reached for the remote, but was stopped by the next face that appeared on the screen. Adam. Her heart raced. She leaned forward, taking him in as if it had been years instead of days since she'd seen him. He was surrounded by reporters yet appeared relaxed, managing to smile despite the tough topic. Even though his angular face was sharper than she remembered, as though he'd lost weight, the camera loved him. Ryan did, too. Which was probably why she spent more time than she should wondering about the gorgeous woman standing just behind Adam, along with what she assumed were execs from the ranch. In all the coverage watched or read there'd been no mention of charges or jail time for Dennis, and no mention of Luke at all. Time would tell if Ryan's hunch was correct, that even when wronged Adam could be the bigger, better man. Instinctively, she picked up the phone to call him. But memories of his parting words stilled her fingers. Adam had moved on. When her phone rang a short time later with the name Victoria on her Caller ID, Ryan couldn't have been more surprised.

"This is Ryan."

"Hello, Ryan. It's Victoria."

"Hi, Victoria."

"How are you, sweetheart?"

Her interest seemed genuine. Ryan was floored. "Okay, I guess. Busy."

"Then I won't keep you. I'm following up on the call I made a while back and the information regarding our event that my assistant sent you. Did you get it?"

"Not that I remember. It may have gone to spam." As

for the call received in what felt like a lifetime ago, Ryan had forgotten it until now. "I'm sorry, there's been a lot going on."

"I can only imagine how difficult this time has been for you, which is why I hope you'll forgive my extreme presumption in placing you on the program for our affair. You don't have to attend, of course, but I wish you would."

As Victoria talked, Ryan scrolled through emails and found an unread one from the CANN Foundation. It explained that Integrative Healing had been listed on the program and Victoria would love it if she could attend. Ryan was very surprised, and grateful. She asked a few more questions and then told Victoria she'd most definitely be there.

Ryan arrived early, per Victoria's request, ready to offer the services of massage and Reiki energy healing to as many of the one hundred women in attendance as she could. There'd been so many surprises about that day, starting with the fact that Victoria had not canceled her appearance, that she'd invited her even after what happened with Adam.

"You two still haven't talked?" Victoria asked, as they walked from the foundation offices to the ballroom.

"No. I'm pretty sure that's not going to happen."

"Breedlove men are very proud and when angered, or hurt, can be very stubborn. What you did was honorable and courageous, and I applaud your actions. They told me that you're exactly the type of young lady that those attending this charitable event need to see."

Victoria was the only person besides Brooklyn who'd agreed with her actions. Ryan didn't know what to say.

"How's your family handling all this? There must be friction."

"To put it mildly," Ryan said, the understatement producing a smile. "My dad's been in touch, keeping me updated. They're grateful that Adam didn't press charges that would have likely sent Dennis to prison. But neither him nor my mother is speaking to me."

"Stay encouraged," Victoria said, placing an arm around her. "When it comes to family, we never give up."

They entered the elaborately decorated ballroom to more surprises. Ryan had expected to see well-heeled women wearing their favorite designers and enough diamonds to cancel the national debt. Some of the women indeed fit this description but others, though nicely dressed, were clearly out of their element. Victoria explained that every donor had purchased two tickets, one for themselves and one to be donated to a woman of lesser means. Victoria wanted them to experience a little bit of luxury, to be treated like queens for the day.

With everything set up, Ryan thought it would be a good time to run to the restroom. She'd just begun to head that way when Victoria waved her over.

"Are we ready to start?" Ryan asked.

"Yes, lunch will begin in about twenty minutes."

"I thought that was happening after the show."

"No, the fashion show takes place as the women are eating. You didn't read the email?"

"Not entirely," Ryan sheepishly replied.

"You're forgiven. Listen, I waved you over because I need your help. There's someone we've invited who's just a little nervous about this whole affair. She's in one of our smaller dining rooms and I thought if you could go in and work some of your magic, she'll feel more comfortable coming out."

"Oh, of course. I'd be glad to help. Where is she?"

They walked out of the main ballroom and down a hall where smaller, private dining rooms were located. "She's in the last room on the right." Victoria's phone rang. "I've got to get back."

"Oh, Victoria…"

But she was gone. Ryan wished she'd gotten the woman's

name. But it didn't matter. Once treatment began, her body would tell Ryan all she needed to know.

Ryan gave a soft knock, and then opened the door.

"Hello," she said softly, as she stepped inside.

"Hi, Ryan."

Ryan froze before slowly turning around and coming face-to-face with her birth mom.

"What…are you doing here?"

"Don't be mad," Phyllis said, her eyes searching Ryan's face. "That lady, Victoria, asked me and Ida to come here. Ida couldn't make it but she called me, the first time we talked in years. She said that Joe told you everything. She told me about the transplant, too, and you giving him a kidney. The best part is that she finally forgave me, Ryan, and if you will have me she gave me her blessing to be in your life."

# Twenty-Four

Ryan pulled into a parking space at the far end of the Strip, turned off her car and walked toward the sign with deep blue coloring and white lettering bearing her name. In the days since all of the secrets were revealed, and all the lives that they had affected were being mended, Ryan had finally allowed someone long denied a voice—the little girl inside her. The inner child who from a very early age had longed for her real mother. She placed a key in the lock and stepped into the interior painstakingly designed to bring peace to those who entered, a thought that was bittersweet because missing Adam denied her that serenity.

A tinkling bell signaled the inner door opening. Brooklyn walked into the foyer. "Ryan!" She rushed over and gave her a hug.

"Come on, I just made tea and don't have an appointment for another thirty minutes." They began walking toward the back and the mini kitchen. "Needless to say I've been very concerned about you."

"I'm sorry to have worried you."

"No apology needed. I saw your brother's press conference. When you left the message about canceling clients and taking time off, I thought it was a wise thing to do."

Brooklyn busied herself making the tea. For several seconds, Ryan watched her, realizing that the woman she considered to be her best friend knew almost nothing about her past. Brooklyn finished dressing the tea and handed her a steaming mug.

"Okay, sit," Brooklyn commanded, in a voice that was soft yet firm. Ryan pulled a chair away from the quaint bamboo table and sat down. Brooklyn took the seat next to her. "Talk."

Ryan hesitated, but only briefly. "I'm adopted."

Brooklyn nodded. "I had a feeling that you were."

"Your intuition?" Ryan asked.

"I guess so."

"I should have known."

"That time you told me about a client looking for her parent, I had a gut feeling it might have been you." Brooklyn smiled, and squeezed Ryan's arm. "It's okay."

"I know that now, but for twenty years that was a secret I felt forced to keep."

Brooklyn set down her cup. "Hang on a minute, I'll be right back."

"I shouldn't—"

"No, you're fine. I just need to grab my phone."

Ryan waited, sipped her tea, amazed at how much a lie could weigh and how much lighter she felt since learning the truth surrounding her birth.

"Okay, I'm all yours."

"But your clients?"

Brooklyn waved a dismissive hand. "I just silenced the ringer. Besides, right now, you're more important."

Ryan shared everything about what had happened that culminated with Ryan seeing her biological and adoptive mothers together for the very first time.

"All of us were suffering individually," she finished. "Afraid of a bogeyman created in our minds. There's still a lot of work to do, and we'll probably never go on a girls' trip, but we realized there's room to be civil. My birth mom Phyllis understands that Mom isn't the devil, and Mom understands that Phyllis isn't a threat. I never thought this day would come."

"I'm so glad it did." Brooklyn leaned over and hugged Ryan. "What about Adam? How does he feel about it?"

Ryan sighed, realizing that even with the bomb she'd dropped about being adopted, there was another explosive topic to deal with.

"You watched Dennis's press conference, right?"

"Yes, but I didn't really understand the apology."

When Ryan finished the short version of what had happened a few minutes later, all Brooklyn could say was "Wow."

"I know. It's like I've been trapped in a really bad movie and can't get out."

"You love Adam! What are you going to do?"

Ryan shrugged. "I've reached out to him. He hasn't called back, but he knows how I feel. Right now, I'm focusing on Dad and the upcoming surgery. I can't live in the past."

Brooklyn's phone buzzed with a call she had to take. Ryan reheated her tea and walked into the office she hadn't seen in a week. She hadn't planned on working but now didn't want to leave. So she retrieved her laptop from the car, fired it up and within two hours had rescheduled the clients from the past several days, giving a discount for the inconvenience her unexpected absence had caused them. She called the web designer and discussed ideas for her upcoming blog. Life lessons were never only for the person who learned them. She knew there were other adoptees out there navigating the sensitive waters flowing between the moms who birthed them and the moms who raised them. Too many families kept too many secrets, leaving wounds sometimes not recognized and scars that never healed. As she finished up the notes on what she wanted to send over, her phone rang.

*Dennis.*

What did he want? He was back at their parent's home in Bakersfield. How could she help him? A favor perhaps? Something to ask her ex-lover and his former boss? She let the call go to voice mail. Adam was currently not speaking to her, and with Dennis there was no more to say.

The week passed quickly. Ryan tried to embrace her new normal. Work helped. The pavement-pounding, networking and social media presence was paying off, along with referrals and repeat business. Learning that Joe was her birth dad had filled her heart with more love than she thought she could hold. Still, she missed Adam with every breath. It was crazy to believe he'd contact her after everything Dennis had done and how he felt she'd betrayed him. She tried to not think about him, to bury her emotions beneath a pile of paperwork and scheduling screens. Just when she'd managed almost an hour without a thought about Adam, he called.

"This is Ryan."

"Hello, Ryan. It's Adam."

"Hi."

"I got your messages but have been out of the country. I'm still out, but will be back on Saturday."

"I thought you might still be upset with me."

"I'm not angry with you, Ryan. Not anymore. What happened wasn't your fault."

"At times it felt that way." Ryan's honesty was met with silence. "Adam?"

"I should have contacted you sooner," he said. "My schedule's been crazy. How are you?"

"I'm okay."

"Ryan, what else did you want to share that day you came to my office? I was so angry at the news about Dennis that I couldn't hear anything else."

"I've tried to put myself in your shoes and can somewhat understand you being so upset."

"Still, it was wrong of me to cut you off that day without hearing everything you wanted to tell me. I'd like to have that chance again."

"I don't know, Adam. It's probably not necessary. What we had is over and—"

"You still deserve to be heard. It wasn't until my schedule slowed down that I remembered part of your text mentioned having incredible news. What did you want to tell me?"

"I'm adopted and have been looking for my birth father. The day I came to your office, I'd found him."

Ryan told Adam about her childhood, about finding and building a relationship with her birth mom, Phyllis, and what she'd learned of her dad.

"You've dealt with a lot. I'm proud of you, Ryan. You sound really happy."

"I am. No more secrets. It's good to not hide it anymore."

"It also solves a puzzle that I couldn't figure out," Adam responded.

"What?"

"How you can be such an angel while Dennis is the devil in disguise."

They shared a laugh, reminding Ryan of the easy camaraderie that used to exist between them and making her wonder if they could ever get it back.

"I've been very selfish."

"Why do you say that?"

"Since the scandal broke, my complete focus was on the business and how I'd been affected. I was too angry to consider what you'd gone through, more than I ever suspected. While crisscrossing the globe to meet clients, I've had time to reflect on the whole situation and the strength it took to do what you did. I treated you unfairly, Ryan. I'm sorry."

"It's okay."

"No, it's not. I'm a better man than the one you've seen recently. I've missed you terribly and if given the opportunity, I'll do everything I can to make it up to you. Will you forgive my past actions and give me that chance, Ryan? I didn't mean what I said that day at the office. Will you see me again?"

"Of course," Ryan managed, while fighting back tears. "I appreciate the kind words but just so you know, life's been pretty miserable without you, too."

"Then let's end the misery for both of us. I'll call you as soon as I land."

"Sounds good."

"There's one more thing."

"What?"

"I love you, Ryan."

Ryan hadn't expected the *L* word but answered from her heart.

"I love you, too."

# Twenty-Five

*A few months later*

Adam took one last look around the en suite bath, then returned to his bedroom. He closed the top of the carry-on luggage that rested on the bed, zipped it up and reached for the phone he'd tossed next to it earlier. Seconds later, a groggy voice answered the phone.

"Adam?"

"Good morning, Ryan."

"What time is it? Is everything okay?"

"Everything's fine. Look, I've got something cool to show you. A car is on the way to pick you up."

"Now?" He could hear what sounded like her moving around, perhaps getting out of bed.

"I know it's early but if we're going to do all that I've planned, we have to start now. Don't worry. I've taken care of everything. You're spending the night. So throw a few toiletries in a bag and dress comfortably. Elvis will be there in about thirty minutes."

"What if I said I didn't want to come over?"

"Then I'd have to come kidnap you."

"I appreciate that, babe, but there's a reason I didn't plan anything this weekend. I'm really exhausted and just want to chill out."

"Then that's exactly what we'll do. Now, please, go get ready. Elvis will be there soon."

Adam ended the call, pulled the luggage to the floor

and rolled it behind him as he left the room. Passing by the counter he picked up his keys, phone and sunglasses and continued out of the house to the wraparound porch. He stopped and put on his shades, taking a moment to breathe in the smell of freshly cut grass and to appreciate the cool morning breeze. The day was new and fresh, like his relationship with Ryan.

Adam couldn't wait to see her reaction to the plans he'd made. Her happiness meant everything, a fact that Adam found quite surprising given the chain of events that had led his heart there. Dennis Washington had cost him a chunk of money for a scheme that could have caused his business to fail before hardly getting started. Still, Adam could never hate his former friend. Knowing him is how he'd met Ryan. Since that Sunday when they'd reconnected, their love had blossomed. For that, he'd do it all again.

He crossed over to where a profusion of colors burst from the aspen trees he'd had planted for that very reason—because of how their leaves changed in fall. Shades of red and orange and yellow were highlighted, backlit by the sun. The leaves actually looked happy and free, the way that he felt since admitting his struggles with dyslexia to a business blogger. The article went viral. Adam became an inspiration for others who struggled, proof that the challenge could be overcome. Owning that truth allowed him to fit fully and comfortably inside his own skin and realize that others knowing about his disability made him no less of the person he'd been before that truth came out. This realization and newfound appreciation for authenticity would have never happened except for Ryan. Meeting that woman had changed his life in so many ways. He hoped to return the favor.

Adam heard the sound of a car. He turned to see the executive SUV he'd sent to pick up Ryan coming down the drive. He strolled over to where he'd left his luggage and, after making sure the door had been locked, headed toward the drive. Once the car had pulled in and parked, the driver quickly exited the car.

Adam waved him away. "Thanks, Elvis, but I've got it."

"You sure?"

"Positive. Hey," he quickly continued, motioning for Elvis to come toward him. "You didn't tell her, did you?"

"She doesn't know a thing," Elvis replied with a wink.

Adam placed his luggage in the back, then opened the door and climbed inside. Ryan sat cross-legged, her back against the door, looking as fit as a fiddle. Not at all like someone with only one kidney.

"I thought we were just going to hang out" was her *good morning*.

"We are."

"Then why are you getting in the car?"

"To take us to where we're hanging out." Adam stretched his body over the seat for a quick kiss. "Good morning, gorgeous!"

"You woke me out of a deep sleep and had me picked up before breakfast, even coffee. We'll see how good it is."

Adam took in her black skinny jeans, sweater and faux leather jacket. Her face was devoid of makeup, and the hair that often had a mind of its own was held away from her face with a band. She looked adorable.

"I didn't bring a change of clothes."

"You look fine."

"But you brought a suitcase. Where are we going?"

"Just relax, Ryan. Since you're a business owner, I know you are keen on the details and like to be in control. For today, let taking care of you be my job. Okay?"

He kissed her once, and again, and watched the pout she'd worn slip away. "Okay." She looked out the window. "I can't get over the beauty of this estate. It's like being in a whole other world."

"In many ways, it is. Mom wanted to create a type of fantasyland for family, guests and clientele. With every renovation or new edition, she outdoes herself."

Ryan looked over at him. "What were some of the changes?"

The car stopped. "I'll answer that question after we get on the plane."

"Plane? Adam, where are we going?"

"Not far. I'll get your door." Long strides made quick work of covering the distance. "Come on, babe."

"No." Ryan crossed her arms. "I refuse to go where I don't know where I'm going!"

"Ha!" He held out his hand. "Do you trust me? Well, do you?"

She gave him the side-eye but placed her hand in his and allowed herself to be pulled out of the car. In the meantime Elvis had retrieved Adam's luggage. Still holding Ryan's hand, Adam grabbed the luggage handle and led them toward the plane.

"Thanks, Elvis!"

They reached the airstairs of a private plane. Ryan looked up. "We're going in that?"

"Yes, isn't it a beauty? Come on."

Adam entered the plane and stopped near the cockpit, where the pilot and flight attendant were standing. He introduced Ryan.

"Nice meeting you, young lady," the pilot said. "Check's all done, Adam. We can take off anytime."

Adam gave him a thumbs-up. "Let's go!"

He stopped at the first set of seats. "Aisle or window?"

"Window." He stepped back so Ryan could pass him, watched her eyes scan the plane's interior, which even after all the times he'd flown in it was still impressive.

"Buckle up, babe."

Ryan reached for the belt, still looking around. Her eyes landed on a shiny plaque. "Christian Breedlove, President,

CANN International." She looked at Adam. "Ah, so this is the company's plane?"

Adam shook his head. "It belongs to Christian, a birthday gift from our parents."

"Wow. Mom and Dad gave Dennis a toy plane one Christmas but...oops, sorry."

Adam laughed. "Don't worry about it. He's still your brother."

He pulled Ryan into his arms as the plane barreled down the runway and began its ascent. There was a companionable silence as the two looked out the window, first at clouds and blue sky and then at mountains bathed in different hues once the plane leveled out. Angie, the attendant, walked out carrying an ornate silver tray holding two flutes, a basket of miniature rolls, a covered dish and a small bouquet of perfectly formed roses.

"It's only an hour flight but this will get you started," Angie said.

"Can I help you?" Adam asked.

"Oh, no. I've got it." She pulled down a tabletop from the wall in front of them and put down the tray. "I've got coffee on as well and there is hot chocolate available, along with champagne if you'd like to turn that juice into a mimosa. What else can I bring you?" She looked from Adam to Ryan.

"Hot chocolate sounds good," Ryan said.

Adam nodded. "Make that two."

Ryan leaned forward and pulled one of the roses from the bouquet. She touched it to her nose and deeply inhaled. "This smells amazing. I've never smelled a rose this fragrant, or seen one this big. These are huge! I also don't think I've ever seen an orange rose."

She placed the flower to her nose again, looking at Adam with love in her eyes. "Were these brought on board just for me?"

"Absolutely." Adam reached for the two flutes. He gave

one to Ryan. "To celebrate the woman who's touched my life and captivated my heart. This day is for you."

"That's so sweet, babe." Ryan gave Adam a quick kiss on the lips before they clinked glasses and took sips. "Thank you. What's under the dome?"

Adam raised the silver top to reveal two beautifully plated servings of eggs Florentine.

"Yum!"

He reached for one of the small plates and handed it to Ryan, then picked up the other and began eating.

"How's Joe doing?" he asked, and was immediately rewarded with one of her life-giving smiles.

"Dad's recovery is amazing. The first couple weeks were scary. We didn't know whether or not his body would accept my kidney. With the time that's passed the doctors are increasingly optimistic. They've even made plans to visit…"

"What?"

"Never mind."

"Is it about Dennis? Baby, I've made my peace with what he did. I lost all of the trust and respect I had for him, and he'll never again work in the meatpacking industry, or any part of the service industry, most likely. But I don't hate your brother."

"I appreciate that," Ryan said. "The way he was treated in Bakersfield after the press conference was worse than being in jail. A month ago he got engaged to the neighbor and moved to Texas with her and her kids. My parents will visit him soon."

"And you?"

Ryan shook her head. "I'm still working on forgiving him for the pain he's caused me. Not just what he did to you but from the time I was adopted. I don't hate Dennis, either, but I honestly can't say I like him much right now."

"Then have Brooklyn do some of that woo-woo stuff to help you heal. Unforgiveness hurts only you."

"Woo-woo stuff?" Ryan laughed. "Listen to you! But

you're right. I tell my clients that all the time and need to take your advice."

They chatted about the past week's events and raved about the food. Angie returned with their hot chocolate, and to refill their flutes. Shortly after they'd finished eating, she returned for their dishes and picked up the tray.

"We'll be landing shortly," she said. "Time to buckle up."

Ryan looked out the window. "This isn't Los Angeles," she said, stretching her neck this way and that. "Are we going to Phoenix?"

"A few more minutes and the destination will be revealed."

The plane landed and the captain announced, "Welcome to Sedona."

"Babe! I love Sedona!" As she turned and threw her arms around his neck, the brightness of Ryan's eyes and smile were enough to add years to his life.

"We'd better get out of these seats and get to it, then."

Ryan released the belt and stood. "How did you know?"

"I talked to Brooklyn. She told me this was one of your favorite spots."

They said goodbye to the crew and walked down the stairs to a waiting car. Once inside, Ryan reached for his arm. "This is really special. Thanks again."

"You're very welcome."

"Did Brooklyn tell you anything about Sedona? There's lots to do here depending on what you're in the mood for, and places where we can eat later on. Ooh, babe, had I known we were coming here I would have worn different clothes!"

"Don't worry, gorgeous," he replied. "You're the most beautiful woman in town. Now—" he pulled her into a gentle embrace "—tell me about Sedona and why you love it."

"It's beautiful, for one thing," Ryan said, resting her head against his arm and sounding dreamy. "It feels good and when I come here, no matter what my mood is beforehand,

I soon feel good, too. It's because of the vortexes, these pockets of energy that can heal and transform. People come from all over the world to experience them. It's pretty cool."

They chatted a bit more, him asking questions, Ryan answering them, until they pulled into an über-luxurious hotel and spa called, appropriately, Vortex.

"Unbelievable," Ryan whispered with an almost child-like wonder. "This place has been on my bucket list for years!"

"Brooklyn said I'd score points by bringing you here."

"My bestie was right. You. Are. Winning!"

Adam had grown up in luxury, but from the lobby to their penthouse suite, he was impressed. Ryan was overwhelmed. He'd wanted her to feel like Cinderella and had pulled out all the stops. They toured the town, attended a festival and took a ride in a hot air balloon. When they returned to the car, Ryan nestled against him. "I'm so deliriously happy right now."

Adam kissed her temple as he placed an arm around her. "Have I worn you out yet?"

"I'm strangely invigorated," she murmured, placing a hand on his thigh while looking at him coyly, a clear message in her eyes.

He gently gripped her hand, stopping its movement toward his crotch. "I've had that on my mind since we got on the plane," he admitted. "But later, after dinner, when I can take my time and—" he ran a finger down her face, neck and the top of her breast "—do things right."

"After dinner, huh?" Adam nodded. "Can we make it quick, like go through a drive-through?"

"Ha!"

When they arrived back at the hotel, Ryan was shocked to see a closet filled with shoeboxes and clothes, courtesy of a designer Victoria had recommended. He'd had every clothing item delivered that a woman needed, from lingerie to Louboutins.

"Baby, you've thought of everything. You've turned me into a big crybaby with all of these gifts!"

"I don't mind. I'm just happy you like them."

"I love them," Ryan responded. "I love you."

They showered—separately, amid Ryan's protestations—and went to dinner dressed to the nines. Adam's tailored umber-colored suit shot through with gold thread made him look dashing and complemented Ryan's shimmery, one-shoulder silk delight that hugged her curves the way Adam planned to later. The menu was a symphony of vegetables, grains, starches and legumes that created gastronomic melodies over olfactory harmonies so good that Ryan requested the chef be brought to their table and thanked in person.

Ryan reached over for Adam's hand. "You know, babe, I think this might be the best day in my entire life."

"Really?"

"Definitely. You're an amazing man, Adam Breedlove. It's seems such an inadequate statement given all you've done, but thank you, for everything."

"You're welcome, babe, but the night's not over."

"Oh, I know that," she said, her voice flirty and low.

Adam chuckled. "Are you ready?"

"Sure."

They walked out of the restaurant. She headed toward the elevator. He caught her arm and began walking toward the exit.

"Where are we going?"

"My last treat of the day."

"What else is left to do?"

"You'll see."

The same car that had driven them around all day idled in the circular drive. The driver stood by the opened car door and nodded slightly as they entered. Adam immediately pushed a button to raise the privacy screen and pulled a more-than-willing Ryan into his arms. He slid his tongue along the crease of her mouth as a finger tickled her nipple.

She gasped, providing the opening he wanted. His tongue darted inside her mouth, touching the tip of hers, which eagerly awaited to touch, taste, dance together.

When Ryan's hand once again crept toward Adam's burgeoning erection, he put on the brakes.

"Babe, if you let the snake out of the cage we won't reach our destination."

"Releasing that snake is my destination," she whispered against his mouth. "But I'll behave."

The car turned off the highway onto a dirt road that ran along the edge of a mountain. It was a cool, clear evening, almost dark, and the higher the car climbed the brighter the stars shone.

"It's so beautiful out here," Ryan whispered, almost reverently. "I can't imagine where you're taking me, though."

"To heaven, I hope," Adam replied.

The car pulled over. Adam instructed the driver to open the trunk. "Wait here," he said to Ryan. He retrieved items from the trunk and returned to the car. Once inside he handed Ryan a large cashmere shawl. "It's bit chilly out," he told her.

"You've thought of everything," she said.

"I try." He reached into a large canvas bag in the trunk and pulled out a pair of slip-on sneakers. "I love those stilettos but these will work better on the mountain."

"I love being out here in all of this beauty, but, babe, I'm not exactly dressed for a hike."

"What I'd like to show you isn't far and won't take long." He removed his suit jacket and donned a pullover sweater. "You ready?"

"Sure."

Adam stepped out of the car, hoisted the bag on his shoulder and reached back in for Ryan. There was a blanket of stars across a clear, dark sky; some seemed almost low enough to touch. Adam held Ryan securely as they followed the rocky trail going up the mountain until the path opened up onto a wide plateau. From here they couldn't see the car or the road. Rock formations isolated them from everything, created a world with Ryan and Adam only, no one else. Ryan stepped away from Adam, dropped her head back and spun around. Her eyes landed on an object a short distance away. She walked over and squealed.

"A telescope!"

Hurriedly, she put her eye to the lens. "Wow, this is amazing. There's the Big Dipper," she said, while swiveling the machine in different directions. "And there's the North Star. Babe, you've got to see this. It's like I really am in heaven and can catch these stars in the palm of my hand."

Adam took a turn to look in the telescope. After a while he turned to her. "Ryan, I think you're right."

"What?"

"The stars. They're so close. I believe we can catch them, too." He walked over to Ryan. "Hold out your hand."

Ryan cocked her head. "It was a figure of speech, Adam. Even if a star fell, which they really don't, having it land in my hand would be a long shot, even for a Breedlove."

"Everything is possible," he responded. "That's what the woman at the festival who worked with crystals said." He paused, stepped closer and looked deeply into her eyes. "Do you believe that's true?"

"Yes."

"Good. Hold out your hand and close your eyes."

Ryan's eyes slowly closed as her hand lifted.

"Now, make a wish upon a star and ask it to come to where you are." He waited. "Abracadabra," he slowly said, releasing what he'd pulled from his pocket and letting it fall.

Ryan jumped as she felt an object hit her hand. She opened her eyes and saw something sparkling, a ring with so many carats that it shone brighter than Polaris or any of the other stars. Her eyes slowly raised from the ring to Adam's face, glimmering with unshed tears.

"What's this?" she whispered.

He picked up the dazzling princess-cut rock set in platinum and held it between his fingers. "It's not a falling star," he said, "but it represents my wish for us. My world hasn't been the same since you entered it. Everything's brighter. I'm a better person, a better man. I might not be able to give you the world or even a planet, but I can give you my heart."

Adam watched a single tear slide down Ryan's cheek as he got down on one knee. "Will you marry me, Ryan, and fulfill all my wishes?"

"Yes," she said after a pregnant pause, where her lips trembled and she composed herself. "Because you just made all of mine come true."

Adam stood and pulled Ryan into his arms. They kissed with passion and desire amid a shower of falling stars. Adam had fallen for the vegetarian practitioner. Ryan was ready for the cattle-raising rancher. Together, they planned to weave those differences into a lifetime of harmonious love.

* * * * *

# COMING SOON!

We really hope you enjoyed reading this book. If you're looking for more romance, be sure to head to the shops when new books are available on

## Thursday 17th October

To see which titles are coming soon, please visit **millsandboon.co.uk/nextmonth**

# MILLS & BOON

## THE HEART OF ROMANCE

---

## A ROMANCE FOR EVERY KIND OF READER

**MODERN**

Prepare to be swept off your feet by sophisticated, sexy and seductive heroes, in some of the world's most glamourous and romantic locations, where power and passion collide.
**8 stories per month.**

**HISTORICAL**

Escape with historical heroes from time gone by. Whether your passion is for wicked Regency Rakes, muscled Vikings or rugged Highlanders, awaken the romance of the past.
**6 stories per month.**

**MEDICAL**

Set your pulse racing with dedicated, delectable doctors in the high-pressure world of medicine, where emotions run high and passion, comfort and love are the best medicine.
**6 stories per month.**

*True Love*

Celebrate true love with tender stories of heartfelt romance, from the rush of falling in love to the joy a new baby can bring, and a focus on the emotional heart of a relationship.
**8 stories per month.**

*Desire*

Indulge in secrets and scandal, intense drama and plenty of sizzling hot action with powerful and passionate heroes who have it all: wealth, status, good looks…everything but the right woman.
**6 stories per month.**

**HEROES**

Experience all the excitement of a gripping thriller, with an intense romance at its heart. Resourceful, true-to-life women and strong, fearless men face danger and desire - a killer combination!
**8 stories per month.**

**DARE**

Sensual love stories featuring smart, sassy heroines you'd want as a best friend, and compelling intense heroes who are worthy of them.
**4 stories per month.**

---

To see which titles are coming soon, please visit

**millsandboon.co.uk/nextmonth**

# MILLS & BOON

## MODERN

# Power and Passion

Prepare to be swept off your feet by sophisticated, sexy and seductive heroes, in some of the world's most glamourous and romantic locations, where power and passion collide.

# DARE

## *Sexy. Passionate. Bold.*

Sensual love stories featuring smart, sassy heroines you'd want as a best friend, and compelling intense heroes who are worthy of them.

# MILLS & BOON
*True Love*

## Romance from the Heart

Celebrate true love with tender stories of heartfelt romance, from the rush of falling in love to the joy a new baby can bring, and a focus on the emotional heart of a relationship.